MERMAID COVE

MERMAID COVE

A SMALL BATCH MYSTERY

MICHELLE BENNINGTON

First published by Level Best Books 2023

Copyright © 2023 by Michelle Bennington

All rights reserved. No part of this publication may be reproduced, stored or transmitted in any form or by any means, electronic, mechanical, photocopying, recording, scanning, or otherwise without written permission from the publisher. It is illegal to copy this book, post it to a website, or distribute it by any other means without permission.

This novel is entirely a work of fiction. The names, characters and incidents portrayed in it are the work of the author's imagination. Any resemblance to actual persons, living or dead, events or localities is entirely coincidental.

Michelle Bennington asserts the moral right to be identified as the author of this work.

Author Photo Credit: Michelle Bennington

First edition

ISBN: 978-1-68512-383-3

Cover art by Level Best Designs

This book was professionally typeset on Reedsy.
Find out more at reedsy.com

Anthony Pierce.
Your faith, strength, wisdom, sense of humor, and equanimity will always be my North Star.

Chapter One

Rothdale was abuzz about the upcoming Bourbon, Bands, and BBQ festival, and no one was more excited than the distilleries in the bourbon community. Each distillery was going to put their finest bourbon on display in hopes of winning the grand prize of ten thousand dollars, the prestigious Kentucky Distiller's Guild award, and an interview in the *National Bourbon Review* magazine, which could catapult an unknown distiller into international fame.

My boyfriend and I had stopped by Mermaid Cove for the purpose of loaning them a canopy for the festival. Even though I worked at a competing distillery, Four Wild Horses, one of the owners of Mermaid Cove, was my best friend, Millie's mom.

I shook off the feeling of being watched as my boyfriend, Deputy Jimmy Duvall, and I parked in front of the Mermaid Cove Distillery. Though I was now fully healed, the sensation of being watched or followed lingered around me, along with weird and downright horrific dreams and memories. No matter how strong I tried to be, the trauma from my best friend's murder, and my own close call, came rushing back to me at the sight of any distillery. It didn't help that I still worked at Four Wild Horses Distillery.

The dreams were worse, though. Several nights a week, I'd have dreams of my best friend that morphed into nightmares of my mother's murder or faceless monsters attacking me. Then I'd wake to spend the rest of the day in a jittery mess and my mind in a sleep-starved fog.

Yet, life went on all around me. Prim was hanging on in spite of her late-stage cancer, bless her heart. My neighbor, Batrene Bishop, and my ex-husband, Porter "Cam" Campbell, were my biggest saving grace in assisting my recovery and helping Prim live with her illness. And Millie kept me sane with welcome distraction. Jimmy was around when he could be, but his work kept him tied up a lot. With funding and staffing shortages, he was called on more than ever.

Jimmy turned off the truck. "What's wrong?"

"Nothing." I forced a smile. "I'm fine."

"You look a little spaced out."

I shrugged. "Just thinking."

"You've been through some stuff. I can recommend a counselor that—"

I lifted my hand, cutting him off. "I said I'm fine." I threw open the truck door and grabbed my near-empty bottle of Kentucky Spice soda. "Let's go." I didn't want to go through the counselor issue again. I was eyeball-deep in school loans and medical debt. I couldn't afford a counselor too. I downed the rest of my soda to fuel the Southern social graces I'd need to face the people inside.

Patrice Dawson stood behind the black granite counter in the Mermaid Cove Distillery gift shop, which also doubled as a lobby.

"Rook Campbell, are you here to spy on us and learn all our secrets?" Patrice looked over the rim of her wire frames from under a mop of tousled gray hair. Her eyes were blue mingled with green, rendering them nearly teal in color.

"I wouldn't dream of it." I grinned, but my smile felt tight. "Besides, if I told you, that'd make me an awfully poor spy."

She laughed and stepped out from behind the counter. She was country chic in black denim and a black boat neck shirt. Patrice opened her long, skinny arms. "Come here and give us a hug."

Patrice Dawson was Millie's mom. Millie and I had practically grown up together, joined at the hip from kindergarten through high school until I went off to college, and she went into yoga and massage therapy training.

We hugged. Her delicate violet perfume tickled my nose. "I haven't seen you in a dog's age." She held me at arm's length. "How've you been keeping yourself?"

CHAPTER ONE

"Fine as frog hair." I tucked my hands into my pockets and rocked back on my heels.

Her gaze drifted over to Jimmy Duvall, Rothdale's finest sheriff deputy, who, for the past two weeks, was doubling as my beau. Her brow lifted. "Mm-hm. I see." So *not* subtle.

My face grew warm. Time to deflect what was shaping up to be an awkward encounter. "You look great."

She did. Her skin was clear and pale, with only the faintest smile lines around her eyes and mouth to signal her fifty-eight years. Young and fit for her age, she might've looked younger if she still dyed her hair chestnut brown. But she let her gray hair take over, which gave her a magical, witchy quality that I adored. Especially when she wore all black. A small silver mermaid dangled from a chain around her neck.

"That's a pretty necklace."

She touched the mermaid. "Thank you. Dee Dee and I got ourselves these little necklaces to celebrate our five-year anniversary of owning the distillery." Patrice looked over my body wrapped in dark jeans and a thin, red cotton shirt. "You're looking good, girl." She winked at Jimmy. "I bet that has something to do with you."

Jimmy chuckled, I blushed, and Patrice laughed, nudging Jimmy with her elbow. She sobered. "Oh, honey, Millie told me all about Prim's cancer. How's she doing?"

"As well as can be expected, I guess. She has good days and bad days."

"She still refusing treatments?"

I nodded. "Yeah."

She shook her head and squeezed my arm. "If there's anything at all I can do, you don't hesitate to tell me, okay?"

I nodded again, biting my lip to keep from getting emotional.

Delia "Dee Dee" Winslow floated from the back room, wearing a daffodil-yellow jacket and flowy skirt. A large gold statement necklace lay flat against her radiant bronze skin. Her black hair was plaited into several braids, which had been coiled into a bun at the back of her head. She smiled. "Well, look what the cat dragged in. Patrice, why didn't you tell me Rook was here?"

"They just now walked in."

Dee Dee and Patrice had been friends since kindergarten. Much like my bestie Millie and I, they went to the same college together, shared dorms and apartments, stood at each other's weddings, and helped each other shoulder all of life's ups and downs in the way only a best friend will do. Their friendship had weathered the test of time, lasting far longer than most marriages. In its own way, it was a kind of marriage.

Dee Dee swept me up in a tight embrace. She smelled fresh and bright, like sunshine. I introduced her to Jimmy. After asking after each other's families, Dee Dee said, "What brings y'all out this way?"

"We wanted to take a tour of Kentucky's only female-owned bourbon distillery, and I brought that loaner canopy for y'all to use at the festival tomorrow."

"Thank you so much," they said in unison.

Patrice said, "Our canopy has a huge tear in it. I don't know how that happened. Clem must not've been very careful when he put it in storage. And we didn't have time to order a new one when we discovered the tear."

"Think nothing of it. My boss didn't mind one bit loaning it to y'all, since we had extras. Everything's in Jimmy's truck...." Both women looked at Jimmy with a curious light in their eyes. I tried to ignore their questioning gaze and continued. "Do you have someone who can help us get them out before we leave?"

Patrice acknowledged me with a nod, but she was already honing in on her target: Jimmy. "Now then...." She extended an elegant arm with a charming and sneaky side smile. Her voice oozed honey tones. "The infamous Deputy Jimmy Duvall." He chuckled and accepted her hand. "I'm not sure how infamous I am."

Patrice flashed me a knowing look. "Oh, I do."

And with that, the dam of Patrice's politeness and hospitality broke into a flood of questions leveled at Jimmy, who tried to maintain an equilibrium of courtesy and respect in the face of her interrogation. Meanwhile, Dee Dee, in the vein of older women who have no filter and whose one mission in life was to embarrass all younger people, snapped her head around and

CHAPTER ONE

descended on me. "Y'all are dating now? What happened to Cam?"

My skin crawled with fire ants, and a thin film of sweat broke out under my arms. "He and I are no longer together."

Her usual velvety voice tripped up two octaves. "What? Patrice, were you aware of this?"

Patrice stopped her interrogation long enough to answer. "I've known it for a while. Millie told me. How did you not know that? I'm certain I told you."

Dee Dee smacked her lips and tapped Patrice's arm. "Noooo. You did not, missy. Why didn't you tell me?"

Patrice ignored the question and turned back to Jimmy, drilling every ounce of significant information out of him while he tried to keep up with both conversations.

Dee Dee latched on to me. "What happened to Cam?"

"He and I divorced about nineteen months ago." I tried to keep my answers short and as polite as possible. But I did *not* want to discuss Cam. Things were always so complicated with him. We had problems. In short, we had both contributed to the dissolution of our marriage. He moved on much faster, which hurt. And a few weeks ago, when he'd declared he still loved me, it had freaked me out because he'd been engaged to another woman at the time, and I doubted his love. Not because I thought he was manipulating me, but because we'd been spending a lot of time together, and I thought he was mistaking nostalgia and sentimentality for love.

"Aw, I thought you two were forever and ever amen." She crossed her arms over her ample chest.

I pulled at the front of my shirt to fan the heat building in my face. "It's really complicated," I muttered.

The doorbell rang as a visitor entered the distillery. *Millie. Thank heavens!* I waved, "Hey, girl."

Her long dark hair was thrown into a loose ponytail. She labored under a large box. "Hey, y'all."

Jimmy jogged toward her. "Let me take that." The small ropes of muscle in his biceps and forearms bulged as he took over the box.

"Thank you," Millie breathed, rubbing her arms. "Whew! That sucker was heavy."

"Are those the T-shirts for the festival?" Patrice trailed after Jimmy.

"Sure is." She pushed her sunglasses up on her head to reveal teal eyes like her mother's. Classically pretty, she reminded me of a Pre-Raphaelite model with round, limpid teal eyes and a straight nose over plump lips. Dressed in a white peasant skirt and coral tank top, the teeny bells on her ankle bracelet jingled as she walked, harmonizing with the soft *flip-flop* of her sandals. She reached to greet me with a hug.

I whispered in her ear. "I'm *so* glad you're here. They're putting Jimmy and me through the wringer."

"Mama, are y'all bothering Rook and Jimmy?"

Patrice waved a hand. "Not at all. I was just curious about a few things." Patrice and Dee Dee rifled through the boxes, and each pulled out a peach T-shirt with teal writing that read *Mermaid Cove Summer Nights*. They held them up, chattering and inspecting the cotton shirts.

Clement Sikes, the custodian, limped from the back of the building, the keys jangling with each step like spurs on cowboy boots. He was a big, burly man, about six feet tall, wearing a Mermaid Cove T-shirt and worn jeans. His arms were brown and leathery from a life of working outside. "Miss Dee Dee, I want to show this spot back here. I think we're going to need new equipment."

"Oh, dear. Let me go look at this. I'll be right back."

"We also have a fan out in the tasting room," Patrice told him. "It's been out for a few weeks."

Clem glowered at her. "There's only one of me," he snapped. "Y'all act like I'm some kind of Superman. There's only so much a body can do. Maybe if y'all hired me a little help around here—"

Dee Dee clapped her hands and jumped in. "Let's not get into that now."

Patrice put her hands on her narrow hips. "Now, Clem, you know we appreciate you."

He hmphed as Dee Dee stepped around Clem and started down the hall. "Show me what you're talking about." She glanced back at us. "Excuse me.

CHAPTER ONE

I'll be right back."

Clem flashed the stink-eye at Patrice one last time before following Dee Dee out of the room.

Patrice rolled her eyes and waved at me. "Never mind Clem. He's a good worker and does everything we need. After he grumps about it a bit."

Trying to break the awkwardness, I looked around, taking in the track lights and shiny oak walls. "It looks like y'all've put a lot of work into the place since I was here last."

"Oh, we have. You want to see what we've done outside?"

Millie added, "You should. It's gorgeous."

I locked fingers with Jimmy's. "Let's go. You haven't seen the place yet."

"Sure." Jimmy reached for his wallet. "How much are the tickets for the tour and the tasting?"

Patrice waved her hands at him. "Put that away. We won't take your money."

After a few minutes of obligatory polite arguing over payment, I said to Jimmy, "You aren't going to win this. Let it go."

"All right." He put his wallet away and held up his hands in defeat.

Patrice told Millie, "When Dee Dee comes back, tell her we're touring and that I need her to look at that paperwork on the desk."

Mille leaned on the counter and laughed. "You're just trying to get out of paperwork."

"Every chance I get," Patrice guffawed. "I sure love spending the money, but I hate keeping track of it. I'll do the ordering when I get back." She patted Millie's arm. Patrice turned to us. "C'mon, y'all. Let's get this party started."

The Mermaid Cove Distillery lobby and gift shop was similar to most bourbon distilleries inside with the oak barrel décor, but it was blended with touches of beachy flair in the form of fishing nets, mermaid wall hangings, turquoise glass mosaics, and nautical-themed pictures. Together it created an elegant, rustic chic environment. Patrice showed us through the distillery itself, which contained the copper distillers, great oak fermenter bins, and bottling line all distilleries needed to function. Where Mermaid

Cove separated itself from all the others was the green space outside the buildings.

We passed out of the production building into a veritable paradise. We walked along a seashell path—quite unusual for Kentucky—to a man-made waterfall that equaled in beauty and magnificence anything Mother Nature could produce. Out of the brush of honeysuckle and ivy, a stair-step of great stones fell under a cascade of rushing water that pooled into a lazy stream wrapping around the perimeter of the distillery. On the other side of the distillery, a bridge arched over the stream topped with lily pads, like a Monet painting brought to life. This bridge led to an English flower garden complete with a hedge maze. Winding back around, we were brought to a covered patio behind the bistro. In the evenings, Patrice explained, it would be lit with a myriad of patio bulbs, which would, no doubt, lend an otherworldly quality to Mermaid Cove Distillery.

When we'd completed the tour, we gathered at one of the patio tables. I sat at a table and scanned the scene around me. Trees on the cusp of autumn colors rimmed the property below a sapphire blue sky filled with enormous puffy clouds. The jittery feeling I'd had all morning melted away in the serene atmosphere. "This place is amazing, Patrice."

"Should be. It cost me a fortune. Money we didn't really have to spend." She looked around proudly. "It's been a ton of hard work and many sleepless nights, but this is our baby. Our pride and joy. We hope to pass this on to Millie and to Dee Dee's son, Roderick, in the future." She looked down at her hands. "If it survives that long."

Millie already owned a yoga and massage center, so I couldn't imagine how she'd manage a distillery, too. But it wasn't necessary to bring up that particular rain cloud to wash out Patrice's hopes.

A server brought out a sampling of the Summer Nights bourbon whisky for Jimmy and me to taste. I examined the bourbon in the light. The amber liquid was clear as a topaz gemstone. Not a single particle. Holding the glass under my nostril to get the "nose," I detected notes of peach, topped with hints of honeysuckle and vanilla. Taking the shot, the flavors exploded in my mouth. If I could drink a sunset, this was it. Warm, golden, smooth,

CHAPTER ONE

tranquil; it fired against my tongue and warmed all the way down my throat into my belly.

"Man, that's good stuff." Jimmy swirled the dark amber liquid in the snifter. "I want a bottle of this to take home."

"Me too. That is delicious. There's no way Four Wild Horses' Devil's Kiss can compete with this at the competition next weekend." I took another sip. My mind was already racing to create cocktail recipes. "This'll make fabulous hot toddies this fall and winter, with a bit of orange and ginger. Or pair it with Kentucky Spice soda to make a Kentucky Mule cocktail. The citrus ginger of the soda and a touch of mint would be really refreshing—especially if you make it frozen."

Patrice tapped my arm. "Oh, that's a good idea. I'll share those ideas with our bartender." She ran her hand through her hair as she studied the landscape. "You think we can beat Fox Trace at the competition next weekend too? Their Totally Foxed Blended Bourbon Whiskey is one of the best in the industry."

I said, "There's no doubt Fox Trace is good, but it's not this good. If y'all don't win next weekend, then that contest is rigged."

Dee Dee was mad as a wet hen when we returned, slamming papers and pens around on the countertop and muttering to herself.

"What's wrong?" Patrice pulled a couple bottles of Summer Nights off the shelf by the counter.

"Oh, that Fox Graham was out here nosing around, trying to get us to drop out of the contest."

Jimmy launched into deputy mode. "Did he threaten you?"

"No." Dee Dee waved her hand. "It was his tone. And I found him back in our office." She rubbed her upper arms as if cold.

"What!" Patrice cried, setting the bottles on the counter by the register. "What was he doing back there?"

"Don't know. I'd stepped away to go to the restroom and found him before he reached the desk. He tried to pretend like he was lost." Dee Dee rolled her eyes.

Jimmy's eyes searched the ceiling. "Do you have any cameras in place?"

"Not yet." Patrice wrung her hands and exchanged a worried look with Dee Dee. "We've been meaning to get some installed, but…"

Dee completed the statement. "We hadn't gotten around to it yet."

Patrice swept her hand through her long bangs. "I guess we'll need to get cameras installed next."

Dee Dee pulled her jacket around herself like a hug. "I wonder how much all that'll cost?"

"There's a good security company downtown called Gate Keeper Plus. They have a range of systems that could run a few hundred to a few thousand. Depends on the package." Jimmy scanned the room, extracting his phone from his pocket.

Both women's eyes glazed over.

Jimmy typed notes on his phone. "Did Fox take or damage anything or hurt you?"

Dee Dee hugged herself tighter. "No. He's just so…aggravating. When I asked why he was here, he started saying stuff about how we should drop out now because we'll never win. That Summer Nights can't compete with Totally Foxed by any standard. Which is complete nonsense if you ask me."

"Don't you worry about that," I said. "Summer Nights is one of the best bourbon whiskeys I've ever tasted. Y'all have every chance of winning."

Jimmy typed notes into his phone. "Why's this important? What would you win?"

Even though I'd been talking about this contest with him for weeks, he apparently hadn't been listening to a word I said.

"For starters, we'd win an interview with *National Bourbon Review* magazine, which would put us on the bourbon map, so to speak. It could really boost our popularity and our sales."

"We'd also win the prestigious Kentucky Distiller's Guild award and about ten thousand dollars," Patrice added.

My eyes popped wide. "That's a lot of money."

Dee Dee pursed her lips and nodded. "That money would come in handy, too. We—"

Patrice cleared her throat loudly and shot an intense look at Dee Dee, cutting off her sentence. Dee Dee pinched her lips together.

Jimmy pulled out his card and handed it to Dee Dee. "If he threatens you or you need him removed from the property in the future, you let me know. If he becomes violent or threatening, you could get a restraining order against him."

"Or I could just get that little jerk in a headlock…." Dee Dee imitated a headlock with one arm. "And razz that silly head of his." She used her other arm to imitate scrubbing an invisible scalp with her knuckles.

We all laughed. Jimmy's presence and the comic relief seemed to soothe the women, returning the atmosphere to its prior ease and warmth.

Patrice rang up our purchases with a deep discount.

As we said our goodbyes, Patrice and Dee Dee commissioned me to give their love to Prim. "Tell her we're thinking about her," Patrice said, holding my hands.

I squeezed her hands. "I will. Thank you for thinking of us. And don't worry. I'm sure y'all are going to win. Then you won't have to worry about Fox Graham ever again. Your star will rise, and he'll be left in the dust where snakes like him belong."

Chapter Two

We began setting up at The Bourbon, Bands, and BBQ Festival around ten in the morning, so we'd be ready to go by the time the festival-goers poured into Rothdale's town square by noon. Folks from all over Kentucky came to check out the vast array of food, clothing, and beverage vendors and sample the best bourbon and BBQ in the world while enjoying live music ranging from Southern and classic rock to country and bluegrass. Fortunately, August's heat wave had abated into the balmy climate of mid-September. The day was perfection.

Since my distillery, Four Wild Horses, had entered Devil's Kiss bourbon-whiskey in the contest, we set up a booth to offer samples and notify folks of upcoming events and bourbons. I'd dressed comfortably in a pair of worn jeans, sneakers, and a long-sleeved gray T-shirt with a blue distressed FWH logo on the back. I pulled my hair up in a high ponytail to keep it out of my face while my co-workers and I worked on organizing the booth and setting up sample flights of our most popular spirits.

My phone buzzed. The federal prison. It was my dad's weekly call. My heart sank under the weight of guilt, shame, and sadness. I hadn't been to see him in about a year. It was too hard to go and too easy to put off. I hated that he was in prison. Truth be told, he probably deserved some jail time for his smaller crimes. He wasn't an honest man. But he didn't deserve a life sentence for a murder he hadn't committed.

I silenced the phone and crammed it in my back pocket. I didn't have time right now. I had work to do. It was crazy how one little thing could trigger a flood of memories. Now, thanks to that call, my past splashed over me

CHAPTER TWO

like cold water. How, in my youth, Prim would take me to the prison to visit dad once a month. Dad had always told me he was getting an appeal and would be out soon. But soon never came. Then as I got older, school, extracurricular activities, and boyfriends ate up my time and my monthly visits dropped to quarterly ones.

By the time I reached college, life had overwhelmed me, and my visits dropped to a couple times a year and weekly phone calls and random conversations with the lawyer. My dad was innocent, but I didn't know what to do about it. I trusted the lawyers to do their jobs. But I realized as I opened a bottle of Devil's Kiss and poured out several samples I hadn't heard from the lawyer in a while.

Millie's face entered my vision and snapped me out of my reverie. "You all right?" she asked. A sequined bandeau she'd crafted herself held back her luxurious waist-length hair and matched her mustard-colored tank top, green batik-printed maxi skirt, and jeweled sandals.

I slapped on a bright smile. "I'm fine."

She eyed me with disbelief. "If you say so." Then she thankfully changed the subject. "Got you a chai latte and pumpkin spice cream cheese danish from Irene's." She held out a paper bag and cup. "I figured you hadn't had a chance for breakfast."

My mouth dropped open. Millie was right, of course. I'd stayed up late looking through my dad's old trial transcripts—for the tenth time—in hopes of catching something. Inevitably, I slept late and was forced to rush out of the house without so much as a coffee. "You are a whole bowl of awesome." I grabbed the bag and cup. "I knew there was a reason you're my bestie." Digging the danish out of the bag, I winked at her and bit into the sweet, spicy flavors of fall. "Fank oo so mush," I said through a mouth full of food.

"It's slow at my mom's booth right now. Thought I'd come hang out with you for a bit." Millie extracted a danish from the bag.

"Morning, ladies." Jimmy strode up to the booth. He said to me, "You've got something on your lips. Hold on." He kissed me, then pulled back, smacking his lips. "Mm. Pumpkin spice> Cream cheese." He stroked the small of my back. "My new favorite."

My cheeks heating up, I nudged him and leaned against his chest.

He asked, "You need help?"

"There're still a few boxes in the van."

He flexed his biceps like a pro-wrestler. "Never fear, Jiffy Jimmy is here." Millie and I exchanged a glance and burst out laughing. He winked at me. "Try not to watch me walk away." He wiggled his hips as he headed to the van.

We giggled at him again. Of course, the way he filled out his jeans made it impossible for me to resist watching him.

Millie leaned over my shoulder. "You're smiling like my grandma with a winning Bingo card."

"I can't help it. I mean, you *see* him, right?" I sipped my chai latte.

She laughed. "Could this be love?"

Almost choking on my drink, I coughed and slapped my chest.

"No." I waved my hand. "Nonononó."

She blinked at me.

"I don't think so."

She tipped her head and smiled.

I shook my head. "I'm not going there. Not even going to think about it. Just enjoying the companionship. That's all."

Patrice stopped by our booth, her arms loaded with a box. "Hey, ladies, how y'all doing this morning?" Her hair, frizzed in untamed curls, was tucked behind her ears. She wore a pair of black capris with black Keds and a teal Mermaid Cove Distillery T-shirt.

I finished off my danish. "Fantastic."

Patrice said to Millie, "Hon, I need your help until Dee Dee gets here. She's running a little late."

"Sure, momma." Millie took the box from her mom, and they walked a few booths down to the Mermaid Cove booth.

Soon after, the festival started. People poured into the streets and I fell into a rush of issuing samples, talking bourbon, passing out pamphlets, and selling merchandise.

At one point, my neighbor Batrene Bishop and her sister, Bonnie, brought

CHAPTER TWO

my grandma Prim with them. Their arms were loaded with bags of fresh kettle corn, cotton candy, and various other items.

Batrene's fleshy cheeks rounded into a smile. "We wanted to stop by to get us each a bottle of this Four Wild Horses maple bourbon barbeque sauce you've been going on about."

A flutter of happiness passed through me to see Batrene smiling and out of the house so soon after Bryan's death. Her son, and my best friend, had been murdered at the Four Wild Horses Distillery a few weeks ago. He was the accountant there and had discovered a bourbon theft ring. Trying to keep their dastardly deeds in the dark, the monsters killed him. We were all moving on the best we could, but we'd be lying if we didn't admit there was a big Bryan-sized hole in all our lives.

While talking to a visitor about the Four Wild Horses Distillery's most popular flavors, Porter "Cam" Campbell, my ex-husband, entered my field of vision. We divorced nineteen months ago but, somehow, had remained good friends. Of course, he wasn't yet aware that I was dating his best friend, Jimmy. I hadn't meant for that to happen, to keep that information from him; it just sort of…happened, and then it became too difficult to tell Cam. I was afraid of his reaction.

Cam—wearing a cowboy hat, a snug pair of jeans, and a worn T-shirt—carried a folding camping chair in a bag slung over his shoulder. He spotted Prim and Batrene and ran up to speak with them. He hugged them both and kissed Prim's head. He offered his sun-baked arm to her to lead her to a nearby food truck. He bought her, Batrene, and Bonnie a lemonade, then led Prim, following the pace of her mincing steps, to a nearby shade tree. He removed the chair from his back, unfolded it, and helped her sit before squatting by her chair to chat with the ladies. Prim patted his cheek. My insides turned warm and squishy. While Jimmy and Prim got along fine, she didn't seem to like him as much as she liked Cam.

Prim said something to Cam and pointed in my direction. He smiled, and gave me a hat tip, turning me into goo. He excused himself from Prim and returned to the lemonade truck. I turned to attend to a visitor, and then there he was. Cam stood right in front of me with electric blue eyes and a perfect amount of stubble. He looked as though he'd just stepped out of a cowboy novel. "Hey there. I was told you might be in need of a frozen lemonade."

For a split second, it was as if our entire history had vanished, and I felt like a fresh-faced high school girl meeting her crush for the first time. Why was I blushing? "Thank you." I accepted the drink.

"I'm impressed Prim is out of the house."

"Yeah, me too. She pushes herself too hard sometimes, but I think she gets stir-crazy sitting at home all day, every day."

He raked his eyes over me. "You look good. Happy. Haven't seen that on you in a while." He reached and brushed something off my cheek and held up his finger.

A wave of nostalgia crashed over me, and I was carried back to when we first started dating about eight years ago. He'd been so kind, generous, passionate, bold. He changed for a bit. Or I thought he had. Maybe I'd been the one who changed and pushed him away. Because, in this moment, he seemed to be exactly the same man I'd fallen in love with all those years ago.

He flashed that crooked, boyish smile that had always made me weak. "An eyelash. Make a wish."

I was afraid to. In this moment, I might've wished for him. To have us restored. To start all over. "Uh, I can't think of anything."

He chuckled. "Really? Because I can think of a thousand things I'd wish for right now."

"You can have my wish then."

He closed his eyes for a moment, opened them, then blew the eyelash off his finger. "Hope it comes true."

"What did you wish for?"

He snorted, his eyes glinting with humor. "C'mon, Rook. You know the rules for wishes. If I tell you, it won't come true." He winked and hat-tipped me again. I swear I melted into my shoes. He turned to leave and said over his shoulder, "If you can get away, maybe you can join me to watch the bluegrass bands." He rejoined Prim, Batrene, and Bonnie, who were preparing to leave. He retrieved his chair and hugged all the women, and

CHAPTER TWO

continued on his course to the bandstand.

The ladies then came over to say bye to me. Batrene said, "Prim's feeling a little weak now. But she had fun and stayed out much longer than I expected. Bonnie and I'll take her home to get her some lunch and let her rest."

"Sounds good. Thank you." We gave out hugs all around, and they began their trek to wherever they had managed to park.

Just then, a girl I recognized from high school, Melissa Dandree, entered my field of vision, running up to Cam. Bad blood had flowed between Melissa Dandree and me since we were freshmen. She was one of those people who hated people just because she could. She hated me for reasons I couldn't fathom and spread a rumor that I had a host of venereal diseases, causing Eddie Epperson to refuse to accept my invite to a homecoming dance. She was nice to my face and an evil demon cockroach to my back. She downright bullied me but in a passive-aggressive way so that, if I had sought revenge against her, I'd look like the instigator.

My blood boiled to watch her long dark, tousled hair cascade down her back to meet the band of her denim shorty-short shorts showing off her tanned, lightly dimpled thighs. She completed her Daisy Duke look with a pair of cowboy boots and a T-shirt knotted at the side to highlight her hourglass figure. She took his hat off and clapped it on her own head, laughing. He laughed, too, and stood to take the hat back. She playfully slapped away his hand. They chatted for a bit while a barbed blade twisted in my gut and released a flare of anger up through my throat into my brain. A visitor asked me a question, forcing me to refocus, sort of, on my job. Handing a pamphlet to the visitor, my heart sank as I watched Melissa and Cam saunter off. She was still wearing his hat. But the pause gave me a moment to realize that something else slicked the underbelly of that anger. Something I didn't want to admit. I was jealous.

"What a B with an itch," I muttered, defeated. I didn't want to be jealous. I wanted to move on. Right? I was *trying* to move on. I liked Jimmy and had fun with him. But I couldn't pretend that he and I were clicking in the same way I had clicked with Cam. Maybe that was because things were so new with Jimmy.

"Hey, beautiful." Jimmy stepped up to the booth when the visitors had dispersed.

"Oh, hey." I quickly averted my gaze and waved at an invisible fly. "What's up?" I pasted on what I hoped was my prettiest smile. "You having fun?"

He crossed his arms and watched the crowd. "Yeah. Been over at the stage. Some good music out here. You want lunch? The pulled pork at the Hacienda Habanero food truck is calling my name."

Melissa and Cam's apparent connection had burned down my appetite and turned it to ashes in my mouth, and my mind had scattered like a jar of marbles dropped on the ground.

When I took too long to answer, he looked at me. "What's wrong?"

I ground my teeth and tightened my ponytail to buy a little time for an answer that wouldn't tick off my boyfriend. After all, I didn't want to tell him I was having a jealous fit over my ex-husband. There was too much to unpack. "Oh, uh…nothing." I shook my head. "I guess I'm struggling a little this morning." I pulled the puppet strings on my smile a little too tightly.

The hint of suspicion in his eyes belied his response. "I think BBQ will cure what ails you. C'mon, let's grab lunch."

In the name of "fake it 'til you make it," I pretended to be excited about the BBQ, though my stomach was twisted into a pretzel. I left the booth in Jeff and Marla's care.

The air was thick with smoke from the various BBQ pits and food trucks and mingled with the sweeter scents of kettle corn and cotton candy. We ate lunch while watching the first half of the Banjo Kings show, who played bluegrass-Southern rock fusion music. My appetite hadn't returned, but in my usual method of emotional eating, I forced the BBQ into my knotted gut. On our way back, I spotted Cam in the crowd. He wasn't with Melissa, and had regained his hat. I dropped Jimmy's hand and put some distance between us.

"What—?" Jimmy tried to reach for my hand.

I twisted away. "Cam's headed over here. He's seen us."

"He's going to learn about us eventually."

"Yes. But I don't want a dust-up here in public. I'm at work. You were supposed to talk to him."

"I was. I am. I haven't had a chance yet. This is the first day I haven't been at work."

"I know." He did work a lot. Surely, it wouldn't always be this way. "You should've let me handle it."

"No. It should come from me. Trust me. It's a guy thing."

Cam appeared in front of us. "Hey, y'all. What's up? Looks like a serious conversation?"

"Oh, uh, nothing," I lied.

Jimmy changed the subject to the music we'd been listening to as I fiddled with my ponytail and swam in a stew of neuroticism. Self-conscious, I analyzed my every move to ensure I wasn't showing preference or attraction to Jimmy while also remaining neutral to Cam. By the time I parted with them on the premise of returning to work, my nerves were frazzled.

On the way back to the Four Wild Horses booth, I stopped by Mermaid Cove's booth to chat with Patrice, Millie, and Dee Dee.

We were interrupted by one of the bourbon contest organizers. "Good afternoon, y'all. I'm Doug. We're going around double-checking everyone's facts and entries." He was a shiny middle-aged man, preened in yellow pants, a bowtie, a pastel plaid sports jacket, glasses, and a Panama hat. He studied his clipboard. "Oh, wait. I don't see your distillery on the list. Sorry for the mistake." He started to turn away.

Patrice waved her hands. "Whoa. Hold on there. We paid our fee months ago and sent in a bottle of Summer Nights bourbon whiskey."

"Yeah. Look again at the paper." Dee Dee tipped back her wide-brimmed straw hat.

Doug scanned the paper. "Oh, yes. Here you are. It says you withdrew."

"We did not!" Patrice came from behind her table.

"I bet Fox Graham is behind this." Dee Dee fumed, pushing up the sleeves of her turquoise Mermaid Cove T-shirt. "Does it say *who* withdrew us?"

He shook his head. "I can't read the signature."

Dee Dee held out her hand. "Let me see that." She held the paper close as Patrice and Millie looked over her shoulders. "I can't make it out. What do you two think?"

They shook their heads. Dee Dee passed the board to me. I studied the sharp stick-like scratches posing as letters and the loop at the end. I shook my head. "It's illegible." I handed the clipboard to Doug. "The person who signed this, what did they look like?"

Doug pushed his glasses up his nose and shrugged, his eyes wide with fear. "I-I don't know. I didn't see them. This was given to me by the competition organizer."

"Is the organizer still here?" Patrice searched the crowd. "I want to speak to them."

Dee Dee jumped in. "We'll worry about that later. Right now, we have to get re-entered. Scratch out that name." She tapped the board with a shiny red nail.

Doug blinked. "But we don't have your bourbon to even enter it into the contest. It was revoked."

"I'll fix that right up." Dee Dee looked around. "Let's find a bottle…" She rummaged through the boxes stacked on the ground along the back of the booth. "These are all empty. And there are only five boxes here. There should be ten." She looked under the table. One by one, she opened the remaining five boxes and inspected their contents. "All these contain our Single Barrel Bourbon." Her voice pitched a couple notches. "It's not even the right bourbon. How did this happen?"

"Clem," Patrice scoffed, balling her fists. "I told him which boxes we needed loaded in the van. I even marked them. He loaded the wrong blasted cases. I could choke him."

Dee Dee pressed her fingers to her temples. "I cannot believe this is happening."

Fox Graham approached, his hands plunged into his jeans pockets and his eyes hidden behind reflective sunglasses. He was a short, muscular man with pasty skin, bright blond hair, and a wide smile full of large teeth. He wore a dark green Fox Trace T-Shirt. "Hey there," he said in a nasally drawl. "How're y'all doing today?"

I'd never cared much for Fox Graham. I'd known him in high school. He was the sort of guy who wouldn't study and then flirt with the smart, plain girls to cheat on homework and tests. He wasn't popular, but a hanger-on and sycophant to the more popular kids who tolerated him or used him as a scratching post. Yet, by making himself seen with the popular kids, he was able to live off their scraps in less popular circles.

Dee Dee half-snarled. "What do you want?"

"I couldn't help but overhear that y'all aren't going to be in the contest." He scratched his nose. "That's a shame." He seemed to be suppressing a laugh.

"Fox…." Millie sighed. "This isn't helpful."

I crossed my arms. "You wouldn't happen to know anything about what occurred here?"

Fox shrugged and threw up his hands. "Beats me. I overheard and wanted to offer my condolences."

"If we can get a bottle of bourbon to you before the contest, will you let us re-enter?" Patrice asked Doug.

"Well…." He hemmed.

Dee Dee "You don't really want that getting around, do you? Because I will tell everyone here. Imagine the embarrassment, the damage to your contest's reputation, and the number of angry people you'll have to deal with."

Doug batted his eyes. "Well, I-uh-uh-I…." He scratched the back of his head and sighed. "Okay. If you can get a new bottle to us, we'll get you re-registered." He marked out the signature. "In the meantime, I'm going to see about locating your proof of payment."

Patrice squeezed his arm. "Thank you so much." Then she said to Dee Dee, "I'm going to run out to the distillery and grab a few cases of Summer Nights. I'll be right back. Millie, hon, will you help Dee Dee until I return?"

"Okay, Momma. Be careful."

As he turned away, Fox chimed in, his tone touched with menace, "Yes. Do be careful."

My gut wrenched as I watched Fox leave. I muttered to Millie. "He's shady. Wouldn't surprise me a bit if he was responsible for this."

I wondered if I should tell Jimmy. I stood on tiptoes, searching for him. He and Cam were still talking. I didn't want to go back over there to swim in those uncomfortable waters. I'd wait. There wasn't much to be done about it right now, anyway. Patrice would be back soon with the bourbon, and everything would be fine. Maybe we didn't need to get the law involved, and we could pretend like nothing happened.

The rest of the afternoon grew warm and busy. Jeff, Marla, and I slung mini-flights of bourbon like our lives depended on it. However, a little niggling feeling in my gut wouldn't leave me alone. I craned my neck to check out Mermaid Cove's booth. I spotted Millie and Dee Dee, but no Patrice. Something was wrong. She should've been back by now. When traffic at our booth slowed down, I stepped away for a moment to speak with Millie and Dee Dee.

"Is Patrice still not back?" I asked, searching the crowd.

"No." Dee Dee worried her red thumbnail. "It's been an hour. She should be back by now. The bourbon contest is going to start soon. I've tried to call and text, but she's not answering me."

"Maybe she was caught up at the office or ran into a traffic issue." Millie bent down and pulled her phone from its hiding spot under the table. "I'll try calling her, too." She tapped her phone a couple times and held it to her ear.

"When did you call her last, Dee Dee?" I asked.

Her thin brows knitted in concern. "I've called or texted her at least six times."

"She hasn't responded to any of them?"

She pressed her peach-glossed lips together and shook her head. "No. I'm beginning to worry."

"She's not answering. That's not right." Millie tapped her phone again. "I'll try Mitch. Maybe he knows." She waited. Mitch was her mother's live-in fiancé for the past two years. Surely, he would know something. Millie hung up, frowning. "He's not answering, either."

Fox Graham wove through the booths with a cocksure swagger, landing at Mermaid Cove like a yellow jacket at a picnic. He glanced at his watch.

"Huh, still don't have your bourbon?" He winced and added with fake pity, "I guess y'all are going to have to withdraw from the contest, after all."

Dee Dee charged around the table, wagging her finger at him. "What did you do to her? Where is she?"

He held up his hands. "Whoa!" He released a wheezy laugh. "I don't know where she is. But the longer she's gone, my chances of winning get better and better." He grinned. "Y'all have a good afternoon." He saluted us with two fingers and walked away.

Millie's eyes widened. "What if something happened to her?" She retrieved her purse and keys from under the table. "I'm going to go look for Momma."

I ran after her. "I'll go with you."

Chapter Three

Marla and Jeff understood my emergency and covered the Four Wild Horses booth while I went with Millie to Mermaid Cove. I called Jimmy on the way and informed him of the situation. "Meet us out there as soon as you can."

Millie floored the gas. "I hope she's okay. Keep trying to call her for me." She clutched the wheel until her knuckles turned white.

We sat in tense silence for the twenty-minute drive to the distillery while I repeatedly redialed Patrice's cell, office, and home. The distillery sat northeast of Rothdale, out in the rural landscape of Franklin County, Kentucky, so we rounded through hills and curves with crops, cows, and barns whizzing by.

"I'm going to stop by the house first since it's on the way. Maybe she stopped there." Millie slowed down at a road squeezed between two horse farms. Autumn Ridge Estates represented some of the wealthiest families in Kentucky, where grand houses ornamented large swaths of land. Many of the residents in the rural subdivision owned horse farms.

We pulled up in the drive of a gray brick, modern cottage-style home with a large bay window on the right.

Millie opened her door. "Wait here." She left the car running as she dashed inside. A couple minutes later, she returned. "No one is home, and it doesn't look like anyone has been there recently. Even weirder, it looks like Mitch's stuff isn't there."

"What do you mean? He's gone?"

"Seems so. His favorite recliner wasn't there in front of the TV. At first, I thought maybe they got rid of it. Maybe it broke, or they were replacing it. But when I checked the bedroom, his clothes were gone, too."

"He's moved out?"

"It appears so." Frowning, Millie threw the car into reverse and peeled out of the drive down the quiet street.

"Have they been having problems?" I watched the trees and fences swish past.

"Mom told me they had been fighting,, but I didn't think it was that bad. Mom never mentioned anything to me about him leaving."

"Maybe it happened really recently. And with the contest and running the distillery, she's been too busy to deal with it. I know I bury myself in work when I don't want to deal with things. Especially emotional stuff." In fact, I was especially thankful for my job in the last few weeks. It kept my mind off the disturbing dreams and the danger I'd been in recently.

Millie adjusted her rearview mirror. "Maybe. Maybe she was embarrassed, or maybe she didn't want me to worry. But we're best friends. It bothers me she wouldn't tell me." She whipped out of Autumn Ridge Estates onto the country road toward Mermaid Cove.

"Well, it doesn't matter right now. The only thing that matters right now is her safety. I hope she's at the distillery."

Mermaid Cove's gray tin roof peeked over a hill covered with goldenrods and tall grass. We flew down the drive and skidded to a halt in front of the building.

There were only two vehicles in the parking lot: a beat-up old blue pickup truck in the center of the lot and a white BMW near the door.

"That's Mom's car." Millie parked beside it, craning her neck to look at the BMW.

We jumped out of Millie's car to get a closer look at the BMW. Millie framed her face with her hands and peered in the window while I scanned the parking lot, looking for signs of life or struggle. Since production didn't operate on the weekends, it gave the distillery an eerie ghost-town quality that made my skin crawl. I rubbed my arms. I wanted to leave. But not without Patrice.

Millie said, "Nothing in there seems out of place. Let's check inside."

We jogged to the building. A large sign on the door announced that the distillery was closed to tours since the staff was away for the festival. We tried the door. Unlocked. Millie and I exchanged a look of concern.

Millie said, "That's not right."

"No, it's not."

Inside, the building was cool and smelled of peaches, oak, and corn mash. The lights were on in the gift shop, and near the black granite counter, several broken bottles of Summer Nights and crate lay in a large puddle of bourbon. Dread filled my chest with ice. This was not good.

Millie shouted for her mother as she ran to the back of the building. I stopped to look around. There didn't appear to be a struggle, except for the broken bottles and crate. I pulled my phone out of my back pocket and snapped a few pictures at different distances and angles, texting them to Jimmy. Millie continued to shout for her mom, the panic in her voice increasing as she searched. But Patrice didn't appear.

I shouted to Millie, "I'm checking out back." I searched the water first, so Millie wouldn't have to in case things had gone really bad. No body. Thank heavens.

The sound of scraping metal echoed several yards away. I followed the sound to the gazebo. Clement Sikes, the maintenance man, shoveled dirt around the gazebo. He wore a T-shirt under bibbed overalls, a U of B-ball cap pulled over his eyes, and Timberland boots. A wheelbarrow of mulch that reeked of dung and a cart of yellow mums, hay bales, pumpkins, and a cutesy scarecrow stood nearby.

"Hey there." I tucked my hands into my back pockets. "I was wondering if you've seen Patrice recently?"

Holding the shovel handle in the crook of one arm, he released a red bandana from his back pocket, lifted his cap, and wiped the sweat from his red face. The right eye looked to the outside corner while the left eye looked at me, and his long bushy beard bobbed up and down as he spoke. "Nawp. Can't say as I have."

CHAPTER THREE

"She seems to be missing. You're Clement, right?"

"Maybe." He frowned. "Who are you? The po-lice?" He clapped his hat down on his head, wiggling it around to get a "just right" fit.

"No." I chuckled to show goodwill, though I wasn't especially feeling it. "I'm Millie's friend. We're looking for Patrice."

He sniffed and rubbed his nose. "Whelp. I ain't seen her."

"Have you been here all day?" I glanced at the spot of fresh earth he'd been working on. It was at least four or five feet long. Long enough for a body.

"Yep. Since this morning."

"Have you seen anyone else here? Maybe someone who shouldn't have been?"

He snorted, then spat a loogie toward the creek about fifteen feet away. "Nawp. Ain't seen a soul." He jabbed the shovel into the ground to make it stand on its own. "Not that I expect to. They all out at the festival whooping it up while I'm out here working." I noticed a colorless tattoo on his arm of a daisy growing out of a broken heart. The flower had only one petal and another petal falling. The name *Daisy* was written underneath. He turned, grabbed the handles on the wheelbarrow, rolled it over to the dirt patch, and dumped it.

"They're working too."

"Pfft. Whatever." He grabbed the shovel from the earth, jammed it in the ground, and pulled up a clump.

"Looks like you're working awfully hard." I put a little extra twang in my accent to signal I wasn't an outsider.

"Always. I bust my butt around here, can't get no help. It's always…." He spoke in a mock female voice, 'Clem do this. Clem do that. Clem, Clem, Clem' I'm sick of hearing my own name."

I blinked at him. What a sourpuss. "Well, Patrice and Dee Dee are your employers."

As if he hadn't heard me, he said, "They work me like a mule but don't want to pay me what I'm worth. They say they can't afford it. But they sure have plenty of money to buy those fancy cars and clothes."

Awkwardness crawled over my skin. It was deeply inappropriate for him to talk this way about his employers to a stranger. A nightcrawler wiggled out of the ground. He bent and plucked it from the dirt. He smiled, his two front bottom teeth missing. "Save that 'un for later. Catfish love 'em." He deposited the worm in a nearby Styrofoam cup. "I sure do love fresh catfish. Fried up in cornmeal. Mm-mm. Good eats."

"You do much fishing?"

"Yeah, buddy. I'd be out on the water right now if the boss ladies hadn't made me come in today to mess with these flowers and such."

I squinted against the sun. "You like working here?"

"You shore ask a lot of questions, little girl." He shifted the mulch around with the shovel head.

Aggravation tickled the hairs on the back of my neck, but I needed to play nice if I expected to get any information out of this guy. "I mean, I figure Patrice and Dee Dee are good bosses."

"They're all right for lady bosses." His voice lowered to a warning level as he shot me a hard glance. "Pretty naggy. Always asking me to do something then complaining when I don't do it *just the way* they want it done." He grabbed a hay bale and dropped it haphazardly on the corner of his dirt patch by the gazebo steps. "Reminds me of my first wife."

There was an air about this man that made my guts squirm like the inside of his night crawler cup. I didn't like him. And what's more, I couldn't help but wonder if Patrice was in the ground beneath the stinky mulch, covered in night crawlers.

My phone chimed with a text from Millie asking where I was. I texted back that I was on my way. After thanking Clem for talking to me, I ran off making a mental note to come back out to poke around in that patch of dirt the first chance I had.

Millie stood in the doorway of her mom's office.

The office was disheveled, as if there'd been a struggle. *Uh-oh*. I'd seen this before. Images of finding Bryan dead flashed in my mind, of his body lying in a disheveled office at the Four Wild Horses Distillery. At least in this case, there was no dead body. Yet. I closed my eyes and said a silent prayer that I wouldn't find a dead body this time. I'd had more than my fill in the past couple months.

Millie motioned toward the office. "Look at this place." She turned her wide eyes to me. "Something bad has happened here. She's been…." She clapped her hands over her mouth, and tears filled her eyes. "What if she's been…k-hurt?"

"Hey, hey, hey…." I wrapped an arm around her. "It's going to be okay. Maybe she was in a hurry or…." I struggled for the right words as Millie's fears seeped into my own body. "Or maybe there was an emergency." True hope fell out of the words that felt hollow and empty in my mouth.

Her voice wrenched a few pitches. "Where could she be?"

"I don't know. We'll find her. I promise." I knew I was looking at a crime scene, and we didn't need to be in here any longer than necessary. I guided her out of the room. "Why don't you call Rothdale General Hospital? Maybe there was an emergency, and she didn't have time to call."

Dazed, she nodded and stepped out of the room.

I stood in the doorway of the office, leery about stepping inside and tainting the scene in case a crime had been committed. I called Jimmy.

He answered. "I'm almost there. What's up?"

"It looks shady here," I scanned the room. "The desk chair is pushed far back in the corner." I craned my neck, then bent over to look at the floor around the desk. "Papers are scattered on the floor behind the desk. The desk phone is knocked onto the floor."

"Anything missing?"

"Hard to tell. Besides, I've only been in this office a few times in my life. I wouldn't know what's normally here. I can only say it doesn't look right. I'll call Dee Dee to come out here to verify."

"Okay, good. Don't go in. Close the door ASAP, and don't let anyone in until I get there. I'll call for assistance."

We hung up. Before I shut the door, I snapped several pictures of the office with my phone and texted them to Jimmy. Then I pulled my shirt sleeve over my hand to prevent leaving my fingerprints on the knob and closed the door.

I met Millie in the gift shop. I scanned the room, looking for anything out of place, but everything seemed in order. Millie paced, pressing her palm to her forehead.

"Any luck with the hospital?"

She wrapped her arms around her middle and looked out of the window into the parking lot. "No. There's no one by her name or description." She turned to gaze at the floor. "I guess I should clean up that mess."

I stepped forward, my hand out like a traffic cop. "No. You can't. It could be evidence."

"You mean you think my mom was murdered?" she squeaked.

"That's not exactly what I'm saying. Maybe she was...." My heart sank at the tortured look in her eyes. I knew her fear. I lived a nightmare when my mom was murdered and taken from me when I was only eleven years old. The thought of Millie suffering the same loss was almost too much to bear. I'd give anything for her to not suffer through the loss of her mom, too. Yet, I couldn't lie to her. There was no way to shelter her, because the sheriff's office would tell her soon enough. "Taken."

She clapped her hand over her mouth, silent tears spilling down her cheeks. She shook her head and fell against me. I held her and whispered comforts. Over her shoulder, Jimmy entered the building carrying a notepad and pen. His badge was hooked to his belt.

"Jimmy's here," I said. "We'll let him look around. Maybe he can find evidence. Okay?"

She pulled away, wiping her eyes and sniffling.

"Go get yourself cleaned up," I whispered.

Millie nodded and disappeared down the hall to the restroom.

Jimmy rubbed the small of my back. "There are people on the way. How's she doing?"

"Freaked out, obviously."

He nodded. "Understandable." His eyes roved over the scene. "Thanks for sending those pictures. They'll be helpful." His boots clomped on the polished oak floor. He carefully scanned the room, then squatted by the counter to make a note of the shattered bourbon whisky bottle and scrutinized the cash wrap.

CHAPTER THREE

"The office is back here." I led him down the short, dim hallway.

Jimmy pulled a pair of latex gloves out of his back pocket, snapped them on, and opened the door to the office.

Dee Dee shouted from the front of the building. "Millie! Rook!"

Leaving Jimmy to inspect the office, I met Dee Dee in the gift shop. "Hey." We hugged. She smelled like jasmine flowers.

"Where is she? Why isn't she answering her phone?" She started toward the office.

"You can't go back there yet. Jimmy's searching the office to see if he can find any clues."

"Clues? Oh, that means something bad has happened." She put her hands to her face.

"We aren't sure yet." I rubbed circles on her back to comfort her. "But I think it's safe to assume there's been foul play since we can't reach her, and the hospital doesn't have her."

Dee Dee's bottom lip quivered. "I can't believe this is happening." She closed her eyes and dropped her head into her hands. Her lips moved in a silent prayer.

Millie joined us, dabbing at her eyes and sniffing.

I said to her, "You should try to call Mitch again to see if he knows anything or has seen her."

She rolled her eyes. "I feel so stupid. Why didn't I think of that?" She tapped her phone screen a few times. After a moment, she said, "Mitch. Have you seen Mom?" She fell into a series of "uh-huhs" and "okays." She met my gaze and shook her head. "Okay." Disappointment entered her voice. She ended the call and sighed. "He says that the last time he saw her was yesterday at home."

The distillery phone at the gift shop desk rang. Dee Dee, Millie, and I looked at each other.

"I'll get it." Dee Dee answered the phone. After a long pause, she snapped, "Who *is* this? Do you have Patrice? What have you done with her? I want to talk to her right now." Millie and I hovered nearby, holding hands and staring intensely at her, as if we could suck information from her brain. "I'm not doing anything until you prove to me she's okay." There was a pause, then frantically, she added, "Patrice? Patrice? Are you okay? We're going to find you, sugar. We're going to…"

Millie's nails dug into my knuckles.

"Okay. Hold on. I need a pen."

Dee Dee grabbed a pen and looked around. She snapped her fingers and air-scribbled, indicating she needed a piece of paper. We all looked around. Millie ran to the book stand and pulled out a book, then flipped to the back blank pages and laid it flat on the counter. Dee Dee made sounds of acknowledgment at the caller and wrote while Millie and I peered over her shoulder. I couldn't make out the message since I was reading it upside down, so I scooted over to get a better view.

Jimmy came from the back, talking loudly. "Well, ladies, I—"

I stuck a finger over my lips to indicate he should be quiet.

He sidled up to me and whispered, "What's going on?"

"Someone is calling about Patrice. I think she's been kidnapped. They're giving Dee Dee information."

Dee Dee said, "Okay. I will. You make sure you take care of her and that she comes back safe and sound. You hear?" She looked at Jimmy, her dark eyes full of terror. "Okay. I won't. No police. I promise. Okay. Okay." She placed the receiver in the cradle and confirmed our worst fears. "Patrice has been kidnapped, and they want money. More than I can possibly afford. They want a million dollars."

My guts dropped into my shoes, and my face went numb. "Holey moley." I couldn't even imagine what a million dollars looked like or how a human even put their hands on that much money.

"They said they're watching me and the distillery, and they'll know if I talk to the police." She gripped my hands. "They said if the police get involved, they'll kill her and then come for me."

Chapter Four

Just when I thought things had hit rock bottom, in walked Sheriff Harlan "Bulldog" Goodman, with Deputy Ladonna Price trailing behind him. His head was as square as a cinder block, and the thick, russet mustache only accented his perpetual frown. He was in plain clothes, a red polo shirt, a pair of dark denims, and cowboy boots. A gun belt and badge hung from his belt line. He scanned the room with cool detachment while Deputy Ladonna Price's eyes darted. She seemed primed for action.

Professional to the core, I couldn't help but like her. She had the great distinction of being the first black woman on the force. But to the basketball-worshiping townsfolk, that paled in comparison to her greater achievement of being the older sister of Billy Reynolds, a.k.a #43 on the University of the Bluegrass Thoroughbreds basketball team. He hadn't played college ball in years and had long moved on to the NBA, but fans in Kentucky still hailed him as one of the greatest point guards the Thoroughbreds had ever known.

Jimmy approached the sheriff and filled him in on the latest events and findings. With arms crossed over his barrel chest and his legs in a power stance, the sheriff nodded and stroked his mustache.

"Have y'all tried to track the phone yet?" he asked Jimmy.

"Not yet. I got here only about ten minutes before you and inspected the office. I'll take care of that now." He shouted in Millie and Dee Dee's direction, "Do either of you know who the carrier is for Patrice's phone?"

Millie shook her head. Dee Dee answered, "AT&T."

Jimmy tapped his phone screen, scrolled, and dialed a number. He paced over to a far corner to complete his call to the phone company as the sheriff placed a call and removed himself to the opposite corner.

Deputy Ladonna approached, pen and notepad in hand. She was a short but solid woman with long, thick lashes edging dark, glittery eyes. Her sepia skin glowed like a polished gem with not a blemish in sight. She was one of those fortunate women who needed no makeup to highlight her natural beauty. "Good evening, ladies. I wanted to get details about what's transpired here."

Dee Dee swiped under her eyes. "My best friend and business partner is missing, and some guy called a few minutes ago to tell us he's holding her for ransom."

Ladonna nodded, one eye squinting. "How much is he asking for?"

"A million," Millie interjected. "How on earth are we going to get that kind of money?" She threw her hands up, defeated. Her voice shook. "She's going to die because I don't have the money."

Ladonna held out a hand, the pen braced between her fingers. "Okay. Hold on. I understand that's frustrating, but I need to collect more information." She turned back to Dee Dee. "What did the guy sound like? Older? Younger? Deep voice? A lisp or accent?"

Dee Dee pursed her lips to think. "His voice was deep. He'd probably sing baritone in a church choir."

Ladonna nodded, scribbling notes, as she scattered a few "Mm-hm" and "Okays" to

encourage Dee Dee to continue.

"He had a regular Kentucky accent, I suppose. No lisp or speech impediments. He sounded like a mature man, but not old. And definitely not young."

"Okay." Ladonna stabbed the paper with a punctuation mark. "Did you hear anything in the background?"

Dee Dee shook her head slowly, fingering her earring. "Mmmm-no. It sounded like he was on a cell phone, because of the static. And it sounded like he was outside. I heard cars swishing by. But I didn't hear anything else."

"Any other people talking?"

CHAPTER FOUR

"Nope. Nothing else." Then her red nail flashed to point at the ceiling. "Except... I think he was a smoker."

"Why do you say that?"

"I heard like a popping of his mouth, a pause, and then an exhale. I've talked to smokers on the phone before, and it reminded me of them."

Ladonna nodded. "Good information. Anything else you can think of?"

"No. I can't think of anything else." Dee Dee shook her head and rubbed the center of her forehead.

The sheriff wrapped up his phone conversation and came toward Dee Dee, Millie, and me. His eyes hardened to little stones when he saw me. "Miss Campbell."

Honestly, just the sight of him aggravated me since he led the investigation that had put my dad in jail for my mom's murder. I was convinced his past with my dad tainted the sheriff's judgment in the case. My dad was a small-scale crook, for sure, and shouldn't be trusted with anyone's money, even in a game of Monopoly, but he was not a murderer.

"Good evening, sheriff," I said, trying to keep a civil tongue in my mouth for Jimmy's sake.

"Why am I not surprised to see you mixed up in yet another nefarious deed in this town? Trouble is like a beacon on the hill for you and your family, isn't it?"

I curled my upper lip with a measure of snark. Jimmy's light, brief touch to the small of my back turned off my mouth. I crossed my arms and turned away to lean against the granite counter. "Whatever..." I pulled my ponytail tighter.

He removed a pad and pen from his chest pocket and began collecting Millie and Dee Dee's identities, how they knew Patrice, and everything they knew about her disappearance up to this point.

"Mrs. Winslow, how is your relationship with Ms. Dawson? Do y'all get along? Any disagreements?"

Dee Dee adjusted her earring. "Our relationship is fine, sir. We've been friends our whole lives. We often disagree on little things, bicker and such, like sisters. But we haven't had any real argument in years."

He nodded, writing. "I see. And how's the business doing? Any reason she might want to disappear of her own volition?"

"What do you mean?"

He circled his hand in the air. "Are you having a lot of financial troubles here? Or has she run off with a large sum of money, anything like that?"

Dee Dee bristled. "Absolutely. Not. Now, I'm not saying we don't need money. We do. We're a fairly new distillery and we're struggling a bit, like any new business. But that's why we entered the contest. If we'd won, it would've boosted our business and established our reputation as genuine and respectable distillers." Her eyes watered. "We were so close."

"You don't think she was cracking under the pressure and ran off with a bunch of money?"

Dee Dee pursed her lips and narrowed her eyes as if to say, *You've got to be kidding*.

Millie interjected, balling her fists at her sides. "My mother would never do anything like that. She's a good, decent woman."

"Understood." Goodman didn't look up from his notes. "I'm only looking at all possible angles, miss."

Dee Dee put a hand on Millie's arm and gave her a back-down-and-be-calm look. "Why're you interrogating me when we received a ransom call."

Millie hugged herself and started pacing between us and a nearby shirt rack.

The sheriff excused himself to look at the office. Jimmy and Ladonna went with him. After about fifteen minutes, they came back.

Goodman said, "Here's the problem I have, Mrs. Winslow. That office isn't very torn up. There's a few things knocked around but, from what I can tell, mostly everything is in place."

"Meaning what?" Dee Dee's brow crinkled.

"Meaning that she seems to have left in a hurry. In fact, it looks a little staged. But I can't rule out other explanations yet."

Anger warmed my blood like a double shot of bourbon. I stepped in. "Sheriff, we received a call from the kidnappers right before you walked in. They were demanding a ransom and told us that we shouldn't call you

CHAPTER FOUR

because they'd kill both Patrice and Dee Dee. If she was being kidnapped, then she probably did leave in a hurry. I don't know how much clearer it could be."

He stroked his mustache. "Miss Campbell, while I appreciate your enthusiasm and evident expertise, I have to consider all explanations. Even the ones that may seem implausible or offensive to you and your friends' sensibilities."

"I have another angle for you. What about that creepy maintenance man who works here?" I pointed at the back door.

Dee Dee tucked her chin. "Clem Sikes?"

"Yes. He's out back right now working a body-sized patch of ground."

As if calling his name had summoned him from beyond, Clem entered the room, his keys jangling. He held his hat in one hand and wiped his forehead on his upper arm. His other hand clasped a glass Coke bottle. "Whew." He clapped the hat back on his head and froze when he saw us. His gaze dragged over us with suspicion. "What's going on?"

I said, "Turns out Patrice has been kidnapped. You know anything about that?"

He scoffed, and his eyes lit with mistrust and humor. "You're kidding?" He drew from his Coke bottle and used his bottom lip to draw the moisture off his mustache. My stomach turned. *Gross.*

The sheriff shifted his weight to one foot. "This is not a joke. Can I get your name?"

"Clem Sikes."

The sheriff wrote in his notepad. "And what's your position here, Mr. Sikes?"

"General maintenance, landscaping, whatever needs fixed."

"How long you been here?"

"Since the place opened about five years ago." He wiped his face on his upper arm again.

"If there's anything you can tell us about Ms. Dawson's disappearance, we need to know."

Clem shrugged, his eyes wide. "I don't know nothing."

Dee Dee interrupted. "Did you see *anyone* here today?"

"Nawp." He tucked the Coke bottle in one of the long, narrow pockets on his leg. He then hooked his thumbs in the sides of his bib overalls and laced his fingers together. "I didn't see nothing."

"When did you get here today?" Jimmy asked.

Clem thought. "About two, I reckon."

"Why so late?" Dee Dee asked.

His brow furrowed. "I'd been here earlier fixing a fan in the production house. Then I went out for lunch and swung by the garden center for the mulch and mums. Then I went out to the Tractor Supply for the hay. Takes time to do all that."

Ladonna added, "Was Ms. Dawson's car here at that time?"

"Yep."

"Her car was here, but she wasn't?" Goodman's tone indicated his annoyance.

"Right. But I didn't think nothing of it. I figured maybe she'd met someone here, and they rode together out to the festival."

"What about that hole out back?" I said.

He frowned at me. "What hole?"

"By the gazebo. It's not a hole now, of course. But it was. What's in it?"

"Nothing but dirt and worms, missy. It was never a hole. It's where I've dug up the old plants that were there to prepare the flower beds for winter."

I said to the sheriff. "Won't you even look? You should at least go check it out."

Jimmy took my elbow and pulled me aside. "Stop. Let us do this. I'll check it out in a bit."

Jimmy pulled his phone from his pocket and began texting. "I'll ask an officer to bring a cadaver dog out here to have a look around. Just in case."

Clem looked between Goodman and Jimmy. "Y'all don't think I did something to that woman, do you? I mean she got on my nerves, but not enough for me to kill her. Geez, man."

Goodman lifted a hand. "That's not what we're saying, but we have to look at all angles. When was the last time you saw Ms. Dawson?"

CHAPTER FOUR

He shrugged. "Yesterday evening at closing. She had me round up a bunch of boxes for the festival and load them in the van."

"Which you messed up, Clem." Dee Dee frowned.

"What are you talking about?"

She pointed at him. "We needed ten cases of Summer Nights. You gave us only half that. The other half was something else."

"That ain't true." He flushed, and his eyes darted.

"It is. And if you hadn't messed up the order, she might still be here. What happened to those other cases?"

His face grew almost purple. "None of this is my fault. And I don't have to stay here and listen to this. I'm leaving."

Goodman said, "Sir, I'd appreciate it if you'd hang around in case we have further questions."

Clem said, "Am I under arrest?"

"Of course not."

"Then I'm going home." He stormed toward the door.

Goodman pulled out a business card and followed him. "Hold on one minute." Clem paused. Goodman held out the card. "If you think of anything related to this case, please let us know. We just want to get Mrs. Dawson back safe and sound."

Clem glowered at the card and snatched it from Goodman's hand. "Fine." Clem threw open the door and stormed outside.

Goodman turned back to Dee Dee. "Are there any other disgruntled employees who might want to hurt Patrice?"

Dee Dee scoffed. "No. We're like a family here. Clem is grumpy, but he's harmless."

Goodman nodded. "I see." After a short pause, he added, "Do you think she's faking her kidnapping to get her hands on more money—"

"Are you crazy?" Dee Dee planted her hands on her round hips and gaped at him like he'd just sprouted a second head. "Patrice would never do such a despicable thing. I don't even know anyone who would dream up such a thing.

Goodman looked around the room. "I'm simply wondering if this might be an inside job."

"No, no, no." Dee Dee closed her eyes and shook her head. "Not possible."

"The papers I saw in the office show y'all owed a lot of money on this place and that y'all have a few maxed-out credit cards. Mrs. Dawson, especially."

Dee Dee gaped and shook her head. "Uh…"

"In other words, it could be possible that you two women have concocted this whole thing to bilk money from folks who would help you raise the ransom. Or that Ms. Dawson is acting alone in bilking funds."

Dee Dee glared at him and held up a hand, her nostrils flaring. "Sheriff Goodman, how dare you make such wild accusations of me and my dear friend Patrice." Her voice timbre lowered a few notches, and she spoke slowly. "I'm going to pretend you've had a real long day and aren't thinking clearly. And when you wake up in the morning, you're going to see the error of one of the most absurd statements I've ever heard in my life."

He nodded with a glint of humor in his eye. "One of the truths of running an investigation, Mrs. Winslow, is that we must think out of the box and be prepared to consider something that, on its face, may seem outlandish."

Millie broke into tears and turned her back on the group.

I stepped up to look into Goodman's face. "Did you consider that maybe she really was kidnapped by a loon? Or maybe that her fiancé may be involved since they recently broke up and he moved out?"

"Is that so?" His dead brown eyes searched my face. He had the hard eyes of a man who had seen and experienced terrible things. Which made me only a smidgen less annoyed with him.

"Well…" I backed down, uncertain. "His stuff wasn't at the house today. So it seems pretty likely, doesn't it?"

He jotted a note and said to Dee Dee, "Ma'am, do you know anything about Ms. Dawson's breakup with her fiancé?"

"All I know is that they had a big fight over another woman, so they broke up over it. She told me that if he came around wanting money or credit cards or anything at all, I should ignore him and not help him. When I tried to get details about the breakup, she said she didn't want to talk about it. But she was angry. I could tell."

CHAPTER FOUR

His mustache twitched. "What's his name?"

"Mitch Thomas."

"How long have they dated?"

She shrugged. "A couple years."

"You said they were engaged?"

"Yes."

"How long?" Goodman wrote notes as fast as he could throw out questions.

"They got engaged around six months ago."

"They lived together?"

"Yessir."

"How long?"

"A couple years."

He locked eyes with Dee Dee, and his eyes lit with intensity. He was like a bloodhound on a trail. "Now, the answer to this question is real important. Does he seem like the sort that would hurt her?"

Her thin brows arched. "You don't think he did something to her, do you?"

He clicked his pen over and over impatiently. "That's what I'm asking you."

She thought, then said, "He *seemed* like a nice guy."

"So did Ted Bundy," I muttered. Everyone looked at me. I lifted my hands. "I'm just saying…"

Dee Dee continued, "I mean, he was always nice to me. I don't think he was ever abusive to her. I never saw any evidence of it, and she never said anything to me. We were best friends. I'm sure if he was abusive, she'd tell me."

"You'd be surprised, ma'am," Ladonna added. "Smart women who get caught in such situations will often keep it quiet out of embarrassment and shame."

Goodman glanced at Millie and continued speaking to Dee Dee. "How *well* do you know him?"

"Well…" Dee Dee shrugged. She looked up at the ceiling and seemed to stare beyond it. Then realization lit her face, and her gaze locked onto his face. "Not as much as I thought, I guess. I know he's a doctor and he lived with Patrice. He was always nice to me, but as for details about his family or friends...." She opened her hands. "I don't know any of that." Her hands slid down the sides of her face to her mouth. "Why didn't I ask more questions about him? I accepted him at face value." She shook her head and closed her eyes.

"Don't be so hard on yourself, Dee Dee." Millie stepped in, wrapping her arm around Dee Dee's shoulder. "You couldn't have predicted any of this."

I said to Sheriff Goodman, "You also need to look at Fox Graham from Fox Trace Distillery. He could be involved.."

"That's right," Millie said. "I'm almost positive he rigged the contest and was responsible for getting Mermaid Cove kicked out of the competition."

Dee Dee perked and shook her finger at Goodman. "Yes! He was out here the weekend before the festival, trying to intimidate us and get us to drop out. And it was because of him that Patrice had to come out here today to get a bottle of Summer Nights to get us re-entered in the contest."

I added, "Maybe Fox had someone out here waiting for Patrice to show up."

Goodman listened, nodding. "That's all useful information, and we will consider that possibility, too. But, as I said, I'm considering *all* angles. And you, Mrs. Winslow, as one of the people closest to Mrs. Dawson, must also be eliminated as a suspect."

She lifted her hands and face to the ceiling. "Oh, this isn't happening. Help me, Lord." She lowered her hands and gaped at Goodman. "Are you serious? I'm a suspect?" She flattened a hand over her heart. "Me?" She shook her head, her mouth twisted downward, and she waved her hand. "Nah. You're out of your mind."

He tucked his chin and stared at her under his thick brown brows. "Ma'am, it'd be wise if you didn't leave town any time soon."

A high-strung German Shepherd on a leash pulled an officer into the building. The dog's tail waved in a happy rhythm, and he panted with a long, pink tongue hanging from his mouth.

Jimmy nudged me. "Let's go." He jerked his head toward the back door.

CHAPTER FOUR

"This way,

Jaeger." The dog pawed excitedly to pull his handler forward, his nails clicking on the floor.

Outside, Jaeger was unleashed and he dashed around the distillery grounds, his tail in the air, waving. We humans stayed on the dining patio watching him.

"Anywhere in particular?" the handler asked.

"Try around the gazebo." Jimmy pointed toward the structure at the back of the lot near the water.

The handler jogged over to the gazebo and whistled at Jaeger. He pointed at the ground and moved his arm back and forth, back and forth, focusing Jaeger's attention. The dog followed with intensity. When the area had been searched, the handler looked at us and shrugged with outstretched arms. He shouted. "He's not hitting on anything."

He removed a stuffed toy from his pocket and threw it across the yard. Jaeger shot like a bullet across the grounds, grabbed up the toy, shook it, and ran back to his handler, where he was treated to a quick game of tug-of-war.

Jimmy said to me, "You heard him. Nothing there. If Patrice was dead and buried, the

dog would've found her. He's the best cadaver dog in the state. We call him in for our toughest cases."

Relief washed over me. "At least there's hope that she's alive and still out there."

But my relief was quickly replaced by doubt and suspicion. "Don't you think there's something *off* about Clem Sikes? I think he's involved." I poked my stomach. "I feel it. In my gut. The way he spoke about Patrice earlier. He doesn't seem to like her much."

Jimmy watched the dog and handler play. "I'll look into him. I promise."

"Can you have Jaeger take one more search? Please? Just to be certain?"

"All right. It couldn't hurt." He jogged across the yard toward Jaeger and his handler.

Millie came out to meet us. Her eyes wide in fear, she clutched my hands. Her hands were cold and shaking. "You have to help me," she whispered.

"You have to help find my mom."

"I'm not—"

"Please," she begged. "You were instrumental in helping catch Bryan's killer. I'm afraid this won't end well if you don't help me."

"You're giving me way too much credit, Millie. Jimmy and Goodman are good at what they do." I mostly believed what I was saying. I had my doubts about Goodman sometimes, but Jimmy was capable.

"But to them, she's just another victim. It's not personal for them like it is for me and you." Her nails dug into my fingers as tears pooled in her eyes. "I'm begging you. You have to help find my mom."

I searched her face. My mom had been murdered when I was young. I knew what it was to lose a mother and live without her. I couldn't let my best friend suffer in that way. I pulled her close and hugged her tight. "I'll do everything I can. I swear it."

Jimmy whistled to get our attention. Running toward us, he shouted, "They have a lock on Patrice's phone. I have an address. I'm going to go look for it."

Pushing out of Millie's arms. "I'll do what I can." I squeezed her arms and followed Jimmy.

Jimmy opened his vehicle door. "Rook, go back."

"Please, let me come with you." I wasn't really asking. I launched myself into his truck seat. I'd made a promise to Millie, and my efforts on her behalf began immediately.

He pressed his lips into a tight line and shook his head as he started the engine. Apparently, he didn't have the time, energy, or desire to fight with me. He threw the truck into reverse and flew out of the parking lot. We rode in tense silence, speeding down light dappled country roads, the low, mellow gold sun flicking through the trees. When we popped out onto a busy highway, Jimmy wove in and out of traffic as I clutched the Oh-help-me-Lord- handle above the passenger window. He whipped onto a residential road that led to downtown Rothdale. Passing through the town square, he took the road to the right toward the warehouse district. We passed a few dilapidated buildings before he whipped into a parking lot on

CHAPTER FOUR

the left behind a mechanic's building. He slammed on the brakes, and the truck skidded to stop.

We jumped out. Jimmy grabbed his pistol from under the truck dash. Boards covered the windows of the business, and weeds grew tall around the building and pushed up through large cracks in the pavement.

Jimmy turned around. "Dang it!" His cheeks blazed bright pink, and aggravation sparked in his eyes. He kicked an empty glass bottle, and it clattered across the pavement. He held up his weapon, ordered me to stay.

"But—"

"Rook, don't argue with me." He yelled. He marched toward the building and kicked the door in.

Honestly, his anger was a tad scary, yet a spark of electricity shot through my center and tickled right below my belly button. I didn't like being commanded to stay like a dog. Even though I understood the necessity for it, it took every ounce of my will to stay by the truck.

He disappeared inside, calling out for Patrice. A few moments later, he reappeared, shaking his head. "Not there." He rubbed his hand over his face in frustration and returned to the truck, looking around on high alert.

"I don't understand. If her phone was tracked to this location, she had to be here." I searched the ground for anything that appeared new or fresh, but I didn't see anything. "Wait. I have an idea." I pulled my phone out of my pocket and dialed Patrice's number.

In the distance, Shania Twain called out, "Man, I feel like a woman," before the guitars and synthesizers chimed in.

Like a couple of hound dogs, he and I perked, searching for the sound. I pointed at a rusted barrel along the fence row. "It sounds like it's coming from there." I dashed for the barrel. He soon overtook me and was looking into the barrel as I arrived.

"It's in there." He had never removed his latex gloves from the scene at the distillery so he tipped the barrel to look inside. The phone had already switched to voicemail. "Call again."

I dialed Patrice's number, and Shania sang out again. Jimmy dug around in the barrel and pulled out a white plastic bag. The blue light from the phone shone through the bag. He lowered the barrel to the ground and squatted. He ripped the bag open. Food wrappings, bottles, napkins, and half-eaten food spilled out. A half-used ketchup packet was stuck to the phone screen.

I watched him. "Even Prim has a newer phone than that."

"Good thing." He wiped the screen with a wadded napkin from the trash. "It'll make it easier on me." He pushed the Home button, and the screen lit up, showing a background image of Patrice dancing on the beach.

"Just like Prim." I shook my head and half-chuckled. "No lock or passcode."

"Another lucky break." He opened the Recent Calls tab. "The last number dialed was Mitch."

"What? Why did she call her ex?" I leaned in to see the screen. "When did she do that?"

"According to this, about an hour before she went missing."

"Why would she call him? They broke up, and she was mad at him."

He searched through other folders. "Here's a voicemail from him, which is about an hour earlier. It looks as though she was returning his call." He pushed the speaker phone and listened to the voicemail. It was a simple statement from Mitch asking her to call him back.

My knees started to ache, so I stood. "He sounded nervous, don't you think?"

"Maybe. Or agitated."

I looked at the pile of garbage spilling from the bag. "I bet that garbage might have some DNA."

He nodded and stood, his knees cracking. "That's what I'm thinking. I'll gather this stuff up and take it out to the station tonight. The lab won't open until Monday, but I'll go ahead and log the evidence and make sure it's there first thing."

"Surely, we'll find her before then, right?" I'd watched enough *Forensic Files* and read enough true crime books to understand that the first forty-eight hours were the most critical in a missing persons case. If we didn't find her by then, our chances of finding Patrice alive dropped exponentially. I searched Jimmy's face for a glimmer of hope, but he turned away.

Chapter Five

Jimmy called the sheriff to update him on what we'd found. Since Jimmy was no longer needed at the distillery scene, he drove me out to the festival so I could help Jeff and Marla pack up our booth. The sun had melted into an amber puddle on the horizon. As we loaded up the company truck, I heard a group of people shout out. The source of the noise was Fox and others from Fox Trace. They huddled around their company truck. Fox held a trophy high in the air, and a friend held up a bottle of Fox Trace's Totally Foxed. Fox slapped high fives all around.

"We won, baby! Woo hoo!" he shouted, a smirk on his smarmy face.

My antennae twitched. He rigged the contest. I wasn't sure how yet, but I was going to figure it out. And I was willing to bet my eye-teeth that it was connected to Patrice's disappearance.

When everything had been loaded, Jimmy drove me home. Fellow Kentuckian, Chris Stapleton's "Tennessee Whiskey" played softly on the radio, and street lights flashed as we passed under them. He had one hand on the wheel, his elbow propped against the truck window, and one finger stroking his upper lip. He was thinking.

I broke the silence. "What do you think happened?"

"You know I can't really talk about it. It's an open case."

"As I see it, now that we're dating, telling me is as good as telling another deputy. And I think I did pretty good detective work on the last case you and I worked on together." I flashed a flirty grin.

He rolled his eyes and scoffed. "Yeah, right. Nice try. *Watson.*"

I laughed. "What if *I* talked about it because it's eating me up? You can listen."

"Rook, can you please just be quiet for a while so I can think straight?"

My hackles raised immediately. "You don't have to be so rude about it."

He glanced between me and the road. "You want your friend found or not?"

"Of course I do, but it helps me to talk these things through."

He slammed his hand on the dashboard of the truck. I jumped. He practically snarled as he spoke, "*You* are not a police officer." He pointed at me. "*You are* not involved in this. You are a citizen who needs to stay out of the way before you mess something up or get yourself hurt. Wasn't the last time with Bryan enough to teach you anything?"

My whole body shook with rage competing with hurt feelings, and it caused my voice to shake. "Millie, my best friend in the world, asked me to help. Period."

He swiped his hand through the air. "Irrelevant."

"How *dare* you speak to me this way. I don't care who you are or what your job is, you're not going to talk to me like this."

He tapped his head against the headrest. His voice was high-pitched and tight. "I'm trying to do my job and keep you safe. How do you not see that? I'm under an immense amount of pressure here, Rook, and you want to run around playing detective."

"You think I'm playing. I'm not playing. No, I'm not a detective or an officer, but…" I poked myself in the chest. "My mom was murdered. My best friend was murdered. I know the pain and suffering that causes. I know how murder rips apart families, and if I can keep my best friend from living through that hell, then that's what I aim to do."

"Rook—"

"Don't even talk to me right now." I crossed my arms and legs, winding myself into a tight knot. I stared out the window and wiped away silent tears.

Prim was already in bed when I entered the house. Batrene relaxed on the couch watching *20/20*.

CHAPTER FIVE

"Hey, sugar." She stood and entered the kitchen, where I kicked off my tennis shoes. "You're home awfully late."

"Yeah. I'm sorry. Millie's mom is missing. We've been busy trying to find her. Then we still had to go back to the festival and help break down the booth."

"Oh, heavens!" Batrene gasped, clapping her dimpled hand over her heart. "How awful! What happened to Patrice?"

I told her the basic story while I poured myself a glass of iced tea and rummaged through the pantry for a Moon Pie and cheese puffs. I planned on sitting up to do some research since it was Saturday night, and I didn't have to work the next day.

She fiddled with the crucifix necklace lying against her chest. "What has this world come to? It's getting so I'm too afraid to stay in my home by myself or go out alone."

That hadn't been an issue a few months ago when Bryan was alive. "I know," I said, squeezing her arm. "I hate it for you living over there alone. Maybe you could get a companion to come live with you. A niece or cousin? Or maybe one of these college kids that go to the university. They always need money." I sat at the table and opened up the chip bag.

"That's a good idea." She blinked behind her glasses. "Maybe. Maybe I will."

I crunched a cheese puff and smiled. "Or you could always live with us. You're over here helping with Prim all the time anyway." I crunched another puff. "Which I appreciate more than you could imagine."

Her nose crinkled, and her chin doubled. "Nooo." She laughed, waving at me. "I'd never be able to get up and down the stairs with my messed up knees." She patted my arm and sat down at the head of the kitchen table. "You've got your hands full enough."

The phone rang. I rushed to pick it up in hopes the noise wouldn't wake up Prim. "Hello?"

The caller breathed into the phone, but didn't say anything.

"Hello? Are you there? Who is this?"

Again, the breath with no words.

"Stop calling here."

Then a click and the flatline noise. I slammed the phone into the cradle.

Batrene fluffed her curly hair with her nails. "I bet that's the same fool who's been calling here all night."

"This has been going on all night?"

"Yep. They never say anything. Only breathe heavy or laugh."

"Aggravating." I sat down beside her, one knee under my chin. "I'm sorry you had to deal with that. Thanks for watching Prim tonight. How did she do?"

"Very well. Took her medicine and went out like a light. I had to help her in and out of the chair and help her a little with going to the bathroom." Her eyes glistened with unshed tears. "She's gotten so frail so fast."

My throat clenched. I quickly stuffed a couple of puffs in my mouth as a distraction. "Don't you start crying, Batrene. I couldn't stand it." Especially tonight after such a bad ride home with Jimmy.

She flapped her hands. "Oh, honey, I'm sorry. I won't. I promise." She lifted her glasses and swiped her eyes.

I guzzled my tea to force down the lump in my throat. "Come on." I licked the cheese dust off my fingers. "You're probably tired. I'll walk you home."

After I saw Batrene safely home, I changed into a pair of cotton shorts and a Bob Dylan T-shirt, then set up my research station in the living room: TV on *Forensic Files*. Check. Cheese puffs, Moon Pie, and Kentucky Spice citrus-ginger soda beside me on the coffee table. Check. Stretched out on the couch with an afghan over my lap. Check. Laptop on and Google ready. Check.

I stared at the multicolored Google logo. Where should I begin? The debt. I couldn't look up Patrice and Dee Dee's credit reports or debt balances without social security numbers and such, along with running the risk of hefty fines. But I could establish a history of luxurious spending, which *could* indicate debt and, therefore, a motive.

I started by looking up the neighborhoods where Patrice and Dee Dee lived. Patrice lived in Autumn Ridge Estates. I went to the Property Value

CHAPTER FIVE

Administrator website. Ten years ago, Patrice and her ex-husband paid three hundred grand for that house long before she owned the distillery. Five years later, they divorced. The ex had been an equine veterinarian, and she hadn't worked. I then went to Zillow and looked up how much a house costs in today's money, and it was a whole lot more than that. The land alone was worth tens of thousands.

I ran Dee Dee's property through the same rigors. She lived in Beaumont Acres, which was a heavily developed suburb where grand houses sat almost on top of each other. She and her husband had paid about the same for their house. Only it didn't come with any land, which I thought was a rip-off. And they had to pay enormous HOA fees. Pfft. No, thank you. Her husband was a financial planner at a big accounting firm in downtown Lexington. He worked in one of those sleek, glassy buildings that smelled of money when you walked inside. Again, Dee Dee had been a stay-at-home wife and mother, too.

Both Patrice and Dee Dee had lived among the elite crowd for many years. Both husbands had good jobs, but they all had lavish lifestyles: fancy homes, fancy cars, country club memberships, fancy vacations—the whole kit and caboodle. Granted, the husbands made good money, but they all spent like drunken lords, so it could've been a facade. After all, people didn't go into thousands of dollars of credit card debt when they had plenty of money to spend.

Then I opened my phone and looked at the pictures I'd taken at Mermaid Cove: the broken bottle, the messy office. I expanded one of the images. One of the pictures I snapped showed a credit card statement of at least ten thousand dollars. And there was more than one credit card statement on the office floor.

Here's what I knew: I couldn't do this alone.

I needed to speak to Millie. I hated to—she was probably worn out—but the sooner we could catch a lead, the sooner we'd find Patrice and, more importantly, have a better chance of finding her alive.

I dialed her number. She answered, her voice quavering with emotion.

"It's me."

"Hey."

"I really hate to do this, but I need to ask you a few questions. tThey may seem offensive at first, but the information is super important."

"Well, you can't make me any angrier than Sheriff Goodman has." Her voice cracked, and she sniffled.

I bit down on my lip and tapped my foot to divert the emotion. *Focus. Don't get emotional now. Time to work. Time to think.* "

"Were your parents in a lot of debt before they divorced?"

"Yeah. I think it was pretty bad. I think it was the main reason for the divorce. According to my dad, my mom was too free with the credit cards." I heard the rattle of her ice maker in the background as she put ice in a glass.

"Their divorce was overall pretty peaceful, right? Nobody threatened anyone?"

"If you think my dad did this, you're crazier than I suspected. He's living in Georgetown with his new wife. He and Mom don't even think about each other."

"You're sure?"

"Absolutely."

"Okay. I'll check him off my list." I pulled at my bottom lip, wiggling my toes to poke them in and out of the Afghan holes.

"Now I have a really offensive question."

"Shoot." She sighed.

"Your mom. We all love her. But would there be any reason you know of that she might go off the deep end and need to score a crap ton of money? Would there be any reason at all for her to manufacture this whole thing?"

Millie scoffed. "You sound like Sheriff Goodman." She inhaled deeply then exhaled loudly. "My mom drinks money like water. She's always spent it faster than it came in. I won't deny that. But to go to such lengths…." Her voice broke. She sniffled. "Sorry." She blew her nose. "I won't believe that."

"I promise I'm only trying to help."

"I know. I appreciate it. I'd be lost without you."

"Okay. An equally offensive question. What about Dee Dee? You know her way better than I do. What do you know about her spending habits, her

CHAPTER FIVE

debts? Or the distillery debts?"

"Dee Dee is a lot like my mom when it comes to spending money. You see the way she dresses. You won't find her picking over the sales racks at Target." She paused. "My mom told me that she and Dee Dee did get into a minor tiff about money a few weeks ago. About the distillery. I think it's in financial trouble. I mean, you've seen how they've decked out that place."

There was no denying that. Mermaid Cove was nothing short of exquisite. They could open a spa resort on-site.

Millie continued, "Mom told me all about it. Dee Dee was accusing her of mismanaging the books, and Mom said Dee Dee was as much to blame as anyone."

"Why don't they have an accountant?" I played with the fringe on the afghan, twirling it around and around my finger.

"Good question. I guess they thought they could do most of it themselves. Maybe Dee Dee's husband helps out with the books, too. Or at least that was the solution to their fight."

" What was Mitch like with money? Do you think he latched on to your mom because he thought she had money?"

"Possibly." She sniffled and blew her nose. "He loved the high life too."

"They met at the country club, right?"

"No. They met at his clinic. It's one of those walk-in clinics. Mom thought she had the flu and didn't want to go through the hassle of making an appointment, so she went to his clinic."

"What do you know about him?"

She grew quiet. "You know, when Goodman was asking Dee Dee these questions, and she admitted that she didn't know Mitch very well, I realized then that I'm in the same boat. I feel like the worst daughter ever. How could I not have looked out for her better? I should've asked him more questions about his background, get to know him better?"

"You can't beat yourself up over this. Nothing about this is your fault. What *do* you know about him?"

She sighed. "The basics. Born in Indiana. His dad was a steel worker, moved the family down here when Mitch was a baby. He became a doctor and was married once before, but she died. No kids."

My intuition fired up like a sparkler. I sat up, pulling my feet to the floor as I set my laptop aside. "How did his wife die?"

"I never asked. It seemed…inappropriate."

"How long had they been married?" My nose tickled, and I sneezed. Fall allergies were kicking in. I blew my nose while she answered.

"I don't know. I didn't ask."

"Did he ever tell you her name?" I unwrapped my Moon Pie and took a big bite out of the chocolate-covered cookie marshmallow treat.

"No." Her voice raised a few pitches. "Why didn't I ever think to ask? Gah!"

"I guess you don't know where he married?"

"No."

Frustration fizzled around my ears. I shook my head and washed down my food with soda. How on earth could I get anywhere if she didn't have any information? It dawned on me that this was the sort of stuff Jimmy probably encountered all the time. I softened toward him a little. A very little.

"Did he ever give any indication that he was using Patrice for her money, or was he ever absent for long stretches of time without explanation or anything weird like that?"

"What are you talking about?"

"Haven't you heard those stories about men who are broke, but pretend to be what they're not to snag rich women? Or about the men who are living double lives? Maybe he has a wife and family in Arizona or something."

Silence. I could almost hear her eyes rolling. Then she laughed through her sniffles. "You've got the wildest imagination. This isn't one of your *Law and Order Cold Case* thingamajigs. They were engaged for two years. I think if he was a nefarious criminal, he would've gone off the rails by now."

I made a mental note to tell Jimmy to look into Mitch's first wife's death, even though, in the moment, the thought of talking to him made my stomach twist into a pretzel.

"Not if he was smart. Which clinic does he work at?"

CHAPTER FIVE

"The Franklin County Health Walk-in Clinic, out on Blantonboro Road, before you reach Lexington City limits."

"Okay, I know where that is.'?"

"What if we paid a visit to Mitch tomorrow?"

"He usually doesn't work Sundays, but I can find out where he lives. Maybe we can visit him at home. I don't think he's involved, though. I'd bet my life savings Fox Graham is connected to this."

"I aim to find out for sure."

When I hung up with her, my phone rang. Jimmy. I stared at the screen, debating whether or not I should answer the call. Well, I did need to tell him about Mitch's first wife.

Begrudgingly, I answered. "Hello."

"You sound like you're still angry at me."

"Not as much as I was. I didn't like the way you spoke to me. I get that you're protective, doing your job, and so on, but you don't get to order me around like I'm a dog."

"Understood. I sometimes get carried away. I didn't mean to talk to you like that. I guess I was all worked up about not finding Patrice."

I waited for an apology, but he didn't say anything else. I changed the subject so I could tell him the most important information. "I just spoke to Millie."

"Yeah?"

"I found out her mom's ex-fiancé, Mitch Thomas, had a wife before. She died."

"Now that's interesting. Did she mention how she died?"

"No. Turns out Millie didn't know much about him."

"That's unfortunate. Guess I'll have to find my leads elsewhere."

"Guess so. Millie's convinced Fox Graham is involved. I wouldn't put it past him, but Mitch is awfully suspicious, too. He and Patrice recently broke up. All his stuff is gone. Apparently, he, Patrice, and Dee Dee all liked to live awfully high on the hog. Big homes, fancy cars, high-end clothes and purses—all the trappings of either great wealth or great debt. And I sent you all the pictures I took at the distillery. Have you looked at them yet?"

"Briefly. I'm going to go back over them when we hang up."

"Look close at the ones with the credit card statements. One of them was at least ten thousand dollars. And there were several statements laying around."

"Huh. Maybe she was desperate." I heard a can pop open in the background. "You need to delete those photos, though. I don't want this case compromised in any way." He sipped his drink.

"I will." I thought for a moment. "What if she was desperate and there's way more debt than anyone realizes? Dee Dee did seem awfully desperate to win the bourbon award."

"She did. You think she might be mixed up in this somehow?"

I stared at the TV, flicking commercials at me. Then I recalled our fight on the way home. "Why are you even talking to me about this? I thought you didn't want me involved."

"We're just two friends talking. You know these people better than I do—"

"So you're using me for leads." I rolled my eyes. "Nice."

"I wouldn't put it that way…"

"Whatever." I was too tired to fight. I stared at the Granny Square pattern of the afghan and wove my finger in and out of the holes while I thought. I'd known Dee Dee as long as I'd known Patrice, though I didn't know her as well. However, because I knew Patrice and Millie so well, I operated under the Birds of a Feather Theory.

"You still there?" Jimmy asked.

"Yep." Then I added, "Dee Dee's good people. She wouldn't be involved in this either to hurt Patrice or help Patrice scheme. You saw how tore up she was tonight."

He sighed. "I want to take your word for it, but I've seen people do some crazy things in my line of work. I can't count the number of times I've seen so-called *good people* do bad things."

"I get that. I'm not stupid. But I also think I'm a pretty good judge of character and I'm one hundred percent sure Dee Dee doesn't have anything to do with this." A light chill settled on me, so I pulled the afghan tighter around me.

"It looks like I'm back to square one then."

"Yep. Fox or Mitch." I relaxed back against the sofa. "Fox is obvious. He wanted to win the prize. Ten thousand dollars and an established spot in the bourbon game. That's big."

"True. Definitely worth looking into."

"Except he doesn't really seem like the sort to get his hands dirty."

"He could've hired someone."

I thought about the scores of *Forensic Files* and other crime-solving shows I'd seen over the years. "But usually, the perpetrator is whomever is closest to the victim, right?"

"Usually. That's why our investigations always start there. Spouses, lovers, and so on."

"Right." My mind raced to concoct a way to get close to Mitch to question him. We knew each other, but I didn't know him really well. He and Patrice had only been engaged for a couple of years.

He yawned. "Well, I guess I need to jump off here. I should get some work done before I go to bed."

"Okay."

"Goodnight."

"Night." The call disconnected, and I put down my phone, emptiness creeping into my core. He never did apologize.

Chapter Six

The next morning, a fine mist laced the ground as I made coffee. I opened the kitchen window and breathed in lukewarm morning air. A hint of yellow and red brushed the tree leaves. Squirrels hopped and raced, stuffing their cheeks with acorns littering the ground.

I inhaled the sweet, spicy scent of hay, aging leaves, and earth that hearkened to the impending autumn. I loved fall. Normally at this time of year, I would be filled with joy. But Patrice's disappearance provoked a host of nightmares about my mom and when I was attacked during my friend Bryan's case. I leaned on the counter, drained of energy. Sipping my first of what would be a few cups of coffee, I made pumpkin-spiced pancakes and bacon for breakfast to lift my spirits

After giving Prim her medication, we settled in the living room with breakfast to watch church service together on the local programming channel. She picked at her food while I told her about Patrice.

She shook her head. "I sure hate what's happened to Patrice. Millie must be beside herself." Her voice was weak and gravelly. "She is."

She stared pensively at the television as she nibbled on a slice of bacon. She grabbed the cordless phone from the table beside her and began dialing.

"Who are you calling?"

She lifted a finger, then said, "Hey, Oda Dean. Prim here. We've got a situation."

The realization dawned on me. She was firing up the OLN, the Old Lady Network.

"Patrice Dawson is missing, been kidnapped." After a few "mm-hms" she

CHAPTER SIX

continued. "Here's what we need to do. Since you're church secretary, you get hold of all the elders. We need to start a prayer circle, and we need to raise some money to help Millie. A fall bake sale would be perfect, but we're going to need a mighty bundle more than that. One million. I know. Isn't that something? Make sure you ask Brother Steve to make an announcement for donations. Mm-hm. Yep. I'm watching him on the TV now. Well, the music could be better. I don't know why they insist on letting Gina Maplewood sing. That poor woman can't carry a tune in a bucket. Why aren't you there? Oh, okay. Well, I hope you feel better soon." After a little more gossip, Prim hung up the phone. "We're going to get some money for Millie one way or the other."

"She'll really appreciate that."

The doorbell rang. Prim and I looked at each other. It must be a stranger because they were the only ones to go to the front door. Family and friends came through the back door in the kitchen. I set my plate aside and answered the door.

A delivery person stood on the step with a beautiful bouquet full of stargazer lilies, red roses, sunflowers, and purple statice. "Delivery for Rook Campbell."

I batted my eyes. "Uh, that's me." I couldn't remember the last time I received flowers. I signed for the flowers and shut the door.

"Well, look at you," Prim said, "Who are those from?"

"I don't know." I plucked out the card and read it. *To Rook, from Jimmy.* He wasn't exactly a poet. "They're from Jimmy."

Prim gaped at me. Then she seemed to come to a realization. "He must be in the dog house. What did he do?"

I didn't want to talk about it and maybe it wasn't important anymore. Maybe he didn't actually say he was sorry for talking to me the way he did last night, but the flowers were apology enough. "Nonsense," I said, carrying my flowers to the kitchen, almost dancing. "Maybe he's trying to be nice."

Prim scoffed. "Yeah, right. I wasn't born yesterday, missy."

I placed my flowers on the table and doted on them for a few minutes. I called Jimmy. "Thank you for the flowers."

Noise from the gym filled the background. "You're welcome. You like them?"

"Of course! They're beautiful."

"Maybe I'll top it off with a nice dinner tonight. How about The White Tulip?"

My breath caught. "Oh, wow. I don't know if I even have clothes to wear to that place. It's so fancy."

"I guess you'd better find something. I'll pick you up at six tonight."

"Shouldn't you be working the case?"

"I am, but I think I can make time to take my lady out to dinner. A man has to eat."

I hung up with him and danced into the living room. "Jimmy is taking me to The White Tulip tonight. Can you believe it?"

"He must've really messed up." Prim stuffed a piece of pancake in her mouth.

"We did have a fight, but it's all better now."

"What did you fight about?"

My head was too full of fantasies about The White Tulip to care about the fight now. "Oh, it doesn't matter."

"Hm." She chewed. "You sure about that?"

I lifted my chin. "I have to pick out something to wear." I left Prim to her TV and jogged upstairs to rummage in my closet for a dress that would suffice.

Thirty minutes later, I finally settled on a little champagne-colored dress I'd worn on my first date with Len Ashfield, who was my former supervisor at Four Wild Horses and who was now in jail for his part in the crimes committed there. Thinking of Len only brought back a rush of bad memories of Bryan's murder, the attacks on me, and my apparent bad judgment in men. Just seeing the dress called back, the date we'd had at The Castle and the ER visit when Prim was rushed there in pain. But it was the only dress I had. I couldn't afford to go buy a new one. All my money, after buying groceries, went to put gas in my car, pay for medical bills, and pay student loans.

CHAPTER SIX

Millie texted me **U still want to visit Mitch? I have his address. Can meet you in an hour.**

K. Sounds good.

Pick you up at your house.

After a quick shower, I dressed in a pair of jeans, a black peasant blouse and sandals, and light makeup; then I returned downstairs. Church had ended and *The Andy Griffith Show* played while Prim slept. Her medicines and poor sleeping habits made it difficult for her to stay awake during the day.

I settled on the couch with my laptop. Since I wanted to visit Mitch, I needed to know when his clinic opened, so I looked that up first. According to the Franklin County Health Walk-in Clinic website, they wouldn't open until noon. With some time on my hands, I figured it'd be a good time to perform a little research on Fox Graham.

I started on Facebook. His top post announced that Fox Trace had won the bourbon contest. There was a picture of him grinning broadly, holding up the trophy and the check. *Jerk.*

Dee Dee and Patrice really needed the win to uplift Mermaid Cove. And, given the amount of debt they'd amassed both professionally and personally, they needed the money, too. It was ridiculous, and a little scary, how easy Facebook made it to get a glimpse of his life with a single visit to his page. Pictures alone told much of the story of his character, what he valued, and what he spent time and money doing.

Within fifteen minutes, I discovered he liked the high life. He owned a brand-new Cadillac Escalade, with the obligatory picture of himself leaning against it. Golfed at Idyllic Acres, which was a country club filled with all the highfalutin folks in the Lexington-Fayette County area. Hung around at the Keeneland racetrack—a lot. Probably too much. Based on his posts, he liked to bet on the horses a lot, too. There were pictures of deep-sea fishing expeditions, vacations to Hawaii, and courtside seats behind Coach Jimmy Bianchi of the University of the Bluegrass Thoroughbreds basketball team. Since basketball in Kentucky was a veritable religion, those tickets were akin to sitting behind the Pope.

Fox's house was as lavish as either Dee Dee's or Patrice's. He lived in a rural residential area surrounded by horse farms. It looked a lot like the small town of Midway. Apparently, there was a certain image to uphold in the bourbon world.

Next, I went to Google Maps, got on the satellite view, and took a virtual tour of Midway, soon locating the neighborhood where he lived. Then I looked up the address on Zillow. His house last sold for five hundred thousand. I whistled. *Good Lord.* There were people in the world who wouldn't blink at a house that price, but to me, it was unimaginable. Those houses were beautiful, and there was a time when I had dreamed of owning such a house. But taking care of Prim and the house, while working, taught me one valuable lesson: never buy a house that's too much trouble for one person to care for.

I needed to figure out if Fox had a motive, other than winning the bourbon competition, to kidnap Patrice. That was going to be hard to prove without getting inside information on his finances, or information from someone close to him that he was simply out to destroy the competition. I needed to give that more thought. I peeked in the living room at Prim. Still sleeping. I made a mental note to ask her if she knew anyone connected to Fox Graham. As a founding member of the Old Lady Network, she'd be sure to have all the latest gossip—or know someone who did.

The clock on my computer read eleven-thirty, which meant I needed to high-tail it to the clinic before the crowds gathered.

Prim woke up. "What's going on?"

"You want lunch before I leave?"

"No, I'm not real hungry right now. Where are you going?"

I didn't want to be specific. "I need to run out for a minute. Will you be all right?"

She eyed me suspiciously. "Yep. I'll be fine."

"One thing. Do you remember Fox Graham?"

"Is that Buddy and Nora Graham's boy?" She hit the lift button on her recliner remote.

"I think so. He owns Fox Trace."

CHAPTER SIX

"What about him?" I swiped on some lip gloss.

"What do you know about the family or about Fox?"

She screwed up her face. "I don't like any of them. I love them because I'm supposed to, but I don't trust them as far as I can throw them."

"Why?" I dug in my purse for my car keys and sunglasses.

"Not a bit of integrity among them." She shuffled into the kitchen.

"Why do you say that?"

She reached in the fridge for a ginger ale. "Fox used to work for his daddy out at the farmer's supply. He sold a lemon lawnmower to Birdie Harper's husband. Said it was brand new. It didn't work for more than a week. When Walter Harper tried to return it, Fox claimed he couldn't return it or get it fixed. Come to find out the mower wasn't new at all. He's not an honest man."

That wasn't proof that Fox fixed the bourbon contest, but it highlighted a lot about his character.

As I stepped out the door, I called Batrene to tell her I was leaving. "I won't be gone long. Maybe an hour or hour and a half, tops."

"Should I come over?"

"That's not necessary, though you're welcome to, if you want. If you could at least call and check in on Prim, I'd really appreciate it."

"I think I'll come on over. I got a new jigsaw puzzle at the Dollar General yesterday. Maybe we can work it together."

"She'd love that. It'd be good for her, too. I appreciate you." It occurred to me, since Batrene was part of the Old Lady Network, she might have information about Fox Graham or Mitch Thomas. "Hey, Batrene? What do you know about Fox Graham?"

"Buddy and Nora's boy?"

"Yes."

"You're not buying anything from him, are you?"

"No."

"Good. He can't be trusted. He stole money from the church bazaar back when he was a teenager."

"What!" Surprise popped my eyes wide. I suspected he was a rascal, but I didn't realize he was rotten to the core.

"Yes, ma'am. I've never trusted him since. I mean, I always thought he was a little crooked, but in a mischievous way, like most teen boys. But when he did that, I wouldn't trust him to watch my grass grow. That boy is liable to do anything to get what he wants."

I lowered my voice. "Like kidnap an innocent woman?"

"Do you think he kidnapped Patrice?"

"I hope not, but do you think he'd actually do that?"

"I don't know. I don't trust him around money for sure, but kidnapping? That might be a stretch even for him."

"What about Mitch Thomas? Patrice Dawson's ex-fiancé. What do you know about him?"

"Not much. I've only met him once or twice. He must be a hard worker, though, because every time Patrice is at church or at a gathering, he's almost never with her. He's always at work. I figure what's the point in marrying a man you never see? But that's none of my business."

"Did she ever seem threatened by him or afraid of him?"

"Threatened?" She chuckled. "Lord, no. The way she talked about him, you'd think the sun rose and set with him." *Interesting.* Maybe I was headed in the wrong direction to question Mitch. Maybe I should be talking to Fox instead. "That is until about two or three weeks ago."

My antennae shot up straight and sharp as a needle. "What do you mean?"

"Well, remember when we had that food drive out at the church? She came out with a big bag of food, but she looked rough. No makeup, hair pushed back in a head band, and rumpled clothes. I don't think I've ever seen Patrice without makeup and dressed neat as a pin. I asked her what was wrong. She said 'nothing' and that she 'didn't want to talk about it.' But she looked like she'd been crying. Real puffy face, and all sad and tired looking."

I was all too familiar with that look. When Cam and I divorced, that was my go-to look for at least a month. But that put Mitch back on my radar.

Millie pulled up in the drive and honked the horn. I hung up with Batrene and kissed Prim goodbye, and jumped in Millie's silver Honda CR-V. It smelled of patchouli and lavender, probably from the incense and oils used

CHAPTER SIX

at her yoga/massage studio. A sparkly bandeau held back her long hair, and a black tank top revealed her lightly sunburned arms.

She turned down The Decemberists as she backed out of the drive, her gold bangles jingling. "Do you really think Mitch may have taken my mom?"

"I can't say for sure, but from what you've told me, he doesn't seem as concerned as a fiancé should be."

"But they're exes." She turned off the AC.

I checked my image in the visor mirror. "That may be, but I figured that if Cam ever went missing, I'd want to know where he is."

She snorted and glanced at me, my warped face flashing in her mirrored glasses. "You and Cam are different."

"What do you mean?"

"Y'all are so in love, it's almost sickening."

I slapped the visor back into place. "We are not."

"Oh, puh-lease. You're not fooling anybody. Y'all never fell out of love."

"You're crazy," I said dismissively. I didn't want to talk about this right now. "Anyway..." I swiped my hand through the air. "The issue at hand is that Mitch loved your mom enough to want to marry her. And not that long ago. It stands to reason that he would want to be more involved with finding her."

"I guess..." She screwed up her face and stopped at a light. "I can't picture him as the sort of man who would do something like that, though."

For the rest of the drive, we chatted about our respective jobs and relationships until she pulled into a high-end gated condominium complex on the outskirts of south Rothdale. Tuscany Pointe was full of two-story condos with white stucco exteriors and red Spanish tile roofs.

"Wow, fancy place." I breathed, taking in the tall windows and the arched entries on the façades.

"Yeah, he really likes nice things." She pulled in next to a champagne-colored Jaguar. "That's his car. Looks like he's home."

"On a doctor's salary, he can probably afford it."

"Mm. Maybe. It's amazing how quickly he found this place and moved from my mom's house." She turned off the car.

"What do you mean by maybe?"

"Well, last night, after you and I hung up, I thought more about the things you were asking me. I remembered one fight. I'd stopped by and had walked in while they were in the kitchen, fighting. He was griping about how much money she spent, and she said, 'We have plenty of money' and he…" She pushed her sunglasses up on her head. "He froze, like a deer in the headlights. As if that caught him off guard, which I interpreted as a signal that they didn't have a bunch of money."

"What happened then?"

"They saw me and changed the subject, pretended like nothing was going on."

"Hm. Interesting." And suspicious. I tucked that nugget away in my mental file.

We knocked on the mahogany door.

Mitch opened the door. Though he was at least twenty years my senior, Mitch Thomas was a good-looking man. He was around six foot, with gray-streaked dark hair, and dark olive-gray eyes fringed with deep laugh lines. He had a largish Roman nose and a bright, appealing smile. He was sweaty in a damp T-shirt and a pair of exercise shorts. He clearly spent a lot of time working out.

"Hey, what's up?"

Millie said, "Can we talk for a minute?"

He hemmed. "Sure. I guess." He stepped back and let us in. " If you don't mind my appearance. I was on the treadmill."

Cool air greeted us as we stepped into the condo. The décor was modern minimalist with a white sofa and chairs, gray shag rug over a white tile floor, and glass tables. It was an open floor plan, and large windows at the back of the condo allowed light to pour in. Yet, the space was pretty messy. Discarded clothes lay on the floor and on the furniture. Unpacked boxes sat stacked against the wall. The kitchen table was loaded with sundry items. Golf played on the large flat screen over the fireplace, and a treadmill stood along the wall, facing the television.

He muted the television and sat in a chair. "Have a seat. Sorry for the

CHAPTER SIX

mess in here. My cleaning lady hasn't come by yet this week, and I'm still moving in."

"No worries." Millie motioned to me as we sat on the couch across from him. "You know my friend, Rook?"

He pulled a towel off the golf clubs by his chair and wiped his face. "Yeah, yeah. How you doing?" He flashed a bright, but tentative smile.

"Good, thanks."

He half-stood. "Y'all want anything to drink?"

"No thanks. We won't be long." Millie flipped her hair off her shoulder and leaned forward to speak, but he interrupted her to speak to me.

"How's your grandma?"

"Good," I said. "Prim's holding on the best she can." I ran my hand over my jeans.

He frowned, leaned his elbows on his knees, and ran his towel through his hands. "Yeah. Patrice told me about her. I hated to hear about the cancer. How's it progressed?"

"It was stage four when we learned about it, so it was already advanced." I pressed my knees together and clasped my hands in my lap.

He frowned with concern. "How's she handling the treatments?"

"She's refused treatment." My throat tightened.

"Really?" His brows shot up. "Wow. How's she handling that?"

I shrugged one shoulder and gnawed on my lower lip. "As well as could be expected." I didn't want to talk about Prim's decline, so I flipped the subject. "And I'm sorry for *you*. You must be beside yourself with worry since Patrice went missing."

Sadness flickered over his features. He looked down at the towel he twisted over and over in his hands. "It's inconceivable."

My first instinct was to jump off the couch and slap him all about the head and shoulders, demanding him to tell me why he was being a jerk and running on the treadmill instead of going out to find Patrice. I reined myself in. "Have you heard anything from her or the kidnappers?"

"You think it was really a kidnapping?" A hint of humor gleamed in his eyes, which only rekindled my desire to punch him square in his pie hole.

Millie crossed her arms over her chest. "There was a ransom call asking for money for her return, which tends to indicate a kidnapping."

He shrugged, a smarmy twist to his mouth. "Unless it was staged."

Millie had always been slow to anger, but now her eyes blazed. "My mom would never do such a thing, and you know it."

He sat back in his chair with a grunt and a satisfied air. "Is it? What about that time she got mad at me, packed all her stuff, and took off to Lexington to stay with you? She didn't leave a note, didn't answer her phone or nothing. She left me to sit here and worry about her for a whole week."

"This is different. I wouldn't be here if she wasn't really missing."

"And we've received a call from the kidnappers," I added.

He looked between us. "Really? No joke?"

I flashed a glance of exasperation at Millie. "Really. We last saw her at the Bourbon, BBQ, and Bands Festival yesterday. She left to get more bourbon and never came back. We went out to the distillery to find her and she was gone."

"Huh…" He leaned an elbow on the chair arm and stroked his chin. He sat, dazed, staring up at the silent golf players on the screen. As an afterthought he muttered, "I can't believe it."

That wasn't exactly the reaction I was expecting. Millie and I glanced at each other then she said, "Well, have you not seen or heard from her at all?"

He gawked at us as if we'd appeared out of thin air. "Uh, no." He rubbed his face. "I, uh, can't believe it. I didn't think—" He stopped himself.

Millie's voice raised a few notches. "Mitch, if you know anything about my mom's disappearance, you have to tell us now."

I narrowed my eyes, certain I detected guilt clouding his features like a little kid who was caught scribbling crayon on the wall. "You didn't think what?" I asked.

"Oh, uh, nothing." He stood and paced, rubbing his hand over the top of his damp hair. "Hey, um, I'm sorry, girls, but I've got to get dressed to go to work. So, I need to ask you to leave."

"I thought you didn't work on Sundays."

"I do now. We're short-staffed at the clinic these days."

CHAPTER SIX

Millie and I stood. She said, "The kidnappers haven't called you? You don't know anything?"

"No." He shifted from foot to foot, nervous. He continued to walk forward, corralling us toward the door.

"Well, can you at least assist with the ransom?" I asked. "They're asking for a million dollars."

He opened the door and waved us out. "I'll see what I can do. I'll be in touch."

As we stepped outside, I spun and held up a finger. "Wait, one more thing. Do you know Fox Graham from Fox Trace Distilleries?"

He hemmed, and his eyes filled with knowing. He averted his gaze. "No. I don't think so. Why would I?" He shut the door in our faces and locked it.

Chapter Seven

Millie and I gaped at each other.

She said, "Is it me, or was he acting weird?"

"He was acting really weird."

We jumped in the car. I pulled out my phone. My first instinct was to call Jimmy and tell him how shifty Mitch had acted when the subject of Patrice had come up. But I was still a little raw about the way he'd spoken to me last night. While the flowers had helped soothe my hurt feelings, it didn't make up for the missing apology. Besides, if I told him what we'd been up to, he might shout at me again. .

Dropping my phone in my purse, I said to Millie, "I think we should wait for him to leave and follow him."

She pulled her long hair from behind her and let it cascade over her shoulder. "He said he was going to work."

"Maybe he was lying. Wouldn't hurt to find out, right?" I pointed to a big SUV at the top of a hill and across the street. "Go park in front of that SUV. And when he comes out, we'll follow at a safe distance."

"Won't he know it's us? He knows my car."

"I doubt he's going to be looking for us. Why would he?"

We didn't have to wait long. Within about twenty minutes, Mitch eased out of his front door. Wearing sunglasses, he glanced around, ducked inside his car, and sped off.

We trailed him at several car lengths behind and let a couple cars get in front of us to help camouflage us. We followed him out of Blantonboro Road toward the clinic. But instead of going to the clinic, he turned right

CHAPTER SEVEN

into a large park. It was a massive park and a favorite hangout, not just for Rothdalians, but folks in surrounding communities and counties. A few large playgrounds and picnic cabanas with grills bordered an enormous lake for non-motor boats and fishing. In the distance stood an amphitheater, behind which lay an arboretum and butterfly garden, several hiking and biking trails, a water play area with a variety of sprinklers and sprayers, as well as a fenced dog park.

Mitch wound his way to the back of the park. Locals wanting a family-friendly day at the park avoided the back area which had a reputation for catering to seedier elements. Mitch pulled into a parking spot in front of the bathroom building. Beside him was an island of pine trees, a garbage receptacle, and a dog poop bag stand. There was also a large sign listing park rules.

Millie parked on the other side of this island where we couldn't be seen. Unfortunately, we couldn't see him, either, so we eased out of the car and ducked into the trees. We peeked around the feathery pine branches. Mitch left his car and got into a dark silver car. I was horrible with car types so, unless it was an obvious model like a Corvette or a Mustang, I had no idea what I was looking at. It was sporty and sleek with a squarish front. It wasn't anything I recognized. Unfortunately, the windows were tinted black as coal dust, and because the windows were rolled up, we couldn't hear their conversation.

Mitch had only been in the car a few minutes before his door popped open and he stepped out. He leaned on the door, finishing up his conversation.

"I'm going to see if I can get on the other side of this tree and get a picture of the silver car's plates." I stood and moved, tripping over a root and falling into the pine tree. *Crap!*

Mitch snapped his head around as Millie and I ducked back behind the tree. My heart raced, blood thrumming in my ears.

"Who's there?" Mitch said.

The silver car flew backwards, tires squealing as it peeled out of the parking lot.

Mitch moved toward the trees.

Dang it! I shoved at Millie with both hands and mouthed, "run." We ran, threw ourselves in her car, and sped away in the other direction. I turned in my seat and watched out the back window to see if Mitch spotted us. He came from around the pine tree as Millie and I rounded the curve and disappeared into the woods.

With a sigh of relief, I turned and sank into the seat.

"Did he see us?" Millie asked

"I don't think so, but keep driving and get us out of this park as fast as possible." I opened Google on my phone and typed in "sports cars" to see if I could figure out what kind of car it was. A menu of popular sports car images populated my screen. I scrolled through and found a car that looked similar to the car I saw. Dodge Challenger. I opened the image to get a closer look.

Robert Plant howled the opening bars of the "Immigrant Song" from my phone, and I about jumped out of my skin. It was the ringtone I'd set for when Jimmy called. I answered the phone. "Yes?"

"Hey, what's up?"

Glancing at Millie, I rubbed circles over my chest to calm my pulse. "Nothing much. Just hanging out with Millie." It wasn't necessary to tell him anything right now. He'd just yell at me again. Maybe I'd wait until I had something definitive. Then it would be worth the risk of telling him.

"Sorry. I need a minute to calm down." Millie pulled over in the parking lot of a Dollar General. Shaking, she looked around. "I don't see him. I think we're clear." She white-knuckled the steering wheel. "That was scary." Her eyes watered, and her nose grew pink. "Mitch isn't acting right. I think he has my mom. How am I going to get her back?"

"Jimmy and Sheriff Goodman are working hard on the case. They're going to find her."

She whispered, "What if they don't?"

I squeezed her hand. "You just have to keep hoping until there's none left."

Chapter Eight

Sitting on my couch, fuming in my cocktail dress, curled hair, and pristine makeup, I waited on Jimmy for over an hour. Yet, he still hadn't called or texted to tell me he was running late, or to cancel, or anything. Silence. Even when I called him, he didn't respond. I was now on the verge of tears, which would only add fuel to my growing fire.

Prim didn't help.

She stood at the window in her purple floral house dress. "What kind of man leaves a woman waiting like this? I've got a good mind to call up his mother and ask her if she let coyotes raise her son."

Normally, I would've defended him. Or I would've asked her to stop being so grouchy. But I was afraid to speak. If I spoke, I might cry. Or break something. So, instead, I chose to stew in my silent anger. Even now, I was tempted to explain it all away. Maybe he was on the job, got called in to an emergency, and couldn't get away to call. Maybe he found an important lead in Patrice's case. Maybe he'd been hurt. Guilt twisted in my gut. Maybe I was the one being selfish.

I closed my eyes and rubbed the tight spot on my forehead. Surely, it wasn't being unreasonable to expect at least a quick phone call or a text to let me know something. Even if the message came from another officer—anything to release me from this limbo of guilt, anger, hurt, and worry. How long was I expected to wait? Now, the result of sitting on pain began to take shape: my head began throbbing, acid rose in my mouth as my stomach twisted into knots. Even if he showed up in the next five minutes, I probably couldn't eat supper with him anyway. The sight of him would turn my stomach. But I couldn't sit here either. Prim's fussing was only feeding my anger, my heartache, and my headache.

There was only one place I could think of to go to and get away.

Tangled up in Brew, Cam's bar on Nyquist Street in downtown Lexington, was packed with football fans and the atmosphere was, thankfully, loud enough to drown my thoughts. The University of the Bluegrass Thoroughbreds challenging the Florida Gators lit up every television in the bar. Bob Segar sang about standing "Like A Rock" on the jukebox in the billiard corner, and the scent of fried foods filled the room.

Cam stood behind the bar in a navy Tangled Up in Brew T-shirt and blue jeans, dishcloth on his shoulder, mixing a cocktail. Behind him was a well-lit mirrored wall lined with an array of liquor bottles. I hopped up on a barstool. I had thrown on an oversized sweatshirt over jeggings, wiped off most of my makeup, and thrown my hair into a messy bun.

When Cam saw me, his face it up. He looked like one of those guys playing volleyball on a beach in a beer commercial, all toned and tan, but adorably scruffy.

"Hey there, pretty lady. I wasn't expecting to see you here tonight. What brings you out?"

It was likely Jimmy hadn't spoken to him about us dating yet and, given the way things were going, we might not need to reveal our little secret. Either way, I didn't even want to think about Jimmy right now. So, I was going to keep quiet about my situation. "I just needed to get out of the house for a while."

"Who's watching Prim?" He pulled the handle on a beer tap, filling a glass with gold, foamy liquid.

"Batrene. Can I get a Guinness and a slice of chocolate cake?"

"Uh-oh. What happened?" He slid the beer over to a waiting server.

"Nothing. I don't want to talk about it."

He studied me. "Fair enough. One order of Distressed Damsel coming up." His blue eyes lit with humor.

"Ha. Ha. Very funny." I made a face at him and propped my face against

CHAPTER EIGHT

my hand.

He laughed and filled a frosted glass to the brim with the espresso-colored stout. Cam shouted to the server. "Hey, Ronnie, grab a large piece of cake. Make it extra sweet."

The guy with a goatee glanced my way and understood. "Sure thing."

In a flash, I languished in my Guinness with a side of chocolate cake with a scoop of ice cream drizzled in fudge.

Cam gave Ronnie his dish towel and asked him to take over the bar. Cam stepped from behind the bar and sat on the stool beside me. Just having him near brought some relief. He nudged me with his shoulder. "You sure you don't want to talk about it? We bartenders have a reputation for being good listeners."

I gazed into his blue eyes. It was like looking into bright summer skies. There was nothing but kindness, interest, and tenderness there. I felt like I was being wrapped in a warm blanket. I couldn't bear to tell him the truth. Why on earth did I get involved with Jimmy, of all people? Cam's best friend. I rubbed my face and shook my head. "Thanks, but I really don't want to talk about it." A bunch of fans shouted at the television.

"I see. So, have you heard anything about Patrice?"

"No. And it's hard watching Millie go through this. It reminds me a lot of my mom and how I lost her. I can't stand to see Millie go through the same thing."

He nodded. "Have you talked to your dad recently?"

I shook my head and jabbed my fork into the moist cake. "No. He called a couple days ago, but then Patrice went missing. Between that, work, and taking care of Prim, I've been swamped." My phone screamed out "The Immigrant Song." Jimmy. I hit silent and returned the phone to my back pocket.

"You said awhile back he had a new lawyer...."

"Yeah. Stu, the lawyer, gave me some files to read. I started reading them, but ..." I flipped my hand as if that completed the thought.

Cam circled back to Patrice. "Has Jimmy said anything about Patrice's case? Surely, he's found some leads by now."

I shrugged and stuffed a bite of cake in my mouth. I glanced around as I chewed and noticed a familiar face walk in the door. Mitch Thomas. He was dressed in a U of B pullover, dark skinny jeans, and black vans. He seemed to be trying too hard to look younger. Then I saw why. Behind him came a young, very young, doe-eyed woman in a pink baby doll dress and brown ankle boots. A mass of wavy brown hair surrounded her round, freckled face. The home wrecker was cute enough, well-built, in a stocky, athletic way. In her late twenties, maybe early thirties, she was young enough to be Mitch's daughter.

I swallowed the chunk of cake in my mouth and washed it down with Guinness. "I can't believe he's here. What a jerk!"Cam leaned back on his seat and followed my gaze. "Who? What?"

I turned to him. "That's Mitch Thomas, Patrice's ex-fiancé."

"Ooooh. So?"

"He's with another woman while Patrice is missing. And when Millie and I went to see him this afternoon, he acted really weird when we brought up Patrice's name."

"Are you saying he might be involved in her disappearance?"

"Not sure, but I think he knows more than he's letting on." I put another bite of cake in my mouth.

"What makes you say that?"

"Even though he didn't realize Patrice was kidnapped, he didn't seem too surprised about it either when we told him. As if he knew she was missing. But he actually said that maybe she'd staged it. Can you believe that?"

He lifted his brows. "I can't imagine. I mean, if you went missing, hell fire couldn't keep me from finding you."

Our eyes locked for a moment. Heat bloomed in my chest and spread down into my belly. I looked away and took another bite of cake. I wanted to know who that woman was. I took another drink of Guinness and slid off the stool. "I'm going to go talk to him."

"Whoa…" Cam said.

But I was already pushing my way through the sea of blue U of B shirts. I approached the table and smiled down at the mismatched couple. "Hey,

CHAPTER EIGHT

Mitch. Long time no see."

He looked at me like I'd slapped him.

I stuck my hand out toward the woman. "Hi, I'm Rook Campbell. A friend of Mitch's fiancée's daughter."

Mitch laughed nervously. "My ex-fiancée."

The woman took my hand and smiled apprehensively. "Hi. I'm Savannah."

"Savannah…." I let my voice drop, leaving a space for her to fill in the blank.

"Stewart."

"Ah. Nice to meet you. So, are you Mitch's daughter?"

"Um, no. We're dating."

Mitch's demeanor clouded as if he was one number short of a winning Bingo card. "Not that my personal life really any of your business, Miss Rook."

I ignored him. Playing the part of just-between-us-girls, I playfully tapped her arm. "Oh, wow. Good for you, girl. You snapped him right up before another girl moved in. No reason to let that get cold. Amiright?" I laughed.

Savannah pasted a tense smile on her face as her cheeks took on a sunburned hue. "Uh, I guess."

Mitch looked around. "Where's our server?"

Cam sidled up to me. "Evening, folks." He put his hand on the small of my back. It was a delightful spot of heat. He smiled down at me. "Rook, you over here causing trouble?"

Flashing happy innocence up at him, I said, "Never in my life." Then I turned to Mitch and Savannah. "This is my ex-husband, Cam. He and I are still great friends, though."

Mitch's olive-gray eyes flashed with heat. "How good for you. If you don't mind—" His phone rang. He pulled it out of his pocket and whispered a curse. "I have to take this. Excuse me."

He stepped away from the table.

I turned to Savannah. "So, how did you and Mitch meet?"

She played with her bracelet. "I work at Mitch's clinic. I'm the receptionist there."

I lifted my brows. "Oh, okay. You like that job?"

She seemed to be relaxing. She nodded. "Yeah. It's okay. It pays the bills."

"And how long have you and Mitch been dating?"

She flushed and shrugged one shoulder. A shyness seemed to overcome her. Yet, she seemed to be calculating something. "Why do you want to know?"

My irritation flared, but I suppressed it. "I'm just curious because Mitch and Patrice broke up only a few weeks ago, and now she's missing. You might want to consider that before getting too involved with him."

"I'm sorry to hear about her disappearance. I don't know what you've heard, but Mitch and I have been dating for several months. I think someone misled you about their relationship. And I don't need to explain myself to you or anyone else."

"You're right." I lifted my hands. "I meant no harm. I was just curious." Mitch re-entered the bar and made his way to the table. "No worries. Y'all have a nice meal."

"We just want to live our lives. People fall in and out of love every day. I hope your friend is found soon."

"It was nice to meet you."

Mitch sat at the table. He glanced between us. He seemed on edge. "Everything okay?"

"Yes." Savannah nodded.

I gave my parting shot. "Bye, Mitch. I'll tell Millie you said 'hi' and that you're doing everything you can to help find her mother. I mean, I'd think you especially would want Patrice found soon since you'd be the prime suspect and all."

The server approached to take their order.

Cam put his arm around my shoulders as we walked away. "Did you find what you were looking for?"

"I wasn't really searching for anything. I just wanted to meet the woman who came between Mitch and Patrice." I returned to my seat at the bar and tucked in to my cake, glancing, from time to time, at Mitch and Savannah, who both tapped intently on their phone screens.

CHAPTER EIGHT

At one point, when I looked over at them, Mitch wiped his mouth on his napkin, then reached across the table, grabbing her phone from her hand. He scrolled through it and then held it up. His face was red, and his eyes a little buggy. He shook the phone at her. She leaned back, shocked.

Savannah grabbed for her phone, and he jerked it away, still speaking. Though I couldn't hear what he was saying, his thin lips seemed to be pinching off a long line of barbed words. Whatever he was saying, it wasn't pleasant. That much was clear. He tossed the phone at her chest, and she fumbled it as it fell under the table.

Mitch downed his beer, stood, and threw a wad of cash on the table. He stormed off while she scrambled to get her things together and tripped along behind him.

I jumped from my stool and followed them. I chased them outside. Numbness fell over my ears as I stepped from the din of the bar into the relative quiet of the street. The air had cooled, and cars swished by.

Savannah ran along the sidewalk after him with short, mincing steps as if her shoes hurt her feet. She caught up to him at his car. She grabbed his arm and said, "For the last time, I'm not sleeping with Shane Decker. We're only friends. If you can't trust me, then this is over."

Mitch looked up to see me. His mouth dragged downward.

I reached in my pocket to extract my car keys and moved toward a car parked on the street to pretend I was getting in.

Swiping his hand through the air, he said to Savannah, "Get in the car."

They climbed in the car, and he sped away.

Chapter Nine

When I arrived home around nine, buzzing with chocolate and hops, Jimmy was sitting in his truck, waiting on me. *Oh, crap.* I wasn't getting out of this one. I took a deep breath, steeling myself, and muttered, "Okay, let's do this." I got out of my car. A light, cool breeze washed over me. A chorus of crickets and tree frogs permeated the night air.

He was already out of his truck, leaning against the grill, arms crossed over his chest. "I've been calling you. Where've you been?" He was in his uniform, but the shirt was untucked and unbuttoned to reveal a white T-shirt underneath.

"I decided to go out and enjoy my evening since you stood me up. What? Did you think I was just supposed to sit here and wait on you all night? How long have you been here?"

"About an hour."

I crossed my arms. "And why didn't you call or text to let me know what was going on? I sat on the couch, all dressed up, over an hour, waiting on you. And you didn't contact me once to explain. I might've understood if you had just done that. I know you have an important job, and you're likely to get called away, but it's not fair to leave me to worry and wait."

He hooked his thumbs in his belt loops and dropped his chin to his chest. "You're right."

"Where were you? Why didn't you let me know something?"

"I was interviewing suspects in Patrice's case and doing some investigation. Then I called out to assist with a wreck that killed two people. But you're right. I should stop and worry about a dinner date."

Guilt tightened my throat. Yet, something wriggled in the corner of my mind. Something wasn't sitting quite right, and I couldn't pinpoint what it was. It's not that I expected him to drop everything. Or that I thought our dinner date was more important than a fatal accident. But was I wrong to want to be told something? "That's unfair. You're making it seem like I'm asking too much. Don't you think I deserve to know *something* so that I don't sit around all night waiting?"

"But you didn't sit around waiting, did you? Where've you been?"

"Tangled Up in Brew."

He lifted his brows. "Hanging out with Cam, I guess?"

"He's your friend and mine. Is that a problem?"

"He's also your ex."

He seemed jealous. "You accusing me of something?"

Jimmy pinched his lips together and shook his head. "Nope. Where'd you go after that?"

"Home. I went to the bar, had cake and Guinness, played a game or two of pool, and came home."

"You bounced back awfully quick from being stood up. Good for you."

"I can't do this. I'm cold and tired. I want to go inside. If you want to fight, I guess you'll have to do it by yourself. Good night." I started toward the door.

Jimmy ran up and grabbed my arm. He was faster than I'd realized. "C'mon. Let's not fight. I'm tired. You're tired. Let's not do this. C'mere." He pulled me into his arms. He was warm and smelled of sweet musk. I melted against him and hugged him back. "I promise next time, I'll call. You're the first girlfriend I've had in a couple years because my work has kept me running, so I'm not used to…all this."

"I understand. But next time, call or text. It takes thirty seconds."

"10-4, chief."

I yawned and pulled away from him. "You want to come in for a bit?"

He glanced at his watch. "Don't you have to go to work tomorrow?"

"Yeah, but I can stay up a little longer."

Prim was in bed by the time I returned home, which was expected.

Batrene tucked her crochet into her yarn bag, her face drawn and the corners of her mouth weighed down with concern. "She's feeling poorly this evening." She shook her head and pushed her glasses on top of her head. "I put her to bed with a cold compress for those lumps under her arms." She rubbed her eyes. "She didn't eat much. I made her some mashed potatoes. She ate a few spoonfuls with a little dry toast. Poor thing." Her voice cracked. "She's plain wilting away."

I sighed. "Thank you. You did your best. I appreciate it." I turned to Jimmy. "Would you care to escort Batrene home while I check on Prim?"

"Sure." He swept his hand toward the door. "After you."

She gathered her things and patted my cheek. "You call me whenever you need me. Day or night." Batrene and Jimmy left me in the quiet of my kitchen, trying to stand under the weight of my burdens.

I heard Prim coughing from her bedroom. I gathered a few cough drops and a ginger ale and ran upstairs. I cracked the door and peeked in.

"What do you need, child?" Prim croaked, her back to me. She coughed again.

"Just checking on you." I stepped in. "You're coughing a lot. I have ginger ale and cough drops for you."

"Thank you." She rolled over. "Get the light."

I sat on the bed and flipped on the lamp, then I helped aim the straw into her mouth and unwrapped a cough drop for her.

She patted my hand and lay back on the pillows, closing her eyes. "Where'd you go tonight?"

"Cam's bar."

She lifted her brow and popped the lozenge in her mouth. "Now, don't get mad at me…." She lifted her hand weakly. "Why are you with that man, child?"

"You mean Jimmy?"

She nodded.

"I like him. And I figure it's time for me to move on. I've been divorced for nineteen months now. Why don't you like him?"

"It's not that I don't like him. He's all right, I guess. But, honey, he's not Cam."

"You have a sweet spot for Cam, though."

A gravelly laugh escaped her bony chest. "Of course. Because he's your man. Always will be. What you two have is…special. Like what me and your papaw had." A spark entered her eye. "Electricity. Fireworks."

It was hard for me to imagine my papaw, who had lived in bib overalls and John Deere caps, as the sort of man who would elicit electricity and fireworks, but he sure did for Prim, which was apparent in the smile blooming on her lips.

She said, "You're wasting your time. Life is short, child, and every day you lose time you could've had with the only man who will truly make you happy."

"I don't think I have a choice now."

She frowned and patted my leg. "You always have a choice. You only need to make up your mind what you want and go get it. And I hope you do it soon. Don't waste any more precious time."

I heard the kitchen door open downstairs, and Jimmy called my name. I shouted. "Just a second."

I re-settled Prim then, fighting back tears, descended the stairs to Jimmy.

Jimmy and I settled on the couch in front of the TV while Jimmy scrolled through Netflix options.

Now that we were reconciled, I needed to tell him the things I'd learned today. I cuddled up against him, but felt like I was cuddling a cactus. "I hate to do this because I know you just came off a long shift and have been working hard today. But…" I took a deep breath. "I've come across some information. Kind of."

He looked down at me. "What are you talking about?"

I told him everything about Millie and I visiting Mitch, his weird behavior when Patrice's name came up, his meeting with a mystery person in a silver Dodge Challenger in the park, the run-in with him and Savannah at Tangled Up in Brew—all of it.

He sighed and rubbed his face, then scratched the back of his neck.

"There's so much there. I don't even know where to begin." He shook his head. "And it doesn't seem like anything I say would be listened to anyway."

I moved back from him a little.

"Why did you and Millie go to Mitch's?"

"I told you. We wanted to see if he'd heard from Patrice, if he knew anything about her disappearance. Or, better yet, if there was something he would do to help."

"And did he offer to help?"

"No. Which don't you think that's horrible? I mean, I know they're broken up, but it's a recent split. They were engaged, so he must still care about her. Why wouldn't he be helping more?" I grabbed the afghan from the corner of the couch and pulled it around my legs, more for its calming effect than for warmth.

"In regards to the car at the park, did you at least get any plate number or a description of the driver?"

"No. The windows were too dark. And the car was parked at an angle where I couldn't get the numbers. And it drove away really fast—"

"So, you and Millie put your lives in potential danger for...nothing?"

I toyed with my turquoise and silver ring, a memento of my late mom, shrinking internally from the admonishment. His arrow had hit the mark. "Okay. That was a fail, for sure. It wasn't a complete loss because we got a description of the car."

He nodded. "Mitch is certainly on our list of suspects, and we've already talked to him once. I'll call him in again. Now, can we watch this episode of *Better Call Saul?*"

Chapter Ten

Six in the morning on Monday came early. I stood in the shower, hands against the turquoise subway tiles, letting the hot water rain over my head while I tried to fire up my brain after a night of fitful sleep fraught with anxious and nightmarish dreams. I could only remember snippets. I was being attacked, but Jimmy wouldn't help me. He couldn't even see me. My mom was dating Mitch in the dream, too. The mind played strange games. At any rate, I'd risen early so I'd have extra time for visiting Fox Graham out at Fox Trace before I went to work. I'd talked to Mitch. Now it was Fox Graham's turn. Hopefully, the visit would prove fruitful.

I scrubbed my hair with a happy apple-scented shampoo. Prim's cough reached from the hallway as she passed by. Each night the coughing worsened. I couldn't think about Prim without wondering how many days or hours I had with her. My days and nights were spent balancing on a line of floss stretched across a canyon. Once I realized she was breathing, breath returned to my lungs. As if her breath was my own. I choked down, rising emotion. I couldn't think about that now either and turned my thoughts to Millie and Patrice. Every time I thought of Patrice, my own mother popped into my mind. But there was hope for Patrice, so that's where my focus had to be.

The first forty-eight hours were critical, and we'd been looking for her since Saturday. Technically, we were already out of time. The realization of that seized my heart and breath. *Heaven help us.* I worked apple conditioner into my ends. I didn't know how to work faster or how to get Jimmy and Sheriff Goodman to work faster. Mitch had behaved so oddly when Millie and I spoke with him. He had to be involved. I didn't want to completely discount Fox Graham, but Mitch would've had easier access to Patrice.

I didn't have anything solid against Mitch, but my gut told me he was shady. He didn't seem particularly concerned about Patrice, and he was dating his receptionist. A vague notion squirmed through my mind's surface that maybe he and the receptionist were working together on Patrice's disappearance. I squeezed rose-scented body wash into a pink loofah and scrubbed my skin in quick strokes, as if the vigorous movement would spark an idea while I considered the suspect list.

Dee Dee had believed Fox Graham might've had a hand in Patrice's disappearance. It was important to at least eliminate him as a suspect then I could focus all my energy on Mitch. I couldn't show up at Fox's house out of the blue; it would be too weird, and he'd get suspicious. Maybe I could speak to him at his work too. I could take some flowers or candy to Fox Trace, and say it's a congratulatory gift from Four Wild Horses. I needed only a few minutes of his time. It was worth a shot. Of course, I was still upset with him about rigging the contest. I hadn't forgotten that and was going to inform the Kentucky Distillers' Guild as soon as I had confirmation of his cheating. The KDG would probably do nothing more than strip him of the title and prizes, but that was enough. It wouldn't necessarily go to Mermaid Cove, but at least it wouldn't go to a cheat.

I jumped out of the shower, dried off, and began my dressing routine, opting to braid my wet hair and pin it in a chignon. I donned a navy wrap dress with white polka dots, and red Mary Jane pumps. I applied a coat of natural makeup, heavy on the under-eye concealer to hide my lack of sleep, and cheek highlighter to grant a near-awake and dewy-fresh appearance.

I jogged downstairs to make oatmeal for Prim's breakfast. She was outside on the screened-in porch trying to stuff her feet in her gardening boots.

I opened the door and poked my head out. "What are you doing?"

"I'm going to get the weeds out of my turnip greens and pick up a few apples off the ground before they rot. I want to set up more apple butter soon."

Only heaven knew where she was going to get all the energy to do those

CHAPTER TEN

things. "Aren't you going to eat breakfast?"

"When I'm done."

"I'm making it now before I go."

She nodded with impatience. "Fine, fine, fine." Her illness made her less tolerant of people fussing over her. She clapped her broad straw hat on her head and grabbed her spade and a bucket. "I'll eat it when I get back. Leave it on the stove." She clomped across the wood floor and out the screen door, holding the door to ease herself down the steps. She let the door slam.

The television blared from the living room. I was about to turn it off when the corner image showed side-by-side still shots of Holly and her accomplices. The anchorman reported that they would go to trial soon, recapped the details of Bryan's murder case and the bourbon-thief ring at the Four Wild Horses Distillery. My heart sank. Every time I saw them was a reminder of my friend's death and his absence. They all looked unkempt and wild-eyed. Holly's dark roots bled through her fading blonde hair. Without her layers of makeup, she looked downright evil. Images of her trying to kill me flooded back to my mind. I shuddered as hatred wove between my ribs, pulling a dark cloud around my mind. I turned off the television. I was free. My life went on, and they were going to jail. Good enough for me. I didn't have to deal with them until I took the witness stand. I'd probably be hearing from a lawyer soon.

I left Prim's breakfast in a covered bowl. I threw together a travel mug of coffee and popped a couple of waffles in the toaster for myself as I watched Batrene make her way into our yard in her black cotton dress topped with a red flannel barn jacket and her reading glasses atop her frizzy brown hair. She needed to go to the salon. Her sister Bonnie usually helped with such things. I made a mental note to mow her yard for her after work tonight. She and Prim walked to the back of the yard, where Prim managed a small family garden.

My waffles popped. I slathered them with butter and apple butter, then wolfed them down before rushing outside to greet Batrene.

"There's fresh coffee inside for you, and her breakfast is in the bowl. Help yourself." Then I added, only half-teasing, "Prim's being ornery this morning, so make sure she doesn't get too tired. Make her take breaks. Prim, you listen to Batrene. Don't give her any problems." I hated leaving Prim again. Though I was thankful for Batrene's help, I hated relying on her so much. She had a life, too. I needed more help. I simply didn't have anyone else, and I couldn't afford in-home care. I looked it up one day, and at twenty to forty dollars an hour, there was no way I could manage that.

Prim waved me away. "Quit your fussing. Go on with you."

I kissed her cheek and winked at Batrene.

My first stop was Martine's Pastry shop—a tiny little store with a pale green and white striped awning on Main Street. I bought their best breakfast rolls, inspired by Kentucky's most famous pie, made in kitchens every Derby Day. The rolls were loaded with chocolate, walnuts, and bourbon and, unlike the pie, drizzled with bourbon cream cheese icing. These pastries were so rich and decadent that even my sweet tooth could handle only one. But these tasty treats were bound to loosen the lips of Fox Graham enough for me to find out if he had any involvement in Patrice's disappearance.

Fox Trace was a pretty little distillery nestled in a valley in northern Franklin County near the Owen County line. The valley rose into hillocks of trees where a few were beginning to take on the fire of autumn colors. The main building housed the visitor's center, gift shop, and administrative offices and consisted of giant windows trimmed in red paint, set in gray siding. The bottom of the building was trimmed in gray stone. This would've been a beautiful place in the fall, but I pitied the landscaper who had to rake up the leaves.

Stone paths wound through a canopy of shade trees to a tiny cafe with outdoor seating under large hunter-green umbrellas. The production center and several rickhouses lined up beyond the cafe. They resembled tall warehouses with aluminum siding and rows of small windows.

I parked in front of the building and entered with my box of goodies. I had toured Fox Trace once before, and it had changed very little in the few years since I'd last visited. The interior was like most distilleries: wood walls and wood floors made to resemble high-polished bourbon barrels, a few

CHAPTER TEN

accent walls of exposed brick, and ceilings of exposed pipes. The ground floor consisted of reception, restrooms, a history of bourbon room, and a lounge area. The second floor housed the tasting rooms and gift shop. My destination was the third floor, where the business offices resided.

A tour guide greeted me first. He was a young, baby-faced guy, probably early to mid-twenties, average height and build, with short dark hair, round dark-rimmed glasses, and a dark, scanty beard. He was a college-aged Harry Potter. He sauntered toward me wearing the uniform of hunter green polo shirt tucked into khaki pants. His name tag said "Turner."

"Good morning. Are you here for our nine o'clock tour?" He pointed as he spoke. "Just pay Darlene here and meet the rest of the group in this room over here. We're gathering in front of the bourbon timeline wall, and we'll start in about fifteen minutes."

"Thank you, but I'm not here for a tour." I turned to cut him off and addressed Darlene. "I'm here to see Fox Graham. I have a gift from the Four Wild Horses Distillery to congratulate y'all on your big win at the competition this weekend."

Turner scratched the back of his head. "Oh, uh..." He flushed and turned away.

The receptionist called ahead, sending me up to an assistant who walked me back to Fox's office.

His office consisted of a large window behind a desk that looked out across the surrounding hills and the rest of the distillery grounds. The decor was streamlined, and modern, with lots of dark, seemingly uncomfortable modern furniture.

Fox sat behind the desk and rocked back in his chair with a smug smile. He wore a white shirt, yellow tie, and black pants. His suit jacket hung on the back of his chair. The bourbon competition trophy gleamed from the corner of his desk: a circle of crystal with a gold circle and black writing in the center.

He leaned forward to pat the trophy. "It's a beauty, huh?"

"Congratulations." I forced a smile. "I brought these on behalf of Four Wild Horses Distillery in celebration of your win." I set the box of pastries on his desk.

He lifted the lid. "Oh, Irene's Derby Breakfast Rolls. Now that *is* special. What spell did you cast to score these? They're always sold out every time I go."

I tossed in a fake chuckle for good measure. "Guess I got lucky." Being friendly to him made me want to throw up my waffles.

He rolled up his sleeves. "I think I'll have one now." He gently lifted a roll and bit into it, nodding his head. He said with a full mouth, "These are amazing." He sipped his coffee to wash down his food.

"Glad you're enjoying them." I sat in one of the chairs in front of his desk. The chair was as uncomfortable as it looked. The ridge of the support rod under the seat pressed into my bottom.

Fox tilted his head, the roll hovering near his mouth. "Was there something else?"

"In fact, yes." I crossed my leg, pulling my skirt over my knee.

He dropped the roll and licked his fingers with loud, sucking sounds. "Make it quick. I have an interview with the National Bourbon Review in thirty minutes. The publicity is coming out of the woodwork. TV stations, magazines, bloggers are calling and emailing, wanting to talk about Fox Trace. We're going to be a national household name before long, like Jim Beam or Maker's Mark. Maybe even international. This award is the best thing to happen to us since we opened." He pushed the box aside.

I stared daggers at him. That should've been Mermaid Cove's award. Patrice and Dee Dee should've received those accolades.

"Fox Trace is pretty new, isn't it?"

"Only five years old."

"About the same age as Mermaid Cove, right?"

"Yep." He clasped his hands together and leaned on the desk. "So?"

"I'd say the competition is pretty stiff between you two trying to establish yourselves among the ones that have been here for over a hundred years, like Four Wild Horses and others. Tough to compete in that market."

He shrugged. "Sure, but every award we get helps in establishing us deeper in the whiskey and bourbon community. Next stop is the World Whiskies."

CHAPTER TEN

He clapped his hands together and rubbed them vigorously.

"And now that you've gotten Mermaid Cove out of the way…."

He leaned back in his chair and rocked. "Why exactly are you here?"

I was tired of messing around with this guy and I needed to get to work. "I'm going to ask you straight out. Did you have anything to do with Patrice's disappearance?"

He frowned. "What do you mean, disappearance?"

"I mean, she never came back from Mermaid Cove the day of the festival. She's *gone*."

He snort-laughed. "Maybe she was too humiliated to come back."

"I'm not kidding." I glared at him. "Her bourbon whiskey was superior to yours, and you know it. You needed Mermaid Cove out of the way, and I think *you* made her disappear."

Fox frowned and stopped rocking. "Whoa. Wait. You think I had something to do with her disappearance?" His eyes darted, and he licked his lips. "You're crazy." His face flushed red, making his pale eyebrows almost white against his skin. He stood and walked to open the office door. "I don't have time for this nonsense. I won that contest fair and square. I'm busy. I've got an interview coming up soon, so it's time for you to leave."

At the door, I turned. "You enjoy that award while you can."

Once in my car, I dialed Jimmy and told him about my interview with Fox. "You need to check out Fox Graham ASAP. He has to be connected to Patrice's disappearance."

"First, you think it's Mitch. Now you're convinced it's Fox," he chuckled. Papers rustled in the background around a low buzz of voices and ringing phones. He was likely at the office.

"I know. They're both strong contenders. Heck, for all I know, they're working together."

Silence. "Huh. Actually, that's not the craziest idea."

A little pride swelled up in me as I started my car.

"I have a crazy idea of my own."

"What's that?" I put the car into gear and pulled out of Fox Trace.

"How about I come get you for a lunch date?"

"That sounds awesome." I didn't want to get my hopes up. "Are you sure you have time?"

"I think so. If anything prevents me, I promise I'll let you know."

That eased my mind some. "Okay. How about the Bourbon Barrel Café on Main?"

"I'll see you at noon."

After an uneventful lunch of Hot Browns at the Bourbon Barrel Café, Jimmy drove me back toward the distillery. I was enjoying the autumn sun and the wind in my face.

Jimmy put his hand on my knee. "Maybe once the new recruits get settled at the department, I can get a little time off, and you and I can go camping. Just me and you down at the lake, under the stars…." His hand sought mine, and we interlaced our fingers. "Doing stuff to startle the wildlife." He waggled his eyebrows.

I chuckled as he lifted my hand to his mouth and kissed it.

A flutter of butterflies crowded my stomach. And not in the warm fuzzies way. Instead, the feeling was more akin to nervousness and uneasiness. *What's wrong with me?*

He squeezed my hand tighter. "Maybe I shouldn't tell you this, but back when you first started dating Cam, I had a *huge* crush on you, and I was totally jealous of him."

The mention of Cam's name brought on a flood of confusion and competing feelings. Each feeling was a snake, and a big pile of them squirmed around in the pit of my stomach.

I threw a smiling mask on my face. "Really? That's why you were always hanging out with us?" I teased.

"Pretty much." He chuckled. "All I know is I'm one lucky guy."

I slid closer and snuggled against his warm, firm body as he wrapped his arm around me, guiding the steering wheel with his left hand. "Speaking of Cam…have you told him about us yet?"

"No. I swear I'll do it tonight. We're supposed to go to the gym. I'll tell him then."

CHAPTER TEN

A tight sensation crossed my chest. I liked Jimmy and wanted to keep dating him. And I still cared a lot for Cam. Maybe even loved him still? But things had always seemed too complicated with him. Maybe it was easier for us to continue as friends but go our separate ways as lovers. I didn't want to hurt him. It was the last thing I wanted to do. Especially since the past month, he'd been incredibly sweet and doting had helped me with Prim and had consoled me when we found out about her cancer.

"Side trip," Jimmy announced. He parked by a gas pump at the Quick-Mart. "I need to stop for gas before I take you home."

On the window of the convenience store was a sign for the Kentucky Lottery. Prim loved scratch-offs, and I was sure Batrene would like some, too. And if she won a hundred thousand dollars, that'd be a good start to paying her back for all the help she'd been giving me with Prim lately. Cam used to help me with watching Prim, but ever since I'd started dating Jimmy, I didn't feel right about calling Cam for help. I guess I didn't feel right about a few things, but loneliness and hormones made for a dangerous mix. I grabbed my wallet from my purse and slid from the truck. I said to Jimmy, "I'm going in to buy scratch-offs for Prim and Batrene. You want anything?"

He stuck the nozzle in the tank and pushed the button. "Gatorade. I like the blue one."

Cool air washed over me as I entered the building. The place smelled faintly of a potato bin and dirty mop water.

I searched out the blue Gatorade and claimed my place in line.

Jimmy finished up at the pump and joined me inside. "Pump isn't taking cards." He wrapped an arm around my waist, laying his hand on my hip. When we reached the counter, I requested several scratch-off tickets. Jimmy insisted on paying for everything when he paid for his gas. I thanked him with a kiss on the cheek, and we clasped hands on our way out.

A silver double cab truck pulled up in front of the store. Cam. His square jaw gaped as he looked at me and Jimmy. He jumped from the truck, his bright blue eyes focused on us.

"Hey," he said, puzzled, his eyes glancing at mine and Jimmy's clasped hands. He flushed and looked out across the parking lot as he rubbed the back of his neck. His arms were dark with sun exposure, a white line peeking from under the sleeve of his red T-shirt. As always, he filled out his jeans well. They were covered in dirt, grass, and grease stains. He'd probably been helping on his parents' farm. "I, uh…" He licked his lips, looked down at his cowboy boots, and blew out a sharp breath as though he'd been punched in the gut. "Wow. I, uh…." His voice cracked, and he cleared his throat. "I guess you two are, uh…."

"Cam—" I reached to put a hand on his arm, but he jerked back as if burned.

He lifted his hand. "Nope. Don't. I-I gotta go. My mom needs a gallon of milk." He snatched open the door with a hard glance in our direction.

Jimmy released my hand and with a touch to the small of my back, guided me toward his deputy SUV. "Don't worry about it. I'll talk to him and get it straightened out."

Chapter Eleven

The rest of my afternoon at work dragged on in an inner turmoil of knotted feelings that lived in a rope of stress twisted around the back of my neck and into my shoulder blades. I tried not to think of Cam, but the anguish I'd seen in his eyes at the convenience store had seared into my brain, and every time I turned to my work, that look reared up to torment me.

After work, I mowed both mine and Batrene's yard, trying to decide if that was worse than the leaf-raking I'd be doing in a few weeks. I'd already finished the mowing and had nearly completed the weed-eating when Jimmy pulled up. The evening sun was settled low in the sky, but hadn't quite set yet, so I needed to work quickly. He jumped out of his truck in a pair of worn jeans and an Air Force T-shirt. He smelled clean and was as polished as a fresh apple. He'd probably come straight from the gym.

He removed his sunglasses to reveal a black eye.

Gasping, I touched his face. "What happened?"

He grinned. "Cam and I had a talk."

Anger flooded my system. "Who threw the first punch?"

"He threw the first and only punch. I wasn't going to fight him. It's my fault. I should've talked to him sooner."

"This is plain stupid. I'm not to be fought over like a couple of dogs fighting over a pork chop. I'm going to talk to him, and he's going to apologize." I spun toward the house.

He grabbed my arm. "Hold on there, champ."

I faced him.

"Please don't get in the middle of this. Cam and I have had our fights before, and we always work it out. This is a man thing."

I glared at Jimmy. Of course, my mind was already devising what I was going to say to Cam, but my mouth said, "Okay. Fine."

He smiled and pulled me close. "Thank you."

I shied away because I was covered in grass and sweat and smelled like wet dog. "Sorry, I'm really gross, but I needed to get this done tonight. The grass was out of control, and there's rain in the forecast."

"No worries." He kissed me, then smacked his lips. "Mm, tastes like pork chop."

Screwing up my face, I slapped his arm playfully as he laughed.

Laughing, I shoved him away. "Get out of here and let me get this work done."

"You need any help?"

"Nah. I'm almost finished. Go keep Prim company."

I watched him walk to the house, enjoying how his jeans hugged his shape. I yelled out, "Hey, don't you tell Prim what happened to that eye. She doesn't need to be worrying about that." He waved his acknowledgment without looking at me.

I revved up the weed-eater and trimmed around the large oak, the house, and the shed, angrily swiping the trimmer over the weeds as I went through all the things I'd say to Cam. I rinsed off the mover, swept the grass out of the weed-eater, and put everything away. Tree frogs and crickets wound up their evening song as a deep amber light covered the yard. I brushed the grass from my body and kicked my shoes off in the screened porch, then entered the delicious air-conditioned kitchen, breathing in the smell of Prim's cooking. By then, I'd burned through much of my irritation at Cam. I'd deal with him later.

Jimmy sat at the kitchen table, iced tea in hand, and Prim stood at the stove in her black pants and pink blouse. They were talking about mutual acquaintances in our church. Jimmy didn't go to our church (neither did we since Prim's diagnosis), but since Jimmy was a deputy and Prim a high-ranking member of the Old Lady Network, they knew many of the same people.

"Prim, I can do that," I said. "Why don't you have a seat and rest?"

She blinked at me through her glittering spectacles. "Why shouldn't I do this? It won't hurt me to get around a little bit. Besides, you're filthy. Get upstairs and get cleaned up. We'll eat soon."

As I ran up the stairs, I heard Jimmy ask Prim if she liked fresh catfish. I smiled to myself, knowing he was looking for any excuse to get back out to the lake and go fishing before cold weather set in. After a record-speed shower, I lotioned up, put on a dab of perfume, slipped into a gray cotton T-shirt dress, and pinned my wet hair into a bun at the back of my head. I ran downstairs, barefoot, to help Prim.

She'd already fried the cornmeal battered squash and was working on the chicken. I layered a few cold tomato slices on a plate, put a jar of dressed cucumbers on the table, and checked the green beans.

The phone rang. I heard breathing, but no one spoke.

"Are you going to say anything?"

There was no answer.

"Fine." I hung up.

A few seconds later, the phone rang again. I let it ring. It stopped, then resumed ringing. I answered with a huff. Jimmy frowned with concern., The breather didn't speak. I hung up and took the phone off the hook.

Jimmy said, "Is that happening a lot?"

"Just enough to be a nuisance."

"You want me to get a trace put on it?"

"I doubt that's necessary. It's probably some kids who think they're being funny."

We sat down to dinner, blessed the food, then started passing the bowls around.

Prim handed Jimmy the squash. "What happened to your eye?"

Jimmy looked at me, forking squash onto his plate. "I got sassy with Rook, and she clocked me one." He winked, and we chuckled.

Prim inspected the bruise. "It looks pretty fresh."

Jimmy reached for the dressed cucumbers. "I got it at softball practice."

"Hm. That's the story you're sticking with?" Prim stared pointedly at me.

"What?"

"You believe that story?" she asked.

"Why shouldn't I?"

She narrowed her eyes and chewed her food slowly, her hands under her chin. "I'd heard a different story from Cam's momma."

Geez Louise...I rolled my eyes, chewing my food. Did nothing get past the OLN? These old ladies should be training the CIA in intelligence tactics.

Jimmy flushed. "Well, I..."

We were saved by a knock at the kitchen door.

"I'll get it." Glad for the interruption, I dropped my fork and jumped for the door.

Millie and Roderick, Dee Dee's son, stood there with red, puffy eyes, indicating they'd been crying.

"What's going on?" I stepped back to let them in.

Roderick was clean-shaven with close-cropped hair and kind, brown eyes. His lean muscular form, dressed in a teal polo and khakis, towered over us. He teared up again. "They've arrested my momma."

Millie's voice shook. "What're we going to do? Dee Dee was in the process of getting the money together to free my mom." Her voice tightened another notch. "The kidnappers contacted us again today. We have until Saturday. That's only five days. What are we going to do?"

Prim and I blinked at them in stunned silence. After a moment, Prim pulled out a chair and guided Roderick toward it. She patted his shoulder. "You come sit. We'll make you a plate." Then she frowned at Jimmy. "Were you aware of this?"

"No, ma'am. I'm just as surprised as y'all are."

"Prim, please." I tossed a panicked and apologetic glance at Jimmy. "The police can't always share everything during an investigation. Sometimes—"

Prim wasn't having it. She slammed the fridge door and held the tea pitcher with both hands. "This ain't got a darned thing to do with any investigation." She set the pitcher down with a thud. "This is about friends and family. He could've at least told us she'd been arrested."

CHAPTER ELEVEN

Prim pulled down a couple glasses, and filled them with ice, then said to Millie and Roderick, "Now you two have a seat and get something to eat. We'll talk about what can be done." She set tea glasses down in front of our guests. "Rook, get place settings."

I jumped up to grab plates and silverware.

"Do you know who made the arrest?" Jimmy bit into a chicken leg.

Roderick propped his head on his hand and pushed at his fried squash with his fork. "Sheriff Goodman."

"Did he say what the charges are?"

"I asked, but he wouldn't tell me. He kept saying it was related to an ongoing investigation."

I asked Jimmy, "Can he do that?"

He nodded. "He's not under any obligation to give any details. But…" He put down his chicken leg and wiped the grease on a napkin. "Let me see what I can find out. Excuse me." He pushed back from the table, removing his phone from his pocket, and stepped outside onto the screened porch. After about ten minutes, he returned. "Looks like they're holding her on embezzlement and kidnapping. To start. No doubt Sheriff Goodman is investigating to add on additional charges."

I squeezed Roderick's hand. "We'll go out there first thing in the morning to talk to her."

He nodded, wiping his eyes. "Thank you."

Jimmy said, "Hold on there, Rook. You have to set an appointment if you're not a lawyer or preacher."

Roderick looked between us. "How long will that take?"

"It could be a couple days before you get to see her."

"Isn't there anything you can do?" I asked Jimmy.

"I'll talk to Goodman to find out what's going on, and I'll try to visit her myself. Look in on her, make sure she's okay."

"Thank you," Roderick and I said in unison.

"Who's running Mermaid Cove?" I asked.

Roderick shook his head. "We have a few people who can run tours. I think the production crew can run on their own at least for a few days until this gets cleared up I guess I'll skip classes in the morning to go out and supervise for a few hours."

Millie interjected, "Except for tomorrow, I can switch my schedule and cover in the mornings for the rest of the week, if you can arrange evenings, Roderick."

I jumped in. "And I can help on the weekend, if Dee Dee is still in jail by that time."

Prim cut her eyes at Jimmy. "Which hopefully she won't be."

Roderick rolled his eyes with relief. "Oh man, that would be a ton of help, Millie and Rook. Thank you. Y'all are the best. My momma didn't have anything to do with Miss Patrice's disappearance."

I said, "Of course, your mom is innocent. We know Dee Dee loves Patrice like a sister. This is hard on her, too. We hate that this has happened."

Jimmy's phone chimed. He looked at it. "Emergency. I've got to go." He jumped up from the table, kissed my lips, and grabbed another chicken leg. "Thank you, ladies, for supper." He said to Roderick, "I'm sorry Goodman arrested your mom, but he must've stumbled on something *appearing* to implicate her. I'm sure there's a mistake. We'll get it sorted and get her out." Jimmy dashed from the house.

Millie pushed back her plate after only a few bits of food. "What about my mom? Where are we going to get the money? With Dee Dee in jail, it's going to cause a major delay. We only have five days."

I leaned back in my chair, looked up at the ceiling, and rubbed my face. I sighed heavily, my mind stewing in a vat of rage, confusion, and powerlessness. "I don't know."

Prim gnawed on one end of a chicken bone. "If it were me, I'd go talk to that rich boyfriend of hers." She discarded the bone and wiped her hands and mouth on her napkin. Elbows on the table, she interlaced her hands under her chin. "They may've broken up, but if he ever really loved her, he'll pay the money." She stood and carried her plate over to the sink, sitting it on the counter.

Millie said, "We tried talking to him once, but he didn't seem too interested."

CHAPTER ELEVEN

Prim said, "That may be, but I think if you explained to him that he might seem less suspicious for providing the money, he might be more agreeable. After all, the officers are going to watch his behavior very closely while they're gathering evidence." She opened the freezer. "Y'all want some Ice cream? I have fixings for sundaes."

Everyone declined.

She said, "You have to have dessert."

Crossing my arms over my chest, I rolled my bottom lip between my thumb and index finger as I considered what Prim had said. It did seem weird that Mitch wouldn't be more involved in saving Patrice. After all, people didn't fall automatically out of love because they broke up. My relationship with my ex-husband, Cam, told me that much. When Millie and I had talked to Mitch, he hadn't seemed particularly bitter. He seemed relaxed. Until we mentioned that Patrice was missing. Only then did he become tense.

Mitch's split from Patrice probably hadn't been especially amicable since he'd been cheating on her. But by my logic, even if he'd moved on, if he had loved Patrice at all, he'd want to help get her back. After all, I was sure Cam would do that for me. Even in his current mood about my and Jimmy's relationship.

Maybe Prim was right about Mitch being willing to help with the funding. I needed to talk to Mitch again, see if he'd be willing to help. I also needed to have a long talk with Cam.

Chapter Twelve

The next morning, I called work to tell them I'd be a little late so I could visit the clinic and offered to bring in a box of donuts from Irene's and to work late in recompense. It was actually no big deal if I was late. We worked a pretty flexible schedule at the Four Wild Horses Distillery. As long as the marketing team completed our jobs well, clocked our forty-hours, and met deadlines, our boss, Pierce, didn't really care how we managed our time.

I racked my brains for a legitimate reason for visiting the clinic. As I pulled out of the drive, I spotted a swath of ragweed. *Bingo! Problem solved.* I got out of the car and grabbed a handful of ragweed. Pushing up my shirt sleeve, I pressed the weed to the inside of my arm and rubbed vigorously. I was quite allergic to many grasses and weeds—especially ragweed. I sneezed. Even being near it triggered my allergies. I smiled, wiping the bits of green off my arm. My arm was already getting pink and splotchy and itchy. By the time I arrived at the clinic, I'd have a good old-fashioned case of contact dermatitis ripe for a doctor's diagnosis.

First, I stopped at Irene's and grabbed a dozen mixed donuts, danishes, and fritters. Thenn I headed out Blantoboro road toward Mitch's clinic. As I pulled into the clinic parking lot, a ragweed fueled fire had crawled up my arm. I scratched and inspected it. The parking lot seemed awfully full for a Tuesday morning. A few people loitered near the door smoking. Ugh. I didn't want to walk through all that secondhand smoke. One person went in, stepping quickly, hands tucked into his pockets, as a lady came out, practically running to her car, scratching her arm and licking her lips. She

CHAPTER TWELVE

had a haggard look about her. As did the folks hovering around the door. In fact, they looked like a bunch of scarecrows. A sense of uneasiness fell over me.

My phone rang. Jimmy.

"Hey gorgeous, what're you up to?"

"You know me." I smiled into the phone. "No good at all."

He paused. He added, his voice serious, "Rook, what are you doing?"

I laughed. "Nothing. I'm going to the doctor." It wasn't entirely a lie. I only omitted the bits that might cause an argument.

"Why're you going to the doctor?"

"Nothing major." I examined my pink, itchy arm. "I think I've got an allergic reaction. Probably from when I was working in the yard last night. I'm going to get it checked out. Can I call you back?"

"Sure."

"Thanks, I shouldn't be long."

I scanned the parking lot, looking at the plates on the cars. Many of the cars were from places at least fifty miles away, as far as Letcher and Garrard Counties. Those counties had clinics of their own, so why were all these people here? If this were Lexington, where there were specialists and advanced medical care facilities, then it might make more sense for all these out-of-town folks to be here. However, this was a little country clinic in Franklin County. So, it didn't make sense for people to drive so far.

I held my breath against the secondhand smoke as I opened the door. The waiting room was full of bedraggled souls.

The receptionist, Savannah, looked up. Her smile slipped when she saw me. "Can I help you?" Her voice was cold.

I utilized the hand sanitizer sitting on the lip of the counter. "Rook Campbell to see Dr. Thomas."

"Do you have an appointment?"

"No. But this is a walk-in clinic, isn't it?"

"Right. Please fill out these forms." She handed me a clipboard with papers and a pen.

I looked around. "It seems pretty packed in here. How long will I have to wait?"

She typed on her computer. "It won't be long. We move pretty fast around here."

I bet.

The waiting room was a small, undecorated room with pale, ugly yellow walls. Wooden chairs lined the walls, and two rows of back-to-back chairs stood in the center of the floor. The chairs were full, and a television anchored high in the corner played a morning news talk show. I felt trapped, closed in, and surrounded by grime. My hands itched for more sanitizer.

I sat beside a wiry young man, a mouth-breather, who smelled of stale cigarettes and bacon grease. He wore a hooded jacket, and his greasy dark hair lay against his face. Acne scarred his pasty face, and he bounced his leg nervously. He sniffled, licked his lips, and shifted in his seat constantly, as if he sat on a cactus. Nearly everyone in the waiting room seemed fairly young; some were grungy, some clean-cut, all antsy. My intuition perked like a deer scenting a hunter. I couldn't pinpoint what caused it, but a vaguely unsettled feeling crawled over my skin. I tensed, sat up in my seat, and pulled my body tighter around my purse, determined to stay alert.

A nurse came out and called, "Clayton Harmon." The fidgety guy beside me in a flannel shirt over a T-shirt, in eighty-degree weather, followed the nurse, his large Red Wing work boots clomping on the tile floor. I opened the note function on my phone and typed his name. A tickle moved through my gut, triggering an instinct that something was "off" with this guy. It was probably insignificant, but I thought it would be good to note it just in case. Then I turned on the video, and holding my phone up, pretending to text, I recorded the folks in the waiting room. I'd show it to Jimmy later. Within minutes, Clayton Harmon came out, tucking a paper into his jeans pocket as he left the building. That was odd. He'd been in the back for maybe only ten minutes. I noted that. Another patient was called back. She, too, came out in a flash. I made more notes. *Interesting.*

The nurse called me back next, though there were many other people who should've been called before me. It was odd, but I wasn't going to argue. I wanted out of this place. I followed the short, squat nurse down the beige

CHAPTER TWELVE

and dingy hall. We popped into a small room to get my weight and height. When we stepped out, Mitch and a man in a green golf shirt and khakis stood at the end of the hall. He was middle age like Mitch and in apparent good shape. Mitch was the shorter of the two. They stood close and, by the looks of it, were engaged in a serious conversation. Mitch's hands were tucked into his lab coat pockets; the other man had his hands on his hips. He was doing most of the talking and seemed annoyed or angry.

The man glanced my way, then froze, staring at me as if I'd suddenly sprouted two more heads.

The nurse said, "Hon, we're going this way." She led me away from the doctor and the man. We turned the corner, and she stopped at the first door.

We went through the usual rigmarole. She took my vitals, asked the preliminary questions, and then left the room. The room was a pale, sickly green and seemed unclean. I used the hand sanitizer, hoisted myself onto the padded, paper-covered table, and idly scratched my arm.

A few moments later, Mitch entered with an iPad. He flinched when he stepped in the room, clearly not expecting to see me. "Rook. How are you doing?" He looked down at his iPad and fiddled with it.

"Good." I scratched my arm. "I'm surprised you're working today. With Patrice missing…." I shrugged and let the insinuation linger.

He frowned and punched the iPad screen.

"Have you heard anything from the kidnappers? Have they called to at least let you speak to Patrice?"

"No, unfortunately. Let's see what brings you out here today?" His eyes trailed over the screen.

"Don't you think that's bizarre? I mean—"

He cut me off. "Says here you have a rash?" He set the iPad on the counter and stepped toward me as he put on latex gloves. "Let's take a look at you."

I showed him my arm. He smelled nice—fresh, mossy.

Since I had a limited amount of time, I needed to get really nosy, real fast. Maybe if I could find out something out about the guy he'd been talking to, I could get some kind of information, another lead to help find Patrice. "I saw that guy you were talking to in the hall. He looked familiar. I've seen him before." I lied.

"Who, Shane?"

I pretended to know. "Yes! That's it. Shane, uh…Oh, what is his name?" I made a big show of trying to recall his name. "Dang. I'm sure I've seen him before."

"Shane Decker." He glanced at me.

I paused, taken aback. Actually, the name Decker really was familiar to me. Then it hit

me. A man named Will Decker had been dating my mother during the time my parents were on a six-month break from each other, shortly before they married. I had just learned about him a few weeks ago. Was Shane related to Will? Maybe he was. Maybe, if I could talk to Shane, he could help me connect with Will. Then I could find out something about who really killed my mom and help exonerate my dad. I rubbed my hands on my thighs and remembered to play my part. "Oh, uh, sort of. I think I met him in passing at a wedding," I lied. "Is he a doctor, too?"

"No. He's my partner. He owns this clinic." He touched my arm, inspecting it.

"Really? He should be happier than he was in the hall. After all, that waiting room is packed. I've never seen such a busy clinic."

One side of his mouth ticked upward, but he didn't look at me. Nor did he acknowledge my insight. Instead, he said, "Does this itch?"

Okay, so he was done talking about Shane Decker. "Like crazy." I shifted, the paper crinkling beneath me.

He nodded. "Have you used any new soaps or detergents?"

Maybe I could get him talking about Patrice. "No. I'm surprised you can stand to work with Patrice gone and all."

He chuckled. "I work to keep from going insane. What about cleaning agents coming in contact with your skin?"

"No." I lowered my voice. "Millie's devastated over all this."

He glanced at me and moved away to pick up his iPad. "Relationships break up all the time."

"True." I chuckled. "I've sure had my share of splits."

CHAPTER TWELVE

He flashed a weak smile in response.

"Um...Savannah seems like a sweet girl."

"She is."

"Where did y'all meet?"

"Shane introduced us."

"Oh, okay." I nodded. "How long have ya'll been dating?"

He eyed me with suspicion. "That's a rather personal question. Do you always ask such prying questions of people you don't know well?"

My face flushed. "Fair enough. I guess I'm too curious for my own good."

"You may be." He looked through me. He sighed and typed into his iPad. "Looks like you have a case of dermatitis. Probably an allergic reaction." He spoke quickly. He clearly wanted to get away from me. "I'll have the prescription for a topical cream sent to your pharmacy. It should clear up within the week. Keep an eye on it. If it gets worse or doesn't clear up, please come back." He studied me with a squinted eye. "You're not experiencing any headaches, severe back pain, or trouble sleeping?"

I squinted back at him. "Um. No. Just the rash. Thanks."

"You sure?" He squinted harder.

This squinting contest with him was getting weird. "I'm very sure."

He nodded, but seemed a little confused. "Which pharmacy do you use?"

"Green's Pharmacy on Main Street."

"Okay." He punched the screen.

I didn't have a neat segue into the hard part of the conversation, so I jumped right in.

"Whoever has Patrice must be in desperate circumstances to ask for that much money for ransom. I mean, a million dollars is a crazy amount."

He stopped and grew pale, gaping at me. "How did you know about that?"

Tipping my head, I looked at him like he had three heads. "Um, because the kidnappers asked Dee Dee for a million dollars."

He frowned. "Wait. They asked *me* for a million dollars, too."

Wow. Apparently, those kidnappers were hitting up everyone they could think of for a million dollars. Did they really think they could get that much money or were they fishing around hoping to snag whatever they could?

He said, "OI received a call not long after you and Millie left."

I tipped my head. "And do the police know you were contacted?"

"I was told not to contact the police, or they'd kill her."

I rolled my eyes to the ceiling. How could a man so smart be so stupid? "You have to tell them."

"I can't. It'll endanger her."

"The police have ways—"

"I'm handling it." He snapped. "And you aren't going to tell a soul about any of this."

The heck I wasn't. Jimmy would be my first call once I got out of this place. Instead, I wanted to gauge his reaction. "Why don't you want to tell the police? Don't you want her found?"

He lowered his voice to a harsh whisper. "Of course I do. But I want her brought back safe and alive. Promise me you won't say anything to anyone. I'm handling this. I'm getting some money together now. Shane is going to help." He stood, tucking the iPad under his arm, and said in a normal voice. "I wish you the best with your rash and with your grandmother. Is there anything else I can help you with today?"

"Yes, there is," I snapped. "Dee Dee has been arrested and is sitting in county jail. She was the one trying to get the money together since she had more at her disposal than Millie."

His brows knitted with concern. He seemed to be working a puzzle in his mind.

"That's why I'm here. Millie and I need your help getting the money together as fast as possible. We have only about four and half days."

His shoulders slumped, and his eyes darted. "Of course, of course." He nodded.

"Can you help us with the money, too? Because now that Dee Dee is locked up, our hands are tied completely."

"Two million dollars." He whispered and rubbed his hands downward over his face, giving it the appearance of a melting candle. He seemed suddenly tired and sickly under the fluorescent lights flickering above us. "I don't have a million for my share and a million for yours, too."

CHAPTER TWELVE

"Geez Louise, Mitch. We have to help her, or she's going to die."

"You're right. You're right." He scratched the back of his neck with his capped pen. "I'll see what I can do."

I slid off the table, ripping the paper. "You need to contact Millie to help her however you can. You owe Patrice that much, at least."

He nodded and ignored me. "Have a nice day."

Pausing on my way out the door, I looked at the framed degree on the wall. *University of Chicago. Internal medicine. Degree issued May 26, 1984.* I needed to remember this so I could provide the information to Jimmy. "Where's the restroom?"

He pointed to the right. "Further down. First door on the left."

I dashed down the hall, repeating the details from the degree under my breath. I passed a few exam rooms and Mitch's office. I paused at Mitch's office door, but it was closed. My hands and feet itched to turn the knob and slip inside to peek around. But Mitch was watching me. "Two more doors down."

Guffawing, I hit my forehead with my palm as if to say "duh" and continued down the hall, annoyed that I couldn't get inside that office. I continued with the mantra of his degree details, locked myself in the restroom, and recorded the details of his medical degree on my phone. After relieving myself, I washed my hands twice because the soap smelled like fresh peaches.

Sniffing my peach-scented hands, I passed down the hall. Tense whispers greeted me as I neared Mitch's office. The door was now open.

"I need more samples and another prescription." That wasn't Mitch. The voice was unrecognizable to me. I pressed against the wall, eavesdropping.

"Okay." There was some shuffling of papers. "I'll see what I can do."

"And you're going to have to get more patients in here."

"How exactly? I can't force people to be sick."

"Not my problem. But we need to increase business. The more people we get in here, the more money we make."

"If I do that, I run a much higher risk…" Mitch lowered his voice, rendering his speech indiscernible. Whatever he said, his companion didn't like it.

"I don't want to hear it, man. It's got to be done. We need the money for the new project."

"Can't you get a loan?"

"I've tried that. This has to be done." Desperation entered the man's voice.

"Well, I need money, too. I need to do something about Patrice. I've got the cops and her friends and family all over my case."

"What's that got to do with this?"

"One of Millie's friends is here asking me to help with the ransom. She wants to know why I didn't call the cops."

"Let me explain this to you. We don't have a choice. You understand? Our partner will be very unhappy."

"Fine. I'll try to figure it out."

The voices sounded as if they were getting closer to me, so I walked quickly in the opposite direction. I glanced over my shoulder. The men appeared in the doorway.

The stranger was Shane Decker. He muttered to Mitch, "We'll talk soon." He dashed away, slipping a paper and a box of pills in his pocket.

I pretended I was lost. "I-uh-" I laughed. "I can't figure out how to get out of here."

Suspicion marked Mitch's features. He pointed to the left. "Down that hall. You'll see a sign that says 'Lobby.'"

Bobbling my head side to side, I said, "Duh. I have no sense of direction at all." I snort-laughed. "Sorry, thanks." I rushed down the hall. Maybe I could catch up with Shane and get him to talk to me.

I jogged out of the door and across the parking lot to catch the stranger. "Hey, mister. Yoo-hoo!" I waved.

He stopped and turned around about twenty feet from his car. It was a shiny white Lexus with heavily tinted windows. I could make out the silhouette of a passenger in the car, but no distinguishing features.

"Can I help you?" he asked. He was middle-aged, in pretty good shape. He looked a bit like Robert Redford with thinning strawberry-blond hair, light freckles, and dark green eyes. He had a long face ending in a pointy chin and an odd-shaped nose with a squared end as if the point had been cut off. His mouth twitched near a half-smile, causing a dimple in his cheek,

CHAPTER TWELVE

but his eyes were hard, suspicious.

"You're Shane Decker, right?"

His eyes darted. "Yeah. Who's asking?"

"Mitch told me you were his business partner."

He nodded, running his tongue under his closed lips. "He did, huh?"

Uh-oh. I hoped I hadn't caused a bunch of problems for Mitch. Not that he didn't deserve them, but until Patrice came back safe and sound, I had to try to find a way to be on friendly terms with the cretin. I continued, coming up with a lie for cover. "The company I'm working for is in need of investors. Is that something you do, invest in businesses? Or are you only interested in medical facilities?"

He seemed to relax. "Actually, I'm a land developer. My brother and I own Decker Properties."

He turned toward his car as he spoke. "Look, if you're interested in real estate, call the off—"

I followed him. "Is your brother named Will, by chance? William Decker? I think he might know my mom."

He stopped and turned. Fear flickered in his eyes. He hesitated. "I, uh, think you have me confused with someone else."

"He dated my mom at one time. A long time ago."

He looked around as if he were looking for an escape route. He ran his hand over his hair. "I really can't…I don't want to, uh…."

"Please. I'm begging you. My father is in jail for murdering her. I think he's innocent, and if there's anything at all that you can tell me, it might help."

He licked his lips, nervous. He chuckled and shook his head. "I can't…I'm not, uh—"

The passenger in the car honked the horn.

"I've got to go." He started toward his car.

I chased with mincing steps while digging in my purse for a business card. "Please, uh, Shane, uh, Mr. Decker." Fishing a card out of my purse, I handed it to him, returning my purse back to my shoulder. "Please give this information to William. Tell him he can call me anytime. Day or night. I want to talk. Just a few questions. We can meet somewhere, if he's comfortable with that. Or talk on the phone. Please. Any information, even the most insignificant thing, might be helpful in getting my dad out of prison and finding my mother's real killer."

He took the card and stuffed it into his pocket with one hand as he opened the car door with the other. His passenger called out. "Hurry up, man."

"Hold your horses," Shane snapped at the passenger as he climbed in.

I peeked in the door, trying to glimpse the passenger. He looked a lot like Shane. They could almost be twins. "Hey! Are you Will? Please, call me. He has—"

Shane slammed the door, cutting me off, and sped away.

Disappointed, I returned to my car, hoping that Will would get in touch with me so I could ask him questions about my mom. I called Jimmy on the way to Mermaid Cove Distillery. It was on the way to work anyway, so it wouldn't hurt to stop by and see if Millie or Roderick needed anything.

Jimmy answered. "What's up? Did you get checked out?"

"I'm out at Mitch's clinic. He looked at my rash."

Silence.

I attempted a preemptive explanation. "It was a good opportunity to snoop around."

"What kind of rash?"

"Ragweed. A little Benadryl'll clear it right up."

""I guess you learned something?"

"Maybe. Have a few names. Maybe you should check out a guy named Clayton Harmon."

"Who's that?"

"A random guy at the clinic, but he seemed a little off."

"All right. What else?"

"Look up Shane and William Decker. Shane is in business with Mitch."

"Right."

"Well, his brother, William, was interrogated for my mom's murder, but was apparently cleared."

"Hm. Interesting. I'll take a look."

CHAPTER TWELVE

"Anything else?"

The tin roof of Mermaid Cove peeked over a hill. "I can't think of anything else. We can talk more at dinner. You're coming over, right?"

"Nah. Can't. Working on this case."

"I can bring you some dinner to the station, if you like?"

"That'd be great. You know what I like. I'm easy. Hey, I got to go. See you later, babe." He hung up.

Chapter Thirteen

I pulled into the Mermaid Cove Distillery on my way to Four Wild Horses to check on Roderick or Millie. I swore I'd only be a few minutes—especially since I had donuts waiting in the car. Tourists lingered around the door. I parked in a visitor's spot and strode inside. A middle-aged man was at the front. I announced that I was there to see Roderick.

He said, "I think he's in the office, hon."

"Thanks." I passed through to the office and opened the door. Clem, the maintenance guy, stood in the middle of the room. He tucked his hand in his pockets, and his face turned pink. He tried to duck past me.

I stepped in his path. "What are you doing? Does Roderick know you're in here?"

His eyes darted. "What's it to you? I was changing a light bulb." He lowered his head to step past me. "Not that it's any of your business."

I wasn't about to get into a wrestling match with an old man. I moved aside to let him pass. "Where's Roderick?"

"Don't know. Don't care."

I made a face at his back and spun around to head back down the hall toward the reception desk. Roderick entered through the back door from the café area. He was handsome in a lime green polo shirt and black pants.

He smiled and waved. "Hey, Rook. What're you doing out here?"

We turned back together to the office. "I came out to see if you need any help while your mom's in jail."

"Nah, I'm good. I got word that they don't have anything on her, so they

CHAPTER THIRTEEN

can't detain her. She'll be home soon."

I jumped up and down with glee and hugged him. "I'm so happy to hear that! Thank heavens! You must be thrilled."

"I am. And I'm glad I don't have to visit her in jail. I don't think I could have handled that." His baleful eyes searched my face.

"I understand completely. My dad's in federal prison and has been since I was eleven. I can't bear to see him in those surroundings."

"I didn't know that. How do you deal with it?"

"Well, it's a little different situation in my case. My dad…" I sighed. I didn't want to go into all the details about my dad. "It's complicated. Anyway, you and Dee Dee are going to be okay."

He nodded, clicking his pen nervously. "But I will say that this little incident has made me change my mind about my major in school. Mom's been on my case to get my MBA and help run the business. So, that's what I'm going to do now."

Gushing, I nudged him. "That's the best gift you could ever give her. Good for you!" I opened my arms. "Well, since you don't need me, I guess I'll scoot along." We hugged. He smelled sweet and woodsy. When we pulled apart, I spoke quietly so only he could hear. "You should know that when I was looking for you here in the office, I found Clem in here with the door closed."

Roderick's brows shot up, and he tucked his chin. "Really?"

"He said he was fixing a light because you'd asked him to, but he didn't have any tools or supplies with him."

He bit his bottom lip, searching the room. "All right. Thanks for telling me."

"Is there anything missing?"

He examined the top of the desk and opened a few drawers. "It looks like everything is here. As far as I can tell." He sighed and flopped down in the desk chair. "I'll deal with him in a minute." He rolled his eyes and shook his head. "There's always one in the crowd…"

"You got that right." I laughed. We said our goodbyes, and I headed to work.

Work was hectic, and the pastries from Irene's vanished in a flash. I felt accomplished, though. I had cleared much of To Do list. Visit Mitch. Check. Mermaid Cove. Check. I had one more item: call Cam and gripe at him about Jimmy's black eye. I'd have to do that after work. I had to finish my tasks for the upcoming fall charity event to raise funds for the Pasture Pals retired thoroughbred horse farm. I called Cam as I left the distillery administration building when my work day was done.

He answered flatly, "What."

That wasn't a good sign. I pulled the seat belt across my body and clicked it into place. "Hey, Cam, I want to talk to you about Jimmy."

He sighed. "I don't want to talk about it." His voice was tense.

I started my car. "Look, I'm sorry. We should've mentioned it earlier. This thing just sort of happened." Checking my mirrors, I backed out. "We never intended to hurt you."

"Jimmy? Seriously, Rook? You go after my best friend?" His voice was tight with rage. "Of all the people on Earth, you had to pick him?"

Guilt wrenched my stomach. "I'm sorry. We'd been seeing each other a lot while working on Bryan's murder case, and we…" My face burned with shame at the admission, as if I'd been caught cheating. But Cam and I had divorced nineteen months ago.

"How could y'all do this to me? My ex-wife and my best friend?" His vocal cords sounded tight enough to snap. "And you knew…I still had hopes…. Y'all betrayed me." I imagined he probably had a purple-red face right now with a vein popping in the middle of his forehead. He didn't get angry often, but when he did, it was a little scary.

"Cam, I swear I didn't mean to hurt you, but we've already tried. I need to move on. I can't keep my life on hold, waiting to recapture whatever you think we can scrape together from the ashes. "

"Then move on," he barked. "Don't let me hold you back." He hung up.

Anger, guilt, and hurt flashed through me, flushing my skin hot instantly. "Oh no, he did *not* hang up on me," I shouted at my windshield. I hated being hung up on. And he knew that. It's how we fought back when we were married. Stomping on the gas pedal, I turned right instead of left and

CHAPTER THIRTEEN

headed toward the Campbell farm.

Weaving in and out of traffic and flying down the road at top speed, I made it to the farm in about ten minutes. I pulled up in the drive by the white farmhouse. Cam was up the hill at the barn. He lifted a hay bale from the trailer and carried it into the barn.

I marched up the hill. He came out of the barn as I reached the door.

He gaped in disbelief and shook his head. He was covered in dirt and sweat, and hay. Sweat had soaked through his white T-shirt in patches.

He stopped and put his hands on his hips. "What're you doing here?" He wiped sweat from his forehead with the back of his forearm.

"How dare you hang up on me."

He pushed past me and grabbed another hay bale. "Shouldn't you be out with my best

friend? Correction. Former best friend."

"Hold up, mister. We're going to have this out right now."

"Nope, we're not." He grunted, lifting the bale, large knots bulged in his biceps.

"You owe Jimmy an apology. You should've never hit him."

"That's between him and me."

"No, it's not. I think I have a say in this, too. I'm not a prize to be won by the strongest caveman. I have a mind of my own, and I'll be the one to make decisions about who I'm going to be with. You owe him an apology."

He dropped a hay bale along the wall and turned to walk out. "Don't hold your breath waiting for that to happen."

I walked beside him. The barn was dimly lit and smelled of hay, chickens, and dirt. "I'm sorry. Jimmy's sorry. We never ever wanted to hurt your feelings. Can't you try to be happy for us? I was willing to let you go so you could marry Jacie."

"We broke up. Because of you."

Hard on his heels, I said, "That's not my fault. I never asked you to do that."

"You didn't have to ask. I realized I still had feelings for you, so I did the right thing." He grabbed the strings on another bale and jerked it off the trailer, grunting. He wouldn't look me in the eyes. "Big mistake. Little did I know that you and Jimmy were sharpening your knives to stab me in the back."

"That's not how it went at all."

He scoffed. "Yeah, right." He carried the bale into the barn and dumped it. I followed.

He turned, lifted his cowboy hat, and wiped his sweaty brow on his bicep. "For all I know, you two were going at it behind my back while we were married."

Before I realized what I was doing, I reared back and slapped him right across the face. Only then did I recognize the blistering rage fizzing under the surface of my skin. "How *dare* you," I seethed. Cam was the one who had stepped out on me. Though I had had an emotional closeness, a flirtation, with a colleague at the university, I'd never broken our vows. Yet, I felt bad as soon as I hit him.

His tongue touched the corner of his mouth, and his face turned red. Now he looked at me. His blue eyes flashed with a mix of pain and anger. Thunder in his voice, he said, "Get. Out."

"Gladly." I spun and stormed down the hill to my car, hot tears bubbling, blurring my vision. Peeling out of his drive, I sped away, driving until I could no longer see. I pulled over in a McDonald's parking lot and cried like a fool.

Chapter Fourteen

Jimmy met me in the lobby at the sheriff's station. He planted a kiss on my cheek. "Thanks for the food. Come on back and eat supper with me. I don't have long, but I could use the break." He led me, the large supreme pizza, and two Dr. Peppers back to his desk in the corner of the bullpen. His side of the room was practically deserted. Most of the other officers were at their desks across the room, filling out paperwork, talking on the phone, interviewing people, or talking to each other over files.

Jimmy moved a stack of files to the floor to create room for the pizza box. Though I tried to put on a smiling face, I was still sulking over Cam.

Chewing his food, he wiped his face with a napkin. "What's wrong?"

"Nothing," I forced a smile, selecting a piece of pizza and shoving my mouth full.

He sat back in his chair, unscrewing the cap from his soda. "That there is what we call an 'untruth' in my line of work." He took a swig from his bottle. "Your eyes are all puffy, like you've been crying. What's going on?"

I couldn't look at him. I picked at an olive. "Nothing. I don't want to talk about it."

"Ah. So, there is something. You just don't want to talk about it." He took another bite of food.

"Right." I leveled a hard gaze at him. "Leave it." I wasn't going to tell him that I'd explicitly gone against his request to go see Cam. It'd only start another fight.

He lifted a hand in surrender. "All right then." He took a large bite of pizza "Well, you'll be happy to know that Dee Dee is out of jail now."

"I know," I said with a mouthful of food. "Roderick told me. What I want to know is why she was being held at all."

He swallowed his food. "Goodman found she had a secret account or something. Looked like embezzlement to him. But it wasn't. There was a misunderstanding."

"That doesn't make any sense."

He shook his head. "I don't have all the details yet. Goodman was called away when we were talking about it. She's free. That's the important part."

"Is she still a suspect?" I wiped my greasy fingers on a napkin.

"Probably."

After a few moments of silent pizza-eating, I asked, "Have you looked into Clayton Harmon and Mitch's degree information?"

"I did. An interesting fact about Clayton. He's a pillhead. Has a ton of priors for drug possession, selling and a few hits for armed robbery. Probably to feed his addiction. Looks like he found a new legal way to feed the demon."

"What do you mean?"

"From what I can gather, Mitch's clinic is likely a pill mill."

I raised my brows as I chewed my food. I'd heard of those on *60 Minutes* and *Dateline*. Pill mills looked like legitimate clinics on the surface, but they were drug operations servicing addicts with powerful pharmaceutical drugs who wanted to get high without the risk of going to jail or dealing with the gang violence that often came with the illegal market. People visited the pill mills, complain of insomnia or back pain, and received a prescription for narcotics.

"Unless an event alerts law enforcement and triggers an investigation, places like Mitch's usually fly under the radar for years. Especially if they can keep from getting too greedy. Greed is usually what gets these doctors in trouble most of the time, though. They start prescribing too many pills too often to the same individuals, or the pharmacists begin to see patterns."

That sure sounded like Mitch and Shane's operation. "Come to think of it, he did seem confused that I was there only for a rash. Before I left, he asked me if I was having insomnia issues or any pain. It seemed weird at the

CHAPTER FOURTEEN

time, but now I get it." Loading my voice with sarcasm, I added, "I thought Sheriff Harlan 'Bulldog' Goodman was tough on drugs and was going to eradicate the drug trade in Franklin County." I rolled my eyes and took a drink of my soda.

"To be fair, it can be hard to spot these things because they look legitimate from the outside. Especially if no one reports anything." Jimmy scratched his stubbled chin, glanced around, and leaned in to speak in a low tone. "Speaking as friends and not as a deputy…." He rolled the edges of a napkin between his fingers. "Now that we know Mitch is likely operating a pill mill, I'm far more interested in him for Patrice's kidnapping. I interviewed him once already. He seemed shifty."

He looked tired. He'd been working a ton of overtime ever since Patrice disappeared because Sheriff Goodman had made him the case lead.

"I've suspected him, too. But…" I screwed up my face and dipped my crust in the garlic sauce. "I'm having doubts now."

"Why?"

"Because he told me the kidnappers called him to ask for a million dollars ransom, too."

Jimmy frowned and nodded, thinking. "He could be lying. To throw suspicion off himself. After I looked into him today, I think he has plenty of reasons to keep us out of his affairs."

"What do you mean?"

He scooted closer and whispered, "When I looked into his license, I found that he last worked in Philadelphia and that he doesn't actually have an active license."

I blinked at him, shocked that he would reveal details of an ongoing investigation. Discomfort and excitement warred in my gut. If I were more integral, I wouldn't have encouraged him to reveal anything else to me, but my desire to be a part of something bigger and to help find Patrice kicked my integrity in the face and slammed it in a dark closet. I widened my eyes. "You're kidding. Are you sure that's good information?"

He nodded, selected another pizza slice, and bit into it. "He's been reprimanded in Delaware and New York and was actually suspended in

Ohio and California. He was dismissed from a practice in Texas, and in Florida, his license was revoked."

"Was there a time when he wasn't in trouble?" I drank from my soda.

"Not really. His whole career, there's been one report after another."

"How could he get away with all this?" My voice pitched a few notches. "How is he still allowed to practice medicine?"

He touched his closed lips to remind me to be quiet. He continued in a quiet voice. "It would explain why he opened his own clinic. It's after hours now, but in the morning, I'm definitely going to start contacting each and every one of these boards to see if I can discover the circumstances behind these issues."

I sat back. "Oh, my stars. Do you think Patrice knew anything about this? Maybe that's why she's missing now?"

He sat back and took another bite of his pizza. "Possibly. Sure sounds like a good motive to me."

"It would certainly explain why he doesn't seem too eager to find her, to work with the cops, or to help with the ransom." My mind rolled over Mitch's past and his current behavior, and how quickly he'd moved on to Savannah. Fear anchored in my heart, sending a chill over my skin. "Do you think he's already killed her?"

The bags under Jimmy's eyes seemed to grow deeper and darker. "I wish I could definitively say no. But, I'm going to be honest, babe, this doesn't look good. This is the sort of information someone would go to *any* lengths to keep a secret. He won't have much of a choice. I've heard from the DEA. They're forming a task force and will conduct surveillance. They've already obtained his DEA number and are researching the prescriptions he's written."

"How long does that take?"

"A week? Two? Maybe three? It'll depend on how many scripts they find, how many patients he has, how many other cases they're working on, and how much of a priority they think this is."

"Are y'all any closer at all to finding Patrice? I know Millie is about to lose her mind."

CHAPTER FOURTEEN

He squinted and licked his lips. "I'm not speaking in my official capacity, you understand,, but we've identified a couple of witnesses who noticed an older model white van in the Mermaid Cove Distillery parking lot the day Patrice disappeared."

"Really? Were there any identifying marks or writing on the van?"

"Not really. The windows were tinted, and there were crossbars on the top. The witness said the van was really dirty, caked in mud, and kind of beat up."

"Huh. That sounds like every single utility van I've ever seen."

"Exactly."

"Could they identify anyone who got in or out of the van?"

"No. They assumed it was a contractor or another worker and didn't pay any attention to it."

My mind wrapped around the details, locking them in. I was going to be vigilant about watching for white vans and getting license plate numbers. I toyed with my mother's silver and turquoise ring, turning it around and around on my finger. "How on earth are you ever going to find Patrice?"

On my way home, I decided to stop by and see Dee Dee just to make sure she was okay and to see if she needed anything. She lived in a large French Country style house in an upscale neighborhood called Beaumont Estates on the south side of town.

She answered the door wearing a navy shirt, navy wide-legged pants, and a large gray sweater. Deep, dark bags weighed her brown eyes, and her long braids were twisted into a large bun at the back of her head. She smiled. "Hey there, lady. C'mon in." She stepped back and let me in her house. We hugged each other in a tight embrace. Her house was an open floor plan with a palette of white walls and furniture with touches of gold and peach. A low fire burned in the fireplace, and candles were lit around the room, making the room smell like spiced apples. The TV played softly. "Can I get you something to drink?"

"No, thanks. I'm good." I sat on the modern L-shaped sectional, wishing I could run my bare feet through the plush shag area rug. "I just wanted to stop by and see how you're doing. Prim and I have been really concerned about you being in jail."

She sat down, pulling her cardigan over her midsection. "I'm fine. They treated me well. The worst part was trying to sleep on that hard cot." She put on a smile, but her eyes flashed with fear, pain, and anger.

"Is there anything you need or anything we can do?"

"Nah, thank you, baby. Just pray for me. They don't have any kind of evidence, because there is none, but I have a feeling they may not be finished with me."

"Why do you say that? The way Jimmy spoke, they have no interest in you."

She shrugged a shoulder. "A feeling I get. They've frozen my assets until the investigation is officially over. I'm free in body only."

"That's a start. I guess. Hopefully, they won't keep you locked down for too long."

"I'm more concerned about finding Patrice alive. Do you know anything?"

I shook my head. "Not really. We still haven't located her, but we're working as hard and as fast as we can. Millie texted me earlier that the kidnappers are supposed to call again tomorrow to tell her the drop-off point for the ransom." Recalling what Jimmy had told me about the white van, I said, "Did you or Patrice call for anything to be fixed at Mermaid Cove? Pipes or something?"

She pursed her lips and glanced up at the ceiling, thinking. "Mm-No. I didn't. Why?"

"There were witnesses who saw a white van on the property that day, and it had racks like a utility truck or a van used on construction sites."

Dee Dee frowned with concentration, then shook her head. "Patrice might've called someone. We'd been having issues with the toilets, and Clem couldn't seem to address the issue. Maybe he called them."

I leaned my ribs against the plush peach pillow. "Do you think Mitch would've hurt her?"

She paused. "I don't think so. They seemed to care deeply for each other. But I've been thinking…" She glanced around the room. "After all, I've had

CHAPTER FOURTEEN

some time on my hands..." She lifted her hands to indicate the room. "But I've been wondering if maybe Patrice cared for Mitch more than he seemed to care for her."

"Really? What makes you say that?"

"I recalled last night that the first time I met Mitch, my husband and I had gone to dinner with Patrice and Mitch when they first started dating, and every chance that rat had, he was eyeballing the waitresses. I guess I'd forgotten about that when the sheriff was asking me questions the other night."

That didn't mean he was a kidnapper or murderer. "That makes him a dog, for sure, but...." I scrunched my face.

"It means he wasn't invested in her. I don't mean he was only glancing at a pretty woman. Most men do that. I mean he was looking them up, down, and all around like a pitbull hungry for a pork chop. And he was watching the young women." She pointed a finger at me. "That behavior, especially on a date, says something about a man's character."

"Huh..." I toyed with the tassel on the pillow. That behavior would indicate he might've been looking for an alternative to Patrice before he became too deeply involved with her. And it pointed to a level of callousness and a proclivity to objectify women that would be present in a potential user or abuser.

"And you know what else?"

I perked.

"I think money was a big problem between them and it might be the main reason they split. She never told me details, but when they fought, she mentioned the fights were over money. And before she went missing, they were fighting more and more. It must've been embarrassing to her, so I didn't press her on the issue."

"You need to tell the police."

"I did. They're looking into it." She sighed. "But that's not helping my current situation."

I recalled seeing a *Forensic Files* episode about a man leading a double life and liked to give the impression of great wealth, however, he was marrying rich women to get his hands on their money before leaving them or killing them and moving on to another woman. And after seeing the clinic he worked at and learning about his issues with former hospitals, it wasn't obvious to me that he was raking in the dough. Maybe he was latching on to women he thought were wealthy and draining their money before moving on to the next. "I have what might seem to be a strange question, but did he have money coming into the relationship? Or did he rely on her for financial support?"

Dee Dee thought for a moment. "Well, he is a doctor. So, I guess he had plenty of money."

"Why were they fighting about money then?"

She shrugged. "I assumed Patrice was spending too much. She does like to spend." She rolled her eyes. "I love her dearly, and it almost kept me from wanting to get into business with her, but I thought I could manage it."

She crossed her arms over her chest and sank against the couch arm. "He seemed like he had money, but now I'm not so sure. She never went into details with me about their financial life."

"See, I'm thinking that Mitch's philandering wasn't the only reason they fell out. I think money might've been a big issue too. At first, I thought it was *her* spending, but now I'm wondering if it was his." I leaned on my knees. "Maybe she finally figured out all the ways he was cheating her and kicked him out."

"If he was going to hurt her, that sounds like a good reason to me."

"Jimmy's working on this. I'll tell him everything we've talked about."

I searched Dee Dee's sad face. "Why did you hide money in a separate account? Please tell me you had a good reason?"

"Of course. It wasn't for dishonest measures. With all the money troubles surrounding Patrice, I was afraid it would hurt the business. I shifted that money solely to protect Mermaid Cove. I didn't want the business to go bankrupt."

"Were y'all in danger of that?"

"Not yet, but we were headed in that direction because of her erratic spending. I love Patrice, but her heart is bigger than her wallet. My husband advised me to do it. He's a financier. He'd said it'd be safest for the company. But that account was earmarked strictly for the company. And, frankly, with the issues she and Mitch were having, I was afraid it would start to affect the business." Her whole body slumped, and her face melted with sadness. Her voice shook, and she wiped under her eyes. "Since the police have frozen my assets, I can't even give you money to help with her ransom."

"Don't blame yourself. We're going to figure this out somehow."

When I arrived home, Prim greeted me with twinkling eyes and a cookie tin. "Lookit what I have here. Oda Dean Spurlock and Birdie Harper dropped this off today." She struggled with the lid and popped it off to reveal a store of cash.

"Omigosh. How much money *is* that?"

"It's at least five thousand. This is just what was collected from the congregation. There's more on the way once Oda Dean and Birdie have finished organizing the fall bake sale. I bet we'll make another five thousand, easy. Maybe more."

Five, even ten thousand, wasn't even a drop in the bucket toward one million dollars. Yet, she was so happy and proud of their small achievement. There was no way I'd take that from her. I hugged her, tears in my eyes. "Thank you so much, Prim. Millie will be thrilled."

"You tell her not to worry. We've got her back."

Chapter Fifteen

Some of my best ideas came to me in the shower. I was in the middle of lathering my hair with apple-scented shampoo, inspecting my split ends, and resolving to get a haircut, when I remembered the coffee can of cash Prim had given me about a month ago. It was soon after she'd been diagnosed with terminal breast cancer and she'd refused treatments. She gave me about fifteen grand as an advance on my inheritance. She'd wanted me to pay school loans with it, but I hadn't yet developed the fortitude to deposit it into my bank account. That turned out to be a fateful bit of procrastination because now I could give it to Millie to put toward the ransom money. Of course, the hope remained that we'd find Patrice soon before having to turn over any money to the kidnappers.

Now with a new errand added to my busy day, I needed to hurry. I brushed on natural makeup, then shimmied into a pair of black wide-leg pants, a pumpkin-colored blouse, and a pair of black, thick-heeled pumps. I accessorized with silver hoops and my mother's silver and turquoise ring and headed to Prim's room to get her dressed. Batrene would be over soon.

Prim coughed and croaked. "I don't want to get up right now."

That wasn't like her. My spirit drained out of my body. If my bones weren't holding me up, I would've melted into a puddle on the floor. Each morning, Prim seemed to have a harder time getting out of bed. I feared the day she became permanently bed-bound. I wasn't ready for it and hoped today wasn't the day my life would begin to change forever.

I cleared the lump out of my throat and tried to steady my voice. "Okay. You don't have to get up right now. I'll go make your breakfast and get your

CHAPTER FIFTEEN

pills. Maybe after your pills kick in, you'll be ready to get dressed before I leave."

I wished I was as strong as Cam or Jimmy. Either one of them could pick up her delicate frame and carry her downstairs. If I hadn't destroyed my friendship with Cam, he'd probably be here now, carrying her down as though she weighed no more than a sack of potatoes.

I wolfed down a couple of waffles topped with peanut butter and started on Prim's food. As I threw together Prim's oatmeal, dry toast, and ginger ale, the phone rang.

When I answered, I heard only a heavy breath.

"Who is this? We're getting sick of this. Don't you have anything better to do? My grandmother is sick, and we don't need this."

The breath broke into a wicked laugh which faded into a distorted voice. "You're going to die. I'm going to get you." *Click.* Then a monotone hum. Ice trickled down my spine. I returned the phone to the cradle and stared at it. I didn't recognize the voice. I couldn't even tell if it was male or female. It sounded inhuman, demonic. Another chill ran over me. I rubbed my arms and shook it off. I didn't have time for this. I needed to get Prim together then get to work as early as possible because I needed to take a long lunch break.

I ran upstairs. Prim had managed to sit up. After wiping her down with adult-sized wet wipes, I helped her into a loose-fitting yellow dress, brushed her hair, and clipped yellow sparkling barrettes on each side of her head to keep the hair out of her face.

By that time, the meds had taken the edge off her pain enough that I could help inch her downstairs and settle her in her recliner in front of the television with breakfast. She'd be content there until Batrene arrived to sit with her.

Before leaving, I searched the hall closet for the coffee can of money. It was in the back corner behind the vacuum cleaner and the twice-used tennis rackets. I took the money from the cookie tin Prim had given me last night and combined it with the coffee can money. I texted Millie, asking her to meet for lunch in Rothdale because I wanted to give her something. I didn't tell her I was going to give her money, because rules in the South dictated she would avoid me to circumvent the humiliation of taking charity. There was an entire dance of insisting and declining that was required to take place before someone could accept money, especially a sum as large as twenty grand.

I kissed Prim goodbye and waved to Batrene as she crossed the small field between our houses. It was seven-thirty already. I needed to hurry.

When I reached my car, I stopped dead. Almost as dead as the poor opossum on my windshield. The critter was obviously a recent roadkill victim, and whoever put it there made certain to smear it all over the car first. Dried blood streaked my already scratched paint job. I blanched. It reeked of decay. I dug into my purse for my phone and snapped a few pictures.

Batrene gasped. "Oh, heavens, how did that get there?"

"Someone put it there. That's how." I typed a message to Jimmy and forwarded the pictures to him.

"Who would do something like that?"

"I have no idea, but it's disgusting." I opened my car and threw my stuff inside. I ran to the shed, grabbed a shovel, and scraped the poor creature off my car while Batrene went inside to see Prim. Cradling the critter in the shovel, I carried him to the back of the lot and dumped him over in the tall grass between mine and Batrene's properties. I shuddered with disgust and terror as I returned the shovel to the shed. Maybe the caller who threatened me this morning was more serious about that threat than I'd realized. As I started my car, my skin crept as if I were also covered in the slime of the roadkill. Now I needed to run by the Flash-Wash auto car to clean this mess off my car.

I sat in the wash bay under the soapy spray and rotating brushes, wondering who might've put a dead animal on my car and who called me that morning. In spite of Mitch's troubled professional record, this seemed beneath him. This even seemed beneath Fox, though he was a weaselly, spiteful cheater.

Jimmy called. "Sorry it took me such a long time to call you back. I was in a briefing. Did you find out who put that critter on your car?"

CHAPTER FIFTEEN

"No. Not yet. I received a death threat call this morning, too. They called the landline."

"I'm going to get your phone records, put a tap and a trace on your line."

"Fine by me. I hope you catch this jerk." The big brush lifted, and the giant dryer clicked on to blow water beads off my car. My car rocked.

Millie responded to my request for lunch, wanting to know where I wanted to meet. I responded **Noon. Thai Palace in the Rothdale Shopping Plaza.**

Once I'd made it to work, I gathered my morning cup of coffee. When I sat in my cubicle, a copy of the FWH newsletter lay on my keyboard. Right in the center of the page was Fox Graham's weasel face smiling up at me, holding the trophy from the weekend's contest. That reminded me. After Googling the contact information for the Kentucky Distillers' Association and the Kentucky Distillers' Guild, I contacted both offices and reported Fox Graham for cheating. I then proceeded to tell them that there's an on-going investigation to see if he's been involved in the disappearance of his competitor, Patrice Dawson. If that jerk did mess with my car, then I considered reporting him sufficient revenge. Then I turned my focus to working on the upcoming Pasture Pals event until I had to meet Millie for lunch.

Rothdale Shopping Plaza on Cherry Street wasn't near as grand as the name suggested. It was little more than a strip mall hailing back to the 1980s, complete with a Big Lots, Thai Palace restaurant, the Blue Lotus Massage Parlor, and Daisy's Beauty Salon, among a few other mom-and-pop establishments and some empty storefronts.

Millie was sitting in the window and waved at me as I approached. Her smile was tense, and her face haggard with lack of sleep. Everyone was looking like that lately. She said, "Hey. How's Dee Dee holding up? Have you talked to her since her release?"

"I have. She's doing well. As well as could be expected, I think." I already knew what I wanted, so I didn't bother to look at the menu. "How are you? You look upset?"

She rubbed her face and poked at the ice in her glass with the straw. "I'm worried about Mom. The kidnappers called me again, said they're watching me to make sure I don't talk to the police, and that they'd call soon to establish a place, day, and time to drop the money." Tears filled her eyes. "I tried to tell them that I can't get that much money, but they didn't want to hear it." She gulped her water. "I don't even have a fraction of the money together. I've called Mitch. He's no help and has stopped answering his phone. Roderick has given me what little bit he's managed to save, but I feel awful. Combined with my savings, I think I've managed to scrounge up about ten grand." She swiped the tears rolling down her cheeks. "I'm never going to get all this money together."

"I'm glad you brought that up. Prim and I want you to have this." I pulled the coffee can out of my purse and plopped it on the table.

She frowned. "You brought me Maxwell House?"

"No. Look inside."

She lifted the lid and peeked in. "Omigosh. How much is that?"

"About twenty grand. It's not much. Not even a drop in a million-dollar bucket. But if it can help at all, it's yours. No strings. Prim and some of the church ladies helped raise some money. And Prim says there's more on the way once they have their bake sale."

She clapped the lid down and pushed it toward me. "I can't. That has to be everything you have."

"It is, but I insist. We have to find your mom however we can." I couldn't help but wish that money could bring my mom back. I shoved it back at her. "You have to take this and I won't take 'no' for an answer. I won't be able to sleep at night if I think I haven't done everything in my power to help you."

The server came by to collect our order.

Millie sighed and took the coffee can. "I'm only accepting this because I know you're way more stubborn than me, and I don't want to end up in a headlock in the middle of the restaurant." A weak smile bloomed before falling away. "I'll never be able to pay you back."

"Don't worry about it. Having your mom home is worth all the money in the world. I'm sorry I can't give you more. We should probably look into taking out loans or something and make a list of people we can borrow

CHAPTER FIFTEEN

money from."

She dropped her face into her hands. "I pray the police find her before we have to pay a dime."

After a quick lunch, Millie and I walked out together. I said, "I'm going down here to Daisy's to set an appointment. I've been meaning to call her, but since I'm already here, I'll pop in."

We stepped into the salon. Daisy's was a paradise of white wicker furniture, old hair magazines, purple walls, and black salon hardware. It even had a tanning booth in the back. A strange potpourri of flowers, herbs, vanilla, and chemicals hung in the air. Eighties pop music played in the background, and art created by local artists ornamented the walls. Daisy herself, the only woman I trusted with my hair, didn't appear to be at work yet. The scheduler was on the phone and held up a finger to indicate she'd be right with us. A cacophony of laughter rose from behind the screen beside the scheduler's desk. I peeked around the screen and noticed Savannah Stewart, of all people, sitting at the nail desk. She was getting gel nails like cat claws decorated with pink glitter and rhinestones. How anyone could function with nails longer than a quarter of an inch was beyond my comprehension. I ducked away from the screen before anyone saw me. But I sat in the puffy purple vinyl chair on the other side so I could eavesdrop. Millie joined me, pretending to look at a hairstyle magazine.

The nail tech said, "I love your engagement ring."

Millie gaped at me and whispered from behind the magazine, "Engaged? Already?"

"Thanks," Savannah said.

"Do you have a date picked out yet?"

"No, not yet. He just popped the question last night."

I gaped at her.

"Who's the lucky man?"

"Dr. Mitch Thomas."

"Oooh. A doctor. Lucky you."

A customer walked in as the scheduler hung up. "She was here first." She pointed at me.

133

"Oh, that's okay. Go ahead. We're looking at hairstyles."

The scheduler turned to assist the customer while Millie and I continued to eavesdrop.

The nail tech said, "You must be so excited."

"Oh," Savannah released a deep sigh. "Tough to say. We have a couple of issues to work out. He's a little jealous and possessive. Always wanting to know who's texting me. Ugh."

"Oh. Dontcha hate that?"

Savannah chuckled. "That'll be an easy fix. The worst part is his ex."

Millie perked. She and I lifted our brows at each other.

The tech said, "Exes are always a big pain in the butt. My second husband had an ex from the ninth circle of Hades. She was awful. We'd go out, and she'd show up at the same places and cause big scenes. She followed me to work. She broke into his house and stole things. He had to get a restraining order. I hope you don't have to deal with something like that. Does he have kids? Because if he does, you'll never get rid of her. Children bind the parents together forever."

"No, he doesn't have any kids. And, I think the way things are going, his ex isn't going to be in our way."

"That's good."

Millie's face blanched, and her eyes bugged a little, a sure indication that she was getting angry. In all the years I'd known Millie, I could count on one hand all the times I'd ever witnessed her anger. But that was also what made it scary, because when it did happen, it was unpredictable as to whether she was going to cry or go on the attack. Millie jumped up.

I popped to my feet, too, and grabbed her arm. I whispered, "Please don't."

Millie's bloodshot eyes searched my face. "Did you hear her? She's practically gloating over my mom's disappearance."

The scheduler finished up with the other customer, then turned to me. "Ma'am, I can help you over here now."

I whispered to Millie, "Please wait a second." I stepped over to the counter and scheduled an appointment to have my ends trimmed in a couple weeks.

Millie disappeared around the screen.

CHAPTER FIFTEEN

"Crap," I hissed and chased after Millie.

Millie stood frozen and blanched, her mouth agape. Her whole body shook. I'd never seen her so angry. Not even in high school when Mark Applebaum pulled down her elastic-banded shorts to reveal her pink heart undies in front of a bunch of boys, which included her crush at the time. "You venomous Jezebel. That's my mother's engagement ring." Millie stood over Savannah, shaking with rage.

I sidled up to Millie and spoke soothingly to her. "Millie, stop. Please."

"I want my mother's ring." Millie shoved Savannah's shoulder, and Savannah's mouth and eyes shot wide open as she propelled backward in her rolling chair, her hands in a defensive pose in front of her.

"That's my mother's ring. You dirty, slimy...." She lunged again, and I threw my arms around Millie's waist and dug in my heels, hoping I could hold her back since I had a good twenty pounds over her. I really didn't care a frog's fart about Savannah. She deserved what she got. But I didn't want my best friend going down for assault. As Millie and Savannah argued over the ring, I shouted for the receptionist to call the police.

Savannah shot out of her chair and darted around us. The staff and customers looked at us with fear and disbelief.

"Stop her," Millie shouted. No one stepped in to help.

My arms and legs were depleted of strength from holding Millie. Savannah was already in her SUV and pulling out of her spot. We chased her car a few yards through the parking lot, shouting at it as it sped away. Millie broke into tears and fell into my arms, her sobs broken with apologies and explanations.

"Don't worry about that," I said. "I understand. Don't get yourself into trouble. That's not going to help your mom."

We paid for Savannah's nails because the salon owner didn't deserve to get stiffed, and I finished setting my hair appointment while we waited for the police. They flew to the scene, sirens blaring and lights flashing. Jimmy and Ladonna exited their vehicle.

I whispered to Millie, "At least Jimmy's the one who showed up."

He questioned Millie. She said, "My mother was wearing that ring when she was taken."

"Are you sure about that?"

Millie hemmed. "Uh, I think so. I mean, I'm pretty sure."

"They did break up," I said. "Are you certain your mom didn't give the ring back?"

Millie rubbed her face. "I'm pretty sure."

"Are you one hundred percent?" Jimmy asked.

Doubt twisted Millie's mouth. "About eighty percent. It was my mom's ring. He gave it to her. It was my mom's."

Jimmy and Ladonna exchanged an unsure glance. Ladonna shrugged. "Won't hurt to check it out."

Chapter Sixteen

When I arrived at Four Wild Horses, the parking lot was full, and a herd of tourists were heading into the visitor's center. There, they bought tickets for tours and tastings, purchased bourbon memorabilia, and bourbon-infused items from the gift shop. It was common practice among all distilleries.

I parked my lime green Fiesta beside a white Corolla. The driver, likely a tourist, was still inside. She was a chubby blonde with poofy hair and large round sunglasses that practically covered her entire face. She was digging through her purse.

Grabbing my purse, I raced to my desk and set immediately to work on the Pasture Pals event. The rest of the afternoon flew by, and there was no time to be bored.

At around four, the receptionist buzzed a call through to me.

"This is Rook Campbell," I typed some information into a spreadsheet.

A man's voice said, "It was you, wasn't it? You evil witch."

I couldn't place the voice. I frowned into the phone. "Who is this?"

He ignored my question and charged forward. "I won that contest fair and square. Then you report me to the board, accusing me of kidnapping that woman from Mermaid Cove in order to rig the contest?" *Fox Graham.* His voice raised a few pitches and became squeaky. "What's the matter with you? Why on earth would I even consider something like that? That doesn't even make any sense. Thanks to you, I'm being investigated by the Guild and the Association."

"You know what you did. Soon enough, everyone else will too."

"You'd better hope we don't meet in person. I'll get you for this, you little…." He called me the usual sort of names reserved for women who make people angry, then hung up.

It's hard to say which made me angriest, being cursed out or hung up on, but I was too busy and tired to give the matter much attention. Instead, I made a beeline to the breakroom for a cup of coffee and a Snickers bar.

I worked a little beyond five to make up the time I'd missed at lunch and then dashed out of the building to head home. When I reached my car, I noticed one of the tires was flat, and someone had keyed the alternate name for a female dog into my driver's side door. The attacker had also written "die" with red paint or dye on the driver's side window.

Rage fired like a bottle rocket through my veins. There were a few cars parked near the visitors' center, but it was clear they were at such a distance and angle that visitors wouldn't have noticed anything fishy happening with my car.

Most of the admin staff was gone. The only staff remaining was the rickhouse and production workers who parked lower in the lot, closer to their buildings, so there were no witnesses to talk to. Pierce had cameras installed in the admin building, the rickhouses, and the production houses. He'd also planned on installing them outdoors, but, unfortunately, that hadn't been done yet.

"Geez Louise." I sighed. Growling to myself, I poked out a text to Jimmy about what had happened.

He texted back. **Working wreck. Be there ASAP.**

Angry tears flooded my eyes, and I quickly swiped them away. My brain was a swarm of hornets—unclear, irrational, and filled with a primal urge to lash out. A couple of the production house workers approached and got in their vehicles. One in a dark green, old model Highlander pulled up behind me and rolled down his passenger window. "You alright there, hon?"

He was old enough to be my dad and best described as grizzly. Probably late fifties with a bulbous nose under sunglasses, he had thick, gray-white hair and a full gray beard.

"Not really. Someone vandalized my car."

CHAPTER SIXTEEN

"You're kidding? Hold on." He pulled up beside me and got out, tugging his sagging jeans into place on his narrow hips. His work shirt, a black T-shirt with white writing, stretched tight over his barrel chest. His shirt was tucked in, and a large, ornate silver belt buckle glinted from under his belly. He came around to my driver's side. "If that don't beat all." He scratched the back of his head with his thick, work-worn hands. "The first thing you want to do is take pictures for your insurance. You done that yet?"

Feeling like an idiot and a failure at adulting, my bubble of rage deflated. I smacked my forehead as I dug my phone out of my purse. "Not yet. I'll do it now." I snapped pictures of the damage while he talked. The insurance agency was closed, so I'd have to report it in the morning.

"I can't believe someone would do that. And here in the parking lot where people come and go all the time." He chuckled. "You must've made somebody big mad."

"Maybe." I took a picture of the tire. My anger dissipated, and my thoughts pushed through with more clarity. This guy could be right. Fox was awfully mad at me when he called and cursed me out earlier that afternoon. Of course. It had to be him. That low-down, skeevy, stinking weasel-faced. I balled my fists. I was going to get him. I wasn't sure how, yet. But he wasn't going to get away with this.

The man said, "You got a spare, young lady? I'll at least change that tire for you. I'll get my jack." He dug around in the back of his vehicle and came out with a jack and a tire iron.

When I'd finished taking pictures and video, I pulled the spare out of the trunk. "I'm sorry, I don't know your name."

With a grunt, he eased onto one knee to remove the flat. "I wouldn't expect you to." He breathed heavily as he worked at the lug nuts over his belly. "You admin folks don't get down our way too often unless there's a problem. My name's Cyrus West. Folks call me Cy."

"It's nice to meet you, Cy, and I appreciate you more than I can say. I'm Rook Campbell."

"Nice to meet you, too, young lady. I saw you out at the festival the other day. Didn't know your name, but I never forget a face." He dropped another lug nut in the hubcap and started on the third one. "I shore thought we had a chance of winning with Devil's Kiss, but I guess it wasn't meant to be."

"Really? I hate to say it, because I work here, but I thought Mermaid Cove had us beat hands down. Their Summer Nights is delicious."

"Huh. Haven't had it yet." He dropped the third lug nut and started on the fourth. "But I didn't think they were eligible, anyway."

"What do you mean?"

"Well," he grunted, struggling with the final lug nut. "I volunteered at the event and was helping to set up the judging tent. Some guy in a suit coat and derby hat came by, said he worked for the distillery and asked for the Mermaid Cove bottle. The girl working there wanted to know why, and he said because it's being withdrawn. She handed him a paper, he signed it, and he took the bottle away."

"Is that so?" My brain worked on the puzzle pieces. We'd already discovered that the signature on the form was faked. But we didn't know who had faked it. Maybe Cy could confirm it was Fox. If so, I was going to come down on him so hard. I was going to report him, have his award stripped, and his reputation ruined. "What did the guy look like? Did he have pale blond hair and pale skin?"

"Nah. This guy had short dark hair, dark round glasses, dark beard, not fully grown. He looked young, had a baby face. Maybe early to mid-twenties?" He dropped the tire iron with a loud clatter. He removed the old tire, set it on the ground, then pointed to the spare.

I handed him the tire, and he affixed it. That sounded like Turner, the tour guide I'd seen at Fox Trace. *That skeevy little rat.*

When Cy had finished, he used the tire iron to stand with a loud grunt. "There you go."

"Thank you so much, Cy. I'm in your debt. If you need anything at all—"

He waved away my offer. "Nah. Happy to do it. If my daughter or granddaughter were stranded like this, I hope somebody'd help them out. It's what you do for people." He returned his tools to his vehicle and shut the door. "Now, you don't want to drive too long on that spare." He picked up the old tire and dumped it in my trunk. "Get it to a body shop as soon as you

CHAPTER SIXTEEN

can. Get a police report and take it with those pictures to your insurance agent."

"I will." I offered him my hand. His hand swallowed mine, and he gave it a hearty shake. "And thank you again."

"You take care now."

I watched him drive away as I thought two things: one, I needed to find a way to repay Cy for his kindness. And two, since Fox Trace would be open for a few more hours for tours, I was headed there immediately.

Chapter Seventeen

I called Jimmy on my way to Fox Trace. He didn't answer, so I left a message telling him where I was going and asking him to please go by the house to relieve Batrene from Prim watch, if possible. Then I called Batrene to explain my situation to her.

She answered the phone and snapped. "What do you want?"

"Excuse me?"

She breathed. "Oh, Rook, honey. I'm so sorry. I didn't mean to bark at you. I didn't know it was you. Some idjit has been calling her about every hour or so. Most of the time, they don't say anything. Sometimes they breathe heavy. But the last couple times, they say something like, 'I'm gonna get ya. Ya can't hide,' and then they laugh like a demon." She sounded scared.

I rubbed my head, wishing desperately I could be in two places at once. This was more important. I really needed to talk to Turner. I needed to narrow down the list of suspects so we could find Patrice. I'd promised Millie I would help. I couldn't let down my best friend and helping her mother when I hadn't been able to help my own would've been the greatest act of friendship I could offer to Millie. I ran a quick mental calculation and deduced that Patrice was likely in more danger than Batrene and Prim. "We've been receiving those calls off and on for about a month. It's probably some stupid kid with nothing better to do. Call the sheriff, okay? And have them send someone out. Also, my papaw's rifle is in the hall closet. Have it close by."

"Prim's already dug it out. I have it right beside me on the couch." She sighed again, her voice cracking. "I sure wish Bryan was here."

CHAPTER SEVENTEEN

The mention of his name hit me in the chest. Hard. "I know. Me too."

"You be careful out there. We can't lose you, too."

"Don't worry. I'll be fine. Jimmy might be on his way for dinner. I hope he is, but call the sheriff anyway. I shouldn't be more than an hour."

"All right. We'll be right here crocheting dish rags and dish towels for the ladies in our Bible study group."

Ending the call, I added Batrene to my people-to-thank list.

Parking in front of the visitor's center, I didn't have time to waste. I marched into the building, still shaking with fright over Batrene and Prim. I wove in and out of the tourists and searched the crowd. Turner was standing by the rack of Fox Trace apparel, talking to a tourist.

He didn't see me coming. I sidled up behind him and tapped him on the shoulder. "Excuse me. Can I talk to you, please?"

He beamed. "Sure." He parted from the conversation and followed me to a quiet corner. "You were here yesterday, weren't you?"

"I was."

"You couldn't stay away from our award-winning bourbon, could you?" He laughed.

I scoffed. "Actually, I wanted to know why you cheated Mermaid Cove out of winning that award. They had the best bourbon whiskey in the whole competition. Everyone knows it. And you cheated them out of their rightful place, the money, and the reputation."

His face reddened behind his freckles, and his eyes darted. "I don't know what you're talking about."

"Oh, don't play dumb with me, mister." I pointed at him. "You know exactly what I'm talking about."

He started to walk away. "You're crazy. I have guests—"

Raising my voice, I said, "You'll listen, or I'll scream and tell everyone everything I know." People looked in our direction. I held up my phone. "I've got it all on video, and you'll lose your job."

That spun him back around real quick. He pushed his hands down like dribbling invisible basketballs. "All right. Shhhh." he hissed. He said to the gaping crowd, "Everything's okay. The tour will start soon." He said to me,

"C'mere." He beckoned me over to a corner.

I crossed my arms and assumed a power stance. I'd seen Jimmy and the other officers do it. "You'd best start talking. You cheated my friends."

"I was the one who removed Mermaid Cove from the competition, but Fox told me to. He gave me a bunch of money to do it and promised me a good job when I graduate if I keep my mouth shut."

"How much money?"

"A thousand bucks."

That was like winning the lottery to a college student. I remembered those lean days. Heck, with my mountain of student loan debt and Prim's medical bills, I was still living those lean days. Nevertheless, integrity was more important. "So you sold out for a little money and a job?"

"Hey, times are tough. It's hard finding a job that'll pay more than minimum wage, with full-time *and* benefits. And I needed that money for rent, food, and school books. Do you realize how expensive they are?"

Boy, I sure did. When I was in school, books cost hundreds of dollars, and at the end of the semester, during sell-back, I'd only get the tiniest fraction refunded. And if a new edition of the book was going to be released, I'd get zero money back on my used book, regardless of its condition. I stepped down off my high horse. "Well, that's true. I know how hard it is. But do you realize the damage you've done?"

"I'm sorry. I truly am. But please don't tell anyone. I need this job."

I glared at him, biting my lip. *Dang it.* I melted. I understood Turner's predicament all too well. And I didn't know what else his situation was like. Maybe he had sick parents at home. Or he had a serious illness. "Is Fox still here?"

He turned and looked out the window. "That's his Escalade right there." He pointed at a champagne-colored car.

"What time does he normally leave?"

"Should be any minute now."

"Thanks." I turned to leave.

"Thanks for not telling anyone."

I looked him up and down. He shouldn't feel too comfortable and think

CHAPTER SEVENTEEN

he'd won me over. He needed to sweat a little. "I never said that." Maybe that would make him think twice about fixing contests and cheating people. I marched out of the building and waited by the Escalade.

I didn't have to wait long before Fox showed up. As he approached, I opened the voice memo function on my iPhone, hit record, and held the phone so he couldn't see the screen.

"What're you doing here?" he asked, hitting the key remote to unlock the car.

"I know what you did. You rigged that contest and cheated two decent women, my friends, out of their rightful prize. Everyone knows Mermaid Cove should've won that contest, and they *would've* won had you not interfered."

He snorted. "Prove it." He opened his door and threw his messenger bag inside.

A few tourists milled in the parking lot, slowly making their way toward the visitors' center.

"Don't worry. I have the proof."

"You must be out of your mind to show up here." He moved toward me. "I know you reported me."

My breath increased as panic began to set in. I hadn't exactly thought this through. But my mouth had a mind of its own. "That's right, I did. Because you rigged that contest, and you know it."

He put his hands on his hips, his eyes darting around. He ran his tongue under his bottom lip. He was worried and changing tack. "Fine," he hissed. He held his hand out as if to steady himself. "Okay. Now, listen. I tell you what. You withdraw your report, and I'll give you half the winnings."

He thought since I hadn't submitted to his threats, he could now buy me off. Yeah, right. "I could care less about the money." That wasn't entirely true because five thousand dollars sure would help me pay down some school loans, but I couldn't think about that.

"I don't understand what you want!" He waved his arms in the air, his voice tightening several notches into squealing pig territory.

"Justice for my friends. That's what I want." A price far dearer than anything money could buy. "All you have to do is tell me what happened to Patrice and why you vandalized my car."

Perplexed, he shook his head and held up his hands. "Wait. Whoa. You're saying a lot of things. First off, the car. Whatever. I didn't do crap to your car. I don't even know what you drive."

"I don't believe you, but that's the least of my concerns. You need to tell me about Patrice. Where is she? And what did you do with her? You know something about it. You needed her out of the way so you could win the prize. Everyone believes Mermaid Cove's Summer Nights was primed to win."

He pointed, his pale face flushing bright pink. "I'm telling you I know nothing about that woman, where she is, or who took her, or why she's missing."

"Her family and friends are desperate to have her back."

He crossed his arms over his chest and shook his head in disbelief. "You actually think I'd kidnap someone just to win a prize? You think I'm that crazy?"

"It's an awfully big prize. And ten thousand dollars'll bring out a whole lot of crazy. Since you were willing to rig the contest and cheat, I reckon you're liable to do anything."

He threw up his hands in frustration. "Fixing a prize and kidnapping are very different things. I have no idea where she is, and I don't have time for this stupidity."

"That's a shame. Good thing I have time to talk to the KDG. Now about my car—"

His pink cheeks turned cranberry, causing his pale blonde brows to nearly glow. In a flash, his hands flew out to make contact with my shoulders, shoving me back.

I stumbled back, thankful I was wearing ballet flats instead of heels.

"If you report me, I'll make you regret it." He poked me hard in the shoulder.

Anger swarmed in my blood like hornets. "Oh? Like Patrice?" I returned the shove. "And my car."

CHAPTER SEVENTEEN

He teetered, surprise flashing in his eyes. Maybe he thought he could intimidate me. Maybe he thought I couldn't push back equally hard. "Don't you threaten me, you lying, cheating jerk. My boyfriend is a deputy."

He closed in on me. "Yeah, but he's not here right now, is he?" He grabbed my arm, his fingers digging painfully into my tricep.

I tried to pull away.

He sneered. "You and I are going for a ride." He tried to pull me toward his vehicle, but I dug my heels into the asphalt. Unfortunately, my ballet flats offered little traction. I skidded along behind him.

"Let go of me," I screeched. Instinctively, I tried to claw at his face, but my nails were too short and brittle to do much damage.

A sinewy guy in a plaid shirt and jeans from the tour group called out, "Hey, buddy. Let her go." He ran toward us.

"Mind your business," Fox shouted.

I kicked at Fox, aiming for his crotch, but missed. My arm swung to punch him, but he blocked it and grabbed my other arm. *Dang it!* This guy was slick as a greased pig. I bent over to try to bite his arm, but he kept moving it. He jerked and twisted me around, grabbing me from behind.

The stranger, followed by a couple other guys who looked eager for a fight, surrounded us. Plaid Shirt planted himself behind Fox and wrapped him in a chokehold. "Let her go, man."

Another guy punched Fox in the ribs, shouting, "Let her go. Now."

Fox dropped my arms to defend himself.

The third guy, bouncing on his toes, itching to get involved, jumped in to punch Fox in the face. The men surrounded him like wolves on prey.

Maybe it wasn't my proudest moment, but I let them get in a few licks before I grabbed one of the men's elbows and pulled. "Fellas, fellas, stop!" I inserted myself between Fox and the men. "Please! Stop!" While I didn't like Fox, and part of me wanted to see him beaten to a pulp for cheating my friends and trying to abduct me, three athletic guys against one doughy one wasn't a fair fight. Also, I didn't want any of these heroic strangers to get in trouble for coming to my aid.

"You all right?" Plaid Shirt guided me away from Fox.

Fox climbed in his vehicle and yelled threats from his window. "This isn't over. I'm calling my lawyer."

"Yes. Thank y'all for helping. I'm fine."

The other two flanked us, walking backward to keep their eye on Fox.

"Do you have a car here?"

"I'm over there." I pointed to my lime green Fiesta.

Plaid Shirt took me by the elbow. "C'mon. I'll walk you to your car."

Fox flipped us a vulgar gesture as he sped away.

I got in my car and hesitated to leave. Fox could've been lingering nearby to follow me home. Or worse. I called Jimmy.

He answered. "Just finished work. I'm on my way to your house."

"I'm at Fox Trace. Leaving now. If I'm not home in twenty minutes, come looking for me."

"Okay."

"Did you talk to Savannah about the engagement ring yet?"

"We did. She didn't know that it had been Patrice's ring." He chuckled. "She sure didn't seem too happy about it."

"I bet she wasn't. Did you ask Mitch about it?"

"I tried to contact him. Left a message for him to contact us as soon as possible. I'll keep trying to get in touch with him."

I ended the call, fully appreciating the benefits of dating a deputy. Cam's face popped in my mind. He would've come looking for me, too, actually. And since he wasn't a trained deputy, didn't that make him an eentsy bit braver? I slammed the door on that thought. I couldn't go there. I shook my head. I couldn't think about Cam right now.

I started the car, but didn't leave. I sat, staring at the skyline, trying to empty my mind. But the scene with Fox crept back into my head. Unease pulled at my shoulder blades. Fox seemed sincere when he'd claimed he didn't know anything about Patrice. That bothered me. Because if he really didn't know anything about her disappearance, then who did? I dropped my head on the steering wheel. I wasn't any closer to discovering who had kidnapped Patrice.

My phone chimed with a text notification. It was a text from an unknown

CHAPTER SEVENTEEN

number. Probably spam. Or Jimmy. I opened it expecting to find a message about pleasing your wife with genital enlargement. Instead, the message read: **Ur not home. But ur granny is. She's all alone. You'll never escape me.**

Then another message popped up to call me a female dog.

My heart jumped into my throat. *Prim. Omigosh.* My hands shook.

I forwarded the text to Jimmy and threw my car into reverse. I spoke my text message into the phone. My tires squealed as I peeled from the parking lot. **Leaving Fox Trace. Can you check on them or send someone? I'll be home ASAP.**

He texted back **10-4. OMW.**

Chapter Eighteen

I released a deep sigh of relief when I saw Jimmy's police-issue SUV in the drive. The house lights were on at Batrene's house next door, and she was moving around in the kitchen, so she must've gone home when Jimmy arrived. I blew out another breath, gathered my things, and got out of the car. Still shaken from my interaction with Fox and the creepy message I'd received, I wanted to rush into Jimmy's protective arms and just stay there.

Jimmy was helping Prim make supper when I walked in. Still in his uniform and wearing Prim's apron splashed with the words, "A little sugar, a lot spice," he stood at the stove, stirring something in a pot. His gun belt hung over a chair. It was a comforting, homey scene that made me feel warm and gooey inside.

I cuddled against him, staring over his arm into the pot of macaroni and cheese. "You know how to cook?"

"I do all right, but Prim's a good teacher."

"Hey, hon," Prim dumped her special sauce in the pot of pulled pork. Her movements were stiff, turning the warm fuzzies Jimmy gave me into something akin to drinking orange juice after brushing my teeth. Each day was evident that I was one day closer to living without the most important person in my entire life.

I wrapped my arm around Prim's frail shoulders and kissed her cheek while swallowing the lump in my throat. "How can I help?"

"Pour the tea, set the table," Prim stirred the pork. "Get the buns out of the pantry and pour those green beans into a bowl. And get him out of here."

CHAPTER EIGHTEEN

She pushed one of his beefy arms and pointed away from the stove. "He's already messed up my macaroni cheese. Who ever heard of cooking it in a pot? That may be how you make that boxed stuff, but homemade ought to be baked."

Jimmy and I chuckled. I let him believe Prim was joking. She wasn't. It didn't help that her illness made her grouchier than normal.

Jimmy held up his hands. "I give up." He removed the apron and held up his hands, laughing. "I'm sorry, Miss Prim. I give up. Lock me up in macaroni jail now."

"If I could, I would." She pushed her glasses up on her nose.

"Don't antagonize my grandma. Get the buns out of the pantry." I took the apron from him, hung it up, and nudged him in the right direction.

We sat down to our simple supper over a conversation about our respective days. Prim picked at a bowl of macaroni and cheese and spent most of her time pushing around the elbow noodles, occasionally stabbing a few and popping them into her mouth. Her illness destroyed her appetite.

"Tell me about Fox Trace?" Jimmy bit into his sandwich.

"I went out there to talk to the tour guide, Turner." I told him what unfolded at the distillery, adding, "I have some voice recordings. I'll let you hear them later." I wasn't sure if Jimmy heard me, because he grew as still as a pointer on its quarry.

"What'd you say about him shoving you?" His hazel eyes filled with an intense light best described as cold rage.

I didn't want anyone to worry or put the focus on me when the focus should've been on Patrice. "It wasn't that big of a deal. I handled it. Kind of." I filled my fork with green beans and told him about the strangers helping me out. "I was scared. But mostly mad." Really it was the other way around, but I'd never admit that out loud.

Prim lowered her fork. "You're telling me some man put his hands on you?" A dark glimmer entered her eyes. "And it's no big deal? He could've run off with you like that." She snapped her fingers.

She was right, of course. Fox had been surprisingly strong, and the reality is that if those guys hadn't shown up, I'd likely be...My stomach knotted, and I shook off the idea of what might've happened. "Well, some other guys there stepped in to help. They beat him up a little." I really didn't want to talk about this any longer. "I'm fine. Nothing happened. I—"

"All right." He nodded, smashing the bun down on his pulled pork sandwich. "Sounds to me like you weren't handling it very well if you had to have help from some guys in the parking lot."

He had a point there.

"Mm-hm," Prim said. "That's what I'm saying." She pointed her finger at me. "You shouldn't have been out there in the first place."

My voice tightened with defensiveness as I reiterated my point. "I went out there to talk to the tour guide, Turner, because someone at my distillery said he'd seen Turner messing around with the Mermaid Cove entry at the festival. I thought he might know something about Patrice, too. And my car. Maybe Fox put him up to more than just rigging the contest. While I was there, I ran into Fox, and we had words."

Jimmy said, "As for your car, do you have proof that Fox was involved?"

I shrugged one shoulder. "No. I thought he did it to get back at me for reporting him to the Distillers' Guild. He seemed like the most natural choice since he called me and cussed me out."

He sipped his tea. "Without proof, there's little we can do. You understand that, right?"

Prim poked the table with her bony finger. "I bet my bottom dentures that Fox Graham did it. He was a vandal when he was a high school brat running around, and I'm sure he hasn't changed much." She poked her noodles. "Can't you at least dust for fingerprints or something?"

Jimmy had finished eating. He pushed his plate back and leaned on the table. "I can if it makes y'all feel better, but it's not likely he left anything."

Pushing her glasses up on her nose, Prim added, "It would make me feel better."

"All right, then. I'll call the latent print examiner and have him come out tonight, if he can." He pulled his phone from his pocket and stood. "Excuse me while I place a call." He stepped out on the porch and made the phone call.

CHAPTER EIGHTEEN

"Prim, why are you so hard on Jimmy? Why don't you like him? He's trying his best to get along with you and to be friends."

"He's not for you."

"How do you know that?"

"Because he's not Cam. I can't explain it, but he will never love you the way Cam does. We've talked about this. That spark isn't there."

"But he's a good man."

"That may be. But you'll always come second to his job and...."

My skin prickled as if a thousand ants crawled over me as my irritation grew. "Do I need to remind you that Cam cheated on me? That he's the reason our marriage ended?"

"Nonsense. That's only part of the story, and you know it. Remember that man you developed feelings for in grad school?"

"We didn't do anything."

"But you were headed in that direction. Your attention was divided. You wasn't giving your all to the marriage either. You and Cam both were having issues. Neither one of you understood what marriage was when you got into it, and you let too many other distractions get in the way. The divorce was a mistake."

I frowned. I didn't like that Prim couldn't accept Jimmy. "The only reason you don't like him is because he's not Cam. He's your favorite, and that's the end of it. And it's not fair that you won't even give Jimmy a chance. You've made up your stubborn mind, and that's it."

Prim shook her head. "Nope. That's not it. I'm telling you—" Jimmy opened the door and stepped inside and, as if she hadn't been talking about him at all, she redirected her statement. "I have a hankering for some peach cobbler and ice cream." She pushed herself to her feet. "Y'all want any?"

I jumped to my feet. "I'll get it." I cleared the dinner dishes and deposited them by the sink on my way to the fridge.

If Jimmy knew we'd been talking about him, he didn't give any indication of it. "I called the fingerprint tech. He'll be out here in an hour or so." He sat at the table.

Icy air from the freezer blasted me in the face. "Oh, no. We don't have any ice cream for the cobbler."

"What? I could've sworn I had some." Prim sidled up to me and peeked over my shoulder. "What about behind that pork butt?"

I moved the meat. "Nope."

"We can go without ice cream," Jimmy said.

We both looked at him as if he'd suggested we all buzz the hair from our heads.

Prim said, "It's not cobbler without ice cream."

Jimmy smiled and held up his hands. "Sorry, I didn't realize. Rook, how about we go out to the store?"

"I think that's best. Prim, we'll be right back." I kissed her cheek. "You'll be okay for ten minutes, right?"

"I'm fine. *Family Feud* is about to come on anyway."

Jimmy and I jumped in the truck.

"Can we talk about earlier?" I closed the air vent to keep the air out of my face.

"What's on your mind?" His tone was still a bit prickly under the surface.

"You can't take Prim personally. She's old and sick."

"I don't pay any attention to that, babe. She feels how she feels. She doesn't like me, and it's okay."

"She likes you. She doesn't know you well enough."

He rolled his eyes to give me a *Yeah, right* look. "I'm not stupid." He turned to head toward the store. "It's okay. I'm a big boy. I can accept that not everyone will like me. I'm a cop, after all. I'm used to it."

That bothered me. While he was right, it seemed like it should've been more important to him that he'd want to impress or ingratiate himself to the one person I cared most about in the world. Maybe there was some truth to what Prim had said. No. Prim had gotten in my head. I wondered what my mom would've thought of Jimmy. Of Cam. Of this whole situation. I reckoned it'd be nice to have a mom to talk to about all this love drama. Prim was a good fill-in, but I couldn't help but wonder if my mom would've felt differently.

He must've felt my eyes on him because he glanced at me. "What?"

CHAPTER EIGHTEEN

"Uh, nothing." I turned to look out the window, and as we pulled into the parking lot at the Big Blue Market, I noticed a white van. Clem Sikes was putting gas into the tank.

As Jimmy pulled into the parking lot, I said, "Hey, that's Clem Sikes. You know that grumpy custodian from Mermaid Cove?"

"Yeah. And I notice he happens to be driving a white van." Jimmy parked in front of the store and looked out his back window at the van. "It doesn't have the plumber racks, but those can be removed." He tapped my leg. "Hurry up and get the ice cream. We're going to follow him. See what he's up to, if anything."

I jumped out and ran into the store for the fastest trip I'd made to the Blue Market to date. I grabbed the ice cream, bought a few scratch-offs to improve Prim's mood, and rushed out of the store as Clem was driving off.

"Let's go," Jimmy called to me as I opened the door and launched myself into the truck. He sped off after Clem.

"Do you think he could have Patrice in the back of his van?" I clicked my seatbelt into place.

"If so, he'd be a special kind of idiot. But he might have some tools or other items that have evidence on them. Or he could be leading us to a location where Patrice is being held."

He closed in on Clem and flipped on his siren. Clem slowed down and pulled over. "Ah, crap. I left my gun belt at your house. I'll have to improvise. Hope I don't need to arrest him." Jimmy pulled his badge from his sun visor and hooked it on his belt, then extracted a pistol from under his dash. He jumped out of the truck and tucked the gun in his belt line at the small of his back.

"Hand me the flashlight out of there." He pointed at the glove box.

I retrieved the flashlight and handed it to him.

"I'll be right back. Stay here." He approached the van cautiously. He spoke to Clem and

directed him to get out of the vehicle. Clem stood on the side of the road, paled in the SUV headlights. I rolled down my window, hoping to hear what they were saying, but I couldn't make out distinct words, only mumbles of voices. But the body language spoke clearly enough. Clem was nervous, shifting from foot to foot.

The men walked toward the back of the van which, for me, was a little exciting because I could hear their conversation.

"I don't understand why you need to see in the back of my van," Clem said.

"I appreciate your cooperation."

"What are you looking for anyway?"

"We've had reports of illegal activity. Drugs, guns, and the like."

Clem crossed his arms over his chest. "If you think I'm running drugs and guns, you've got to be out of your mind, son. And I'm thinking I'm going to need a warrant."

"Sir, I am within my rights to search your vehicle if I suspect drug activity of any kind. Now, I can do this with your cooperation, or I can cuff you and do it without your cooperation."

"This right here is a load of crap." Clem jerked open the doors. "Go wild. But you ain't going to find anything."

Jimmy lifted his flashlight and shone it inside the vehicle. I scooted forward and stretched side to side to see. There was a chest and a rolled-up rug in the back. They both looked big enough to hold a woman the size of Patrice. She wasn't very big. "What's in that chest?"

"Heck if I know. It ain't mine."

"Whose is it?"

"My cousin's. Ain't none of my business what he keeps in it."

"Why do you have it?"

"I've been helping him move. Is that a crime now?"

"Mind if I look inside?"

"No skin off my nose."

Jimmy climbed in the van, and my stomach lurched. He was in an incredibly vulnerable position right now. There was a shotgun sitting between the seats beside me. I hoped I wouldn't have to use it. I wasn't sure I'd be able to. I'd shot other rifles, but maybe his police-issue rifle had special features I didn't know about.

Trying to keep an eye on Clem, I searched the cabin for another weapon

CHAPTER EIGHTEEN

in case I needed it. Clem watched Jimmy, stroking his beard nervously. He seemed anxious, fidgety. Jimmy opened the chest, shined his light inside. He looked at Clem. "That's a lot of bottles of bourbon."

Clem licked his lips. "Yeah, so? I get a discount at the distillery. I bought it with my own money. Is that a crime?"

"Depends. You reselling it?"

"What's it to you if I am?"

"For starters, it's illegal."

Clem adjusted his ball cap. "No. I ain't reselling it."

"What do you do with all that then?"

His eyes darted, and he licked his lips. "I drink some of it. I give the rest away for gifts. After all, we've got Christmas coming up in a few months."

Jimmy smiled. "All this is Christmas gifts?"

"Yup."

I didn't believe Clem for a second. I'd caught him nosing around in the office at Mermaid Cove the other day, and he'd lied about changing a lightbulb. He probably stole that bourbon. Unfortunately, if no one at the distillery had reported it missing, then there wasn't anything to be done about it.

"Whose carpet is that?" He stepped on it in a few places. "That your cousin's too?"

"Yup. I'm taking this stuff out there right now."

"Where's your cousin live?" Jimmy shined a light on the rug and knelt down to inspect it.

"Franklin Avenue in Miltonville."

"What's your cousin's name?"

"Jesse Sikes."

Jimmy reached for a roll of masking tape. "Can I use a strip of this?"

"Whatever. Why?"

Jimmy put the light under his arm and tore off a strip of tape. He then shone the light on the rug again and patted the tape strip against the rug, and pulled it off. "Thanks." He returned the tape to its spot, stood, jumped out of the van, and closed the doors. "I appreciate your cooperation, Mr.

Sikes."

"So, can I go now?" Clem snapped. "Or are you going to keep me here all night asking me stupid questions and getting all up in my business?"

"You can go. Thanks for your time."

Clem marched back to the driver's door and climbed inside his van as Jimmy returned to the SUV, watching Clem the whole time. He reached in a side door pocket and pulled out an evidence bag. He dropped the tape inside.

"What's with the tape?"

"I found a hair. It's probably not a match, but it doesn't hurt to get it checked out." He locked eyes with me.

The van sped away. Jimmy climbed into the SUV and pulled onto the road.

"Do you think Clem has anything to do with Patrice's disappearance?"

He shook his head. "Possible, I suppose. There's that hair."

"He seemed pretty nervous."

"He did. I'd like to think it's just because of the bourbon he had in that trunk. There were at least a couple dozen bottles."

My eyes popped wide. "What? That's almost a thousand dollars worth of bourbon. He has to be selling it."

"I'm sure he is. There's no way he's giving all that away for Christmas." He snorted.

"I bet he stole it. Because Patrice and Dee Dee were missing bottles the day of the contest. Clem was supposed to give them ten cases and they only had five. That was part of the reason Patrice had to go back to the distillery in the first place. Then I caught Clem in their office at the distillery the other day. Said he was changing a light bulb, but that was a lie."

"Hm. I'll check with the distillery in the morning. It should be easy enough to prove if he bought it. Though, to be honest, the bourbon is the least of my concerns. I'll definitely keep an eye on him. Might call him in for questioning. I mean, what if Patrice caught him stealing the bourbon? Or threaten to report him for reselling it? That might be motive enough to get rid of her if she was interfering with his ability to make money on the

CHAPTER EIGHTEEN

black market."

I handed a dish of cobbler and ice cream to Prim while *Family Feud* segued into *Wheel of Fortune.* Jimmy and I joined her on the couch with our own bowls of dessert, neither of us able to solve the word puzzle as quickly as Prim. She took a few bites of her dessert and set it aside.

By the time we finished eating, the fingerprint tech had arrived to dust my car. Jimmy and I joined him out in the yard while Prim shouted her guesses at *Wheel of Fortune.*

Jimmy shook hands with him. "Thanks for coming out. Find anything?"

The tech was a wiry guy with dark hair and glasses, and a large nose. "I found a couple prints different from each other at first glance. I'll need to get these scanned into the computer to do a point-by-point analysis." He looked at me. "I'll need to get your prints to eliminate you."

"Sure." We circled the back of his Camry, and he pulled out an ink pad and a card with ten boxes labeled with the finger type. He pressed each finger and thumb of both hands in the ink, then pressed and rolled them on the card. He handed me a wet wipe. "Thanks. I'll have the results back within three to five business days."

Jimmy shook the tech's hand. "Thanks for coming out, man. 'Preshatecha."

"Anytime." Bony man collected everything into his bag and drove off.

Jimmy walked around my car, inspected it. "Have you called the insurance yet?"

"Not yet. The offices were closed by the time it all happened. I'll call in the morning."

"Of course, if you want to press charges against Fox, I'd be happy to arrest him."

"What would I need to do?"

"Come down to the station, fill out the paperwork."

"I don't have to do that tonight, do I? I'm flat tuckered out."

"No. But don't put it off too long. If you can come to the station tomorrow, that'd be ideal. You should probably talk to one of the other deputies to be sure there's no conflict of interest with me."

"Sounds good. I'll come down as soon as I can."

He wrapped an arm around me and pulled me close. I rested my head on his shoulder, taking in the sunset and the rise of the cricket song. A chill entered the evening air. Jimmy said, "Let me ask you something. What if those guys hadn't been there? Where would you be right now? What would Fox have done to you? Because you said he was trying to get you in his vehicle."

I focused on the light mist that had descended over the fields in the distance. "I don't know."

"I really need you to think about that, Rook. We have one missing woman already, and then you go out to Fox Trace to aggravate a man who may have been responsible for her disappearance."

"I wasn't trying to aggravate him. I wanted—"

He turned me to face him. "Rook, look at me."

I looked up into his hazel eyes.

In a gentler tone, he said, "This isn't a game, babe. I've seen too much in my time as deputy. I could be pulling your body out of a ditch tonight instead of standing here talking to you. Fox has clearly reached a point of desperation if he was trying to force you into his vehicle. Desperate men are capable of terrible things."

"Don't you think I know that?"

"I've got creepy people calling and texting me, threatening me and my family. Patrice is missing, maybe dead. I, of all people, know this is a serious situation."

He wrapped his arms around me. I snuggled against him, inhaled his fresh cologne reminiscent of sun-dried laundry, and listened to the music of his heartbeat. "I'm not trying to beat up on you. But I don't want anything to happen to you, either. I'd never forgive myself." He popped a kiss on top of my head. "Come to the station in the morning and file a report against Fox. Then I can get his prints for comparison on the vandalism done to your car. And I'll take care of the phone situation."

I sighed. "I'll be glad when Patrice is found."

Chapter Nineteen

Sleep eluded me. I couldn't turn off my brain. A carousel of suspects and scenarios danced round and round in my head. Mitch: pill mill, double life, maybe a black widower who moved on when he discovered Patrice had no money left to bilk. Fox: cheater, liar, scrambling for bourbon fortune and fame, and Patrice got in the way. Clem: liar, thief, hateful old coot who got busted stealing, and Patrice got in the way. Just like Bryan had got in the way a few weeks ago when he was killed. My mom must've got in someone's way, too. But whose? Neither Will nor Shane Decker had called me yet. I wished they would. Maybe one of them knew some little thing that would solve my mom's case and free my dad. Then back around, I'd go. Mitch, Fox, Clem, Bryan, and Mom.

My cell phone rang. I fumbled for it on my nightstand, knocking a few books and a bottle of hand cream on the floor.

Batrene. "Hon, I'm sorry for waking you." "I wasn't asleep. What's wrong?" "I think there's someone sneaking around your house. I don't know who it is or what they're doing, but—"

"What?" I threw off my blankets. "I got to go. Stay inside. When we hang up, call 911 or Jimmy for me." Not bothering with a robe, I slipped downstairs in my bare feet, a long T-shirt, and cotton shorts.

In the hall closet downstairs, I pulled my late papaw's Ruger .22 rifle from the corner and a magazine out of the box on the top shelf. Clicking on the closet light, I locked the magazine into place. Grabbing the small LED flashlight off the top shelf, I eased out of the house and the screened porch, careful to keep the doors from making noise, and tiptoed through the cold, dew-laced grass. Impending autumn chilled the air. Though there was a security light on the shed, the light didn't reach the side of the house.

Pressing my back against the wood siding, I inched around. When I came close to the corner, I adjusted the rifle against my right shoulder, finger hovering over the trigger, and gripped the flashlight in my left hand, holding it under the rifle. It wasn't the most stable shooting stance, but it would have to do. I needed light to see who was creeping around my house.

It all happened in a blink.

Adrenaline was strong enough to power a rocket pumped through my body. I clicked on the flashlight, then jumped around the corner and screamed, "Freeze," aiming the gun and light at a short figure dressed in a black ski mask, black jacket, and pants. The person froze only long enough for me to detect the acrid fumes of gasoline. As it registered in my brain, the figure threw the can at me. I raised the gun up and twisted my body to block the can, but that didn't stop it from splashing out on my torso and legs before thudding to the ground at my feet. The figure struck a match, threw it into the shrubs, and ran top speed across the yard to a car parked in the darkness at the end of my drive.

Splattered with gasoline, nearly retching at the detestable odor, I leveled the rifle, taking aim. I was less interested in actually shooting someone than just scaring them off, hopefully permanently. I squeezed the trigger, and the blast tore through the night, drowning out the tree frogs and crickets.

The stranger jumped in his car and sped off. I shone my flashlight at the car and squinted to try to make out the type of car, but the light didn't reach that far, and there weren't street lights in the country where I lived. The scent of the burning bush under the kitchen window turned me around. I hit the safety on my rifle and slung it on my shoulder. Grabbing the garden hose, I pulled it to the side of the house.

Sirens sounded in the distance as I sprayed the fire. The bush had caught quickly, and the fire licked at the side of my house, catching to the wood slats and blackening the yellow paint. I couldn't seem to get enough water pressure to adequately attack the flames.

Two sheriff vehicles, a fire truck, and an ambulance sped up my drive.

CHAPTER NINETEEN

Jimmy had barely parked before he jumped out and grabbed a fire extinguisher from his truck seat. He came running in his T-shirt and jeans, his badge clipped to his beltline. He sprayed the fire while the firemen came running up through the yard with extinguishers.

Once the fire was extinguished, Jimmy pulled me away to allow space for the firefighters to inspect the area. He hugged me.

"You probably shouldn't touch me. I'm covered in gasoline."

"Yeah. I smell it. I don't care." He looked me over. "You all right?"

"I'm fine. Just…" Baffled. Scared. Angry. I shook my head, struggling to think straight. The thoughts and feelings were jumbled, fighting for supremacy. "We were attacked."

Jimmy stilled, and he stared at me, intensity growing in his eyes. "Who?"

"I don't know." A shudder of fear passed over me. I hugged myself and rubbed my arms.

A voice boomed from the silhouette in the headlights of the second vehicle.

"Rook Campbell. I should've known you'd be smack in the middle of this. Trouble seems to follow you like your own shadow." I could tell by the size and shape of the figure it was Sheriff Goodman.

Great. Just what I needed. "Thank you for your concern for my welfare and safety. I'm beside myself with gratitude."

Jimmy gently nudged me, signaling to me that I should dial back my attitude. Sheriff Goodman brought out the worst in me.

He stopped and snapped his head toward the house. "What happened here? Why do I smell gas?"

While I unraveled my story, Batrene came out of the darkness, dressed in a pair of sweatpants, one of her late son's flannel shirts, untied tennis shoes, and a barn coat. Her ensemble was completed with a head full of pink sponge rollers held in place with a scarf. Maxine yapped from behind Batrene's screen door.

When I'd finished, she said, "Honey, are you okay?"

The light from the screened porch came on. Prim stood in her robe, looking out at us. "What's all this gob-awful commotion out here?" She eased her way down the three stairs by holding on to the open screen door.

When she reached the bottom, she let the door slam. She shuffled to the side of the house and took in the spectacle with wide eyes. "Oh, my. Wh-what's going on? Rook?"

I put my arm around her to keep her warm and whispered I'd explain later.

Goodman turned to Batrene. "Mrs. Bishop, did you see anything?"

Batrene removed her barn jacket and put it around Prim. "I was outside with Maxine, my dog. She's older, so she has to pee all hours of the night. I had just stepped inside and was closing the door when I noticed a car slow down and turn into the drive." She pointed at the end of my driveway. "I peeked through my living room curtain. At first, I thought it might be Jimmy."

"Could you tell what kind of vehicle it was?" Jimmy asked.

"No. It was too dark outside. I saw lights from a car, and then they went out suddenly. I thought that was odd. I turned off all my inside house lights, so I could see better. To me, it looked like some type of sedan, but I couldn't tell you what or the color. I thought maybe the car was turning around, but then I saw a person walking the perimeter of the yard, hanging close to the shadows."

My skin crawled as I pictured the events in my mind and that Prim and I were in our beds, completely unaware of what was unfolding.

Goodman asked, "What did the person look like?"

She patted her foam rollers. "I couldn't tell. Maybe a man—"

"Can you describe him?"

"No. It was too dark. I only saw a shadow moving." She scratched under a roller.

"What about the height? Anything at all…." Jimmy added, his thumbs primed to type notes into his phone.

She squinted, thinking, then shrugged. "He seemed kind of short."

My mind raced through short men who might have enough of a grudge against me to want to kill me. Fox Graham was on the short side. Mitch wasn't very tall, either. And given the distance between my yard and Batrene's, a man six feet tall might appear short.

CHAPTER NINETEEN

"I managed to get a little closer," I interjected. "He wasn't tallHe was probably my height. Give or take an inch or two."

Goodman ran his eyes over me, taking my measure. "You're what? Five, five?"

"Five, six." Jimmy and Goodman made notes. "He was average size, sturdy build. .From what I could tell."

The ambulance drove off while the firefighters prepared to leave.

Goodman said, "Is there anything else you ladies can think of that can help us track this person?"

"I can't prove it," I said. "But I bet this has something to do with those weird calls we've been getting the past couple of weeks."

Goodman frowned. "What calls?"

"At first, someone would call and hang up several times a day. Or call and just breathe heavy or laugh. In the beginning, we thought it was kids being stupid. Then it turned into death threats. The text my phone sometimes, too."

"How long has that gone on?"

"The death threats? A few days."

He wrote down notes. "And what does the caller sound like?"

I shrugged. "Hard to tell. They mask their voice, and they don't say enough to get a clear read on the voice. I've tried doing the reverse call, but no number comes up. And the texts are coming from a fake number."

Jimmy said, "I put in a request for the phone records and to get a trace on the landline."

Goodman's face tightened, and he nodded. He pulled a business card out of the cardholder in his back pocket and wrote something on the back. "That's my cell number. Office number on the front. If you think of anything, no matter how small, please call me." He handed the card to Batrene.

"Am I done?" she said.

"Yes. But we may need to talk to you again."

"Anytime. I got to get back to Maxine before she barks her fool head off." She hugged and kissed Prim. "I'll get my coat later." She hugged me and headed home.

We watched Sheriff Goodman rope off an area with police tape, and he and Jimmy decided to conduct a preliminary search of the property, the beams from their flashlights sweeping back and forth over the grass.

The sheriff stopped and shone his light on the gas can. "This yours?"

"No. The attacker had it. He threw it at me. Splashed gas all over me." My throat burned with the fumes, and the stench nauseated me.

"Hold on," Jimmy said. He ran to his truck for a pair of latex gloves and snapped them on his hands as he ran back to Goodman. He reached for the can. "Let me see that." He picked up the can and turned it around and around while Goodman steadied the light.

Jimmy squinted at a spot on the side. "Lookie here. Hair. Blonde."

"Yessir," Goodman crooned. "Good catch, Deputy. Just a sec." Goodman jogged to his vehicle to grab supplies.

Jimmy used a pair of tweezers Goodman provided to pluck the hair from the can and carefully place it in the plastic bag. They then lowered the can into a larger bag.

Goodman sealed the bag. "I'll take this to the lab in the morning as soon as it opens. I'd say if the perp was sloppy enough to leave hair evidence, there might be print and fiber evidence there, too. I say you ladies get some rest, if you can. And don't hesitate to call if you think of anything else."

"That's it?" Prim said.

"Well, ma'am," Goodman added. "There isn't much we can do right now. We'll have the techs and the fire investigator come out in the morning to thoroughly process the scene. We have some evidence that we can start on right away, but we don't have much else to go on. No make or model of the car. No real description of the attacker."

"But—"

I put my arm around Prim. "It's okay. They're working on it, Prim. It takes time. They'll catch him." My skin prickled as dread oozed into my center. Was I always going to have a target on my back? Panic filled my head like helium, chasing out everything except a pure animal instinct to run. I staggered a bit, feeling like my yard was closing in around me.

Jimmy steadied me with a hand to my back. The comforting warmth of his hand pressed through the thin cotton T-shirt.

Goodman said, "Rothdale is a small town, and sometimes people who do stupid things like to talk. So, we'll keep our ear to the ground and let you know if we catch wind of anything." He nodded to Jimmy, returned to his vehicle, and drove away.

Jimmy rubbed my upper back. "I'm staying here tonight."

Part of me wanted to put on a brave front and decline his offer, but Prim was the voice of reason. "We welcome your help. You can have the guest bed."

After tucking Prim into bed, I came back downstairs to grab a gallon of vinegar and a box of baking soda, hoping they could extract the gas odor from my skin. Jimmy was already stretched out on the couch, covered with one of Prim's handmade afghans and an accent pillow tucked under his head. His badge and gun lay on the coffee table beside him, and his shoes were kicked off at the end of the couch.

"What are you doing?" I asked. "There's a bed upstairs."

He lifted his head to look at me. "I need to be down here in case something happens."

My belly turned warm and gooey. I suddenly had a strong desire to fill the cover of a spiral-bound notebook with JD + RC surrounded by puffy hearts and rainbows. "Thanks for coming out tonight. And for staying. Sorry I'm so much trouble."

A grin spread slow and sweet as molasses. "I knew what I was getting into."

That gooey feeling returned as I popped a kiss on his head and wished him sweet dreams. I climbed the stairs, ran water in the tub, tossed in vinegar and baking soda, and eased into the tub. In spite of the hot water, I shivered. Though Jimmy was downstairs right now, he couldn't stay forever. I didn't know the identity of my attacker or when, not if, he might return.

Chapter Twenty

Jimmy—in his sock feet, jeans, and a T-shirt—stood at the stove, poking the frying bacon while sipping his coffee. His short fawn hair was spiked all over his head. It was the sexiest scene I'd witnessed in a long time. My insides twirled like a pinwheel.

Prim manned the waffle iron.

I kissed her cheek. "Mm, waffles, too?" I sniffed the air. "Smells like pumpkin spice." I poured my coffee. "My favorite. Thank you."

Jimmy and I pecked lips. "Morning, beautiful lady."

Leaning against the counter, I said, "How did you get Prim to let you cook again?"

He chuckled. "I started before she came down. Then we had a few rounds about it, but she finally let me do it as long as I didn't touch the waffles."

There was a knock at the back door. We all glanced at each other, confused. Seven-thirty was awfully early for visitors. I peeked out of the window above the sink. "It's Cam."

Prim said, "I'll get it. I know why he's here." She shuffled across the linoleum in her house shoes and robe.

Annoyance wrenched my stomach as I pretended to monitor the waffles. "C'mon in, and I'll get the bag."

Cam stepped into the kitchen. The room grew tiny and warm. "What a quaint family scene." His voice was hard.

Jimmy said, "Morning."

I glanced at him over my shoulder. "Hey."

Cam looked, in a word, snuggly in his faded jeans, boots, and a dark plaid flannel shirt. His mussed hair, stubble shadowed jaw, and bright blue eyes ignited a fire in my chest that flashed into my cheeks.

Jimmy said, "How you doing, man?"

A faint sneer tugged his lip. "Been better."

I turned to stare out the kitchen window. My back prickled and itched as if my soft red sweater was made of Brillo. A thin film of sweat broke over my skin as my nerves tightened. I wiped my sweaty hands on my black stretch knit skirt. I hoped that Cam and Jimmy would soon reconcile. I didn't want to deal with this tension forever. Nor did I want to give up either of them to avoid the tension.

Prim returned to the kitchen, clutching a reusable grocery bag in both hands as if it weighed a ton. "Here. Your momma wanted this for the baby shower." Her voice was weak.

"Who's having a baby?" I asked.

"My cousin, Amy," Cam said. "Momma wanted one of Prim's handmade baby blankets." He pulled some money out of his pocket and handed it to Prim. "Momma told me to give you this for your trouble."

Prim held up her hands. "I won't hear of it."

"The yarn costs money, though."

Prim closed her eyes and shook her head. "No, sir. You put that money away..." She shoved his hands back and pulled out a chair. "Sit. Have breakfast with us. We've got plenty to go around."

Oh, Lord. I rolled my eyes to the ceiling. The room grew tighter and hotter. *Please say no. Please say no.*

"Sure. I can stay for a bit."

I dropped my head, staring at the red light on the waffle maker.

Prim stood sentinel by Cam's chair as if she was welcoming an honored guest. "Rook, honey, get him some coffee."

"You remember how I like it, right?" Cam sat at the table, grinning like a fox in the hen house.

"Sure." I grabbed a cup and filled it with coffee, a bit of cream, and two teaspoons of sugar.

Jimmy pulled the bacon out of the pan, laying it on a paper towel-covered plate while Prim scuffled to the waffle maker to extract the waffles and pour more batter. She put a couple of waffles and bacon slices on a plate and handed them to me. "Give those to Cam."

I placed the plate and cup on the table. He thanked me and dug in while Jimmy filled a plate and sat at the other end of the table. The two men chatted a bit, and when the waffle maker beeped, Prim handed me a plate filled with waffles and bacon.

"You sit and eat so you can get to work on time."

The men were almost finished eating by the time I sat. Prim fussed around, wondering if everyone had enough to eat, offering to make more food and refill coffee until we said no enough times that she felt free to sit and drink coffee. She'd clearly worn herself out, but she wouldn't stop until she was certain everyone else was taken care of.

I dug into my breakfast.

"So," Cam crunched his bacon. "Do y'all have breakfast like this every morning?" His blue eyes glittered with jealousy and questioning.

"Nope," Jimmy answered. "I stayed here last night for their protection."

"That explains the police tape outside." Cam's brows lifted, and he searched our faces. "What happened?"

We explained the attack.

"Man. That's crazy. Who'd want to do that?"

"Good question." I stood to put my dishes in the sink. "That's what we're trying to find out."

Cam said to Jimmy, "Don't you have any suspects or leads?"

"Not yet."

"Shouldn't you be out there doing something about it?"

Jimmy glared over the top of his coffee cup as he drank. "I thought it was more important to be here last night in case the attacker returned."

"Well, now it's morning, and you can go find the bad guy, right?" The air around us felt heavy and prickly. Cam sat back in his chair. "But maybe pancakes and bacon are more important."

"Cam…" I warned.

He ignored me as he and Jimmy locked eyes like a couple of bucks locking

CHAPTER TWENTY

antlers. This was shaping up to be a good old-fashioned dance of the alpha male.

Jimmy ran his tongue under his lip, nodding. "Fine." Jimmy stood. "Miss Prim, thank you for breakfast and a comfortable couch." He turned to me. "I'm headed to the station. You coming out to press charges?"

"Yep, right behind you." I grabbed up my purse and keys and cut a look at Cam that I hoped adequately communicated my disappointment and annoyance in his behavior.

Jimmy walked me to my car.

"Sorry about that," I said. "Try not to let it bother you."

"I got what I needed. Good breakfast…" He kissed me—a lingering, heated kiss that packed more octane than my morning coffee. "And a good woman. See you at the station." He jumped in his truck and sped away.

I opened my car door, feeling eyes on me. I glanced over my shoulder. Cam stood in the kitchen window, scowling. I scowled back.

At the station, I wrote out my statement and handed it over. Sheriff Goodman asked me a few additional questions about the incident with Fox. Thankfully, we wrapped up quickly so I could get to work at a decent time.

As I gathered my purse and keys. "Did y'all find a match for the print on my car yet?"

"We ran it through CODIS. It hasn't hit, but if anything comes up, we'll let you know."

Well, that was annoying. That meant whoever vandalized my car didn't have a previous record, but it didn't mean they were any less dangerous. If the prints were run through CODIS and Fox's name didn't pop up, then all that meant was that Fox attacked my car and my house and had no criminal past. What was the likelihood that someone with a clean record would suddenly go off the rails? Fox might if he was desperate enough. But, if he wasn't the attacker, then who was?

On my way out, I noticed Mitch shaking hands with Jimmy as he was led into an interview room. Jimmy saw me, said something to Mitch, closed the door, and came toward me, grinning.

"Hey there. Did you give your statement?"

"Yep. Just finished. Goodman said he'd talk to Fox today."

"Good."

"You're interviewing Mitch again?"

He lowered his voice. "Yeah. Based on fed findings, he's most definitely running a pill mill. And I looked into Clayton Harmon. We've flipped him as an informant. Mitch is in trouble."

"You think any of this relates to Patrice's disappearance?"

"That's what I hope to find out."

"And you're going to ask if he had anything to do with the attack on my car and house, too, right?"

"Of course. What do you take me for, a rookie?" He flashed a wide grin. "Gotta go, babe. Got some bad guys to catch." He kissed my cheek, and we went our separate ways.

Since Mitch was out of the office, Savannah would be alone. It'd be good to run by the clinic under the pretense of an apology to see if we could get any information from her at all.

I texted Millie, **Meet me at Mitch's clinic?**

What time?

Now.

K.

Then I texted Jeff at work. I told him that I was working on the Pasture Pals project and asked if there was anything I could do while I was out.

He texted back. **Pick up signs and banners at Speedy's Sign shop.**

Millie was in the parking lot, sitting in her car and scrolling on her phone, when I pulled in a few spaces away. I knocked on her window, and she jumped, clapping her hand over her chest. She got out of her car and looked over the rim of her sunglasses. "Why'd you want me to come out here?"

"Mitch is being questioned at the sheriff's station right now. I thought we might be able to see if Savannah knows anything that might lead to finding your mom."

Millie blanched. "I'm afraid to see her. I might choke her."

"That's going to be problematic then."

CHAPTER TWENTY

"What do you mean?"

I scanned the parking lot, squinting against the sun. Surprisingly, there were few cars in the parking lot compared to my last visit. "Well, I was thinking if we went in under the pretense of an apology, we might be able to sweeten her up and dig a little info out of her."

She glared at me as if I'd vomited on her favorite suede boots.

"Please," I said. "Keep thinking this is for the greater good. You don't have to be sincere."

Millie crossed her arms and stared across the parking lot. She flipped her hair off her shoulder and adjusted her sparkly silver headband. "Fine. Let's make it quick before I change my mind."

We entered the clinic, where only a couple of people lounged, staring at the television or thumbing through an old magazine. One of them was the guy I'd seen on my first visit: Clayton Harmon. He didn't seem to be in any better shape. Wiry, fidgety, and a little greasy. Deep dark circles haunted his eyes, and he bounced his leg furiously while he picked at his cuticles.

There wasn't anyone sitting at reception, so I stood at the window and peeked around the corner. Savannah was talking on the phone, her back to the window. I lifted my fingers to my lips to shush Millie.

Savannah whispered, "I don't know. He called and said he was called down to the sheriff's station. They want to ask him more questions." She paused. "I don't think so. They haven't talked to me yet. I don't know why they would." She paused. "Oh yeah. Well, I don't think he knows anything."

While she talked, I scanned her desk area. There was a picture of her and Mitch. And another picture of her, Mitch, Shane Decker, and another guy I'd never seen, all sitting in lawn chairs. They were holding beer cans and flashing peace fingers. They were all sitting in front of a silver Dodge Challenger. It looked like the one Mitch had met in the park a few days ago. All the people in the picture wore jeans, sweatshirts, and camo jackets. Browned fall leaves lay at their feet. Now that was really interesting. When I saw Shane Decker, he'd been driving a white Lexus. Mitch drove a Jaguar. Savannah drove some sort of SUV. Perhaps that silver Dodge Challenger belonged to the man I didn't recognize. I wondered if that man was Will

Decker.

Savannah said, "He's here now. Oh, you're worrying too much. Clayton's fine. He's too stupid to…." She glanced around and spotted me. I flashed my broadest grin. She hissed into the phone, "I've got to go." She clapped the phone down and walked toward me, her gaze swinging nervously toward Millie. "Can I help y'all?"

Millie said through clenched teeth, "I wanted to stop by and apologize for attacking you the other day."

Savannah sat down. "Okay." Triumph gleamed in her eyes, and she linked her hands together, resting them on the desktop, the engagement ring glittering in the light.

Millie's shoulders were up to her ears. This was tough for her, so I jumped in to relieve her suffering. "You see, I suppose you've heard that Mitch's ex-fiancée has gone missing."

She cocked a finely trimmed brow. "Right."

"That woman is Millie's mom." I put a hand on Millie's upper arm. "As you can imagine, she's been really upset about it. And then when she saw that you're actually wearing the ring that once belonged to her mother…."

Savannah shrugged. "None of that has anything to do with me." She looked down at her hands. "Although, I'm super annoyed that Mitch gave me a recycled ring. You can bet we'll definitely be having a conversation about that." She said to Millie, "Then maybe I can sell this one to you, since it was your mom's."

Millie glowered and said to me. "I'm done." She went outside and paced in front of the clinic.

I wanted to reach across and pull the hair out of Savannah's head, but instead, I smiled. "How long have you worked here?"

"About two months. Why?"

"So, you started in July?"

She sighed with frustration. "I guess. Do you have an appointment?"

The picture of them was clearly from late fall, which meant they'd known each other much longer.

"How did you and Mitch meet?"

CHAPTER TWENTY

She grabbed a pen and wrote on a sticky pad. "You're very nosy."

"I'm curious. That's all."

She flashed me a look as if I was the dumbest person on the planet. "We met when I got a job here."

I nodded, pretending to believe her. The picture told a different story. "Did you know Shane Decker before you applied here?"

She huffed. "I'm not answering any more of your stupid questions. You aren't the police, so I don't have to say anything to you." She stood and spun on her heel.

"Don't you care that Millie's mother is gone? What if your mom was missing?"

Savannah didn't get a chance to answer because a man appeared behind her at the checkout window. "Hey, babe." He leaned on the counter, nearly pressing his nose against the glass behind her. He must've had back-door access. He was a taller, lankier version of Shane Decker in dark jeans and a form-fitting plaid shirt. He was dressed a little too hipstery for his age, but he got away with it—barely. Where Shane had that square Robert Redford jawline and blue eyes, this guy's face was sharp with a pointed chin, nose, cheekbones, and Adam's apple. His eyes were dark, shiny as onyx. I glanced at the picture on her desk. It was the same guy. One tiny mystery solved. Now, I wondered, was he the owner of the Dodge Challenger? Was he Shane Decker's brother, Will?

Savannah glanced over her shoulder. Though I couldn't see her whole face, I could see that she offered him not a friendly welcome-to-the-business smile, but more of a let's-go-to-bed smile. "Hey there, Will." *Bingo!* Another question answered.

This was Will Decker. Shane's brother. My heart swelled, and my breath quickened. The man who dated my mother when she was briefly separated from my dad before they married. This man knew my mom. Maybe he knew something about her murder, too. Tears formed in my eyes.

He looked at me, then back at Savannah. "I can wait until you're done."

"Oh..." She shot a sharp look at me. "We're done."

He flashed a set of perfect straight teeth. "I won't keep you. Only need to pick up that stuff. I think Shane told you about it?" He shifted from foot to foot, fidgeted with his car keys, and glanced up and down the hall.

"Yes, indeedy." She tilted her head and smiled coquettishly, pulled a set of keys from her drawer, and sashayed to the door at the back of the reception bay. "Come on back."

As they walked away, I stood on tiptoes and leaned to the side to catch him planting a brief kiss to her cheek and a playful pat to her bottom before they left my field of vision. *Oh, my.* Unless my eyes deceived me, Savannah seemed to be tom-catting around on Mitch. Now, *that* was an interesting tidbit.

There was nothing else for me to do here, so I joined Millie outside in front of the clinic.

Millie said, "I've never wanted to hurt one person so bad in my life as I want to hurt Savannah Stewart."

While I shared the sentiment, I needed to think. I pressed my fingers to my forehead. My desire to learn more about this man who knew my mom warred with my desire to see how much, if anything, Savannah and Will had to do with Patrice's kidnapping. First, I knew this was a pill mill. Mitch and Shane were involved in illegal activity. Since Mitch had been connected to Patrice in a relationship, maybe she found out about the pill mill, and she saw or heard something that put her in danger? Or maybe she was too much in the way of Mitch's and Savannah's relationship, and they wanted to get rid of an inconvenience.

Millie and I walked to our respective cars and hugged goodbye. I told her to call me if she needed anything. She climbed in her car and drove off with a wave.

I opened my car door and noticed a silver Challenger pull from behind the building. The driver-side window was down, with Will Decker behind the wheel.

Another puzzle piece fell into place. That was the car from the picture on Savannah's desk and the same car that had met with Mitch at the park and sped away. Now the big question was why would Mitch be meeting Will Decker at the park? Or was Shane in the car, too? It seemed pretty

CHAPTER TWENTY

sketchy to me. After all, Shane and Mitch were business partners, and he could meet Mitch at the office or his home.

So, if Will and Mitch were meeting in secret, why? *Interesting.* And more interesting than this was that Savannah and Will seemed pretty tight. Based on the public tiff I had witnessed between Mitch and Savannah at Tangled Up in Brew a few nights ago, Mitch seemed to be suspicious she was seeing someone else, but he was off by a brother. Or, maybe she was playing all three men against each other. Stranger things have happened. But, if that were the case, what would be her purpose for doing so? I lifted my phone and snapped a picture of the car as it rolled through the parking lot. Then I zoomed in to try to capture the license plate and forwarded both images to Jimmy. I texted **Belongs to Will Decker. Met Mitch in park. Will might be dating Savannah Stewart, Mitch's GF.** I wasn't sure if it would help him in his investigation, but I hoped it might.

Chapter Twenty-One

After a quick trip to Speedy Signs to pick up banners and signs for the Pasture Pals event, I rushed to work. The insurance adjuster called on my way to work and arranged to meet me at the distillery to inspect the damage to my car. He was already waiting for me by the time I arrived. He made a fast examination of my car and made notes of my explanation. Maybe Jimmy or Cam knew someone who could fix the damage in a way that would be cheaper out of pocket than paying the deductible and having the insurance company involved. Maybe I could find a way to fill in the color in the meantime so I could at least hide the expletives carved in my door. I didn't have time to process this now. I'd think about it later. With a brief but sincere thank you, I took his card, gathered my things and the signs, and dashed into the Four Wild Horses Distillery.

I dumped the signs on the conference table in the marketing pit and beelined to my cubicle. Plopping into my rolling desk chair, adrenaline from my already hectic day fired my hands into work mode to lay out plans for the Pasture Pals event at the retired thoroughbred horse farm. We were only about two weeks out from the event, and I was really excited about it. And there were other, smaller events and workshops that were taking place at Four Wild Horses Distillery in the meantime.

The day flew by and, in a blink, it was already five and time to leave. As I left the building, the sun sat low in the sky, a deep, mellow gold. Already the days were getting markedly shorter. The scent of burning leaves filled the air, recalling the fire at my house the night before; remnants of the fear and

CHAPTER TWENTY-ONE

panic flooded over me. My heart raced, my breath came quickly, a thin film of sweat broke in my armpits, and my skin grew hot. I turned on the AC and turned up the music, singing along at the top of my voice so I wouldn't have to think about the attack.

Batrene had texted me to bring bread and ginger ale on my way home, so I headed toward the grocery store. I flew down the road as my personal list merged with my work to-do list, my mind slipping from one thought to another in a well-oiled stream of consciousness.

I didn't know how long the car was behind me. But once I caught its lights in my rearview mirror, I noticed it was riding my tail really close. Annoying. I sped up. It kept my pace. Annoyance slipped into panic. My heart sped up, tripping over its beats, sending adrenaline into my hands until they shook and grew sweaty. I couldn't make out anything about the driver because the lights were too bright. I slowed down, hoping she'd pass me, but she stayed on me. Since I was on a country road, I couldn't pull over. The shoulders were too soft and steep. I pushed the pedal deeper.

Spotting the Food Mart, I whipped my car to the right into the parking lot. The car behind me continued straight. I parked and released a deep sigh that did little to abate the fear which prickled my ribs and chest like fiberglass. I gulped several deep breaths to still my nerves. Maybe it was time to talk to Jimmy about getting a concealed carry license. Failing that, I needed to at least get a stun gun or pepper spray.

Before getting out of the car, I looked through all my car windows to search the parking lot. Not seeing anything suspicious, I popped out of the car and jogged up to the store, glancing over my shoulder.

The doors slid open and blasted me with the A/C. I shuddered. The air smelled earthy and mossy, with a hint of onion, like a potato cellar. I wound my way through the aisles, dropping ginger ale and bread into the basket. As I passed the cosmetics aisle, I spotted lime green fingernail polish, very similar to the color of my car. *Perfect*. Maybe I could fill in the scratches temporarily until I could secure an appointment with the body shop.

Kneeling, looking at the polishes, a pair of legs sidled up to me. The jeans and tennis shoes signaled a woman. I glanced up at a short, stout woman with long blonde hair pulled into a ponytail. She was wearing a royal blue U of B Thoroughbreds long-sleeve T-shirt. She reached over me, getting too much in my space.

Trying to maintain my cool, I stood. "Excuse me." An edge crept into my voice that would warn off even the stupidest person. Then, unable to stop my mouth, I added, "So sorry to get in your way."

She ignored me and stepped in front of me. If I didn't know better, it seemed to be for the express purpose of preventing me from shopping. She didn't seem to be a bit interested in shopping.

My mind flashed to Prim, who'd be livid if I was arrested for physical assault in a

grocery store. I reached around her, grabbed a couple bottles of nail polish, and dropped them in my basket, struggling to stamp down the fire growing in my belly and the wild desire to punch her square in her overly make-upped face.

Her green eyes glinted with malice and challenge, as if to say, "Bring it."

I balled my fist. "What's your problem?"

Her upper lip curled in a semi-snarl, but she didn't say anything. Just glared at me.

Reason got hold of me. I didn't have time for a throw down in the Food Mart. I needed to get home to Prim, get supper, and get laundry started. I backed away, not daring to turn my back on this psycho.

At that moment, Oda Dean Spurlock turned down the aisle, pushing a buggy loaded with food. A white Mammoth Cave sweatshirt covered her top-heavy body, and her gray hair frizzed around her face. Oda Dean was one of the main figures in the Old Ladies Network. If she caught a whiff of trouble between me and psycho-girl, the news would catch fire, and Prim would have all the details by the time I returned home.

"Hey there, hon. How you doing?" Oda Dean glanced between me and Psycho-girl as if she expected an introduction. We hugged.

"I'm fine. Out picking up a few things for Prim."

She held my hand. "Oh. How's she holding up?"

"As well as can be expected." It was my standard answer when I didn't

CHAPTER TWENTY-ONE

want to discuss the details. I usually employed it when in mixed company with folks who weren't close to the family and didn't need to know all the details of our private lives.

Oda Dean said, "We pray for her all the time. I thought if y'all didn't care, we could bring some of the Bible study group over sometime."

"She'd really like that. Y'all are welcome any time."

"Good. I'll tell the ladies." She glanced again at Psycho-girl, who backed out of the aisle, glowering at me.

When the girl had disappeared, Oda Dean asked, "Who in the world was that?"

I laughed. "Your guess is as good as mine."

We said our goodbyes, and I moved into line at the Express Lane.

As soon as I started unloading my basket, the Psycho-girl sidled up behind me again, so uncomfortably close that even the cashier flashed her a strange look.

Pretending I didn't know she was there, I stepped backwards on her toe and crammed down with all my weight. I bumped her backward with my hip, then stepped away quickly, causing her to lose balance.

She yowled, stumbled back, and caught herself on the checkout counter.

"Oh, I'm so sorry," I glared at her. "I didn't even know you were there."

The cashier laughed. "Next time, maybe you shouldn't stand so close to people, hon."

"Good advice," I said to the blonde stranger.

The woman stepped forward. "And you should watch where you're going." She shoved

me.

That's it. I balled my fist and readied myself to strike.

"Uh, Flint…" the cashier shouted over her shoulder at a man standing at the exchange counter.

"Whoa, whoa, whoa." The manager ran up between us, the keys on his hip jangling. He jammed his big body between us. He wore a short-sleeved dress shirt with a tie and black pants. Sweat beaded on the edges of his buzz cut. "Ladies, ladies. We can't be having that now."

"She started it," I said. "She's been harassing me since I got here."

The woman shouted a string of obscenities beaded with threats against my person.

"Lady, I've never seen you before in my life."

Unshaken, as if such scenes occurred every day at The Food Mart, the cashier interjected. "Hon, it's $30.95."

I slid my debit card in the machine, so I could get the heck out of the store.

Psycho-girl snarled, "C'mon over here." She reached around Flint. He pressed forward, backing her up while attempting to talk her down.

The cashier handed me the receipt. "Must be a full moon tonight. Crazy people have been in here all day." She lifted the plastic bags off the carousel. "Here you go, baby. Better skedaddle now while Flint's got her distracted."

My body shook with unvented rage all the way home.

The police tape still encircling last night's attempted fire site, fluttering in the wind, only aggravated me more.

I wanted to unload my story in the most vehement terms to Prim, who'd had the pleasure of witnessing many of my fits over the years. But she'd been so weak and frail, and getting worse by the day, that I didn't have the heart to unload on her. So instead, I threw some pork chops in the oven with a can of cream of mushroom and some sliced portobellos. While dinner cooked, I changed my clothes and went outside to run around the perimeter of our yard until physical exhaustion doused my anger.

When my legs had turned to wet noodles (which didn't take long), I dragged myself upstairs to take a quick shower. I felt a lot better. Maybe I needed a regular running routine. I drew on a pair of soft yoga pants, an oversized sweatshirt, and fuzzy socks. Nothing matched, but comfort was a priority. After wrapping my head in a towel, I returned to the kitchen to finish supper. I boiled some potatoes and opened a jar of green beans Prim had canned. Since Prim remained glued to *Family Feud* instead of trying to take over cooking, she clearly didn't feel good. She slowly worked some blue yarn over her crochet needle.

I ran to the basement to start some laundry, my weak legs barely carrying me back up the steps.

CHAPTER TWENTY-ONE

"I think I saw Cam's truck pull in," Prim shouted.

I peeked out the kitchen window. "What's he doing here?"

When he got out of his truck with a shotgun, a box of ammo, and an overnight bag, I met him on the screen porch.

"What the devil are you doing?" I asked.

"I'm staying here tonight." He brushed past me and entered the house. "Jimmy called me. He said he couldn't be here tonight because he's working. He wants me here in case the attacker comes back." He sat his overnight bag and the gun down on the kitchen table. "Jimmy didn't seem too happy about asking, and I'm not too thrilled to be here, given the circumstances, but…." He shrugged. "Here I am."

Prim appeared in the doorway, eyes twinkling like a kid spotting a bowl of ice cream. "I'll get you a pillow and a blanket for the couch. Cam, you hungry, hon?"

Cam smirked with triumph. "Looks like I'm staying…." Then added in a John Wayne voice, touching the bill of his ball cap, "Little lady."

My mouth opened for an argument as my phone rang. The buzzer sounded on the food, so I answered the phone and shimmied my hand into an oven mitt.

"Rook." Millie's voice came out uneven and breathy, as if she were walking. "I received a call from Mitch. I was with a client so I couldn't answer. He left a message. He said he has something to tell me about my mom's disappearance, but he didn't want to tell me on the phone."

"Okay," I coaxed her to continue as I opened the oven and pulled the pork chops out. The cream sauce bubbled.

I heard the sound of her car door closing and her engine starting. "I tried calling him back, but he's not answering. The clinic is closed by now, so I thought I might try going by his house."

I set the glass dish on the stove and turned off the oven. "You need to call Jimmy. He's lead on the case. He needs to know."

"I will." She hesitated.

A little voice in my head nudged me to ask her, "Do you want me to go with you?"

"Would you please? I'm scared he'll tell me something horrible."

"Are you headed there now?"

"Yes."

"Okay. I'm coming. Don't go in until I get there. I'll call Jimmy for you. Maybe he can meet us out there, too." For a moment, my heart leapt with hope that Mitch might confess, but I tamped that down real quick. It seemed too good to be true. "I'll be right there." I ended the call.

Cam crossed his hands over his chest. "Where you going?"

"I'm going to meet Millie over at Mitch's."

His chest puffed, and he turned to grab his gun. "I'm going with you."

I waved him away. "Put that thing away before you shoot your foot off or something. And you can't go. I need someone to watch Prim, help her with supper, and protect her in case that crazy person comes back."

His chest deflated.

Gotcha. I could feel a smile pulling at the corner of my mouth. "Them's the breaks, kiddo." Since my stomach was about to eat itself, I grabbed a Moon Pie and Kentucky Spice. It wasn't the supper I really wanted, but it'd do. I could eat pork chops when I returned. Snatching my keys and purse, I headed out the door before Cam could stop me. "Be back in a little bit."

He followed me outside. "You be careful, okay?"

"I will." The door on the porch slammed shut. From the screened porch, Cam shouted, "You'd better tell Jimmy where you're going. Don't do something stupid and go out there alone."

"Yep!" I closed the car door and started the engine.

A couple bites polished off the Moon Pie then I called Jimmy. When he answered, I said, "Has Millie called you yet?"

"Yeah. Just got off the phone with her. I'm headed out there now." His voice shook like he was running.

Now I had a bone to pick. "Did you tell Cam to stay the night at my house?"

"I did. I thought it was best since I couldn't be out there tonight."

"That wasn't your place."

"My place is I care about your and Prim's safety not only as an officer but

CHAPTER TWENTY-ONE

as your boyfriend. Therefore, in my mind, it was my place to send Cam out there."

"But why Cam, of all people?"

"You know him. You trust him. And we can't spare an officer to sit at your house."

"But—"

"How about this..." he snipped. "How about for once you stop fighting me and give me a chance to care the best way I know how."

*Well...*My eyes widened, and my jaw clamped down like a bear trap. *Alrighty then.* I didn't have the energy to fight, so I snipped back. "Fine."

"I've got to go." He bit impatiently and hung up.

I threw my phone into my purse, cranked Led Zeppelin, and jammed down the gas pedal, feeling some small satisfaction with the climbing speedometer.

The red Spanish tile roofs of Tuscany Pointe appeared through the trees. I whipped the car into the parking lot and slammed it into park next to Millie, who was sitting in her car staring at her phone.

I rubbed my face, shook off my irritation with Jimmy, and got out of the car. Millie looked up and joined me.

"Thanks for coming out."

The lights were on in Mitch's condo, though the curtains were pulled. We approached the door and rang the bell. The television blasted through the door. We rang the bell again. And again.

"What's the deal?" Millie scoffed. She pounded the door. It popped open. We looked at each other.

I pushed the door open and peered inside. Something was burning on the stove. It smelled like beef and onions, but it smelled odd, faintly of burned food, but faintly of something else, something gamey. The taco shell box on the counter indicated the hope of tacos for dinner. The TV blared a car commercial. I shouted his name. No answer. Concerned about the food on the stove, I dashed into the condo to flip the switch on the stove. Millie followed behind me, shouting for Mitch. Then she screamed.

"What's wrong?" I leapt to her side.

We stared down at Mitch, who was sitting on the floor with his back against the plush chair. He was slumped to the right with a gun awkwardly sitting in his left hand. Blood poured from the side of his head. And now I smelled clearly the coppery scent of blood, that gamey scent I thought I'd detected earlier.

Clutching Millie's arm, I pulled her backward. "We need to get out of here and wait for Jimmy. He's—"

A voice sounded behind us, and we both screamed and jumped, grabbing onto each other. Jimmy.

Millie and I, clinging to each other, moved as one unit behind Jimmy. "It's Mitch," I panted. "He's dead. Very dead." We inched toward the door.

Jimmy eased around the side, placing his steps carefully. He knelt, his knees cracking. He scrutinized Mitch, the blood, and the surrounding scene.

He stood and hands planted on his hips. "No sign of struggle. Nothing valuable is missing. Still wearing a fancy watch, TV, car, and computer, all still here. Bled out. Head wound to the left side of the head." He rubbed his bottom lip. "I don't like it. There's something…off."

Though I was still rattled with shock, my heart resumed its seat in my chest as my mind, desperate to make sense of the scene, grabbed at details. Some pillows on the adjacent couch were crumpled and fallen over. "It looks like someone else was here. There appears to be a butt print near those pillows."

Jimmy nodded. "Yeah." He backed away and carefully placed his steps again to trail behind the chair and the couch. He peered over the top of the couch. "There looks to be some kind of shoe print in oil or dirt. That's helpful."

"Can you tell what kind it is?"

"Not from this distance, but it appears to be some kind of work boot. Like the kind my dad used to wear on the construction site."

My memory flipped to when I'd seen Mitch at the clinic. He seemed healthy and happy. Not exactly the sort who would kill himself. "I don't think he killed himself, Jimmy. This isn't right."

"What makes you say that?"

"He was about to get married, was healthy, happy. I don't know." I hugged

CHAPTER TWENTY-ONE

myself. "It doesn't seem right."

He pulled his phone from his pocket and opened his arms to corral us outside. "Let's go. Y'all need to get out of here."

The blue and red cruiser lights reflected on the cars and buildings in the parking lot. Millie and I leaned on my car, standing close for comfort while Jimmy called the incident in to the station, called the coroner, and the forensics team. He sighed and rubbed his palms over his face, then removed his notepad and pen from his pocket. "All right, let's start from the top."

Millie began. "Mitch called me and asked me to come over. He said he wanted to speak to me about money for my mom."

That sent chills over my skin. What if that had been a lure to get Millie to his house so he could hurt her? As if reading my mind, Jimmy said, "You think that was a trap?"

Millie's eyes widened, and she pressed her palm to her head. "Oh, my stars. I never thought of that. I was so eager to help my mom, it never occurred to me…." She dropped her hand to her mouth, and I stepped in to finish telling Jimmy about how we found Mitch dead on the floor when we arrived.

The sheriff showed up, and Jimmy said, "Stay here." He met Goodman, who rolled his eyes at me by way of greeting. Goodman and Jimmy disappeared into the house for several minutes as the coroner and forensics team began to trickle onto the scene.

Millie sniffled and wiped her eyes. "We're never going to find my mom now."

I put my arm around her. "Sure, we will." I wished I was as confident as I was pretending

to be. "Don't say that."

"I'm sure he knew something about it, and he was going to tell me. Maybe he was even going to confess." She rifled through her purse for a tissue and blew her nose. "Now, I'll never know."

Jimmy, Goodman, and one of the crime scene techs came out, and the tech was saying, "There's something strange about the angle of the bullet, though, and the way the gun fell. The exit wound and the resulting hole is in the floor. Not the wall." The tech pushed his round glasses up on his snub nose with the back of his latexed hand. The red and blue lights danced around us like we were at some silent macabre disco. "Imagine you're going to shoot yourself in the head." He held his fingers in the shape of a gun straight to his temple. "You're going to do this, right?"

Jimmy and Goodman crossed their arms and nodded. "Yep."

The tech said, "Well, that means the bullet is going to go out into the wall."

"Right," Goodman said.

"But the exit wound is at an angle, and the bullet hole is in the floor."

Jimmy and Goodman's eyes widened as something dawned on them.

"What's that mean?" I said.

The tech blinked at me from behind his glasses. "It means someone else killed him. I doubt it was suicide. But that's just my preliminary read on the scene. I'll get our ballistics expert to take another look."

My intuition sounded bells. The scene unfolded in my mind. In my mind rose Mitch's corpse, splayed against the door, limply holding the gun in his left hand. Then a memory flashed in my mind of when I'd visited Mitch at the clinic. I closed my eyes and put my fingers to the center of my head as though I could push the memory into place. I focused and replayed when he was questioning me about my rash. He was scrolling through on the iPad and punching things in. With his *right* hand. "Omigosh. I'm pretty sure he was right-handed."

The men all snapped their heads around to look at me. "How sure are you?" Jimmy asked.

About ninety-nine percent sure."

"That's good enough for me," Goodman said.

Jimmy said to Millie and me, "What do y'all know about Shane Decker?"

Millie said, "I think he was Mitch's business partner, but I've never met him. Mitch was always pretty quiet about his business at home. Wanted to leave work at work. And if he got business calls at home, he either let them go to voicemail or he took the call in another room."

"I only met him once," I said. "I saw him at the clinic having an intense conversation with Mitch."

"They were arguing?"

CHAPTER TWENTY-ONE

"Not exactly. But it seemed like Shane was giving Mitch what for."

"Did you hear any of it?"

"A little bit." I slapped a mosquito and brushed it away. "It was something like Shane wanted to increase business, and Mitch said he'd try but didn't think it was possible. Then he'd told Shane that he really needed money to help with Patrice's ransom."

"How did Shane respond to that?"

I squirmed. A sensation of crawling bugs covered my skin. I was jittery in general. "I couldn't see them. I could only hear them, but Shane didn't seem to have much of a response to that. He only said there was no choice but to increase money in order to keep their other partner happy."

"Huh. And did either of them mention the name of the other partner?"

"Nope."

"Have y'all been able to track any of the phone calls from the kidnappers?" Millie asked. "Maybe some of those numbers will match numbers on Mitch's phone."

"No luck yet. They're probably using the Burner app. We did track movement on one phone, but we found it smashed on the side of the road. We'll look at the numbers on Mitch's phone to see if there's any connection we can make there."

"What about that silver Challenger?" I asked.

He blew out a breath and pushed his hat back. "We're working on it. Turns out there are many of those in the Rothdale-Lexington area."

"Really?"

He shrugged. "Lots of guys love muscle cars." He sighed. "Especially in this area."

Millie rubbed her upper arms, and her voice turned watery. "Are we ever going to find my mom?"

Jimmy's eyes flashed with intensity. "I swear to you we're doing everything in my power, and I will not stop until I find your mom."

The sheriff reminded us he might want to speak with us again at some point about our findings at Mitch's house and asked a tech to swab our hands for gun residue since we had both known Mitch. Then he dismissed us and turned back to the condo with the tech.

Millie hugged me. "Thank you so much for coming out here. I wish I hadn't found Mitch dead, but I'm glad I wasn't alone."

I squeezed her tight. "You call me if you need anything at all. Be careful going home."

She nodded, holding back tears, and got in her car.

Jimmy held my hand. "I wish I could protect you better. I hate this case."

I squeezed his hand. "Me too." I watched Millie pull out of the parking spot and waved to her as she drove away. "I hate it most for Millie. This is killing her. I wish we could find Patrice. *Alive.*" What I didn't say was that finding Patrice alive would be a balm for my own spirit as much as for Millie's.

"I'm doing everything I can."

I nodded. "I know you are."

Jimmy looked around to ensure no one was listening to us. "I'm not telling you this in an official capacity, but I spoke to the DNA tech about that hair I found on the rug in Clem Sikes' van. The initial finding is that it's not even human. They think it's a dog hair."

I sighed. "Okay. Does that mean Clem is off the suspect list?"

"Probably. It turns out he did purchase those bottles of bourbon. I will have to investigate if he's reselling them on the black market, which is highly likely. But there's little chance his money-making venture has anything to do with Patrice's disappearance."

I nodded. "Mitch is dead. Clem is probably out. Who does that leave? Fox?" I scanned the scene around me. Was Fox capable of *this*? I didn't like him, and he had proven he could be hot-headed, but *murder*? I rubbed my face and checked the time on my phone. Nine. "Thanks for telling me." I smiled and whispered.

"If you say anything about it, I'll deny everything." He smiled and winked.

"Understood. I really need to go. Cam's sitting with Prim, and it's getting near her bedtime." I gave him a quick kiss.

Turning to unlock and open my door, Jimmy held on to the door frame. "Hey. Watch your back. Whoever killed Mitch could very well be the same

CHAPTER TWENTY-ONE

guy who attacked your house last night."

Chapter Twenty-Two

Thankfully, Prim was already in bed by the time I got home. I collapsed on the couch where Cam was watching *Blue Bloods*, sipping a bottle of Kentucky Spice, a locally crafted ginger-citrus soda. If I was honest with myself, I was happy for his presence—even if he was annoyed with me.

"My heavens, what a day." I grabbed a bottle of soda, kicked off my shoes, and propped my feet on the coffee table.

"Everything okay?"

I unloaded my day on him. The crazy woman at the Food Mart. The discovery of Mitch's body. "I feel like I'm living in some alternate universe. I'm dying for some peace and quiet." I shuddered and pulled an afghan around me. Something about the squeeze of patterned acrylic yarn, faintly scented with Prim's rose lotion, filled me with a deep sense of comfort and security.

"Maybe you should go camping or something. That always makes you feel better."

"Maybe. It's getting to be perfect weather for it in the evenings."

"Yeah." He sipped his drink and wiggled his sock feet.

"But I can't take off on a relaxing getaway while Millie's mom is missing. I'd worry about Millie the whole time."

"I guess they're not any closer to finding Patrice?"

"Jimmy says they're working hard, and I'm sure they are, but from my perspective, they don't seem to be any closer to finding her."

"Well, I'm sure there's a lot Jimmy's not allowed to tell you." There was an edge to his voice.

"That's true."

We stared dully at the TV for a few minutes until sleepiness began to creep over me. I needed to find a body shop to fix my car, so I reached for my laptop on the side table.

Cam stood. "I'm going to grab a snack. You want popcorn or chips or something?"

Buttery, salty popcorn was the perfect snack. "Popcorn, please."

A few moments later, he returned with a bowl of warm popcorn, and he sat it between us on the couch. I stuffed a handful in my mouth while I searched for body shops that would fix my car for an affordable price, lower than the deductible, but I couldn't find anyone who listed their fees.

When I set aside the computer with a huff, Cam said, "What's wrong?"

"Someone keyed my car, so I want to get my car repainted. You know anyone?"

"Oh, yeah. You should talk to Bobby Crabtree out on Maple Street. He's got a little body shop he runs out of his garage. He's real good and won't rip you off. Maybe, if you talk sweet to me, I can get you a good deal."

"Nice try, buddy." I rolled my eyes, smiling. "This is as sweet as it gets."

He laughed. "I'll call him, and I'll go with you. You'll get a better deal."

The good ol' boy network had its advantages for folks on the inside. "Thank you. I appreciate it. Money's tight, so I need the bargain buster special."

"I'll see what I can do." He swigged from his soda. "Who do you think attacked the house last night?"

"I have no idea. Maybe Mitch. But if he did it, we'll never know now. I have to admit, though, it didn't really seem like something he'd do. Doesn't seem covert and slick enough for him. Maybe Fox Graham."

Cam peeled the label on the green bottle. "Do you think Mitch and Fox worked together?"

Crossing my pink polka-dotted fuzzy socks at the ankle, I said, "I guess anything is possible. But I'm not sure Fox and Mitch knew each other. Then there's a guy, Shane Decker, Mitch's business partner, but I can't imagine why he'd target me. I never had any run-ins with him."

"Unless you'd unwittingly stumbled on something that could hurt him."

I shivered, pulling my sweatshirt sleeves over my hands and cuddling deeper under the afghan. "That's possible."

"Thanks." The warm fuzzies bloomed inside me as I cuddled under the afghan. "Maybe I can run by his office tomorrow at lunch. Try to feel him out."

"That's a horrible idea. If the dude is trying to kill you—"

"Shh. Keep your voice down."

"You can't go out there."

"Okay," I said, shutting down the argument while making a mental note to speak to Shane Decker tomorrow. Maybe I could pick up some hints about the case or about who attacked my house.

After a few quiet moments, he said, "You remember that time we went on that Civil War ghost tour in Harrodsburg?"

"Yeah. It was so cold and windy that night."

"And you thought something touched your neck."

"Hey. It did. I was not making that up."

"It was probably a moth."

"No. It wasn't. It felt like someone's finger going across my neck." I rubbed my neck, still feeling the ghostly touch.

He started laughing. "You screamed out. Scared those old people, about gave them a heart attack."

I laughed with him. "And then I tripped and fell in that ditch."

He slapped his knee. "If there were any ghosts there that night, they were more afraid of you than you were of them."

I nudged him with my shoulder. "Hush."

He gazed at me. His blue eyes lingered on my face. I knew that look, that intense look, right before a heated kiss. The desires of my heart and flesh warred with the morality of a woman dating another man. I wanted him still. In spite of everything. But opening that door was a big no-no. Not only because I was dating Jimmy, but because Cam and I didn't work. We'd tried it and failed. We couldn't seem to get on the same page, and there was

CHAPTER TWENTY-TWO

too much between us already.

Averting my gaze to the television, I redirected the conversation. "The news is coming on. Turn it up, just a little."

The news opened with a report on Mitch, but it was a simple report with no additional information that might help me. Likely, the sheriff's department had decided to withhold information to aid the investigation. The report ended with a call to action for the public to notify law enforcement of tips or additional information.

Then the anchor moved on to a report about the arraignment involving Bryan's murder last month. The B-roll showed clips of Holly, Len, and Keith in orange jumpsuits, hands cuffed in front of them to a waist chain. They looked gray, haggard, hungry. Holly's dark roots and blonde fried ends hung limp and greasy around her face, and large purple bags drooped under her eyes. She looked downright evil. Images of her kicking and scratching threatening to kill me, flooded back to my mind. I shuddered and pulled the afghan tighter around me.

"Do you have to testify?"

"I'm sure I will, but I don't know when. The legal system moves slow." My stomach coiled in on itself. "I'll be glad when they're put away, and I don't have to think about them anymore."

At midnight, I finally felt tired enough to go to bed. I stood and stretched, announcing my exit.

"All right," Cam stretched out on the cushions, pulling the rifle from under the couch and resting it on the floor. "Don't expect me to cook you breakfast in the morning like Jimmy did." He rolled over and tucked his hands behind his head, smiling at me. He winked at me. Thoughts I shouldn't have had edged into my mind. I tried to shut them out.

"Good. Because you can't cook to save your life."

"Hey…" He sat up on his elbows. "I can too."

"Spaghettios and frozen dinners don't count."

He patted his chest. "I've learned some things since we were last together. Things that'll blow your mind."

I laughed. "If you say so. I won't hold my breath." I passed him, and he held out his hand for me. I placed my hand in his, and he pulled me closer, kissing my hand. He gazed up into my eyes, serious, intense.

"I'm holding mine for you. As long as necessary."

Chapter Twenty-Three

During my lunch break, I drove to downtown Rothdale, which was essentially a red brick federal-style courthouse stationed in the center of a square of businesses and government offices. I first grabbed a quick lunch of grilled cheese and tomato soup at Betsy Bee's cafe. Sitting at the table, gazing on the town square, specifically Decker Properties, I tried to think of questions I could ask Shane Decker that would indicate any potential involvement in or knowledge about Mitch's murder without making myself a target.

After lunch, I crossed the square to the building that housed Decker Properties. In the early 1900s, the buildings were row houses or apartments, but the buildings had long been converted into businesses and offices. Some of them were still the natural red or white brick, while others had painted the brick in vivid colors with ornate cornices in complementary colors. Some were flat-roofed, others had steep gables. The city decorated downtown according to the season, so now that we were approaching fall, the lamp posts were flanked by barrels of fluffy yellow, orange, and red mums.

Wedged between a lawyer's office and a financial advisor's office stood Decker Properties in an olive-green building with dark green cornices. I entered the building, where a set of navy carpeted stairs led up to the next floor. To the left was a glass door with gold lettering that read: Decker Properties.

A receptionist sat behind the glass window, where I asked to speak with Shane Decker. The waiting area was small, but classy. Beige walls were covered with large abstract prints, under which sat a plush green sofa on one wall and two comfy accent chairs near the window overlooking the street below.

I sat in a chair and thumbed through a travel magazine, developing a deep desire to visit the far-off places I'd likely never get to see; along with that came a deep envy for anyone who could see those places. Half-annoyed, I cast the magazine aside.

Shane opened the door. He wore an orange button-down and pleated olive-colored pants. His strawberry-blond hair, casually styled and wind-blown, as if he'd stepped in from an outdoor hike. He recognized me immediately and hemmed. "Oh. Uh. Miss Campbell?"

I plastered on a bright smile and jumped up to greet him. "Hey there. I won't keep you long. I have only a couple questions about something."

He hemmed. "Okay. Sure. Come on back."

We walked down a short hall to his office. It was decorated much like the reception area. He sat behind a large cherry-finished desk while I took a chair on the other side of the desk.

"What's on your mind?" He leaned back in this chair.

Though Mitch and Shane were only business partners, Rothdale was such a tiny town, he already knew about Mitch's death. "I wanted to offer my sympathies about Mitch."

He blinked and gave a show of sadness that flickered over his features briefly. "Thank you."

"How long did y'all know each other?"

"Several years."

"Really? How'd y'all meet? Did you go to school together or something?"

"We met at the golf course. I'd heard he was looking for investors for the clinic—" He cocked his head, then glanced at his watch. "I'm not sure why you want to know all this. Is there a property you were interested in or something?"

"Mere curiosity is all."

"I don't understand why you're here." He looked at his watch.

"I see you're busy, so I'll cut to the chase. I'm wondering if you know who would want to hurt Mitch? He was found dead at home. And I'm wondering

CHAPTER TWENTY-THREE

why."

He hesitated. "Are you a cop?"

"No."

"Then I don't have to answer anything."

"That's true. You don't have to. But since he was going to be my best friend's stepdad, I'm concerned about what might've happened to him. If you have any insights to offer, it'd be most helpful."

A knock sounded on the office door, and the door opened. A man stuck his head in. "Hey…" Then she saw me, but he didn't seem to recognize me. He sniffed. "Oh. Sorry." He double-sniffed and rubbed his nose. He seemed fidgety, and he blinked rapidly. "Didn't know you had someone in here. I need to talk to you about that property out in Eastern Hills. The painters have seriously screwed up—"

Shane held up his hand to stop him. "Hang out in the front. I'll be right out."

"All right." He nodded and shut the door.

"Sorry for the interruption. That's my brother, Will. Part owner in this company." He rubbed his hands on his thighs. "Since you aren't interested in any of our properties, I need to ask you to leave so I can get some work done."

"I understand."

"I'll show you out."

I was disappointed I couldn't learn more from Shane about Mitch or the clinic. But, since I was leaving early, maybe I could catch up with Will and speak to him about my mom. "If you hear anything about Mitch's death, would you let me know? I'd really like to bring some closure to my friend."

"I understand. Sure. I'll let you know."

He followed me out to the lobby, where Will paced. Large veins protruded from his bony arms. I waited on the sidewalk for him to exit the building.

When Will exited, I approached him. "Excuse me."

He whipped around as if I was a ghost. "Yeah?"

"I'm sorry. Didn't mean to scare you. I only need a few minutes of your time, please."

"Who are you?"

"My name is Rook Campbell. I'm a friend of Mitch Thomas. He was recently killed."

He stared at me intently, fidgeting. "Yeah, I know. That's tough." He squinted. "You know, you look really familiar to me. Have we met before?"

I didn't want to bring up my mom too soon. It might scare him off, and he seemed awfully skittish. "Um, no. I don't think we've met." I flashed a flirty smile. "I think I'd remember if we'd met."

He seemed to relax. He tucked his hands in his jeans pockets. "What can I do for you?"

"Are you also a partner in the clinic?"

He licked his lips, wiped his mouth, scratched the back of his head, and shifted side to side. "No. Not anymore."

Interesting phrasing. It implied he had been a partner at one time. What changed? "Why not anymore?"

He wiped his mouth, his eyes darting. He shifted from foot to foot. "That's personal."

"Do you know of anyone else who might've been a partner in the clinic?"

"I've got to go." He started to walk off toward a dark silver Dodge Challenger, digging in his pocket for his keys.

I followed him. "Did you know Mitch's ex-fiancée is missing? We're desperate to find her."

He waved his hands in the air as if chasing off a fly. "Nah, nah, nah. I don't know nothing about any of that."

"Please, if you know anything."

He stopped and turned. "You a cop or something?" He extracted the keys from his pocket.

"No. Only a concerned friend trying to help my best friend find her mother. That's all."

He wiped his nose, then scratched his arms and legs with his key. The man fidgeted in constant motion. "Sorry, lady. Can't help you." He moved around the front of the car, unlocking it with his key fob. The car beeped.

"Please, a few minutes of time…"

CHAPTER TWENTY-THREE

"Lady, leave me alone. I done told you. I don't know nothing." He shook his head
climbed in his car.
"I shouted and sped away.
A piece of paper fluttered on the sidewalk. I snatched it up, turning over a prescription for hydrocodone between my fingers. It was from Mitch's clinic, and I was pretty sure that was Mitch's signature in the bottom corner. It was dated yesterday. The date of Mitch's death. Was Will one of the last people to see Mitch alive? I tucked the paper into my purse and felt as though I was being watched. Looking around, the Venetian blinds in the window of Decker Properties moved.

I crossed the square to my car, texting Jimmy as I walked: **I need to see U tonight if UR free.**

My phone rang. It was the lawyer handling the Four Wild Horses Distillery case against Holly, Len, and Keith. I was about to answer it when someone bumped my elbow. I stumbled and looked up into the face of Fox Graham, his pale blonde eyebrows like white caterpillars stuck to his red face. He was coming out of the lawyer's office beside the Decker properties office.

"You." He seethed. "Thanks for having my award stripped with all the money. You've destroyed my brand and my distillery. The media is crawling all over me. And now this." He held up a paper and shook it in my face. "I'm being sued by the KDP and the Guild for fraud."

My mouth dropped open, primed for words to fall out, but instead, I stared at him as my brain scrambled to compute what he was saying, how I should respond, or different potential escape routes.

He pointed at me, and I flinched, stepping back. "You stay away from me, you crazy life-eating witch. You've destroyed everything," he shouted, his voice cracking as veins bulged in his neck. "I was minding my own business and trying to have a successful distillery." He stepped around to his car. "Don't ever come near me again." He shot daggers at me before clapping his sunglasses over his blazing eyes. "Ever." He got into his car and sped off.

Stunned, I stumbled back against my car, my heart sinking into my feet, paralyzed with fear. I got into my car, locked the door, and started the engine while I looked around, unable to shake the uneasiness prickling under the surface of my skin.

My phone chimed and indicated a voicemail and chimed again with Jimmy's text. Wow. I was suddenly popular. Jimmy's text read **B there for dinner.** I listened to the voicemail. The paralegal was calling to set an appointment for a deposition in the Four Wild Horses case. Good. I'd call her back Monday. I needed to get back to the distillery and check my schedule. I'd likely need a few hours of time from work.

After work, I filled in the scratches on my car with the lime green nail polish I'd bought at the Food Mart. The days were getting ever shorter. Though it was only five-thirty, the sun was already low in the sky, casting an amber glow over everything. A light chill fell around me. I squatted by the driver's side door, covering the fine lines with broad strokes to conceal the writing. It wasn't a perfect match, but it was close enough. I was almost finished when Cam pulled into the drive.

He jumped out of his truck with a duffle bag and strode toward me. "Evening. What're you doing?" He removed his sunglasses, hanging them on the neck of his T-shirt as he studied the car.

"Covering up the worst of it."

"I called Bobby Crabtree today. He said he can open a spot for you in a few weeks."

"Wow, that's a long wait."

"It'll be worth it. He does good work."

"What's with the duffle bag?"

He lifted it, his bicep flexing. "I thought it'd be a good idea to be here in case anyone else tried to burn down your house again."

I rolled my eyes. "Well, Jimmy will be here soon, so you don't have to— "

"And what if he gets called out, and something happens while he's gone?"

I hadn't considered that. He had a point. But I had a duty to side with my current flame. "Did he tell you to do this?"

"I don't need his permission to do the right thing. You and Prim need someone here until that nut job is caught."

I didn't have the energy to argue with him. "Whatever, Cam," I sighed.

CHAPTER TWENTY-THREE

"Do whatever you want."Jimmy pulled up in the drive. He slid from his truck and strode toward us. "Hey sexy…" he scooped me up in his arms for a kiss. He released me and stood, hands on hips, studying my paint job. "What'cha up to?"

"Filling in the scratches."

"Not bad."

"Cam's found me a good deal on repairing the paint job."

He lifted his chin, his smile tightening a couple notches. "You should've said something. I could've helped you find someone."

I tipped my head at him, wondering why I should have to ask. Wouldn't most boyfriends offer something like that automatically? Wasn't that something a guy would do if he really cared about his woman? Cam had offered right away.

Jimmy seemed confused. "What?"

"Nothing." I shrugged. "No worries. It's taken care of now."

He nodded at Cam, who nodded back. I hated that things were still tense between them. Jimmy ran his eyes over Cam's duffle bag. "You taking a trip?" His lips formed a tight line.

"Nope. I'm staying the night."

"Is that so? Again?" Suspicion filled his eyes, and he looked at me.

I lifted my hands in surrender. "I didn't ask him to. He decided that all on his own. I told him there's nothing to worry about and that I don't need him to stay here."

Cam hooked his thumbs in his front pockets. "And I told her she can't rely on you to be here all night. You might get called away, and the attacker could come back while you're gone."

Jimmy licked his lips. His hazel eyes scanned the horizon. "He's right. You never know when I'll get called out. He should be here." I could tell it cost him a pound of pride to admit that.

"Told you," Cam said, slinging the duffle bag over his shoulder. "I'm going to go say 'hi' to Prim and get a glass of iced tea." He strode across the yard.

I murmured to Jimmy, "I'm not a princess in a tower."

"I know you're completely independent and self-sufficient and all the rest.

But the person who attacked you is really dangerous. Who knows when or if he'll be back. You can't be too careful." He kissed me again, a soft lingering kiss.

I played with the buttons on his uniform shirt, looking up into his face.

"Are you okay with Cam being here?"

"Do I really have a choice?"

"I don't want you two to fight. Can't y'all make up and be friends again?"

"We aren't fighting."

"There's still tension. A lot of it."

"It'll take time, but we'll be okay. If you stay out of it."

"Fine." I wrapped my arms around him and laid my ear against his chest, listening to the steady, comforting beat of his heart. After a moment, I looked up at him again. "You hungry? We're about to eat supper. Cheeseburgers, roasted potato wedges, and peas."

"Sounds great. I'm starving." He kissed my forehead.

We held hands and started toward the house. I said, "So, I had an interesting lunch."

"Yeah?"

I told him about my fruitless meetings with Shane and Will, but explained how Will seemed edgy. "Like all those people at Mitch's pill mill. He was too thin and fidgety, scratching everywhere, like bugs were crawling all over him. How's the DEA investigation going? Are they any closer to nailing them?"

"Slowly. I call them every day to get them to put a rush on it. But they have their methods."

"It's so frustrating."

"Welcome to my world. Bureaucracy and red tape on one side, criminals on another."

I rubbed my face. "I can't see how this all fits together. "I mean, what if it was Mitch, and he's stuffed her somewhere, we don't know where. And now that he's dead, we may never find her. She could starve to death."

He rubbed his chin, thinking. "I don't think it was Mitch."

"Why?"

CHAPTER TWENTY-THREE

"We've interviewed his girlfriend. She seemed pretty certain that the relationship with Patrice was completely over. And, she said that not long before he died, he'd been receiving calls that had, in her words, 'freaked him out.'"

"There has to be a connection between Patrice's disappearance and whatever dirty dealings were going on at the clinic."

"I agree. I've been all over the leads to find a direct connection. I'm not seeing it yet." His jaw tightened. "But I will."

Prim opened the door. "What're y'all doing? C'mon inside. It's almost supper time."

Dinner was tense, filled with idle chatter interspersed with long, awkward silences. Jimmy and Cam put on their fancy dinner manners, obviously avoiding any and all the hot topics that might lead to unrest: basketball, politics, and their relative relationships with me. But their defensive postures over their dinner plates made it clear they were in a territorial frame of mind, and things could turn sideways quickly.

Prim picked at her burger. "Do y'all know anything about the guy who set the fire a couple nights ago?"

"Not yet. It's going to be several days or even weeks. The lab is always backed up. But as soon as they have test results, they'll let us know."

Prim said, "Rook, that lawyer called back again today. They want to set a deposition with you in regards to what happened to you at your work." She was referring to the attacks against me by Holly a few weeks ago.

"Yes. Thanks. They called my cell, too. I'll have to call them Monday." I couldn't wait to tell the lawyers and courts everything, so I could play a part in putting away Holly, Len, and Keith for a very long time, if not the rest of their lives.

As we finished the meal and began serving up caramel cake and ice cream for dessert, my cell rang. It was Millie. I prepared the coffee maker and turned it on, because caramel cake necessitated coffee.

"Is Jimmy there with you?" Millie asked.

"Yeah, why?"

"I'd like to talk to him, if you don't mind."

"Sure. Don't you have his cell number?"

"I tried. But he must have it turned off."

"Is everything okay?"

Jimmy perked, listening to my side of the conversation. Prim and Cam fell silent as they piled cake and ice cream on the saucers and eavesdropped.

The magical aroma of coffee filled the air.

Millie said, "The kidnappers called me again. They said they want me to drop the money off at Johnson's Ferry at midnight tomorrow night."

"You're not going by yourself." I glanced at Jimmy, who studied me with concern.

"I have to. They told me to come alone. If I don't, they'll kill Mom."

"It's too dangerous. I'll come with you."

Jimmy swiped his hands through the air and shook his head vigorously. "Here's Jimmy." I handed him my phone.

He put his hands over the speaker and whispered, "You're out of your mind if you think you're going."

I waved him away. "Talk to Millie." I poured cups of coffee and helped carry dishes to the table.

Jimmy stood by the sink, looking out the window. Most of his side of the conversation consisted of mm-hms, uh-huhs, and okays. Then he said, "Let me think about that." He paused. "How about this. Meet me here tomorrow night at about nine. We'll come up with a plan to make sure that you and Patrice both come back alive."

Then he hung up and resumed his seat at the table.

"What's going on?" I scooped some cake and ice cream into my mouth.

Jimmy returned my phone to me. "What's going on is that you're not going to be involved any further in this."

"That's right," Prim and Cam said in unison.

I gaped at them all with a who-do-you-think-you-are face. "Y'all are ganging up on me now, I see."

Cam said, "I guess you'll have to live with the horrible condition of being cared about and protected." Jimmy's eyes cut to Cam as he drank his coffee. Cam didn't seem to notice, or, if he did, he ignored it. He said to Jimmy, "So

CHAPTER TWENTY-THREE

what are you going to do to get Patrice back?"

Jimmy ate a bite of ice cream. "They want her to make the drop at Kentucky River. Alone, with no police presence, of course."

Cam nodded. "Where at?"

"On the Franklin County bank near the covered bridge at Johnson's Ferry."

"I'm familiar with the place," Cam said.

I knew it too. A chill prickled my skin. "What a creepy place to be at midnight."

Jimmy eyed me steadily. "And a deadly one. Out in the middle of the woods. By the water. Not a soul around. Very easy to disappear someone in those circumstances."

My voice raised a pitch or two as fear dug into my shoulders and neck. "She can't go out there alone, either."

"She won't. I'll go with her." He chewed a bite of cake.

"You just said it's too dangerous."

He looked at me like I had three heads. "Babe, I'm an officer. I do this every day. I'm trained for these situations."

That was true, but that didn't guarantee he'd come home alive. I didn't say that. This was the downside of dating an officer. The constant worry. Instead, I said, "How are you going to avoid detection? They wanted her alone."

He thought for a moment as he chewed his food. "I'm thinking I'll hide in the back seat under a dark blanket or something. Or maybe she can drive my truck, and I'll hide in the bed under a tarp."

"But what if there's more than one guy? You'll need backup. Shouldn't you take backup?"

"Of course I will. If I can."

"I could go," Cam said.

I snapped my head around. "What? Are you crazy?" My voice had officially reached shrill. "You don't know what you're doing. You'll get yourself killed."

"I can help," Cam argued.

Jimmy studied us. "She's right. You can't go, either. Sorry, man. The liability and everything. I can't allow a civilian to get involved."

Cam sank. "I understand. I guess." He said, to me, "Looks like it's just you and me. I'll make sure you stay out of trouble."

I chuckled. "And who will keep an eye on you?"

"I reckon that'll be your job, then."

Jimmy glanced between us, his eyes lit with suspicion.

Prim paused with a spoonful of ice cream near her mouth. "Blind leading the blind right there."

Cam and I laughed. Jimmy didn't seem amused by our apparent camaraderie. He hung around for an hour or so after dinner to watch TV with us. When Prim went to bed, he stood. "I probably need to go. Long day tomorrow."

I stood too. "I'll walk you to the truck."

Cam stared daggers at the TV. He only said "bye" to Jimmy after Jimmy said it first. Wrapped in an afghan from the couch, I followed Jimmy out to his truck. The crisp air hit my neck, and I pulled the blanket tighter. Crickets chirped. The stars winked like sequins on a dress. Being able to see the stars in the sky was the best part of living in the country. Seeing them so clearly always gave me a little happy tickle inside my chest.

Jimmy dropped a pensive kiss on my lips.

"Are you all right?" I asked.

"I'm fine. Why?"

"You seem annoyed or upset."

He worked his mouth, puckering and straightening his lips. He sighed and looked down at the ground, hands on his hips as he kicked at a clump of grass.

"What is it? What's the problem?"

"I don't want to get into it." Defensiveness edged his voice.

This wasn't my first rodeo. My upper back tightened, and my body braced for an argument. "Something's clearly wrong. You might as well spit it out and get it over with."

"Fine. I don't like Cam hanging around. I don't want him here. With you. Alone."

I lifted my hand and tipped my head as anger pumped through my veins.

CHAPTER TWENTY-THREE

"Hold on a hot minute while I try to figure out which part to be angry at first. The part where you're insinuating you don't trust me to be alone with Cam? Or the part where you're being a hypocrite after, not two hours ago, you stood in my kitchen and said Cam should be here to protect me in case the attacker returns? And where you had him stay here last night for my protection."

"I know, I know." He cupped his hands over his nose and mouth. "I'm acting like a jerk. I don't like it either."

"Then stop."

"I can't. I'm—" He sighed again.

"Jealous? Seriously?" Shaking my head, I rolled my eyes up to the sky. "Well, do you want me to send him home?"

"No. Definitely not. You do need the protection."

"I have a shotgun."

"And so does Cam. You need the backup in case things go sideways. Forget I said anything. I've got to go." He opened the truck door, and the overhead light came on. A moth fluttered around our heads.

"Hold on, mister. You're not getting out of this that easily." He stopped and faced me, leaning one arm on the door. "If you're jealous, it's because you don't trust me. Or him. Or both."

He slumped, defeated. His face was drawn in dismay. "It's clear y'all still have feelings for each other, Rook. It's *so* obvious."

"You're crazy. I mean, I still consider him a friend and all, but—"

"No." He shook his head. "It's in the way you look at each other." He pinched together his thumb and index finger. "In that little split-second-too-long eye contact. The way your eyes, and his, shine with a certain light. A light that isn't there when you look at me."

My breath caught, and guilt like a stone lodged in my throat. I swallowed, and the stone inched down my esophagus and dropped into my stomach. "I don't know how I look at him. I don't do it on purpose."

"Of course. I'm not saying that."

"I-i-it's probably because I've known him longer a-a-and we have a shared history. For all I know, I probably look at Prim the same way." Boy, I was desperately reaching for an explanation. I didn't want to be in love with Cam. Things were too complicated with him. I wanted to move on. I had moved on.

He chuckled. "No. You definitely don't look at Prim the same way. And Cam looks at you like a Rottweiler ogling a steak dinner. I sat there at that table tonight and felt like a fool." His voice tightened with emotion. "I can't do it, Rook."

Tears pressured my eyes. "You can't do what?"

"I can't be caught between you and him. I can't spend time with you, growing close to you, knowing that you're thinking about him, wanting him. All while destroying my friendship with him. If I thought for one minute you could love me the way you love him, I'd give up my friendship with him like that." He snapped his fingers.

My voice turned watery. "But I don't want him. I'm not thinking about him."

"Babe, I'm a cop. I read people for a living. I know what I'm seeing, and I can't be a part of it. I've got to go. Goodnight." He started to get in his truck.

"Wait. What are you saying? Are you saying we're breaking up? You don't want to see me anymore?" Tears brushed my cheeks. I turned my head and swiped them quickly with the afghan.

He climbed up in his seat and stared out the windshield. He released a heavy sigh and rubbed his face. "Maybe taking a break wouldn't be the worst thing. "

"But I don't want to take a break, Jimmy. I want to be with you. "

"Darling, I don't think you know what you want. I've got to go. 'Night."

"But, wait—"

He slammed the door and started the engine.

I watched him drive off, like Scarlett watching Rhett walk away. Numbness and confusion overcame me. I didn't know what I felt.

I returned to the house and fumbled around in the back of the pantry, pulling out the bottle of Mermaid Cove's Summer Nights I'd recently bought when Jimmy and I had toured the place. I grabbed a couple of snifters in case Cam wanted a drink too.

CHAPTER TWENTY-THREE

I flopped down on the couch, broke the seal on the bottle, and poured a drink. "You want one?"

"What's wrong?" Cam asked.

"Jimmy and I might be breaking up. Not sure."

"How can you not be sure?"

I didn't want to talk about it, and I certainly didn't want to discuss it with Cam. I wanted him to go home so I could sit with myself and pick apart what I was feeling—or not feeling. Then I wanted to re-numb it with bourbon. It was Friday night—I didn't have anywhere to be the next morning—so I didn't care if I woke up with a hangover. "You want a drink or not?"

"Uh, sure. I guess. What is it?"

"A peach bourbon whiskey. Summer Nights. Patrice's distillery makes it."

"Sure. Pour me some."

I poured two fingers in his snifter and filled mine at least half full. I sat back on the couch, wrapped the afghan tight around me, slammed back my drink, and poured another. The summery peach bourbon lit my throat on fire, and a warm tingly sensation oozed through my body.

"Whoa there, tiger." Cam drank from his glass. "This ain't that kind of bourbon. This is for sipping."

"I know that, but this is all I have in the house."

"You want to talk about it?"

"Nope. What's on Netflix?"

"Everything seemed fine when he left."

I glared at the TV. "I don't want to talk about it. Play a show. Any show. Now, please."

He grabbed the remote and scanned through a few shows until he landed on *IT Crowd*. "I like this show. It's pretty funny."

"Fine." I didn't care. I was too busy ruminating on what Jimmy had said. It didn't track. I swallowed the last of my drink and poured another, my head swimming. Maybe he was seeing someone else and was looking for a way out. Because I didn't believe I was behaving any differently toward him or Cam or anyone. Maybe that was the problem. I wasn't behaving any differently. Did I love Jimmy? Of course not. We'd only been dating a few weeks. And then he'd said I looked at Cam as if I still loved him. Nonsense. I scoffed aloud.

Cam paused the show. "What?"

The room was swirling now. I turned to him. "Look at me." He did. I searched his face. I didn't see anything out of the ordinary. He always looked like that. Messy hair, brilliant blue eyes, sensual, plump lips. Kissable lips. Velvety soft. Yet strong. Never mind that. "What do you see? Am I looking at you funny, or different, or in a sexy way?"

Befuddlement and amusement intertwined, sporting over his features. "Uh." He chuckled. "No. In fact, I can hardly see your eyes because you're too tipsy to hold them open."

"I'm not thipsy." I forced my eyes wider. "Look again."

"I don't know what I'm looking for, Rook."

I rolled my eyes and polished off my drink. I reached for the bottle.

He grabbed the bottle away. "It's time to stop with this and start talking."

Though my head swam in a peachy bourbon haze, I wasn't so drunk that I'd spill my guts. Besides, what if I said something that would make Jimmy even angrier with me? Or what if I triggered another fight between Jimmy and Cam?

Cam sat the bottle on his end table, brushing my hair from my face. "I don't know what's going on with you and Jimmy..." His hand slid down my arm and held my hand. "But I'm here for you if you want to talk. Okay?"

I nodded. "All I want is to be happy."

"And you deserve to be."

His phone rang. He looked at the phone, then silenced it. He sent a quick text and tucked his phone away.

"I don't want to make anyone else unhappy."

He smiled. "You should probably go to bed."

I nodded. "Yup." I shot up from the couch. That was a mistake. The room tipped sideways, and I fell forward. My arm came down on the corner of the coffee table as I landed on all fours. Fortunately, I was too numb with drink to feel the cut on my arm.

"Whoa. Hey there, champ." Cam jumped up.

CHAPTER TWENTY-THREE

I broke out in laughter.

"You okay?"

I nodded, snort-laughing as I rolled over to sit on my bottom.

"Is that blood?" He grabbed my arm and flipped it over to examine it. "Yep. Party's over. Let's get you cleaned up and put to bed." He grabbed me around the waist and helped me stand. "There's no way I can lift you. I'm too sore from my workout this afternoon."

"I can walk," I pushed back from him, staggering several steps before falling against Prim's chair.

"Get over here." He grabbed me around the waist. "Lean on me. But don't get blood on me. Hold your arm like this." He twisted my forearm upward and held it in place.

I started singing "Lean on Me."

"Shh. Don't wake Prim."

Lowering my voice, I whisper-sang "Lean on Me" through giggles all the way up the stairs to the bathroom. Cam shut us inside and washed the blood off my arm. He whispered, "Just a scratch. We should still clean it. Hold this rag on it." He clapped the wet cloth over my arm, and I held it in place while he searched the cabinets. When he found the peroxide, he poured it over the wound then taped some gauze over it. He walked me to my room, clicked on the light on the bedside table, and pulled back the covers. I dropped down on the cool white sheets. The room twirled as he removed my shoes and placed my feet on the bed. It was nice not being in control for once. It was nice not caring or worrying. It was nice to exist with this happy, dancing feeling inside my skin without any concern for tomorrow. But the twirling slowed and subsided with each passing minute.

He pulled the blankets over me. "Goodnight. Sleep tight," he whispered. He bent down to place a kiss on my forehead, but I shifted my face to grab his lips with mine and pulled him down on top of me, kissing him fervently. He wasn't backing away. He wasn't saying no. And neither was I. Kissing him felt like home. Like putting on a pair of cozy PJs and drinking cocoa after hours of shoveling snow. Jimmy wasn't a bad kisser, but it was different, like traveling to a foreign destination. It was exciting, new, but not home.

Even though I enjoyed traveling, it didn't compare to home. Being away only made coming home even better.

He stopped. Panting, he pushed away and sat on the edge of my bed.

"What are you doing?"

"I can't do this. Not if you and Jimmy aren't officially over. And even if you were, this would be only a rebound. Plus, you've been drinking. And I didn't want to tell you…"

"Tell me what?" I sat up in bed, a sense of doom lowering around me.

"I started dating a girl about a week ago…."

My stomach bottomed out.

My mouth dropped open, and I tried to process what he was saying through the bourbon fog in my brain. "Who?" I suspected I knew, but I was hoping I was wrong. *Please don't say Melissa Bantree. Please, not Melissa.*

"Melissa Bantree."

It was as if he'd punched me in the gut. "You've got to be kidding me. You *know* how horribly she treated me in high school. I've told you those stories. And *she's* the one you chose?" I couldn't breathe. "You low-down, scum-licking…." I couldn't think of anything bad enough to call him. I grew still, hard, and icy. Yet, I was pretty sure flaming daggers shot out of my eyes. I growled, "Get. Out. Get out of here this instant" If I were completely in my head, I'd know that I was being unfair and unreasonable. But none of that mattered as I grabbed the covers and jerked them over me, and flopped onto my side with my back to him. I felt only betrayed.

He touched my shoulder and tried to roll me over to face him, but I resisted. "Come on, Rook. Don't be mad."

"Leave. Now." My head throbbed with rage and bourbon. "I just want everyone to leave me alone." A case of the self-pities was crashing down hard on me and that was better indulged alone.

He sighed, and I felt his weight lift off the bed. "Fine. I get it. It's okay for you to date my best friend, but I'm not allowed to move on at all. Good night, Rook."

The beauty of bourbon was that I didn't sit up all night worrying about my problems. I went straight to sleep. Or passed out. *Tomayto- tomahtoh.*

CHAPTER TWENTY-THREE

I woke in the morning, mouth full of cotton, head thick as cement, and full of the heebie-jeebies. I'd had bad dreams about being chased and attacked. Again. And then there was something about my mom from my dream that I couldn't remember. I squinted at the morning sun. Breakfast scents touched my nose.

Groaning, I squeezed my head between my hands. Not just to stop the throbbing, but to maybe force some thoughts, any thoughts, and memories through the deep fog. Inexplicably, annoyance and guilt, and shame pulled a dark cloud around me. As if something bad was about to happen. Or maybe it had already happened. That sounded closer to the truth.

I pushed myself out of bed and staggered to the bathroom to tend to my morning routine. After a hot shower, I donned fleece pajama bottoms, sloppy T-shirt, and fuzzy socks. I slumped down the stairs to the kitchen. Coffee would make everything better. It always did.

Cam sat at the table with Prim, eating gravy and biscuits.

I froze in the doorway. Seeing him opened the floodgate on the memories from last night. Lightning strokes of anger, embarrassment, humiliation, shame, and all their variants flashed through my body as a thin film of sweat broke out in a few uncomfortable places.

"Morning." He chomped his food.

He had a lot of nerve to sit there at my table, eating food my grandma had prepared, pretending like nothing at all had happened the night before. Scratching his eyes out would be too good for him. Glowering, I grunted and lowered my head, beelining to the coffee pot without speaking.

"Morning, hon," Prim said to me. "You in a bad mood?"

"Yeah. I guess," I muttered, preparing my coffee. I grabbed a couple of biscuits and sat at the table on the other side of Prim, where I didn't have to face Cam directly.

"Don't you want any gravy?" Prim asked. "I thought you loved my gravy."

"I do, but my stomach is a little messed up. I'll settle for biscuits right now."

Cam said to Prim, "She had a rough night."

"Why?" Prim sipped her apple juice.

"Her and Jimmy…." Then he pulled a face that indicated we'd ended unhappily.

"Shut. Up." I glared at him over my coffee mug.

"Hey now," Prim warned. "Let's not get ugly at the table. What's going on with you and Jimmy? Did y'all break up?"

"Not really. I don't know. We might."

"What happened? Everything was fine when I went to bed."

"It's complicated. I don't really want to talk about it." Certainly not while hungover and sweating from humiliation at recalling my behavior with Cam. And certainly not in front of Cam. "Maybe you should go home, Cam. You've caused enough trouble here, don't you think?" I jumped up from the table with my biscuit and coffee. "Prim, leave the dishes. I'll get them later." I retreated to the living room with the remains of my meager breakfast.

I flopped on the couch, cross-legged, and pulled an afghan around me. I flipped on the TV to catch the local news. Cam followed. I tried to ignore him, but he sat next to me on the couch. My skin grew hot again.

"What's wrong with you?"

"I'm fine." I snapped my head around and hissed. "You seriously need to get out of here. I can't stand the sight of you right now. Also, I don't need you telling things to Prim that'll make her worry. I guarantee she's in there ruminating on what could've happened between me and Jimmy."

"I didn't think about that. Sorry."

"That's right. You don't think. Ever. Unless it's about yourself." That wasn't true. I knew that. He'd done a lot to help me and Prim lately, and his own parents, but I couldn't be fair and angry. And lashing out at him was the only thing making me feel better. And worse. Gah! I wished I could cut the wires on my emotions and live as an unfeeling Vulcan like Mr. Spock. "You go through the world breaking things and breaking people."

He clamped his mouth tight, little knots in his jaw bulging. He nodded, then stood. "I'm going to pretend you didn't say any of that." He grabbed his duffle bag and fished his keys out of his pocket. "I've got some stuff to do for my parents on the farm today, anyway. I'll be back tonight in case Jimmy and Millie need help with the ransom drop-off. Because I'm such a

CHAPTER TWENTY-THREE

selfish jerk."

That stung, but I didn't back down. "You betrayed me. Melissa Bantree? Melissa-freaking-Bantree!"

He stood over me. "How dare you even think of being jealous about her when you're dating my best friend. *You* couldn't have picked anyone else? Was that your little way of getting revenge for Jacie?" He pointed his finger in my face. I slapped it away. He continued, "But the best part of your little plan is that you waited until Jacie and I were broken up, the engagement called off. Then you decided to hop into bed with my best friend. He's like a brother to me."

I shot up to my feet. "We did *not* hop into bed," I whispered. We were having one of those fights like parents have when the kids are in the next room.

"Yeah, right."

"Ask him yourself. But what about you and Melissa?" I crossed my arms over my chest. "Are you dating her on purpose just to get back at me because of Jimmy?"

"No. And what about last night when you wanted to take me to bed?"

"That was the alcohol." And the loneliness that Jimmy hadn't managed to assuage, but I'd rather eat broken glass than say that out loud. "Because I guarantee, if I'd been in my right mind, I'd never even let you touch me."

He poked my arms and shoulder. "Like this? Or this? I'm touching you. Touching. Touching."

"Stop it." I slapped his hand away again. "You're so immature. Are you ever going to grow up?"

He smirked. "I wonder how Jimmy would've felt about that if he were to find out? And you say I'm the one who goes around breaking people? Seems to me we're pretty much even on that score." He glared at me, his eyes full of pain and anger, maybe even a little disgust. "I'll see you later. Whether you like it or not." He stormed out.

"Not," I shouted as he slammed the door. I growled and threw myself down on the couch. I punched a pillow several times and pulled the afghan over my head, watching the TV through the little holes in the granny squares, swimming in my cesspool of mucky feelings: anger, distress, guilt, shame, sadness.

Prim stood in the doorway. "What in the world was all that about?"

"Cam being Cam."

"And Rook being Rook?"

"Hey. What's that supposed to mean?" I pulled the afghan off my head and looked at her.

She draped a dish towel on her shoulder and planted a hand on her hip. "You two are in each other's blood. I hope y'all will accept that soon and work it out."

"Don't you like Jimmy?"

"Jimmy's okay. He's fond of you and would be good to you, even if you had to compete with his job. But we all know the truth."

"What truth?"

She stuck out her bottom lip, and her eyes gleamed with knowing. The corner of her mouth inched upward as if she knew a great secret she was itching to tell. She turned and went back to the kitchen.

Great, now I was going to be forced to think it through. I hated it when she did that to me.

The news came on, and the anchorwoman discussed national news, then the sports anchor talked about the upcoming University of the Bluegrass Thoroughbreds basketball season, which, in Kentucky, was second only in popularity to Christmas.

Then the main anchor returned. "In local news, a pre-trial hearing is scheduled to take place on Monday in the case of a bourbon theft ring involving the Four Wild Horses Distillery last month."

I pushed away thoughts of Jimmy and Cam and sat forward on the couch.

"Holly Parker, Len Ashfield, and Keith Morton, all of Rothdale, Kentucky, are each expected to plead guilty in the theft of the rare Devil's Kiss bourbon from the Four Wild Horses Distillery last month. Additionally, Ms. Parker is expected to plead not guilty to two counts of first-degree murder in the deaths of co-workers Dewey Stiggers and Daryl Morton. Mr. Ashfield is expected to plead guilty to one count of accessory to murder in the Stiggers

CHAPTER TWENTY-THREE

case. Their bail has been set for two million dollars each. The third member of the theft ring, Mr. Keith Morton, is expected to turn state's witness in exchange for reduced charges. ."

While the anchorwoman relayed the story, B-roll filled the screen of Holly, Len, and Keith, all filing into court in orange jumpsuits, cuffed at the ankles and wrists. Without makeup, she looked hard and mean. Deep lines pulled down the sides of her mouth, and her eyes were hard little pebbles. Len and Keith both had been shaved, nearly bald, and hunched over as they shuffled, haggard, and defeated.

The anchor continued, "The attorney for Ms. Parker says that she had been lured into committing the crimes by Mr. Ashfield and plans to pursue a separate trial."

"That's not true," I said to the TV. "She was the mastermind."

Outside the courthouse, the attorney, a long-faced man with wavy silver hair and glasses, spoke, saying his client was innocent of the charges. He was surrounded by red-eyed, puffy-faced people I could only assume were Holly's family. There were two men. One older, one younger. Presumably, her father and husband. The older woman dabbing her eyes was clearly her mother. But there was another woman, younger, short and stout, with fawn-colored hair. Her hair was frizzy on the ends, dull, and one-dimensional, as if she'd recently had a bad box dye job. She wore sunglasses and looked away from the camera. I stared at her. If I didn't know better, she seemed to be ducking behind her parents. Yet, she looked familiar. The news broke for a commercial. If I could've stared at her longer, I might've been able to figure out where I'd seen her before. I squeezed my eyes shut and pressed my fingers to my forehead, trying to recall her face and features. But they were already morphing and warping into someone else and fading from memory completely.

Did I go to high school with her? Did she work at the Waffle House? I couldn't think straight enough to pull her name out of the fog and the headache. I needed Tylenol.

After rummaging through the kitchen pantry and the medicine cabinets in both bathrooms, I jogged down the stairs. "Prim, we're out of Tylenol.

I'm running out to the Blue Market. Do you need anything while I'm out?"

Prim settled in her recliner with her crochet work. "Nope, I'm okay." She flashed a pointed look over the edge of her glasses, looped the yarn, and pulled it through. "You know, I suspect Cam dating that floozy won't amount to a thing."

"I don't understand why he would date her, of all people."

Prim shrugged her bony shoulder, studying her last few stitches. "Sometimes we don't know what we want until we're forced to fight for it or lose it forever."

Chapter Twenty-Four

It was a typical autumnal day in Kentucky. A brilliant sun set against a blue sky the color of a robin's egg and enormous white clouds. Folks mowed their yards, raked the grass into piles. People crowded the grocery stores to prepare for barbecues, tailgates, bonfires, and game-watching parties. Yard sales and garage sales created congestion so I had to slow down to pass the cars parked on the shoulder. A boxy maroon sedan followed me at a healthy distance. After a left turn off my road and a couple miles' drive, I turned into the Blue Market parking lot. The maroon car pulled in behind me and parked at the gas pump. I didn't think anything of it. My primary concern was Tylenol.

The store was freezing inside and smelled faintly of dirty mop water. I wove through all the aisles, grabbed a packet of BC Powder, which was way better than Tylenol when downed with a caffeinated beverage. I picked up a Coke Zero and circus peanuts for Prim. She loved those spongy orange sugar puffs, though I couldn't for the life of me understand why. I wanted to stress eat every piece of chocolate in my field of vision. My mouth watered. No. There was plenty of junk food at home.

When I exited the store, I noticed the maroon car was still sitting in the gas bay. I couldn't make out the driver, because he or she wore a ball cap and was looking down, probably at a phone.

I locked myself in my car, poured the bitter BC Powder in my mouth, and chased it with a swig of Coke Zero. Sweet relief was not far behind. I cranked up the music, put on my sunglasses, and started home.

When I turned left out of the Blue Market, the maroon car was behind me, but at a distance. I sang along with "Kashmir." My headache began to fade.

Turning right on my road, I passed a few yard sales, slowing down to rubberneck. Maybe I could spot something I couldn't live without. I honked and waved at Birdie Harper and her sister Oda Dean Spurlock. Birdie was our resident hoarder and could be counted on to hit all the yard sales every weekend. Once I cleared the yard sale congestion, I continued on and noticed a large tree branch lying in the road. The car in front of me swept into the other lane to pass it. But I was concerned that it might cause someone to get hurt. I put on my hazard lights and parked my car on the shoulder. The maroon car rolled by. I got out of my car, grabbed the branch, and tossed it in the ditch.

A little voice in my gut warned me to be aware. The air grew still around me. The maroon car had stopped up ahead. The door was open, and a figure stood at the rear of the vehicle.

That's odd. The person lifted their arms, and a shot fired, missing me and striking my windshield. I ducked and ran around the passenger side of the car, trying to put distance between me and the shooter. Another shot rang out, hitting the ground beside me as I leapt out of the shallow ditch and ran hunched over around the back of my car.

Who was this whackadoo trying to kill me? I crawled into my car, and as I moved to shut the door, the bullet struck right below the side window. I screamed, slammed it closed, and scooted down in the seat. My windshield had a hole in the driver's side where the bullet had passed, and the glass around it was cracked, impeding my vision. I panic-honked my horn to warn any oncoming traffic, threw the car into reverse for several feet, as another bullet hit the front of my car. My car began idling roughly and jerked and knocked as I cranked the steering wheel to turn my vehicle in the opposite direction. A shot passed through my back glass and into my CD player. Screaming, I flew down the road as fast as my dying car would allow, but I could feel it giving out, sputtering, and jerking. One of the shots clearly hit an important component in my engine. My car rolled to a stop about a hundred yards from the closest yard sale.

With my car's last breath, I eased it into the ditch, grabbed my purse and

CHAPTER TWENTY-FOUR

keys, and popped out of the passenger's side, abandoning the dead car. I ran up the hill into the copse of trees and far enough into the tree line that I couldn't be easily spotted from the road in case the nut job in the maroon car had decided to come after me. I headed in the direction of the yard sale houses I'd passed. I decided not to stop at the first house because that would be expected if I'd been followed, so I stopped at the second house. I went deeper into the woods that trailed around behind the houses, running as best as I could through the fallen limbs and uneven ground.

Losing my breath, I stopped, leaned against the backside of an enormous oak, and pulled my phone out of my purse. A bullet had blown through it. The breath left my body. "Ohmigosh." I dropped the phone into my purse.

My right shoulder stung. I rubbed it and touched a warm, wet spot. Blood covered my hand. I was wearing a long-sleeved T-shirt and didn't have time to inspect the wound. I needed to get to safety. Continuing through the woods behind the houses, I ran at full speed which, given that I wasn't a runner, wasn't as fast as it felt. Trailing behind the second house, I rounded the far side of the home and blended in with the other yard salers. Mr. and Mrs. McTaggert owned the house and were deeply involved in our church. He was an elder, and she was the children's minister.

Skittish and glancing over my shoulder, I approached Miss Peggy, a chubby middle-aged lady sitting in a lawn chair inside her open garage. Her frosted blonde hair was pulled into a poofy ponytail. She wore jeans and a red cardigan over a gray T-shirt with an American flag splashed across the front.

She popped her gum and greeted me. "Hey, sweetie." Then she did a double-take and realized who I was. She let out a hoot and jumped to her feet to hug me. "Oh, honey. I'm so sorry I didn't recognize you at first." She smelled of roses and lilies. "It's so good to see you."

I stepped into the garage and ducked into the shadows, glancing over my shoulder. "It's good to see you too."

She picked up on the tension. "You okay? What's wrong?" She scanned the yard. "Why're you on foot?"

I spoke low so as to not draw attention of the shoppers. I lied to keep from scaring her. "My car broke down. Can I wait here until my ride gets here?"

"Sure. I don't mind one bit. I'll get you a lawn chair."

"Oh, no, please. Don't trouble yourself. I've been sitting all day." Truth be told, I didn't want to get comfortable. I wanted to be ready to run, if necessary. "I'll stand here against the wall, if that's okay. I won't be here long, anyway."

"Suit yourself." She looked me over, and her face filled with suspicion. "You know your arm's bleeding?"

"Yeah, uh, I scratched it really bad on my car door when I got out."

She tipped her head in disbelief. "Can I get you a drink?"

After running, I was pretty thirsty. "I'd love a glass of water if you have it."

"Sure." She opened the door to the house and shouted inside for Mr. McTaggert to bring a glass of iced water. She looked back at me. "You want me to clean that wound?"

"That's okay. I'll do it when I get home." I hung out by the garage door and peered outside, watching for a maroon car and the whacko driving it.

I borrowed Miss Peggy's phone and called 911. When the operator answered, I spoke in the calmest voice I could muster, "Hello, my name is Rook Campbell. I'm at the McTaggert residence on 112 Boone Creek Road. Someone tried to kill me. Ran me off the road and shot at me. A maroon sedan. I don't know what kind. Please send an officer."

While I waited, Miss Peggy expressed her concern for Prim and wanted to ask all sorts of questions about her health and care. I didn't want to talk about Prim in much detail, because I didn't want to start crying. I tried a few times to redirect the conversation to herself, her kids, and the church while I watched the road. Mr. McTaggert brought out a glass of ice water, waved, and smiled. He didn't hang around. He quickly disappeared inside the house. Smart man.

Then she said, "I heard you're seeing Deputy Duvall these days."

I about choked on my water. Oh Lord. I definitely wasn't about to discuss my love life with Miss Peggy.

Thankfully, I didn't need to answer. Deputy Ladonna Price arrived, lights

CHAPTER TWENTY-FOUR

flashing, attracting the gapes and stares of the yard sale crowd. I handed the glass to Miss Peggy, thanked her for her hospitality, and ran to meet Deputy Ladonna, glancing around for a maroon car and maniacal killer.

Deputy Ladonna's soft vanilla jasmine perfume jarred against her tough policewoman persona. She reached for the radio on her shoulder. "You reported a shooting?"

"Yes, ma'am." I told her everything.

"What sort of sedan?"

"I don't know, and I can't look it up because my phone is dead."

Deputy Ladonna typed something into her phone and then handed me her phone, the screen lit with a ton of boxy sedans. "Any of those look like the car?"

I scanned through them and found one that looked most similar. "This one, I think."

"A Caprice." She sat in her car to radio in the details. A scratchy voice on the radio issued a BOLO for the maroon Caprice in our location and warned the driver is considered to be armed and dangerous.

"I'll run a search on the car when I get back to the station. In the meantime, let's get you an ambulance."

"No, that's okay. It's not bad. The bullet only grazed me."

"Let me see." She inspected the wound through the hole in my T-shirt. "Hm. I have a first aid kit in the car. I think I should at least clean the wound and patch you up before it gets infected. C'mere." She led me to her car and pulled a first aid kit out of her trunk. She opened the back door and directed me to sit.

Great, the OLN was going to have a field day with this one. Now poor Prim was going to get a slew of calls about her outlaw granddaughter.

She cleaned the wound. Then I asked if she could take me home. I pointed up the road. "It's only about a mile that way. I don't have another ride right now and I don't feel safe walking."

"Do you feel well enough to take me to your car first? I won't keep you there. I only want to check for evidence before something happens to it."

"Sure. I understand. I feel fine."

A corner of her full lips flashed a hint of a goodwill smile. As she closed the door, she addressed the crowd. "Nothing to see here, folks. Go on with your shopping. Have a nice day."

I guided her to my poor little car, surrendered in the ditch.

"Stay here." She got out of the car and, with a hand on the butt of her gun, she eased toward my lime green Ford Fiesta. She peered in the window and studied the bullet holes, and searched all around the car. The late afternoon sun fired up the leather seats in the back of the cruiser. A thin film of sweat formed along my hairline, and the air grew stuffy. She made a call, then got back in the car.

She cranked her neck to look at me over her shoulder. "We'll wait for the tow truck. It's going to take the car to the police impound, where we can get our forensics team to look for bullets. Maybe we can identify the type of weapon. Then I'll take you home."

As soon as I entered the house, Batrene and Prim met me at the door.

Prim said, "Why on earth is Deputy Ladonna bringing you home? What happened?" Her eyes bugged, and her raspy voice pitched a few notches. "And what's that bandage on your arm?"

Oh, Lord, help me. Here we go. Parched and sweaty from sitting in the squad car, I poured a glass of iced tea, my arm tender under the gauze and the tape pulling against my skin with my movements. I downed that glass of tea and poured another. "Can I go change my shirt first? I feel naked with only one sleeve."

"No, ma'am." Prim sat in a chair at the table, her veined bird legs spread open as she leaned her bony arm on the table. "You're going to sit right here and tell me what the devil is going on. Why on earth are Peggy McTaggert, Birdie Harper, and Oda Dean Spurlock all calling me to tell me you got a bloody arm and the deputy has picked you up? You ain't going nowhere until I hear the truth." Prim glared at me over the rim of her sparkly glasses.

Batrene sat down at the table, too, tugging her purple floral T-shirt into place over her stomach rolls. "Are you okay?"

"I'm fine."

"What've you got yourself into, girl?" Prim asked, clearly in no mood to

CHAPTER TWENTY-FOUR

be trifled with.

I sighed. "I was ambushed." I relayed the story, *again*.

Prim and Batrene blinked at each other. Prim said, "That's the craziest thing I've heard."

Batrene offered another idea that I'd already considered while I sweated in the backseat of Ladonna's cruiser. "I wonder if it was the same person who tried to burn down your house?"

Sheriff Goodman was not happy about being called to my house again for the second time in a matter of only a few days. He removed his hat as he stepped into the house and hung it on the back of the nearest chair at the kitchen table. He nodded to Prim and Batrene. "Ladies."

Prim and Batrene each occupied the head of the table. Prim offered him a cup of coffee or iced tea. He politely declined both.

He hooked his thumbs in his belt, sighed, and looked down at me. "Let's talk." He pulled out a chair and sat down, the chair creaking with protest beneath his weight.

Once again, I told the story.

He leaned an elbow on the table. Stroking his mustache. "I've never in my life seen one woman involved in so much drama."

"Ain't that the truth," Prim grumbled, munching on soda crackers and ginger ale. "Got my stomach all in knots."

A stone of disappointment sank cold and jagged into my stomach. "I'm sorry." I swiped at the condensation on my glass with my finger. "I don't want to have all these problems or to cause you grief. All I've ever wanted is peace and quiet and to go about my little life without people trying to take it from me or hurt my loved ones."

Goodman sat back, clasping his hands in his lap below his paunch, studying me with suspicion, disbelief, and exasperation. "I don't understand. Why would someone want to kill you?"

"Seems to me it's related to the ongoing kidnapping case. Which is probably also related to the attack on my house and car and the weird phone calls." "What makes you say so?"

I relayed the story of my visit to the Decker Properties office and how Will seemed shady, possibly involved in drugs, and Shane was a business partner with Mitch Thomas, now dead, who, as it turns out, is most likely running a pill mill.

A different light entered Goodman's eyes: curiosity, interest, and questioning. "Now that is interesting." He cocked his head. "Why didn't you bring this information forward as soon as it happened?"

I hemmed. "I told Jimmy."

His mustache drew downward.

"He didn't tell you?"

His hesitation before answering told me everything. Jimmy hadn't spoken to Goodman. The sheriff recovered quickly. "Yeah, um…" He looked down at his chest pocket, fumbling for his notepad and pen. "Seems I recall him mentioning it earlier. I've been working another case that's got me a little distracted."

I pretended to believe him so he could save face, making a mental note to talk with Jimmy when I saw him. If I saw him. I wondered what else Jimmy hadn't told Goodman. I wanted to ask, but I also didn't want to get Jimmy in deeper trouble. "Did you happen to get any plates on the car or a description of the shooter?"

"No. The car was parked too far away. And the shooter…." I sighed and rolled my eyes to the ceiling to think. "Was far away, so it was hard to tell. He seemed short, medium build. White. He wore a camo jacket, jeans, tennis shoes, black ball cap, sunglasses." I shrugged. "Pretty nondescript, really."

He jotted notes. "Hair color?"

"Couldn't tell."

"Anything else at all that you can think of?"

Prim said, "You think it's the same person who was out here the other night?"

He nodded. "It's more likely than not."

She pushed her glasses up on her nose. "Why do they want to hurt her?"

"Evidently, she's seen or heard information that has upset someone." He turned his attention back to me. "Rook Campbell, you've got to be one of

CHAPTER TWENTY-FOUR

the unluckiest people I've ever met."

"What can I say, I'm a magnet for drama. So let me guess…." I sighed and sat back in the chair. "You have no idea, no leads, and if you hear of something, you'll let me know."

That actually evoked a half-laugh. "That's about the sum of it."

His phone rang. "Excuse me, ladies." He stood and stepped into the living room for a few moments. I heard a few "uh-huhs" and "okays" before he said, "Keep me posted." He returned to the kitchen, dropping his phone in his pocket. "Deputy Price got a few hits on the maroon Caprice. She and another officer are starting the hunt now. Maybe we'll soon flush out our shooter."

"That's good news." Prim and I smiled at each other. "Have you discovered anything at all from the clues collected out here the other night?"

"I'm sorry. It's all in the state police lab. It can take weeks."

Nodding, I cupped my tea glass. "What about Patrice? Have y'all stumbled on any leads as to who might have her?"

"Not yet. We're still looking into the people who were closest to her."

"What about Mitch Thomas' background and his connections? He's definitely shady."

"We're especially interested in him." He stood and tucked his notepad and pen in his chest pocket. "I appreciate your concern and understand your fear. I think your attacker may be connected to this kidnapping. It's a matter of finding one or two pieces to make the whole puzzle fit together."

"I want to believe you…" Something felt wrong, like when my pantyhose got twisted tight around one leg while gaping around the other. Yet, I couldn't think of who else would want me dead.

A car door slammed outside. I stood to peek out the window over the kitchen sink while Goodman lowered his head to follow my gaze. Jimmy had arrived. Goodman and I started toward the door at the same time. He turned and said, "If you don't mind, I need a moment with my deputy."

I stepped back.

He clapped his hat on his head and stormed out of the house.

I bit down on my tongue and stood at the kitchen sink, looking out the window. Goodman crossed the yard making it apparent how he'd earned the nickname "Bulldog." His broad shoulders rounded, and his head lowered between them, his chin jutting and his belt struggling to keep his pants on his narrow hips. He stood toe to toe with Jimmy and hands on his hips. Though I couldn't hear what he Bulldog sai, it was clear he was chewing Jimmyup one side and down the other like a squeaky toy. Jimmy kept his head up, but his eyes lowered. When Goodman finished, he climbed in his police SUV and flew out of the drive in a cloud of dust and gravel.

Jimmy blew out a breath and watched Goodman drive away. He rubbed his face, shook his head, and started for the house.

I threw on a jacket, stuffed my feet in a pair of tennis shoes, and went out to meet him. A chill snaked through the evening air, and the scent of hickory smoke from distant fireplaces and stoves tickled my nose, exciting in me a sudden desire to go camping and roast marshmallows over a fire. One of my favorite autumn activities. Maybe Jimmy would want to go with me. That is, if he didn't break up with me. Actually, maybe it was best if Millie and I went. A girls' glamping trip might be the just the thing when all this was over.

I threw my arms around Jimmy's neck and hugged him, my arm aching. He accepted the hug stiffly and pulled away. His eyes were hard.

"What did he say to you?"

"He told me if I keep information from him again, he was going to take my badge."

"Why did you do that, anyway? He's your boss."

"I know. It was stupid. But I thought I could make a name for myself. I'd like to be sheriff one day. I thought if I could close some big cases, I could run against him in the next election."

"That's crazy. He has a ton more experience and more connections than you."

"Yeah, but a lot of people are upset with him because he hasn't been keeping his promises."

"I imagine it's been pretty difficult weeding out the drugs. I mean look at the case we're…you're…dealing with now. I wonder how many other pill

CHAPTER TWENTY-FOUR

mills there are."

"Whose side are you on?"

"Yours, of course—"

"Sure sounds like it." He rolled his eyes.

My voice rose a couple notches. "I am on your side. But you could use a little more experience. He's been doing this for at least thirty."

"We'll see…" he said, which was his way of changing the subject. He continued, "Why didn't you call me when you were attacked?"

"You heard?"

"Yeah. It was all over the scanner. I came out as soon as I heard."

I crossed my arms, my wound screaming at me. I shrugged. "I thought you were still mad at me, and I didn't want to bother you."

He sighed. "I'm not mad at you."

"Seemed that way to me last night. And you're talking about breaking up with me. What do you call it?"

"I was being stupid. Jealous of Cam. That's all."

"You don't need to be jealous of him. If anything was going to happen, it would've already." I shoved back the memory of the kiss with Cam the night before. In my mind, it didn't count because it was the alcohol talking, not me.

He scratched the back of his neck. "You're right. I'm sorry. It was stupid."

I stepped closer and slipped my arms around his waist. "So, you're going to keep me?" I smiled up at him.

Smoothing his hand over my hair, he said, "Mm. Maybe for a little while longer."

"You want to really prove you're no longer angry at me?"

He lifted his brows and pulled me closer. "Now, this sounds interesting." He smiled crookedly, displaying a dimple. He leaned down and kissed me.

"Take me to get a new phone. Mine's been shot."

We had just returned from the store with my new iPhone and were getting out of Jimmy's truck when a pair of headlights swam over us. We froze like a couple of deer and squinted at the lights.

Jimmy said, "Looks like Cam."

Unfortunately, it had already been decided that he was going to stay with Prim and me for our protection tonight. I could hardly stand the sight of him. All I could see when I looked at him was Melissa Bantree and her too-short-shorts flirting with him at the festival.

Cam stopped and saluted Jimmy. "Deputy Cam reporting for duty."

Jimmy smiled. "Glad you're here. You can keep a close eye on Rook since she can't stay out of trouble."

"What do you mean?"

"It's not important," I said, trying to re-route where this conversation was headed. "Let's go inside and get dinner while we wait on Millie." I turned toward the house, and the men fell in step behind me.

Jimmy told Cam what had happened to me with the shooter.

"What?" Cam squeaked. "Are you serious?" He was beside me as I stepped up to open the screened porch door. "Why didn't you say something? You could've called me…or-or-or—"

"Or what? What could you do? You're not the law. And furthermore, you're not my daddy, or my husband, or my boyfriend. I don't have to tell you a darned thing." I stomped away, letting the screen door slam.

Behind me, Jimmy asked Cam, "What was that about?"

A supper of chili and grilled cheese sandwiches developed out of a fume of my venomous feelings and a bit of slamming things around. The men wisely disappeared into the living room to entertain Prim. By the time we sat down to eat, I'd calmed down, though still sulking to myself.

After supper, we sat in the living room watching the evening news. Rothdale, small town that it was, had limited news, and so we often received repetitive stories. Right now, the story was repeating the information about the scheduling of the pretrial hearing. Then the anchor piggybacked from that intro. She said, "We go now to the family of Holly Parker, who claim that their daughter is innocent. From there unfolded a bunch of nonsense about Holly's supposed innocence

Watching the segment, I did feel sorry for her family because it was clear

CHAPTER TWENTY-FOUR

they'd been blindsided either because she was that good at manipulating them, or because they'd been that oblivious. Holly's mother, a chubby, blonde-dyed, jewelry-bedecked woman, dabbed at her eyes while Holly's husband and father sat with downcast faces.

I looked away from the TV to text with Millie. Millie texted that she was on her way to my house. I was about to invite her to eat supper at my house if she wanted. But I glanced at the TV, catching a glimpse of Holly's sister on the television. I put my phone down. The woman had rough skin, green eyes, and fading fawn-colored hair. I remembered those malicious green eyes. My stomach bottomed out as if I was in a roller coaster car that plummeted from a steep incline.

"Oh my gosh, that's her." I pointed at the TV and set aside my laptop.

"Who?" Jimmy said.

"That's the crazy woman I saw in the store that day. The one who gave me a hard time."

"Are you sure?"

I turned up the volume. "I'm one hundred percent sure. That's her."

"Huh." Jimmy squinted at the screen. "Now that's interesting."

Holly's sister, whose name was apparently Lynne, spoke to the camera. "We aim to prove my sister's innocence and will stop at nothing to clear her name and set her free." The determination and fierceness behind her words and demeanor sent a chill through me.

I looked at Jimmy. "What are the chances she drives a maroon car and has an affinity for setting houses on fire?"

"You think she's the one who attacked you?"

"Makes sense to me. Think about it. She's blonde. And we found a blonde hair outside where the attacker had dumped a bunch of gasoline. She knows who I am. She harassed and shoved me at the store. Further, she seems unhinged enough to attack me, even kill me, in order to keep me from testifying."

Jimmy nodded, frowning, running the information around in his mind. "I'll look into it in the morning when I get to work. If that is her, she's going to be in a world of hurt. Tampering with a witness. Obstruction. Assault.

Attempted murder. Arson. Just to start."

There was a knock at the kitchen door. Millie stood on the screened-in porch, holding herself, looking around. She wore black leggings, ankle boots, a gray T-shirt, and a long dusty rose cardigan. I let her in and hugged her. Her long hair smelled of sandalwood and vanilla. I inhaled deeply, feeling creepy for sniffing my friend's hair, but I loved the scent.

"You want some tea or coffee?"

"Hot tea? It's pretty chilly outside."

"Sure." While I prepared the tea, the men joined us in the kitchen. They all exchanged quick hugs and sat at the kitchen table.

Millie pulled her cardigan around her. "I really appreciate y'all helping me with this. I hope I can get Mom back tonight. Alive and well. I'm scared."

"That's understandable," Jimmy said. "These are dangerous men. You should prepare yourself. They may have abused her. She may look pretty rough. And there's always the chance…" He paused. "That…" He was trying to choose his words carefully. "That we might not get her back at all."

Millie rubbed the center of her forehead. "I understand. Totally. I've been preparing myself for the worst. I mean, they could take the money and kill her anyway."

"How much money do you have?" I asked Millie.

"Only fifty thousand. That's all Dee Dee, Roderick, and I could scrape together on such short notice."

That was considerably less than the million they wanted. "Are they going to fall for that?" I asked Jimmy.

He shrugged one shoulder. "It's a risk. But we have to try."

"Let's focus," Cam interrupted. "What's the plan?"

Jimmy said, "Simple. Millie's going to drive my truck. I'm going to—"

"I can't drive your truck. It's too big."

The teapot whistled. I filled the mug and handed it to Millie. She accepted it with both hands and blew into the mug.

"You could try," Jimmy said.

She shook her head vigorously. "No. If I wrecked, I'd never forgive myself. And it'd take me forever to pay for the damages. It's too risky."

CHAPTER TWENTY-FOUR

I poured a hot tea for myself. I didn't really want it, but holding and sipping a hot drink was comforting. I rested my foot in the empty chair at the table. "I could drive her."

"No," Jimmy said.

Cam folded his arms and sat back. "Okay then. Another plan. "

I stared at the golden-brown liquid in my cup, sulking and thinking. Then it hit me. "What if Millie drives her own car, and you get in her trunk with the money. When she gets there, she pops the trunk, but doesn't close it. That way, you can jump out when you need to."

Jimmy nodded. "That'll work."

Millie checked her phone. "I guess we should probably hit the road. It's already eleven."

Nervous for them, my stomach twisted into a dozen knots. I stood to hug them goodbye and begged them to be careful and to call us as soon as everything was over and they were safe.

Cam and I stood in the yard, watching Jimmy climb into the trunk with the bag of money. I hugged myself and bit my lip. Millie backed out of the driveway.

Cam nudged me. "Hey, Jimmy's a good cop. They're going to be okay."

I spun and headed toward the house, Cam following behind. I pulled a barn jacket out of the hall closet and shrugged it on. "You still have your rifle in the truck?"

"Why?"

I grabbed my purse and keys. "Because you and I are going to follow them out to Johnson's Ferry."

"Oh no, we're not. We're going to sit right here like Jimmy told us."

"You have a choice. You can stay here with Prim, or you can come with me. But either way, I'm going to need that rifle."

Chapter Twenty-Five

Cam and I pulled down the dark, wooded road on the hill above the ferry. Aout forty yards ahead of us stood a sign that indicated the lane leading to the ferry was to the right through the woods. Cam muttered, "You've got to be the most stubborn, pig-headed—"

"Well, you could've stayed home. Now hush and park over there in that open area. We'll walk the rest of the way. And don't slam your truck door."

We slid out of the truck and pushed the doors closed. Cam slung the rifle on his shoulder and we stepped softly, as if tracking a deer, toward the ferry entrance. The path trailed down a steep hill and curved to the right. It was difficult to step quietly because the steepness of the hill increased the difficulty of landing a foothold without skidding and crunching the gravel. Something skittered around in the trees and leaves on the forest floor. Trying to adjust my eyes to the darkness, to make out shapes and silhouettes, I stared so hard my eyes felt like they were bugging out of my skull.

A chill filled the air, and the smell of mud and dank earth indicated we were getting closer. We were now on the hill above the water. The river whispered at a distance and lights from the ferryhouse's exterior reflected on the water. About a hundred yards away was Millie's car, parked under a single streetlight. The gates to the ferry dock were closed, and the ferry house was empty. I checked my phone. Ten till midnight.

Millie got out of her car, the phone pressed to her ear and popped the trunk. She pulled a bag from the trunk and left the trunk open. She walked toward the water, climbed under the entry gate, and walked onto the ferry

CHAPTER TWENTY-FIVE

car dock. The further she walked down the dock, she became half-shadowed, making it difficult to see exactly what she was doing, but it seemed she was leaving the bag there. Meanwhile, Jimmy slid from the trunk and duck-walked around the car, crouching by the headlights.

Cam and I eased our way further down the hill closer to the ferry until we were at the edge of the woods where the tree line met the small parking lot. Cam slid the rifle off his shoulder, adjusted the scope, and stood behind the tree, rifle aimed.

A loud buzzing sound emerged from the distance, and as it grew nearer, I realized it was a motorboat. Millie ran back up the dock toward her car, stopped, and turned before she reached the gate. The jet ski had two riders, all in black, wearing bright headlamps. The vehicle paused for one of the riders to lean over and grab at the bag.

Then chaos broke loose. Jimmy jumped up and screamed, "Freeze!"

The jet ski started up and pulled away from the dock as the rider grabbed the bag of money. Several shots rang out from the river, presumably from the jetski, hitting the side of the ferry house and the dock around Jimmy's feet. The shooter clearly had a semi-automatic weapon.

Jimmy braced himself and fired off several shots of his own. I pressed my fist against my mouth to keep from screaming. Every muscle in my body tensed. Why the devil did he stand there in the open instead of looking for cover? Did he always take such crazy risks?

Another round of shots came from the river, zipping along the gravel, kicking up dust all around Millie's feet.

Millie screamed, covering her ears, and ran to her car, jumping inside. Cam followed the jet ski and fired off a round. One of the lights fell backward into the water.

Jimmy spun around, looking for where the other shot came from. He aimed his gun toward the woods and ducked behind the nearest form of shelter he could find, a light pole on the dock. "Who is that?" He shouted, glancing behind him at the river. "Come out with your hands up."

"You'd better tell him it's us." I tapped Cam's arm, and we stood, brushing sticks and leaves off our legs. "Or he might shoot at us."

"It's us, Cam and Rook!" Cam shouted. "Don't shoot." We stepped out of the woods with our hands up. Cam held the rifle over his head. "

Jimmy hissed what was likely a curse word as he shook his head like an angry bull. He lowered his weapon and ran up the dock full speed, shouting, "Stay there. I'll deal with you in a minute." He then barked into the radio on his shoulder and shuffled down the embankment, his flashlight bobbing in the darkness. The roar of the jet ski had grown fainter and fainter.

I stood, frozen, searching the darkness, but I couldn't see or hear Jimmy. When everything had been quiet for several minutes, I assumed we were safe. "Let's go check on Millie," I said.

We ran down the hill to Millie's car. I tapped on the window, and she jumped. When she realized it was me, she jumped out and hugged me.

"Are you okay?" I asked.

She was hysterical, screaming and crying. "They took the money, but they didn't bring my mom. That probably means they've already killed her and hoped to get the money anyway."

"We don't know that. Until we know something for sure, we have to keep hoping. Okay?" I hugged her tighter, my heart breaking for her, and smoothed her hair, but she wasn't listening.

After several minutes, Jimmy emerged from the darkness and stormed toward us. "What in Sam Hill are y'all doing here?" He holstered his weapon.

Ignoring his anger, in spite of my quivering insides, I said, "I'm pretty sure Cam hit one of the guys. You should probably be thanking your lucky stars we did show up. He may have saved both yours and Millie's lives."

Sirens wailed in the distance.

"Dang it!" he shouted as he punched the side of the ferry house, leaving a dent in the aluminum siding. We all stood in uncomfortable silence while Jimmy rubbed his hand and stared out at the water.

Cam seemed agitated and scared. "I did hit him, didn't I?"

Jimmy rubbed his face. "I don't know, man. Maybe." He shone his flashlight in the river. "There are a few bills floating in the water. But I can't tell if the bag fell open and they lost the money or if the guy you hit took the bag with him when he fell in."

CHAPTER TWENTY-FIVE

"You think he drowned?" I asked.

"Tough to say. The currents are really strong, so he'll likely end up downstream. But the water is rough and cold, so the chances of him surviving aren't good."

Cars began to arrive, the sirens silenced, but lights swirling. I turned from the bright headlights.

Jimmy said, "Here's the team. We're going to drag the river. See what we can find." He sighed deeply and clapped Cam on the arm. "As your friend, I'm going to say, good shot. I'm glad you were there, man." He stood straighter. "But as an officer, we're going to take statements from all of you." Lines deepened around his mouth, and the bags darkened under his eyes. "I hate to say it, but I can't guarantee you won't get arrested over this."

"What!" I said. "You can't arrest him."

Various officers and techs climbed out of their vehicles. Jimmy shouted up at Deputy Ladonna. "Hey, Ladonna, I'll be there in a minute. Hang tight."

She nodded and turned back to convey the message to the people gathering around her.

His eyes locked with mine. "I don't want to, but I might not be able to prevent it. He shot a man."

"Yeah, a kidnapper and maybe a murderer."

"I'll do everything I can under the law to help, but you need to be prepared for the worst."

Cam nodded and puffed out his chest. "I did what I had to do. And you'll do the same."

Jimmy squinted as if in pain. "I've got to take your gun, man. Evidence. We'll have to match bullets."

Cam blinked as if Jimmy had just spit in his face. "Will I get it back? My dad gave me this gun for my twenty-first birthday. I've shot an eight-point buck with this gun."

Jimmy nodded and reached out for the gun. "I understand. I can't guarantee anything, but I'll see what can be done. But if this thing ever goes to trial, you won't get this back for a long time. If ever."

I stepped away from Jimmy as Cam laid the rifle in his hands. "Just so you know…" A steely glare entered Cam's frosty blue eyes. "I'd do every bit of it again."

Jimmy nodded, understanding the silent but clear communication in Cam's eyes. "As your friend, I understand that. However, as an officer, I need to warn you that you have the right to remain silent and should definitely not repeat that. Y'all wait here. I'll get an officer to take your statements."

Deputy Ladonna took Cam aside for his statement while the other officers and techs filed down to the river and began their search.

After Deputy Ladonna had gathered all our statements, she handed us a card. "We will likely have more questions in the future. If possible, it would probably be a good idea to stay in town for the next few weeks."

"Yes, ma'am." Cam tucked the card in his back pocket. "Can we go home now?"

She dismissed us and trotted off to the river.

I said to Cam, "I'm going to ride with Millie."

He nodded, his face marked with exhaustion. "That's best. I'll see y'all later." He squeezed my arm and slumped up the hill toward his truck, his hands tucked in his pockets.

Millie and I climbed into her car. My foot knocked against something in the floorboard. "What's this?" I asked, lifting the plastic bag.

"A Peach Nehi and a homemade lemon blueberry muffin. My mom's favorite snack." Her voice caught. "I was really hoping…." She broke into sobs, hiding her face in her hands.

I put my arm around her and squeezed her. "I'm so sorry, Millie. This is awful. But I'm sure the police will catch these guys."

"I don't know how," she squeaked, falling into another crying fit. Between sobs, she said, "We don't know where my mom is, and they didn't bring her tonight. We didn't see the kidnappers, so we can't identify them. What in the world are we going to do?"

There was nothing I could say or do to alleviate her suffering. Listening was the best I could offer.

"I'll drive," I said. We switched seats, and she wiped her face on a wrinkled

CHAPTER TWENTY-FIVE

napkin from the glove compartment as she cried over her mom. I couldn't help but shed a few tears of my own, knowing her pain.

Prim and Batrene were sitting at the kitchen table with a Scrabble board between them when we returned. They cupped coffee mugs in their hands and looked up, owl-eyed.

Prim only had to see us to understand the horrible truth. "Oh, child. What happened?"

Millie broke into tears again and ran to the bathroom while I explained everything to Prim and Batrene, between a scattering of "oh, no," "mercy me," and "heavens."

"Poor child," Batrene said. "My heart breaks for her. It's awful."

Prim shook her head. The ring on her finger gaped and wiggled, stopped only by her large knuckle. The bones jutted so severely they looked as though they might poke holes right through her paper-thin skin. "I can't believe there's nothing at all that the sheriff or Jimmy can do. Why can't they catch these nimrods?"

"We all wish it were that easy, Prim. But it's not. There haven't been many clues. They're working on getting the call logs to see who's been calling Millie, but that takes time. And I'd be willing to bet that the numbers won't be traced back to anyone. If the kidnappers have a brain at all, they'll use a burner phone and use a different one every time."

Millie came out of the hall, blowing her nose.

Prim pressed herself to her feet. "You sit down here. I'll get you something to eat. I have chili left over and—"

"No, that's okay, Prim. Thank you," she said.

Not to have her hospitality gainsaid, Prim added, "Well, you're staying the night here. Rook, get her clothes to sleep in and get the guest bed ready. It hasn't been used in a while, but the bed is clean."

Batrene stood. "Now that we know y'all are safe and in one piece, I'm going home and putting these old bones to bed." That set off a round of hugs and kisses and bids to take care and to try to have a good night's sleep.

After walking Batrene home, I prepared the guest room and gathered PJs for Millie to borrow. Meanwhile, Prim was downstairs, closing cabinets and quizzing Millie about breakfast foods she liked best and telling her to sleep as long as she wanted in the morning. When everything was finally settled, and Prim was in bed, Millie and I sat on the guestroom bed crying about the grave misfortune of not being able to reclaim her mom. I stayed with her until she passed out, then I went to my room, where I proceeded to toss and turn and stare at the shadows on the ceiling, missing my own mom, missing my dad, going through the list of things I needed to do in terms of calling lawyers and reading the old trial transcripts. Most of all, I was trying to predict what law enforcement's next move might be, though, for the life of me, I couldn't imagine what it would be.

Chapter Twenty-Six

A noise downstairs jolted me awake. It took me a few seconds to realize where I was and that I was hearing Prim's breakfast preparations. Since we'd found out about her cancer diagnosis, my primary goal was to keep her from working whenever I could. But the woman, bless her heart, didn't have an "off" switch.

Groaning, I kicked off the blankets to face the chill in my yoga pants and T-shirt. Autumn was officially here, but we waited until the cold was intolerable before turning on the central heat. I slipped into an old cardigan and tucked my feet into a pair of faux sherpa-lined booties and scuffed my way downstairs. Since I'd forgotten to charge my phone last night, I plugged my phone into the cord on the kitchen counter while I poured my coffee.

Prim cradled a cast iron skillet in her arms. The thing probably weighed more than her at this point. With both hands, she lowered it with a loud clatter onto the stove. "Morning, hon. Would you believe we're out of buttermilk? I don't remember using it all, but I guess I did. Would you care to run out to the Blue Market and pick up a carton so I can make these pancakes?"

I mixed cream into my coffee. "Can't you use regular milk?"

She looked at me like I asked her to stick her hand in a running blender, and I immediately regretted my question. I threw up my hands, answering the look on her face. "You're right. I don't know what I was thinking."

"You ought to know better than to think I could use regular milk…"

"We don't have to have pancakes, do we?" But I was already heading for my car keys and purse by the door.

She put her hand on her hip. "We have a guest in our home."

"You're right." I kicked off my slippers and stuffed my feet into a pair of tennis shoes by the door. "I'll be back in a minute." I grabbed a jacket off the hook and shrugged it on as I walked to the car. The morning was chilly, with frost covering the grass, sparkling in the morning sun. When I didn't see my car, I remembered my car was dead and in impound. I returned to the house. "Prim. I need to borrow your car." Grabbing the keys to her behemoth 1990 gold Caddy, I didn't wait for her permission. I hated driving her car. It was unwieldy and cranky. I called it the Road Beast. Still holding my coffee mug, I maneuvered the steering wheel with one hand while concentrating on not spilling the coffee all over me and the car.

Pulling into the Blue Market, I sat tall in the seat to see over the steering wheel and the long, square hood as I parked near the door. Still not awake, I sat in the car, determined to finish my coffee before it got any colder.

A silver Challenger pulled in a few spots away. Will Decker, tall and lanky, unfolded from the car wearing a blue and green flannel shirt and jeans. His breath puffed in front of him, and he tucked his hands deep into his jeans pockets as he slunk toward the door. The lights on the car flashed, and a beep sounded. An automatic lock.

My gut filled with that squirmy, feathery feeling otherwise known as "women's intuition." His eyes darted, and he glanced around like he was scheming. The dude had given me bad vibes from the moment I first met him.

Downing my coffee, I followed him inside. I tracked him from an aisle away, peeking over the tops of packages and cans to see what he was buying. He was kind of cute in the face and looked a lot like his brother, Shane, but more rugged, harder.

He pulled three drinks from the cooler and turned to the muffins behind him. I knelt, pretending to decide between Rolos and Reese's Cups while keeping an eye on him. What had my mom seen in this man? It seemed my momma sure had a thing for the bad boys. My image of my momma shifted in my mind. The hazy two-dimensional image of her long black hair shining in the sun and her silver hoops glowing against her tan skin,

CHAPTER TWENTY-SIX

and her musical laugh gained a dimension. A sense of her as a person with problems, faults, and flaws swiped away some of the fog surrounding her in my memory. For the first time, I began to question if I ever knew my momma at all. Do any of us ever really know our parents? She was a person, like me, before she had me–she had been a whole person with an identity I would never know.

While everything I thought I'd known about my mother rattled and shook, Will moved to stand in the line forming at the counter. I sprang up and jumped into line, cutting off a round man in a John Deere hat and barn jacket. I stood slightly to the side so I could peek around Will to see what he was holding. He had a Mountain Dew, a Monster energy drink, and a Peach Nehi. He also had beef jerky, nuts, and a blueberry muffin. Peach Nehi and a blueberry muffin. That was the same food that Millie had brought with her to Johnson's Ferry. The chances that another person in Rothdale enjoyed that same snack had to be small.

Will placed his purchase on the counter and paid cash for it, digging change out of his pocket. I peeked around him and noticed among the coins was a thin silver chain with a silver mermaid. My stomach dropped into my shoes. That necklace was identical to the one Patrice had worn the day I saw her at Mermaid Cove. I put the pieces together: silver mermaid necklace, blueberry muffin, and Peach Nehi. This man had to know where Patrice was, or—my heart rabbited at the thought—he'd been involved in her disappearance.

If I said or did anything I might not have another chance, so I bit down on my tongue and stepped out of line, raced to The Road Beast, and waited for Will to come out. I dug for my phone in my purse and couldn't find it before Will exited the store. Why on earth was it never easy to find my phone in my purse? Growling to myself, I resolved to figure out that problem in my first free moment as I started the car and pulled out to follow Will.

I followed him at a distance, continuing to dig in my purse for my phone. Panic set in as I searched, but my hands never fell on the thin rectangle. I dumped the purse onto the seat and, glancing between the seat and the road, I searched through the pile of lipstick, pens, papers, tissues, wallet, empty gum, and candy wrappers. In the same moment I realized I had no phone with me, an image flashed through my mind of my phone lying on the kitchen counter, charging. My spirit sank. *Crap.* I needed to call Jimmy or 911, but couldn't. Nor could I call Prim to tell her I'd be late.

However, as I saw it, my only options were to quit following Will to save myself, or to continue following him to find out where he was going and to potentially help Patrice—regardless of the risk. My stomach turned in on itself, my breath came short and shallow, and my hands began to shake. I couldn't turn back. I couldn't abandon Patrice or my best friend.

So, I continued to follow Will through Rothdale's town center, edging the town square around the courthouse ornamented with yellow mums and pumpkins on the stone steps. Will turned right down Jefferson Street toward the industrial side of town. Small factories and workshops neatly lined both sides of the road, but as we neared the railroad tracks, the buildings became older and more dilapidated.

The Road Beast jostled over the tracks, and we continued on where the road forked. The left went downhill to an older residential area full of bungalows, shotgun houses, and cottages dating back to the 1930s or older. The right side remained level and curved back to abandoned factories and warehouses interspersed with operational factories, warehouses, and other industrial buildings. The streets were littered with trash, and weeds peeked through cracks in the crumbling sidewalks.

The Challenger pulled into the lot of the abandoned J.P. Benjamin factory. It had been a canning factory from the late 1800s, finally closing its doors in the 1960s. The building looked very much like a late Victorian or early Modern Era factory of red brick, charred with coal smoke, and a rusted tin roof laced with holes. The name of the company had been painted with the image of a cherub-cheeked girl, but was faded by the elements and partially covered with overgrown ivy. The windows had all been broken out, making the building reminiscent of an eyeless skull.

The Challenger pulled into the narrow opening in the dilapidated chain-link fence. I didn't want to make it obvious that I was following him, so I drove by to the corner, stopping at the intersection. When the light flipped

CHAPTER TWENTY-SIX

to green, I turned left onto Walnut Street and looked for a second opening to the property. There wasn't one, but there was another abandoned building in the adjacent lot, so I pulled in there. I got out and pushed my door closed quietly with my hip, and ran on tiptoes to the ivy-covered wooden fence. The chain-link fence was on the other side, rusted, but still intact. Will entered the factory, looking around.

I wasn't going to attempt to climb the fence. I wasn't that agile, and if I needed to get out in a hurry, I didn't want to have to shimmy up a fence. Also, I couldn't be assured that Will wouldn't see me. There had to be a better way. I scanned the abandoned factory parking lot. The fence seemed to be open or missing at the back of the lot.

I returned to The Road Beast to relocate it under a wimpy maple tree across the street from the factory. I waited for the industrial trucks to pass, stinking of diesel and blowing hot air in my face. Then I ran across the street and toward the back of the factory. An empty parking lot of a recently abandoned warehouse backed up to the abandoned factory. The space was full of thin trees, weeds, bushes, undergrowth, old tires, and other garbage, but no fence. *Bingo!*

I trailed along the back of the factory, finding a few weather-beaten pallets, overgrown with weeds, stacked near a rusted barrel under a window. I tested the wooden pallet with my foot, pressing my weight into it to make sure it would support me, but I was still too short to reach the window. I climbed onto the barrel and arched sideways to peek into the building. It was a large space with pipes and metal rafters, a maze of conveyor belts, and junky machinery and hoppers. The floor was covered with debris, crates, boxes, pallets, and barrels. The wall to the right was broken up with a series of doors. Probably bathrooms and maybe a break room and administrative office, if I had to guess.

In a dark corner, I noticed a shadowy shape and realized it was Patrice, sitting on a dirty mattress, ravenously eating her blueberry muffin and drinking the Peach Nehi. Her hair was sticking out all over her head. A pair of handcuffs dangled from one wrist.

Will stood nearby smoking.

"Do you have to smoke near me?" Patrice said. "I can't stand the smell of those things and it's messing up the taste of my breakfast."

"Shut up and eat. Soon as you're done, I'm locking you back up."

"I need to pee, too," she said. "I'm about to bust."

"All right then. Hurry." Will's phone rang, and he answered. After several "mm-hms" and "yeahs" and "okays," he hung up. "Don't get too comfortable. We're moving you tonight."

"Why?"

"Because that's how it's done."

"Where are you taking me?" she asked, her mouth full of food.

"I don't know," he snapped. "Dang. Always asking a ton of questions."

"When are you going to give me back to my daughter?"

"As soon as she comes up with the rest of the money." He knelt beside her and snarled, drawing from his cigarette. "Or maybe we'll keep the money and get rid of you." He held gun fingers to her temple and pretended to shoot her. "Phew." Smoke swirled out of his mouth and nose.

She cringed as he laughed.

Undaunted, Patrice asked, "Didn't she have the money last night? I heard y'all talking about the drop."

Will rubbed his head vigorously. He seemed agitated. "Ugh. More questions."

"Why didn't y'all turn me over then?"

He shook his hands in her face. "Shut up," he growled, standing up. "Just. Shut. Up. With all your stupid, endless questions. The only thing you need to worry about is doing what you're told."

"If you let me go, I'm sure I could scrape together enough money for you. Only you."

He snorted. "Right. But then you'd no longer be kidnapped, and you'd turn us in to the police."

"No, hon. I wouldn't. I swear. It'd be y our little secret. You could turn them in. You'd have your money, and I could go back home and get a shower and sleep in my own bed. That's all I really want. I'd forget I ever met you."

That was pretty smart for Patrice to try to divide them.

CHAPTER TWENTY-SIX

He swiped his hand through the air. "Why're you still talking? Shut up and eat your breakfast. Besides, you won't be going anywhere except the bottom of the river once we have all our money."

They never had any intention of letting Patrice go. I had to get her out there–fast. But she didn't even know I was there. I had to find a way of communicating my presence to her so she could be ready to run—without alerting that nimrod kidnapper.

The front door opened, and a man-shape filled the space. The sunlight was behind him, so I couldn't see his features, but Will seemed to know him.

"Hey," Will leaned against the office window that looked out on the production floor. A gun peeked from the band of his jeans.

From behind the man shape appeared a female shape. Will definitely knew her.

"Hey baby," he cooed and strode to meet her halfway.

They embraced, and he squeezed her bottom as they dove in for a passionate kiss.

"You two break it up. Or get a room," Man-shape said.

As the other man neared, I could distinguish his features better. He wore a hooded jacket over a flannel shirt, and his greasy dark hair lay against his acne-scarred face. Clayton Harmon. He had a gun holstered to his hip. "You get us something?"

"Yeah, it's in there on the desk."

Will, joined at the hip with Female-shape, fell in behind Clayton. Within a few steps, I could see the woman was Savannah Stewart. My mouth dropped open. Now I was pretty sure they must've had something to do with Mitch's death. Unless it was Shane. But were they working with Shane? Were they also involved in the pill mill, too?

They all entered the office area and sat around eating sausage biscuits and drinking sodas. Clayton slunk into the office as Will and Savannah followed behind. He stood in the doorway, his back to the window. I couldn't hear the details, but they were discussing the ransom money, something about disposing of Patrice,, and splitting the money. While they were distracted with their conversation, I snapped the end off of a twig and tossed it at

Patrice through a hole in the window. It hit her in the chest then dropped to the mattress.

She looked around, confused, then her sights fell on the window, and they popped open wide. I put my finger over my lips, indicating to be quiet. She froze. I mouthed "get ready" and made running fingers.

She squeezed her eyes shut and popped them open again, communicating silently that she understood.

I gave her a thumbs-up and pulled away from the window. My back against the wall, the brick grating into my back through my shirt, I stared at the brush line. There were three people. At least two of them were armed. That deeply narrowed my and Patrice's chances of success. I needed to distract the kidnappers and, ideally, to separate them.

Climbing down from my perch, I ran on tiptoes around the building and scanned the environs. At first, the only thing I could think of was to set something on fire if I could keep the car lighter hot enough, and long enough to set a fire. However, as I scanned the area, I couldn't find anything that would create a substantial fire. Scratch that idea.

As I rolled through a variety of losing scenarios, a loud bang sounded. A gunshot. Patrice screamed. I scrambled back around to my perch to peek in the window.

Savannah shouted, waving a gun at Patrice, shrieking at her. "Shut up! Right now. Or you'll be next."

Clayton Harmon was splayed on the floor in a growing pool of blood.

Will grabbed the sides of his head. "What'd you do that for? Are you crazy?"

"Listen to me," Savannah said. "This was the only way, baby. He couldn't be trusted. I know as soon as he touched that money, he'd turn on us. I've already got one murder on my hands because of Mitch." She pointed the gun at Clayton. "That fool would've squealed, and I'd be sitting on death row."

Oh, sweet heavens, Savannah killed Mitch. I about fell off the barrel.

Will, still holding the sides of his head, paced in little circles. "Ohmigosh, ohmigosh, omigosh. What're we gonna do? What're we gonna do now?

CHAPTER TWENTY-SIX

We're going to be in so much trouble."

Savannah shouted, "Hey!" Her voice echoed through the empty factory.

Will stopped pacing and gaped at her.

Savannah tucked the gun in the back of her pants and grabbed Will by the top of the arms, and shook him. "Listen to me. We need to move his body. At least hide it in case someone comes in here nosing around."

Frozen, Will stared at the body as Savannah looked around. She found a janitor's closet near the bathrooms. "There. We'll put him in there. But first..." she squatted and took Clayton's gun and his wallet. She handed it to Will. "Here. Take these."

Will took the gun and wallet, tucking one in his waist and the other in his back pocket as he stared at the body. He wiped his face on his arm.

Savannah grabbed Clayton's hands. "All right, help me move him."

Disgust marking his face, Will shook his head and grabbed the feet. "Fine. But promise me you ain't going to shoot anyone else."

Savannah tugged at the arms and stepped backwards toward the janitor's closet. "Well, darling. You're the only one left. And if you don't stop acting like such a whiny baby, I'm liable to shoot you next."

"I'm not a whiny baby." He grunted with exertion. "I wasn't expecting all this. All I wanted was the money. I didn't mean for people to die."

I scrambled down from the barrel and dashed around the building, my mind racing for an idea to cause a distraction. I needed to get Patrice and me out of here pronto. Savannah had an itchy trigger finger that I didn't want to tempt.

As I rounded the corner, I glanced all around, panicked. Nothing sprang immediately to mind, and there were no open businesses nearby where I could go to call for help. Then I spotted Will's gray Challenger. It was parked behind abandoned equipment that had been staged in a corner of the parking lot near the building so that it would be difficult to see from adjacent lots or the street. An idea sprouted.

Spotting a metal pipe in the garbage pile near me, I grabbed it up and ducked down behind his vehicle. I put my back against his car and shook it, forcing the car alarm to sound.

A few moments later, the alarm shut off. He likely used the remote fob to shut it off from a distance. I shook the car again to sound the alarm. The alarm stopped. I shook the car again. The alarm blared.

"Dang it," Will shouted. "What's wrong with this thing?" He turned it off and I turned it back on when he turned around.

"Fine," Savannah shouted from inside. "I'll finish this myself."

He shouted back at her over his shoulder. "I've got to silence the stupid thing so it doesn't attract attention. You want a dozen people over here nosing around?" I heard the crunch of gravel and glass under his feet as he approached the car. Muttering to himself, he said, "I'll unhook you. That'll fix your red wagon." He opened his car door to pop his hood.

This was my one chance, and I had to make it count. As he lifted up and shut his car door, I connected the pipe with his head with all my might. He fell to the ground on his hands and knees and grabbed his head. I conked him again, and he fell flat. He was moaning, stunned. I hit him again for good measure and grabbed his gun. I ran to the factory door, peeked around the corner, searching for Savannah. My mind raced through my mental *Law and Order SVU* files. What would Benson and Stabler do?

Savannah was humming and singing in the bathroom. I quickly decided I wasn't Benson or Stabler and did not want to interact with her if I could help it.

To the right was the janitor's closet. A trail of blood disappeared under the shut door. I don't know how they expected to hide a body when Clayton's blood cut a path straight to his hiding spot. Not my problem. I couldn't think about their stupidity and lack of planning right now. Besides, if Patrice and I ever got out of here alive, I'd report the death to the police. Right now, I needed to keep psycho-Savannah from coming out of that bathroom to shoot me.

I pushed the janitor's closet door open. Clayton lay balled up in the corner like a discarded rag. There was just enough light to prove it was a janitor's closet. I grabbed the mop from the corner and shoved the mop handle in the bathroom door's pull handle. The mop was long enough that the ends leveraged against the flanking walls, preventing Savannah's exit. It might buy me a minute or two until Will woke up.

Inside the bathroom, Savannah's voice echoed. "Will? Is that you? I was thinking we should maybe set the place on fire. That would cover up everything. Destroy all the evidence. What do you think?" She pulled on the door handle. The door rattled. "Hey. Wha—" She tried the door again and released a flurry of curse words when the door wouldn't open. "Will. Are you messing with me? Quit playing around and let me out. Will." She beat on the door, still trying to open it. "Will!"

As with knocking down a wasps' nest, I wasn't going to hang around to see what would happen. I ran toward Patrice and waved her toward me, whisper-shouting, "Run! Run!"

Bless her heart. Poor thing was trying her best. Her butt up in the air in a really wobbly downward dog pose, she struggled to push herself to stand. The intense rattling of the bathroom door indicated the mop handle might not hold much longer. We had to hightail it out of here.

Grabbing Patrice by the elbow, I pulled her up to help her stand. She staggered on the uneven mattress. "C'mon. You're going to have to run."

"Oh Lord, help me." She groaned, as I pulled her along. "My knees can't take it."

"If you don't come on, your knees are going to get us killed," I hissed.

She stumbled and almost fell. I helped her up, tugging at her, pulling her forward. "Please, Patrice, you've got to do this. I'll free your hands from the cuffs as soon as possible, but there's not time right now. You can do it. C'mon. Millie's waiting on you. This is the only chance we have."

That seemed to infuse her with a bit of spirit. She pushed forward, and we ran out the door. I thought about the clearer path through the parking lot, but it was too risky. So, I led her along the rougher path through the garbage, around the side of the building toward the brush line.

"Hey! Come back here. Stop!" Savannah shouted. "Will? Where're you at?"

How in the world did she get out? We picked our way over the garbage, litter, and industrial ruins.

Then I heard Savannah say, "What're you doing? Where'd they go? C'mon.

Get up. Where'd they go?"

Patrice stumbled over a metal plank, and it fell against a cinder block.

Savannah said, "They're back here. Get up."

"Oh, hurry, Patrice." I tugged on her. We were only a few feet from the opening in the brush line.

Patrice fell and yelped. "Oh, my knee."

I pulled on her. "Get up. Just a few more feet."

She made it to her feet, and I shoved her through the brush line. We ran toward the car, and I opened the back passenger door and shoved Patrice inside. She fell on her stomach with a grunt. Savannah emerged through the brush, coming toward us, gun in hand.

"They're back here," she shouted.

I shoved Patrice's feet inside the car, slammed the door, and ran around to the driver's

side.

A shot rang out. I ducked and dived into The Road Beast. Adrenaline surged through my arms and hands, causing me to fumble to find the ignition key. Flashes of the silly 80s horror films flicked through my mind: running women falling down or dropping their keys as they tried to get in the car. I could not be one of those women.

I wasn't used to these foreign keys. I located the key and tried to jam it in the ignition, but the key slipped. *Dang it!* Another shot rang out, hitting the tree in front of me.

Savannah emerged from the brush line, her wavy hair like a lion's mane around her scowling face. Finally, my key found the ignition. I turned it, and threw The Road Beast into reverse as Savannah leveled her gun at me through the windshield.

Patrice started to speak and shifted to the back seat.

"Stay down," I screeched as I slammed my foot into the gas pedal. We flew backward, and I jerked the steering wheel to point us toward the exit.

A shot was fired and blew out my driver's side back window. Patrice and I screamed in unison as flying glass landed in my hair and all around me. I threw the gear into drive and peeled out of the parking lot. The car jolted

CHAPTER TWENTY-SIX

hard as we drove over the thick apron and we both grunted with the force of it. Barely avoiding being hit, I cut off an oncoming truck that slammed on its brakes and honked at us.

I flew down the street and avoided stoplights by turning right and plowing down side streets until we popped out on the courthouse square. We trailed around, whipped down a narrow residential street, and skidded into the parking lot at the back of the sheriff's department.

I sighed and dropped my forehead to the steering wheel. Closing my eyes, my breath came hard and fast as I shook all over. I struggled to slow down my breathing and force deep breaths to calm myself.

Patrice sat up in back. "Sweet heavens. You okay, hon?"

"I'm good." I looked over my shoulder at her. "You okay?"

"Yeah. I think so." She brushed glass out of her hair. "I'd sure like to get out of these cuffs and get a shower."

"We will. Promise. Let's go inside and talk to an officer." I stared out the glassless driver's side window. Prim was not going to be happy. This car was Papaw's treasure. He used to talk all the time about how many years he worked and scrimped and saved to buy this car—this mark of his success, of his finally having obtained his long-coveted notion of success. My guts turned to water and dripped into my shoes. "I'm so sorry, Papaw," I whispered as I got out of the car and shook the glass off of me. I estimated I'd have to work at least six months to fix this window and any scratches in the paint.

We entered the warm building, the fluorescent lights reflecting off the tile floors. The receptionist's eyes lit with a blend of humor and concern. When she saw the gun, her eyes widened. "Ma'am, I hope you have an open carry permit—"

I cut her off. "Don't worry. I want to turn it in. It's not my gun. I need to speak to an officer about an incident."

Sheriff Goodman happened to pass down the hall with papers in one hand and a coffee cup announcing *Taking Care of Business* in the other. When he spotted me, he tipped his chin, puzzled. Then he shook his head and came to the door that led down the hall to the offices.

"Rook Campbell. Is your full-time job to torment me and my staff? And why do you have that poor woman in handcuffs."

"This is Patrice Dawson. The woman who was kidnapped. Also, there's a dead body, Clayton Harmon, out at the J.P. Benjamin factory. Savannah Stewart shot him. She was with Will Decker. I also overheard her admit she killed Mitch Thomas."

Goodman's excellent poker face dropped in place, but he couldn't hide the flicker of surprise in his eyes. "I'll be dogged. Hold on." He stepped over to the receptionist's desk. "Get on the horn right now and send a squad to the J.P. Benjamin factory. And put out an APB on Will Decker and Savannah Stewart. They could be on the run. Send officers to their homes and work, too. We might get lucky." He turned to us. "Come on back."

Patrice held up her hands. "Can you take these stupid things off?"

Within a few moments, Patrice and I were sitting in a questioning room with donuts from Irene's and a carafe of fresh coffee. I inhaled one glazed donut trying not to think about Papaw's car. Then Mitch Thomas popped into my mind.

I washed a chunk of donut down with coffee. "Patrice, I'm sorry about Mitch. Even though y'all were broken up, I know it still must be hard…."

A deep wrinkle burrowed between her brows. She nodded. "There's a whole lot about my life with him that was hard." She lifted the Styrofoam cup to her lips. After a drink, she selected a donut. "He took all my money. Sunk it into that clinic." She ate as she spoke. "Then I found out about that little Jezebel receptionist of his and their affair. I kicked him out." She licked the glaze off her fingers and took another drink of her coffee. "One day, when I was boxing up his stuff—I didn't want him back in my house—I discovered records where his medical license had been suspended. So, I started digging and discovered the clinic was a front for dealing pharmaceuticals illegally." She leaned both arms on the table and nested the cup in her hands. "I was in the process of gathering information on him so I could turn him in when I was kidnapped."

"I guess that's why you were kidnapped?"

"Yes. I think the plan was to get all the money they could out of me to

CHAPTER TWENTY-SIX

build another clinic. When I went back through my books, I noticed he'd been siphoning money off me from the beginning. Then he started tapping into the distillery funds." She sat back in her chair and crossed her arms over her chest. "Dee Dee asked me about it, and I covered for that jerk." She glanced at me with disbelief and shook her head.

I etched my name into my Styrofoam cup with my thumbnail. "Dee Dee said she was advised to shelter the distillery money because of *your* spending. That makes more sense now."

"I feel like a big old idiot." She sighed. She lifted her glasses and wiped her eyes.

I put my arm around her. "You're not stupid for trying to love him. I don't like to speak ill of the dead, but he was stupid for abusing your trust."

She sighed again and pointed at the box. "Gimme another one of those donuts. Chocolate glaze."

I handed her a donut and grabbed my second one when Goodman re-entered the room.

He had a pad and pen in one hand as he closed the door. "Let's talk."

Patrice told him everything she could remember about the kidnapping and the kidnappers, then I related the details of the escape while Goodman scratched out his notes on the legal pad. I finished off my donut and licked the glaze from my fingers. I drank down my coffee and poured more from the carafe. As my blood and nerves fired on the high-octane premium Arabica, sugar, adrenaline blend, I bounced my legs under the table, anxious to get home. Prim would be worried if I didn't get home soon.. Since Cam had a connection to fix my poor lime green Ford Fiesta, maybe he had a connection who could help me get The Road Beast's window fixed.

I scanned Facebook and Instagram for photos of Savannah and Will to provide them to Sheriff Goodman.

When the questioning had concluded, Goodman said, "Mrs. Dawson, do you feel safe returning home?"

Patrice picked at her nails. "I hadn't thought about it. I-I'm not sure. What if they come looking for revenge?" She looked at me as if asking for guidance.

"They might," I said. "But if you need a place to stay, you can stay with Prim and me for a while. At least until they catch those creeps."

"Oh, hon, I don't want to inconvenience you."

"You're not. I wouldn't offer it if I didn't mean it."

"I sure would appreciate that. Only for a few days until those pigs are caught."

"Absolutely. Millie's there now. She'll be thrilled to see you again. She and Prim are probably wondering what happened to me and the buttermilk. We should go."

As we stood, Goodman said, "I'm really glad you were found safe."

Patrice said, "Me too. Now catch them and lock them away for as long as possible."

He rubbed his mustache. "You have my word." Then he actually smiled at me. "I'm beginning to think we should deputize you."

I smiled. "One more thing. Will has Patrice's necklace in his pocket. A silver chain with a silver mermaid on it. We need that back."

Chapter Twenty-Seven

We stopped off at the Blue Market to grab a bottle of buttermilk and drove to my house.

Inside the house, Millie sat on the couch, her face in her hands.

Patrice walked in. "Hey, baby girl."

Millie looked up. Her mouth fell open, and she launched herself off the couch and ran into Patrice's arms. They squeaked through tears, clinging to each other. I wiped the tears from my eyes, thrilled for them. Wishing I could hug my mom again.

Millie asked a thousand questions about Patrice, her well-being, her escape. When she learned of my involvement, Millie hugged me tight. "How can I ever thank you? There's nothing I could ever do to thank you."

After a few moments, I said, "Where's Prim?"

Millie wiped her eyes on her sleeve and flipped her long hair from her face. "She went upstairs. Said she didn't feel good."

My stomach clenched. It wasn't like Prim to not push through. "Have y'all had breakfast?"

"No. I wasn't really hungry anyway, and she waited as long as she could, but finally went up to her room."

"I'll check on her. Patrice, come with me, and I'll show you to the bathroom and get you a change of clothes. I think I can find clothes to fit you."

Millie said, "I'll run out to the house and pick up something for you."

"No," Patrice grabbed her arm. "Don't go there, especially alone, until we've heard about the kidnappers being caught. They might know where I live."

"Okay, I'll go to the Big Lots and pick up underwear, deodorant, toothbrush, and toothpaste. Anything else you need?"

"We can supply the rest for now," I said.

Millie nodded and kissed her mom. "I'll be right back." She squeezed her arm and trailed her hand down to the fingertips, as if by breaking contact, her mom would disappear.

We climbed the stairs, and I handed Patrice a robe. "You can start with this until Millie gets back." I looked her up and down. "You're a little smaller than me…" I dug through my chest of drawers and pulled out a pair of red yoga pants, a long-sleeve Mammoth Cave shirt-shirt, and a pair of fuzzy socks. I opened the closet door and flipped on the light. I motioned at the rack and shelves. "And if you want a cardigan or sweatshirt, help yourself."

She nodded. "I really appreciate this."

"Think nothing of it. Across the hall is the bathroom." I motioned for her to follow me. I pulled out a clean towel and washcloth. "Soap, shampoo, conditioner in the shower, of course. Body lotion under the sink. Perfume and hair styling stuff, too, if you want it. Help yourself. I'll leave you to it while I check on Prim."

She squeezed my hand. "I'm so thankful for you…" Her eyes watered.

Mine responded in kind. "Go enjoy a hot shower."

She wiped her eyes. "I can't wait." She chuckled. "I might take two."

I went to Prim's room. The door was cracked, the room dim, and the ceiling fan on. Yet she'd burrowed deep under a pile of blankets and quilts. I stood in the door debating on whether or not I should disturb her. I wanted to know how she felt, but I didn't want to wake her and interrupt the rest she needed.

"Rook?" she croaked.

"It's me."

"What took you so long? I gave up waiting."

"I know, I'm sorry." I stepped into the room. "I had a little adventure while I was out."

"What's that mean?"

CHAPTER TWENTY-SEVEN

"I found Patrice."

"You did?" Her voice brightened. "Isn't that amazing?" She pushed the covers down and patted the bed. "Come on in and tell me all about it. Turn on the light."

I turned on the lamp as she scooted to sit up. I propped her up with pillows, and she squinted against the light, fumbling to put on her glasses. She blinked at me from behind the lenses. Her hair was damp and matted with sweat against her forehead; she swiped it off her face with the back of her bony wrist.

I told her all about the morning's events while she fought sleep. When I'd finished, she shook her head. "You sure are something." She patted my hand. "I am so very proud of you. Many times, I've worried about how you might turn out, but you are such a treasure."

My throat constricted, and I looked down at the floor. If Prim got mushy on me now, I'd crumble into a pile of blubbering goo. I tried to change the subject. "Millie said you were feeling bad earlier. Are you okay?"

Her voice was thready. "I'm feeling poorly today. Nothing to concern yourself with."

"What's wrong?" *Other than cancer.*

"Just tired and weak. That's all. I think I did too much."

"Should I bring you food? Medicine?"

"No pills. I'm not hungry right now. I just want to sleep."

"How about I bring you a ginger ale and peanut butter crackers? You can eat them when you wake up."

"Don't fuss over me." She sunk down and pulled the covers up to her chin. "Go on with you. Let me sleep."

I kissed her damp head, turned off the lamp, jogged downstairs, prepared the soda and crackers, and figured she'd need medicine soon. I laid it all out on a plate, left it on her nightstand, and pulled the door almost shut.

Then I sat on the couch, turned on the television, and cried while watching *Monk* until Millie came home and studied me quizzically. "You okay?"

"I'm fine." I blew my nose and wiped my eyes. "It's been a difficult day."

"You want to talk about it?" She clutched the store bag under her arm.

There were some things far too painful to discuss, and Prim's illness and inevitable passing was the most painful thing I could ever imagine. "I definitely don't want to talk about it."

"If you change your mind—"

"I know. Thanks. Your mom needs underwear, though."

She disappeared upstairs. When Millie re-emerged, I made us tomato soup and grilled cheese, and we ate in a moment of cherished peace.

After lunch, Patrice retired upstairs to take a nap in the guest room.

Millie and I had settled into our respective corners of the sofas and switched on Netflix to watch a movie when Cam walked in through the kitchen, calling out, "Anybody home?"

"In here," I said. "What're you doing here?"

"Had a little time off."

I hated to admit it but he looked like a whipped topping short of delicious in his worn jeans and soft, gray cotton T-shirt and navy ball cap.

He flopped down between Millie and me, closer to me. He patted my thigh in a familiar way and squeezed it. "Thought I would come by and see a few of my favorite people. See how things are going since last night."

"Rook brought my mom home today," Millie said.

He pushed his cap back and squeaked, "What? How? What happened?" He sat between me and Millie on the couch.

I paused the movie and told the story for what seemed the thousandth time that day.

"Wow. That's crazy," he said. "I'm really glad it all worked out okay, though." He turned to Millie. "I know you're thrilled to have her back. And she's doing okay?"

Millie smiled and nodded. "Yeah, she's doing fine now. We're staying here for a while until the police catch the kidnappers."

Cam cast a lingering look at me. "Well, you're in good hands." He patted my knee.

I pointed the remote at the TV. "Can we watch this movie now or not?"

After the movie, Cam said, "Hey, Rook, will you walk me out?"

I didn't really want to, but his eyes pleaded with me, so I begrudgingly

CHAPTER TWENTY-SEVEN

shoved my feet into a pair of tennis shoes.

The air smelled of hay, the sweet, earthy scent of tobacco, and far-off burning leaves. The sun cast a mellow honey-gold tone over everything.

"What did you need me to come out here for?" I said, turning my face to the sun and squinting at the long shadows the trees cast across the road.

He squeezed my arm. "Are you sure you're okay? It sounds like you had a pretty wild day. Heck, a wild week."

I pulled the long sleeves of my T-shirt over my hands, crossed my arms over my middle, and kicked at a lump of grass. I nodded. "Yeah. I'm fine."

He shook his head with a tone of disbelief in his voice. "'I'm fine' is Rook-speak for I'm-not-really-fine-but-I'm-pretending-I-am-so-no-one-will-think-I'm-weak."

"Geez Louise." I rolled my eyes. "Did you bring me out here to pick a fight? I don't need this right now."

"The last thing I want to do is fight. But I'm not going to play along with your denial, either."

I clapped my sleeve-covered hands over my face and spun away from him. Memories of the fear, distress of the morning, and the crushing weight of Prim's impending passing collided with my general annoyance with him as of late. My body grew hot, and my muscles fired up. I spun back around to face him. "Fine! I was terrified. Is that what you want to hear? Down to my very bones because I was afraid of getting both me and Patrice killed. Then I come home to find Prim in bed, which means she's going downhill faster than I'm able to cope with. And I don't know how much time I have left with her. There. I said it." I pointed at my face. "Now look. I'm crying. Happy now? Is that what you wanted? To see me fragile and crumbling, barely able to hold on? Here it is. Get an eye full." I opened my arms. "I'm not trying to play tough. I'm not in denial. I'm trying to hold myself together because if I fall apart, I don't know if I'll go back together again. Don't you understand that?"

He didn't say a word. He wrapped me up in his arms and held me tight, squeezing all my tears, and to be honest, probably a little snot, onto his shirt. But he didn't seem to mind. He held me until my head hurt and my face turned numb with crying and until I had to push away because I couldn't breathe anymore. He reached in his truck and pulled several fast-food napkins off his dashboard, and handed them to me.

I blew my nose several times. Devil take his hide for making me ugly-cry.

He cupped my face in his hands. "No matter what happens between you and me, I'm your friend first. Always. I will help you through this in any way I can. Okay?"

I rolled my eyes. "What can you possibly do? Except listen to me gripe and cry? And what good is any of that?"

"It's not griping, and it helps to talk. If the tables were turned, isn't that what you would tell me?"

He was right. I couldn't argue that point. But this was all too heavy. I didn't want to feel anymore. So I said, "Sure. But that's because I'm nosy." I smiled.

He kissed my forehead and wrapped me in his arms again. He smelled so good, spicy and sweet, manly, and his chest was solid and tight, his arms strong. My insides melted into my toes, and I relaxed all over.

Jimmy pulled up.

Cam and I separated.

Jimmy jumped out of his truck and strode toward us. "What's going on?" he called out. His voice was edged with suspicion.

An awkward tension pushed between Cam and me. He fiddled with his ball cap while I worked at the wad of napkins to find a clean spot for dabbing my runny nose.

When Jimmy saw my puffy face, his tone switched to concern. "What's wrong? What happened?"

Cam stepped back, dipping his hands into his pockets. "Rook's a little upset. She's had a rough day."

I glared at Cam. *Which I was handling okay until you made me talk about it, clown fart.*

"Yeah, I heard about that. I came over as soon as I heard it on the scanner." He hugged me. His voice echoed in his chest. "Are you okay?"

"I'm fine."

CHAPTER TWENTY-SEVEN

Cam rolled his eyes.

"You want to talk about it?"

"No, I don't," I said. I turned my face up to Jimmy. "You came all this way to check on me?"

"Of course…" He shrugged, smoothing my hair.

For a brief moment, I started to feel I might be special in his eyes.

He added, "And to tell you, we caught the guys."

A part of me sank. The job was everything to him. And I reckoned it always would be.

That evening, Jimmy, Prim, Millie, Patrice, and I sat around the table enjoying a supper of fried chicken, green beans, mashed potatoes, biscuits, iced tea, and the last of summer's fresh tomatoes and watermelon.

Jimmy apprised us of the final details of Patrice's case. "We caught the people who kidnapped you, Patrice."

"Oh, thank heavens." She put her hand over her heart.

He showed her his phone. "And we recovered your necklace, but it's in evidence right now. You can claim it when the case is over."

She gasped, studying the picture. "How long will that be?" She cast a pleading look up at Jimmy.

He tucked his phone in his pocket. "Hard to say. All depends on the lawyers and how fast they can build the case. They could move quickly or drag it out for a couple of years."

"What about momma's engagement ring?" Millie asked, biting into her chicken leg.

"Nothing we can do about that. She'd given it back to Mitch when they broke up. He was free to do what he wanted with it. We can't arrest him for being tacky."

"That's too bad," Millie muttered, lifting her tea glass for a sip.

"I was a fool for not keeping the ring anyway, since I'm pretty sure I was the one who paid for it after he bilked a bunch of money out of me." Patrice rolled her eyes and scooped mashed potatoes onto her fork.

Jimmy spooned a second helping of mashed potatoes onto his plate. "We found a body at the river, too. The one who was shot the other night. He floated a couple miles downriver, and some fishermen found him along the bank. We recovered most of the money, but not all. That'll eventually be returned to y'all."

"Who was the guy?" I said with one eye on Prim, poking half-heartedly at her food. She was pushing the food around without eating.

"Shane Decker. Will's brother and Mitch's pill mill partner. The Feds have confirmed the clinic was a pill mill. They shut it down today and confiscated all the records." He bit into his chicken leg. "Turns out Mitch had blown a bunch of the money they made pushing pills through the clinic. And when he couldn't, or wouldn't, pay it back, they took Patrice to force him to pay."

"Idiots," Patrice snapped. "They were too stupid to know that Mitch and I had already broken up. Mitch didn't care if they had me or not."

"It's probably for the best," Jimmy said. "We found a sizable insurance policy on you among his papers."

Our mouths dropped open in unison as Patrice, Millie, and I exchanged shocked glances.

Patrice snapped her mouth shut and shook her head. "I don't like speaking ill of the dead, but I hope he's chained to a lake of fire right about now for everything he put me through."

Prim shook her head and put her bony hand around her tea glass. "I'll never understand this wicked world, how people can be so cruel to each other."

Millie said, "Oh, hey, Rook, did y'all ever find out who attacked you not long ago?"

"That's a question for Jimmy. But I think it's Holly Parker's sister."

"Oh, that woman who worked with you at the distillery?" She sipped her tea.

I nodded and glanced at Jimmy.

Jimmy spoke, chewing his food. "It is her. Her name is Lynne Abbott. She's Holly's younger sister."

"Well, has she been arrested?" Prim asked.

"Not yet." He swallowed his food with a gulp of tea.

"Why not?" Prim's voice raised a few pitches.

CHAPTER TWENTY-SEVEN

A serious cloud fell over Jimmy's face. His eyes darted to me. "We haven't been able to locate her." He stabbed his green beans. "Yet."

Chapter Twenty-Eight

I stayed at work late the next day since the marketing committee landed a new Halloween project with the J.T. Bolton House in downtown Rothdale. We only had a month to pull everything together, so we decided to put in some late evenings. As always, Batrene was kind enough to sit with Prim, which helped a lot.

After putting my things away and changing into my yoga pants and sweatshirt, I threw my hair into a ponytail and peeked in on Prim. She was sleeping soundly. Since I worked through supper, I made a ham and cheese sandwich, grabbed the salt and vinegar chips, and plopped down in front of the TV. Batrene's reading glasses and pillbox lay on the coffee table.

"Oh, she'll need these."

It was already getting late, and since she'd be going to bed soon, I didn't want to delay returning her things. I set my food aside and walked over to Batrene's.

She answered the door with her dog, Maxine, yapping from the couch. Batrene wore a red muumuu and pink foam rollers in her hair.

"Thanks for watching Prim for me. You left these at the house."

"Oh, honey, thank you. I've looked everywhere for these things. I was sure I was losing my mind."

"I won't keep you. Need to finish supper and get to bed."

We said our goodbyes, and I started back toward my house. There was about a quarter of an acre between my house and Batrene's, so our porch lights only touched the edges of our respective properties, leaving the empty land in the dark.

CHAPTER TWENTY-EIGHT

I heard a rustling near me. I paused for a blink to wonder if it was a rabbit or a raccoon, but in the next beat, something slammed into me and knocked me to the ground, my breath flying out of my lungs. The person was hitting me all about the head and torso.

She cussed and screamed as she hit me. The flurry of the attack rendered me confused in trying to figure out who was on top of me for a moment, then it occurred to me: Lynne. Holly's sister.

I wiggled, squirmed, and bucked to get her off of me. When Lynne lifted her hand, she held a knife. She wasn't playing around. She lunged and brought her hand downward, but I rolled out of the way.

I shouted, "Help! Call 911!"

Maxine's faint incessant barking came from inside, bouncing around with the echo of my voice through the night. I struggled to stand, but Lynne tackled me again. I kicked at her, making contact with her gut. She grunted and fell back. She lunged again with the knife, and I rolled again. My only plan was to avoid the knife as long as I could. I rolled onto my hands and knees and tried to stand, but the psycho tripped me.

Suddenly a blast rang out in the night. In the light of Batrene's porch, I glimpsed her large form charge at us with a flashlight and a rifle.

She screamed, "Freeze right now. I've called the cops."

"She has a knife," I shouted, holding Lynne's wrists, the knife tip only inches from my
face.

"I have a gun, missy," Batrene screamed.

Lynne hissed at me, "I'll kill you before that old lady gets close enough to shoot."

My arms were weakening. I wasn't sure I could hold on much longer. I dug my fingers in one of her eye sockets while working my knees to leverage between our bodies.

She screamed out and pushed harder to lower the knife.

Batrene was close enough that I could hear her breathing, which was worryingly heavy. She shined the flashlight on us and lowered the rifle. It was Bryan's old hunting rifle. "Get off her right now and drop that knife or

I'll put a hole right through you."

Lynne sat back on her butt and I scooted away from her.

"Drop the knife," I sidled up to Batrene. "And put your hands up."

Lynne dropped the knife in the grass and put her hands in the air. In the distance, sirens cried out faintly.

Within a few moments, sheriff's vehicles flew up my drive. Goodman and Jimmy jumped out of their respective vehicles, drew their weapons, and ran toward us.

Goodman was dressed in dark blue jeans and a worn green and gray plaid flannel shirt. He cuffed Lynne and placed in the back of his vehicle.

After taking our statements, Goodman said, "I look forward to the day when I don't have to come out here for a situation. In fact, I'm thinking of taking up a collection to help you relocate to another jurisdiction." The mirth in his eyes indicated he was teasing me in the way friendly colleagues do. Lord, were Goodman and I becoming friends? What was this world coming to?

I returned his banter. "Well, the past couple days have worn me out, so I'll try to give you a week or two vacation."

He actually smiled and said to Jimmy, "Can't you put a leash on her?"

Jimmy chuckled. "That'd be like leashing a tornado."

"Hey." I slapped his arm. "I'm not that bad."

"I didn't say it was a bad thing." Jimmy wrapped an arm around me and kissed me. "I wouldn't have it any other way."

Chapter Twenty-Nine

I planned to go extra early to work. But when the alarm went off, every muscle in my body screamed to call out sick from work, but I'd missed so much time in the office, I didn't want to miss anymore. I needed to prove that I wasn't flaking out.

Prim was still in bed by the time the extra strong coffee had finished perking. I ran up the stairs to check on her.

The room was dark. The curtains were drawn, and the ceiling fan churned wildly above the bed, but it didn't seem to faze her. I tiptoed into the room. She lay on her back, her nightshirt drenched with sweat, her mouth open and gaping like the entrance to a deep cave. She'd been struggling with sleep, so I didn't dare try to wake her even though my own skin crawled with the thought of lying in damp clothes and bed covers. I backed out of the room and crept down the stairs to grab my things with the notion of getting breakfast out of the vending machine at work.

I met Batrene in the yard as she crossed from the field. I tossed my things in the car and crossed my arms over my chest. My rayon dress did little against the morning chill. But it was that weird time of year, cold in the mornings and evenings, but warm during the day; it was impossible to dress for the weather. "I hate to tell you, but Prim is still in bed. So, she might need help getting washed and dressed and getting downstairs."

Batrene hedged, and her eyes drifted to the second story of the house. She pulled her flannel barn jacket tighter over her brown cotton top covered with brightly colored glitter-edged fall leaves. "Oh Lord, I hope my knees can carry me up those steps, or we're all going to be in a fix."

I hadn't thought of that. I blew out a breath and rubbed my forehead. Was that a new crease forming? "Okay, um..." I looked around the yard as if the answers were hiding in the dew like little fairies ready to spring out at me. Maybe I could call Cam to help. I hated to do it, especially for the bathing and dressing, but I truly had no one else to call. If nothing else, he could just be there to help both ladies down the stairs or in case something happened. My stomach snaked up my esophagus. "In that case, let her sleep as long as she will, and I'll see what I can come up with. Call me when she wakes up."

"Okay, dear. I'm sorry I can't do more."

Guilt skittered through my head. "Oh, no! You're doing so much to help us." I squeezed her arm. "I wouldn't be able to do anything without you. Seriously." I checked the time on my phone and opened my car door. "I have to go, but I'll call soon. Just do the best you can."

She adjusted her crochet bag on her shoulder. "I will." She wished me a good day and farewell and headed toward the house as I jumped in The Road Beast and raced to work. After making a pot of fresh communal coffee and buying a pack of brown sugar Pop-Tarts, I settled in at my desk. I was alone in the office, so it was safe to call Cam.

"What's up?" His voice was heavy with sleep.

"I'm so sorry to wake you." I explained the situation to him.

"Mm." He sucked in a deep breath, then yawned. The springs of his bed creaked as he sat up. "Mkay. I'm on it."

I hung up, relief in my heart, and called Batrene to tell her to expect Cam. Knowing my precious Prim was in capable and loving hands, I was at ease enough to leap into my work. I had a mile-long list of things to complete to get prepared for the Pasture Pals event, which was only fourteen days away, and counting, and to start the preliminary work on the J.T. Bolton House project.

The morning rolled by quickly, and before I'd realized it, my lunch hour had arrived. The balmy air and golden sunset in a clear sapphire sky beckoned me outside to call and check on Prim.

Cam answered the phone. "She woke up about thirty minutes ago. My mom is upstairs in the bathroom with her. She's going to help her wash and

CHAPTER TWENTY-NINE

get dressed."

For Prim to sleep so late was unprecedented. Even with bouts of flu and stomach bugs, I'd never known her to stay in bed beyond seven. I wanted to believe that the recent events with the kidnapping and the attacks on our house had simply worn her out. But I knew better. I looked up into the tree. The sun spangled in the colorful leaves. Thank heavens for Irene Campbell. She saved Cam and Prim both a lot of embarrassment. "Is Batrene still there?"

"Oh, yeah. She and Mom have been cleaning and cooking this morning."

"And you've been watching TV while they worked," I teased.

"No. I've been working in the yard Miss Smarty Pants. I've been pulling the weeds out of Prim's garden and getting it winter-ready."

A few leaves twirled to the ground and tumbled across the parking lot. On the verge of tears, I protested. "Y'all are doing too much."

"Nonsense. You and Prim need the help. Besides, we're here only long enough to get Prim settled downstairs so Batrene can watch her. Then I've got to take Mom on a few errands and take her back home."

"I really appreciate—"

He didn't let me finish. "Think nothing of it. Happy to do it." A muffled woman's voice sounded in the distance. "I've got to go."

I hung up, guilt and gratitude at war with each other inside me. I hated that I couldn't be there with Prim. Who knew how much time I had left with her? I'd already lost one mom. I couldn't stand to lose Prim, too. Logically, I knew I had to work to make money to support us and pay for Prim's medical care, but emotionally I hated depending so heavily on others to do the things that I wanted to do for Prim. But, at the same time, I was deeply grateful for their help because there was no way I could've managed without them. After a few breaths to still the rising tide of emotion, I returned to work and lost myself in planning for the Pasture Pals event.

When I returned home, I sat in the car for a moment, watching the sunset, and I was suddenly struck with a thought about my dad and the last time he'd seen a sunset with his own eyes. I couldn't put it off any longer. I pulled my phone from my purse and called the prison. After a few minutes, he came to the phone. We only had fifteen minutes, most of which was spent in exchanging pleasantries.

Near the end, he said, "I've got a new lawyer to handle my appeal case."

"That's great, Dad."

"My last lawyer couldn't seem to get the job done. He didn't know what he was doing. This new guy will probably be contacting you soon. I give him all your info. I'm sure he'll want to talk to you about it."

I suddenly felt very heavy. As though the setting sun was pulling me into the earth with it. Would this ever be over? I had given up long ago on the notion that my life would ever be normal or put together again. But I hoped that if I could live without all these extra worries and cares, I could find something close to happiness.

"I'm sure the court documents—"

Dad interrupted. "Just talk to him. Work with him. Give him everything he wants."

"Okay. I will."

"When are you coming to see me?"

My heart twisted. "I don't know." I ran through the schedule in my mind. Jimmy's cousin's wedding, Prim, work. I rubbed my head.

"It's almost Thanksgiving. And then Christmas."

"I know."

"Christmas was always my favorite time."

The automated voice announced we had a minute left.

I didn't want to tell him that I'd lost most of my memories of our Christmases together, that I remembered only meaningless, random snippets of my childhood. "Mine, too." I lied. But it was a good lie. "I've got a lot of work and stuff. It's hard to get away."

"Yeah. I know." His voice dipped with disappointment. "It's tough. Hopefully, I'll be out soon. This new lawyer is good, I think."

"Okay. I'll try to come sometime in October." That was only a couple weeks away.

"All right then. It'll be good to see you. Love you."

CHAPTER TWENTY-NINE

I barely knew my dad. We missed so many of those beautiful father-daughter bonding moments, those moments that build a strong, trusting relationship. Without all that, could I love him? Was the bond of blood enough? But I thought it best to say, "Love you, too," right before the prison phone system disconnected us.

After a good cry in the car, I cleaned myself up with fast food napkins from my glove compartment and dragged myself inside.

Prim and Batrene were planted in front of the television eating tomato bisque and grilled cheese and laughing at wiry Barney Fife fighting to find the bullet from his pocket.

"You want me to make you a sandwich, hon?" Batrene slid forward in her seat in a move to stand.

"No, no. Finish your supper. I'm not very hungry right now." I set my things on the kitchen table. I noticed the flowers Jimmy had given me were wilted and dry. Petals had dropped from the roses onto the table. I poured myself a glass of iced tea and joined Batrene on the couch. Prim sat in her recliner, picking at her sandwich and nipping her ginger ale. Her soup bowl was full of tomato-cracker mush that appeared untouched.

We chatted a bit about our respective days until *Andy Griffith* was interrupted by a local news special report.

The news anchor, a beautiful mocha-brown woman who glowed as if lit from the inside, said, "Pardon this interruption. We are now joining a statement from Franklin County Sheriff Harlan Goodman."

Sheriff Goodman, Jimmy, and other officials stood behind a podium ornamented with the sheriff's department emblem. Sheriff Goodman said, "Thank you for being here. Please hold your questions until the end. I wanted to provide this statement in regards to recent developments. As you all know, when I was elected, I promised to be tough on drugs in Franklin County, and in holding to that promise, I wanted to make you all aware that, with the help of the DEA, we have recently uncovered a pill mill operating in our county.

Two people involved, Will Decker and Savannah Stewart, have been taken into custody in connection to the murder of Dr. Mitch Thomas, who was the prescribing doctor that worked at the Franklin County Health Walk-in Clinic on Blantonboro Road. It is believed by the DEA, federal investigators, and my department that this may go deeper than the one pill mill. Therefore, I reiterate my promise to the residents of Franklin County that I will not stop until we get to the bottom of this. I will now take questions."

Prim scoffed. "The only thing that man's going to get to the bottom of is a bag of chips. He's only doing this because elections are coming up soon."

I kicked off my ballet flats and pulled my feet up beside me. I might've agreed with Prim at one time, but the sheriff had shown me that he was trying and that he did care even if he did get on my nerves more often than not. And I wasn't sure, but he seemed to be easing up toward me, too. Wow. Sheriff "Bulldog" Goodman and I might actually end up friendly. "Mm. Maybe."

She eyeballed me over the rim of her glasses. "You think he cares about what's going

on?"

"I don't know. Maybe he's coming around. He seems to be softening toward me."

She hemmed. "Hm. We'll see." She coughed, set aside her food tray, and lay back in her

recliner.

"I won't be sending him a Christmas card or anything…." I chuckled, rubbing my

aching feet. "But I'm going to try to give him the benefit of the doubt."

The anchorwoman returned. "In other news, there's a scandal in the bourbon distillers' community."

Next thing on the screen was Fox, flanked by a couple of officers and reporters with cameras and microphones.

The anchorwoman continued, "Fox Graham of Fox Trace Distilleries has been arrested for fraud. Sources say he rigged the Kentucky Distillers' Guild Best Bourbon Award in order to fraudulently win ten thousand dollars and a coveted spread in the *National Bourbon Review* magazine, which is renowned in the bourbon world for catapulting distillers to international fame and

CHAPTER TWENTY-NINE

attention. He is also facing charges for assault. We contacted Mr. Graham and his lawyers, who refused to give a comment at this time."

I was glad to see that a heaping helping of justice was being served all around.

There was a knock at the kitchen door, then a man's voice called out, "Hello."

Cam. My heart reflexively leapt a little.

Cam sauntered in wearing worn jeans, red T-shirt, and a blue Ford ball cap. He carried a rose bush covered with little pale purple rose buds. "Hey, ladies. Prim, I got a gift for you."

Prim sat up and floundered to tuck the recliner base. "Mercy. Isn't that pretty? I've never seen one that color before." I jumped up and tucked the recliner footstool to help her get up. She coughed and pushed herself to her feet, meeting Cam in the middle of the living room. She gingerly touched the leaves and buds. "Oh, aren't you the sweetest boy." She put her arm around him as he pulled her against him and kissed the top of her head. "Wherever did you find this?"

"I found it at Kirby's Greenhouse. My mom and I were out there this afternoon. I saw this, and I knew you needed it." He looked at me and winked. "Now I know it'll be winter soon, so this won't bloom for long, but it'll bloom in the spring for sure. And you'll have beautiful lavender roses."

Tears sprang into my eyes. Oh, Cam, bless his heart. In his thoughtfulness, he hadn't stopped to consider that Prim might not be around to see the roses bloom. I bit the inside of my jaw to keep from crying.

She scuffled off. "Let me get my boots and hat. We've got to get this in the ground. I know just the spot."

"Prim," I called after her, shoving my feet into my nearby shoes. "It's too late. It's almost dark."

"All the more reason to hurry. C'mon now. And grab a flashlight just in case." She stepped out on the screened porch, and Batrene followed her to help Prim stuff her thin legs into her rubber boots.

I didn't want to spoil his gift or Prim's happiness, so I didn't mention how she might miss the spring. I forced a smile. "You sure made her day." Which made my day, too. "We'd better hurry, she won't wait much longer."

Cam dug the hole and dropped the rose bush inside, covering it and watering it for Prim. Then he I stood nearby, a chill falling over us, watching Prim and Batrene admire the newly planted rose bush. Prim then got on the phone with Oda Dean Spurlock, gushing over the delicate lavender blooms and complimenting Cam as the most thoughtful man she'd ever known, next to Papaw, of course.

I leaned toward Cam. "You earned a whole bunch of brownie points today."

"Ah." He threw his head back with a chuckle. "It wasn't about that." He rubbed his hand on his worn jeans. "I was actually trying to earn brownie points with you." He flashed a crooked smile and adjusted his ball cap as he looked out across the yard.

I didn't know what to say to that. "So, does that mean you've forgiven me and Jimmy?"

He adjusted his cap. "Maybe I've been too hard on you and Jimmy. I mean, I've dated others, and you accepted it."

"Eh. Kind of." I smiled, watching Prim stand back and admire her new roses as the dusk threatened to envelop them in darkness. "I wouldn't say I accepted it. I tolerated it. Sort of."

"Much better than I did. And I got to thinking maybe I'd rather have my two best friends together instead of you dating some guy I don't even know.." He shrugged. "At least Jimmy and I are friends, and I know he'll be good to you. That's the most important thing."

I play-punched his arm. "I'm sorry if we hurt you. We never meant to do that."

"I know. I finally realized I didn't want to have a life without both of you in it."

Touched by his openness, I linked my arm in his and lay my head on his shoulder. "I've missed having you around, you big goober."

He worked his warm, callused hand into mine. His thumb stroked the back of my knuckle. "I'm not going anywhere. I'm here. Always."

Acknowledgements

Thank you to my agent, Dawn Dowdle, at Blue Ridge Literary Agency, for looking out for me. And thank you to Level Best Books for your tireless efforts in bringing my books to life.

To my family and friends, you keep me going, and I'm so grateful you're on this journey with me.

Most importantly, I'm deeply thankful to my readers—my reason for writing at all. It makes my heart sing to think I can bring someone joy, pleasure, and a moment of escape. Y'all are THE greatest!

About the Author

Born and raised in the beautiful Bluegrass state of Kentucky, Michelle Bennington developed a passion for books early on that has since progressed into a mild hoarding situation and an ever-growing to-read pile. She delights in transporting readers into worlds of mystery, both contemporary and historical.

In rare moments of spare time, she can be found engaging in a wide array of arts and crafts, reading, traveling, and attending tours involving ghosts, historical homes, or distilleries. She lives in the Kentucky Bluegrass Region with her husband.

SOCIAL MEDIA HANDLES:
  Facebook: https://www.facebook.com/michellebenningtonauthor
  Instagram: https://www.instagram.com/michelle.bennington.author/
  Goodreads: ttps://www.goodreads.com/author/show/22406377.Michelle_Bennington

AUTHOR WEBSITE:
  www.michellebennington.com

Also by Michelle Bennington

Devil's Kiss, Book 1 of the Small Batch Mystery Series

Widow's Blush, Book 1 of the Widows & Shadows Series

www.ingramcontent.com/pod-product-compliance
Lightning Source LLC
LaVergne TN
LVHW091533060526
838200LV00036B/585